D1055911

# BURNING MAGIC

## JOSHUA KHAN

### with illustrations by Ben Hibon

Disney • HYPERION

LOS ANGELES   NEW YORK

Also by Joshua Khan
*Shadow Magic*
*Dream Magic*

# To my wife and daughters

First Edition, April 2018
FAC-020093-18054
Printed in the United States of America
This book's interior is set in Adobe Caslon Pro, Caslon Antique Pro, Charcuterie Ornaments, Cartographer Regular/Fontspring; Solid Antique Roman/Monotype.
The cover is set in Adobe Caslon Pro, Caslon Antique Pro/Fontspring.
Designed by Marci Senders

Library of Congress Cataloging-in-Publication Data

Names: Khan, Joshua, author. • Hibon, Ben, illustrator.
Title: Burning magic : a Shadow magic novel / Joshua Khan ; with illustrations by Ben Hibon.
Description: First edition. • Los Angeles ; New York : Disney-Hyperion, 2018.
• Summary: "Lily the sorcerer queen and Thorn the giant-bat-whisperer journey to the Sultanate of Fire to help their friend K'leef in a no-holds-barred contest for the throne"—Provided by publisher.
Identifiers: LCCN 2017021766 • ISBN 9781368008426
Subjects: • CYAC: Fantasy.
Classification: LCC PZ7.1.K53 Bur 2018 • DDC [Fic]—dc23
LC record available at https://lccn.loc.gov/2017021766

ISBN 978-1-368-00842-6
Reinforced binding
Visit www.DisneyBooks.com

Stars, hide your fires;

Let not light see my black and deep desires.

—From *Macbeth*, by William Shakespeare

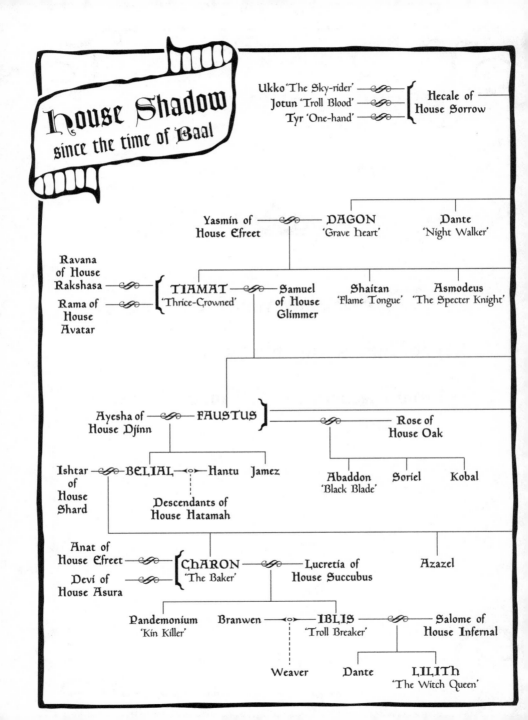

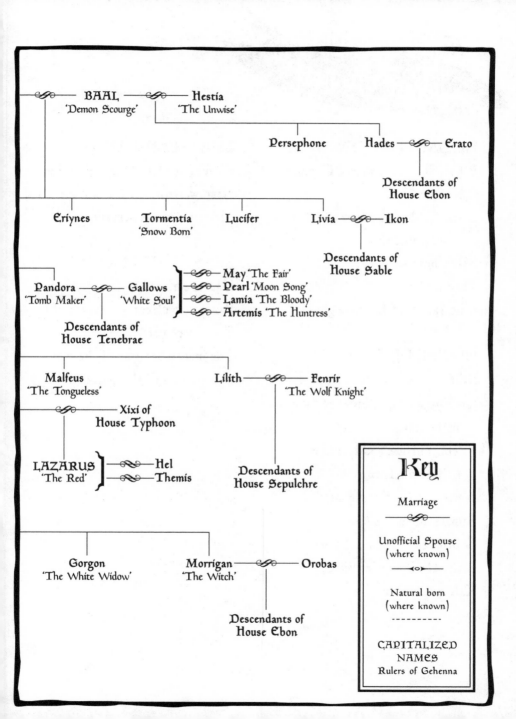

## CAST OF CHARACTERS

### HOUSE SHADOW

Lilith Shadow, ruler of Gehenna,
  a witch
Baron Sable, her adviser and
  loyal nobleman
Mary, her maid
Thorn, a squire
Iblis, father of Lilith, a ghost

### HOUSE DJINN

Sa'if, a prince, soon to be sultan
Jambiya, a prince, blind and known
  as the Lawgiver
K'leef, a prince and friend to
  Lilith and Thorn
Ameera, K'leef's twin sister
Samira, K'leef's sister
Gabriel Solar, fiancé to one of
  the Djinnic princesses
Kali, executioner

### THE SHARDLANDS

Kismet, leader of a nomad tribe
Nasr, warrior of the Scorpion tribe
Merriq, a lowly servant

### BEASTS AND MONSTERS

Hades, a giant bat
Pazuzu, an efreet, a creature of fire
Farn, an efreet
The manticore, one of the many
  predators of the Shardlands

# NAHAS, THE CITY OF BRASS

# ONE

"**H**ey! You got any zombies up on deck?" shouted the girl from her small boat. "Can I see one?"

Thorn leaned over the railings of the ship. "What?"

She paddled her old skiff alongside the ship's hull and raised a mango. "You can have this if you let me have a look at one."

Thorn held out his hand. She tossed it up.

Ah, how he'd missed the smell of fresh mango. It was pure, warm sweetness. He'd used up his stock at Castle Gloom months ago, and ever since he'd been recruited for this trip to the Sultanate of Fire, the thought of obtaining a new crate of that golden fruit had not been far from his mind—or his belly, which gave a gentle rumble.

"You're supposed to eat it, not kiss it," the girl shouted as she waited below. "So can I come up?"

"I ain't the captain," Thorn shouted back. He then returned his attention to the mango.

The skin was orangey-gold, perfectly ripe, and soaked with a mouth-watering scent. He'd mash it up and put it in his sandwich. You couldn't let a mango go to waste, but it was almost a shame to peel it. Almost.

"Hey!" yelled the girl. "Let me up or give me back my mango!"

"Permission to come aboard granted."

The girl lashed the skiff to the nets, then scrabbled up the thick rope with the ease of a sailor. She slid over the railings and looked around. "So where are the zombies?"

Thorn sliced a strip of mango. There was an art to eating these, making sure you didn't lose a drop of the juice. "On the other ship." He tilted his head toward the larger black-sailed vessel a few miles behind them.

He peeled the flesh with his teeth. Oh, wow. It tasted even better than he remembered.

The girl scowled. "You lied to me. You said you had zombies."

"I didn't say nothing." The golden juice dribbled down his throat. His belly responded loudly and gratefully.

The girl braced her lithe legs on the gently tilting deck. She wore a short shirt, much patched and faded, and a pair of calf-length pants belted with a sash of equal patchiness and fade. A bright scarf encircled her long neck, her thick curly hair was held in place by a bandana, and her dark eyes were ringed with even darker kohl. Those eyes were angry. "That'll be a dinar."

"A what?"

"A silver coin." She held out her hand.

Her fingers were thin but tough. Typical wharf rat. Born and raised in the docks. And that was hard living. How old was she? Hard to tell. Her skin was a deep, vibrant brown, and her build was lean and wiry. She was a head taller than Thorn, and he wasn't short, so he guessed sixteen or so. Her two front teeth were capped with gold, probably the only jewelry she owned.

"You mean a crown?" Thorn snorted. "A crown would get me a crate. One mango is worth a couple of pennies, at best."

"A crown," she insisted. "Consider it export tax."

One of the sailors laughed. "She got you good, boy. Better cough up."

Blushing, Thorn searched his pouch and handed over, very reluctantly, one of his precious crowns. "You're a thief, you know that?"

The girl shrugged and tucked the silver coin into her sash. Then she sat on the railing, dangling her legs over the water. "The witch queen's on the other ship?"

Thorn resisted the urge to push her overboard. His pouch felt a *lot* lighter without that crown. "That what they call her here in the south?"

"That's what they call her *everywhere.*" The girl bent a leg to her mouth and bit off a toenail. "You serve her?"

Poor Lily. She wouldn't be happy with the nickname "witch queen," no matter how true it was. "I work for Lady Shadow of Gehenna. I'm a squire." There was more to their relationship, but he wasn't going to give this girl his life story.

She eyed him. "You're not Gehennish, though. Too much color in your face. The Gehennish have skin the color of watery milk."

"I'm Gehennish now."

"But you sound like you come from the Free Duchies. Herne's Forest, maybe." She sniffed. "Yes. You smell of bark."

Thorn resisted smelling his armpit, but he was pretty sure he didn't. Now that he was a squire, he dipped himself in a barrel of water once a week. Sometimes even twice.

The girl swung her legs back and forth. "You're far from home, forest boy."

He didn't like the way this girl was picking at him, as if trying to unravel him. He finished off the mango. "Don't you have somewhere to be?"

"Yes. There." She pointed in the direction of the port ahead. "But that's where you're going anyway."

He gave up. She wasn't going to move until she wanted to. Thorn pushed the pit into his mouth and began working it clean. It made talking impossible, and that was fine with him. He joined the girl on the railing.

The journey was almost over. *Thank the Six.*

They'd spent two months living like sheep, packed in with no room to spread out, trapped by the noise and stink of fifty-three men snorting, snoring, swearing, and sweating as the ship sailed south, through the Lock, past the Lava Isles, and into the Siren Sea, each day hotter than the last.

While the captain had kept the crew busy, Baron Sable had done the same for Thorn and the other squires. They had spent days hanging from the rigging, furling and unfurling sails, and nights mending those same sails. In the time between, they'd learned about knots and navigation and watched the waters for dangers and delights.

One night, they'd heard mermaids singing. The next morning, two men were discovered missing.

Shark riders had followed alongside for two days, lurking in their wake until the captain had ended up, begrudgingly, tossing over a whole cow carcass.

"Best pay the Coral king his toll, before he asks for the whole ship," Sable had said.

Thorn hadn't minded the work, but he'd been uncomfortable for most of the voyage. It wasn't just the constant swaying, and the tight living quarters, where everyone was on top of everyone else. After all, as a squire, he was used to being cramped. But the smells of hot tar and wet rope and the sounds of creaking timbers and flapping sails lit bad memories of the last time he'd been on board a ship. Back then, he'd been shackled and forced to live in the hold with other captives. This time he was accompanying a young queen, and thankfully not as a slave.

He craved firm land. To be able to walk toward a horizon that didn't bob and tilt, to smell trees and earth and anything other than salt and the cook's woeful cooking, the stench of which hung over the whole ship like a poisonous cloud. Sixty days of fish-head stew. Enough!

The seagulls clearly felt very different about the cooking. They circled and fought above the crow's nest as they kept their eyes out for the slop bucket.

"We're coming up to the Twins," said the girl. "Look."

Their ship, the *Ebony Siren*, sailed past rocky ledges into a bay beyond. The city of Nahas sat within the bay's crescent, protected by high cliffs and accessible only through the small gap between the Horns, the point where each cliff ended. And upon each horn stood a dragon.

Radiant light beamed from the twin dragons' eyes, and smoke rippled from their nostrils and partially parted jaws. The evening sun cast red light over their golden scales and the silver wings curled close to their sinewy bodies. The beasts had to be over a hundred feet tall, balanced on curled tails and hind claws, poised to launch into the clouds.

"Did people really build 'em?" said Thorn. "Or was it sorcery?"

The girl shrugged. "You don't have lighthouses in Gehenna?"

"Not like these." He craned his neck to gaze at the closest beast's monstrous head. How big was it? The castle stables could fit inside its mouth!

The *Ebony Siren* passed under the mighty, immobile claws of the dragons and Nahas came into view.

Thorn squinted at the port on the horizon. "It looks like it's burning."

The port started with a thick cluster of warehouses and one-story houses and taverns squeezed together along the docks. Then, gradually, as the city rose on a natural slope—the wall of a smoking volcano—the buildings grew higher, more extravagant, and more spacious, until at the top, lit by the setting sun, was Palace Djinn. Spindle-thin towers surrounded it, and the great halls and chambers were crowned with golden domes. The buildings shimmered and seemed to move, as unsettled as firelight.

The girl stretched, yawning at what were everyday sights for her. "It was, once. Back in the days of the great sorcerers, the walls and towers were carved out of fire. Nowadays, the rich folk clad the walls in metal so it *looks* like flames. The whole palace is made of brass."

"You been up there?"

"I get around."

Countless bonfires sparkled throughout the city and along the cliffs, mixing the salty air with smoke.

Sultan Djinn was dead. During the hundred-day mourning period, it was the people's custom to burn gifts for him to use in the afterlife. Some would cremate extravagant paper models and effigies. In the crueler past, wives, slaves, and animals had gone to the fire, to follow their master.

Lily had loved explaining that, and a whole lot more, to Thorn during the few occasions he had been invited aboard her ship.

He hadn't minded her lessons one bit. The *Shadow's Blade* was bigger and more comfortable than the *Ebony Siren*, as befitting Lily's lofty station. And its cook was vastly more talented than the soon-to-be-convicted-of-poisoning fellow he had. Thorn always enjoyed learning new stuff. His problem was remembering it the next day.

It hadn't all been her teaching him, though. Thorn knew the stars. How the tip of the Manticore's Tail always pointed north. That the Witch's Broom turned during the seasons, and the height of the Six Princes from the horizon told you how many hours were left before dawn. Little tricks that you wouldn't learn while living in windowless Castle Gloom but everyone in Herne's Forest knew. Lily studied her books; he studied the outdoors.

Now the wharf rat seemed fascinated with his friend. The girl glanced over her shoulder at the *Shadow's Blade*. "They say she has her father's ghost trapped in the catacombs beneath her castle, Glum."

"It's Castle *Gloom*, and it's not really like that. Her dad is . . . sort of stuck down in the library, but that's because—"

"And a sailor from Lumina told me she's imprisoned her own brother in a tower of cobwebs."

"Yeah, but that's not the whole story. She had to—"

"What about the trolls? They say even the troll king fears her. That his own daughter is forced to serve the witch queen as her maid?"

"Dott isn't forced to do anything she doesn't want to," said Thorn. "She likes working for Lily . . . I mean, Lady Shadow."

"A minstrel sang a tale about how she cannot abide the living, that even her pet is one of the undead."

"Custard is a fairly unique sort of puppy," Thorn replied, knowing how feeble it sounded. "And he's pretty happy as a, er, ghost."

The girl shivered. "How can you stand it? Aren't you afraid she'll turn you into some monster?"

"What d'you have against monsters?"

She frowned. "What?"

Thorn pondered what—or who—lay sleeping in the hold. "Some of my best friends are monsters."

*Sure, he* does *eat people. . . .*

A fight broke out overhead as new arrivals confronted the squawking seagulls.

Bats poured from caves within the cliff walls and the roofs and lofts of the nearby buildings. They grew thick in the sky above them, and it didn't take long before the seagulls flew off.

"Bats don't usually come out to the boats," commented the girl.

A scream shook the ship. It rose from the hold: a hellish, skull-piercing cry that made one's blood run cold.

"What in the Fire was that?" The girl backed toward the railing, trembling.

The bats flew lower over the deck, and the girl yelled as she tried to shoo them away. "They're everywhere! What's—"

Another terrifying scream broke out from below, and something heavy thudded against the double hatch, causing the deck to shake.

Thorn gasped. "It's breaking free!"

"What? What is it?"

Thorn stumbled back. "No, it was supposed to sleep longer. . . . If it gets loose . . ." He turned to her as the deck shook again. "Save yourself! We have to jump!"

The girl dove off. She slipped into the lapping waves and a moment later bobbed up, already a safe five yards from the hull. "Come on! Jump! Before it gets out!"

Thorn laughed. "Nope. I think I'll stay nice and dry a bit longer."

"What about the monster?"

Thorn stamped on the deck. "You! Shut up!"

The screaming stopped. Instead there was a sullen snarl, promising that Thorn was going to pay for this later. Well, later was later. He wanted to make the most out of this moment. Thorn leaned over the railing. "There. All quiet."

"That was a trick?" She slapped the water. "You dirty, filthy . . ." Thorn didn't catch the next part as it was all in livid Djinnic, but then she switched back to Gehennish. "Hey, what about my boat? It's still tied to your ship!"

"Boat? I thought it was driftwood." Thorn waved at her as the *Ebony Siren* drifted past. "You can pick it up at the docks. Enjoy your swim!"

"That was a bit cruel," said Baron Sable as he joined Thorn to admire the view. "It's about a mile to the docks."

"Cruel? Cruel is being conned out of a crown for a single mango."

"You do get sharks in the bay from time to time."

"Ah. I did not know that." Thorn shrugged. "Still, a whole crown. That was a week's worth of shoveling horse dung outta the stables."

Sable twisted the tips of his mustache into points. "Nahas is a sight, isn't it? I've been away too long."

"Your wife must be pleased about being able to see her family again after so many years."

That was putting it mildly. Baroness Suriya had packed the *Ebony Siren* with crates, trunks, and boxes until there hadn't been room even for the ship's rats in the hold. She'd left her home city of Nahas two decades ago and was determined to catch up with *everyone*.

Thorn sighed. "Wade would've loved this. You should've brought him."

The baron scowled. "You are an idiot, Thorn."

Thorn blushed. Wade was a squire, his best friend back home, and the baron's fourth son. But what he wasn't was the baroness's son. So Wade had stayed up north while the baroness came down south. It was easier for everyone that way. Except Thorn.

What was he going to find in Nahas? Stuck-up nobles and soft-bellied courtiers from all six of the New Kingdoms.

His sigh deepened. This was going to be the very opposite of fun.

Now that the sun was low, the heat of the day was beginning to lift, thank the Six. He wasn't used to the heaviness of the air down south. And the sailors said it wasn't yet summer. How much hotter could it get?

*You're in the Sultanate of Fire. What did you expect?*

The docks came into view.

The last time Thorn had sailed into a port, he'd been in chains. This was much better.

Chants, shouts, and laughter rolled over the sparkling blue water as dockers hauled, merchants haggled, and beasts, great and small, fought for space among all the people.

"What is that?" Thorn blinked, his heart skipping a beat. There was a giant gray-skinned monster lumbering along the pier! "It's got a tail coming out of its face!"

The baron smirked. "It's an elephant. They're mostly harmless."

"But look at those tusks!"

"Eats leaves."

Eats leaves? How could something that big survive on just leaves?

How would he ever get used to this place?

Bells hung from the ivory tusks, and its ears, huge flapping things, were painted with flowery designs. There was a platform on its back, and a richly dressed family was perched on it, watching the crowd from on high.

Thorn took a deep breath. He was a squire of Gehenna now, not some country bumpkin. He shouldn't get so shaken by the first strange sight. There'd be plenty more.

A *thump* came from below.

Sable arched an eyebrow. "He's bored."

Thorn grinned. "The sky's dark enough. I'd better get belowdecks."

Time to free the monster.

# TWO

One of the sailors, Salmon, stopped Thorn at the bottom of the steps. "You letting him out?" he asked anxiously.

"He's been trapped down here long enough. But he's gonna be grouchy." Salmon gulped. "Meaning what, exactly?"

Instead of answering, Thorn covered his nose. The hold *stank*.

The crack in the hatch above him let in some evening light, enough for him to see the massive curve of the sleeping monster. Nets covered it—not to trap it, but to prevent it from sliding around.

A pair of angry red eyes glistened in the darkness. The shape hissed.

"I'm going as fast as I can," said Thorn as he unhooked the nets.

Thorn then went over to the hand that was pegged to the wall. Wax covered the wrinkled old flesh, and the fingertips were black. One of the digits, the thumb, was still alight. A small flame flickered on its tip, producing a feeble thread of smoke. No wonder the creature had awoken.

The Hand of Glory—that's what Lily called it, but Thorn couldn't see anything glorious about the grotesque thing. It was old magic, something Lily had found in the back of the Shadow Library. After a few nights of study, she'd been able to light it and weave whatever dark magic was necessary to make it work. The smoke caused sleep. All five fingers had been lit at the beginning of this journey, but now just the thumb was burning. Thorn pinched off the flame. The wizened digit steamed, and the smoke dispersed.

The beast yawned.

Thorn patted its furry cheek. "Come on, Hades. Time for a stretch."

A flick of a massive wing flipped Thorn over. He crashed into the bundle of nets and ended up dangling upside down.

Thorn met the angry glare of the monstrous bat. "Very funny. Now pull me out."

Hades ignored the request. He shook his body, starting with his ears and working his way down to his saber-long claws, which tore deep grooves in the wood floor of the ship. He nibbled at a tuft of hair on his shoulder.

Thorn freed himself. "I'll give you a proper brushing when we get out of here. And"—he rubbed the bat's hairy belly—"I have a special treat waiting for you."

Hades paused.

"Oh, yes," Thorn whispered. "A yummy treat."

Hades, pretending to be obeying Thorn instead of his stomach, dipped his left wing to let the boy climb onto his back.

Thorn settled himself between the wings and hooked his heels over the bat's shoulders. He rubbed his favorite spot between Hades's ears. "I missed you, boy."

Hades snorted.

Thorn laughed. "Go on, then. Show me what you've got."

The hatch groaned open, revealing the vast cloud of bats in the sky. Also Baron Sable, who was peering in. "You ready?"

How did the bats know that their king had come?

"Well, boy?" asked the baron.

They wheeled above the ship, thousands of them. Smaller than the ones back in Gehenna—no one bred bats like the Gehennish—but they had somehow sensed Hades and now clustered in the night sky to greet him.

Hades hissed.

"Yeah, I think we're ready. How about—"

Thorn's stomach dropped to his heels as Hades launched. One half beat of his immense wings and he was already above the *Ebony Siren*, scattering his smaller brethren in all directions.

Thorn gripped the thick hair around Hades's neck as the bats streamed behind. Hades cried and extended his wings to their full length. Another hard flap and the ship below shrank to the size of a toy boat.

Thorn's heart beat as fast as Hades rose. Two months had been too long. He'd almost forgotten what this was like.

Hades bathed himself in the crimson light of the setting sun, tipping to one side and the next to warm his old wings. He circled over the *Shadow's Blade* and Thorn tried to spot Lily, but they were too high to make out anyone upon the deck.

What was it like? Everyone wanted to know, but Hades never let anyone else get near enough to try riding him.

People called Hades his pet, but that idea was stupid. Thorn didn't command this monster. Hades chose to let him tag along. They had a mutual understanding, a partnership of sorts, but Thorn knew the smelly old bat was in charge. And Hades knew it, too.

"We're expected at the palace," Thorn shouted over the rushing wind. "The big building on the top of the hill!"

Hades slung himself backward, exposing his belly to the sky, and then dropped.

He and Hades often took flights over the villages around Castle Gloom. Thorn loved seeing the villagers come out and wave at the pair of them. Some even brought food over when Hades took breaks. Once, in Graven, a family had baked a bat-shaped cake for him; it was absolutely dripping with chocolate. Thorn wondered what treats he had in store here. Lily claimed Djinnic Delights were the very best candy in the world....

Beast and boy both howled as they swooped over the docks.

And people screamed.

Panic ensued.

It wasn't exactly the reaction Thorn had expected.

A donkey, startled out of its wits, broke free of its rope and bashed through a fruit stand. Horses bolted, tossing their riders. People ran for their lives. Some rushed into doorways, others dove into the sea to escape. And the elephant . . .

It bellowed and lashed out with its trunk. Hades slid sideways with graceful contempt and hissed eagerly. He rose up over the beast, beating his wings to get in position. . . .

"No!" Thorn yelled. "You can't eat it!"

He should have planned this a bit better. Hades was hungry, and here was, in his opinion, a fine feast.

"No!" Thorn pulled back on both Hades's ears. That was usually enough to get his attention.

But not this time.

The elephant rose on its hind legs, tossing its passengers into the water, and trumpeted with rage. Hades tried to get close enough to grip it, but the elephant was a big, mean old bull with tusks longer than Hades's own fangs. And its trunk was an extra weapon to use against the monstrous bat.

Not that Hades was going to quit.

"Let him go!" yelled Thorn, shouting at both beasts.

The elephant beat at Hades with its front feet, but Hades edged back just enough, testing his claws. Then the elephant fled, smashing the gates as it rampaged off.

Thorn scowled. That was going to come out of his pay. He'd be in debt till he was a graybeard. "Now look what you've done!"

Hades shrugged as if to say, *Monsters were made to terrify.*

The bat settled on the now-empty quayside and picked at a pile of abandoned fish. Faces peered through windows and the cracks of doorways.

"He's harmless, really!" Thorn called out. "Come out and see for yourselves!"

Then he spotted the soldiers: men with spears or crossbows and grim-set features. They clambered over the broken stalls and abandoned crates, spearmen at the front, crossbowmen behind.

"We're leaving, Hades."

One beat of his mighty wings and they rose high and away.

They circled a tower twice the height of the Needle in Castle Gloom. Hades snarled at the golden statue of a bird on its roof, its wings as wide as his own. Then, on a flat black patch between two huge brass-clad halls, a pattern of light began to emerge. It was fire, spelling out wavy letters, the flames themselves rising out of the hands of a red-robed boy.

"*T-H-O* . . ." Thorn nudged Hades with his knees. "There! Go down there!"

Hades circled above the flames. The boy waved up at him.

Thorn waved back. "K'leef!"

Hades turned over the gardens and the fiery letters. Then, in his own time—because he was two centuries old and wasn't going to be hurried by Thorn or anybody—he settled back down on the earth.

Thorn slid off the bat and ran up to his friend, who extinguished the flames with a clap. The pair of them laughed as they hugged.

K'leef straightened his golden turban. "Be careful! You have any idea how much this cost?"

"You smell funny," said Thorn. It was true. The boy had the odor of roses.

K'leef wrinkled his nose. "So do you. And not in a good way."

Thorn wasn't willing to be outdone that quickly. "You okay? It's just that you've got a caterpillar coming out of your nostril."

K'leef's hand went to his thin, fluffy mustache. His frown transformed, easily and swiftly, to a big smile. "It's called fashion, something a peasant like you will never understand." He approached Hades and tickled the monster under his chin. "Keeping Thorn out of trouble?"

Hades gave a snort.

"You must be hungry."

The bat's ears flicked at the last word.

"He's always hungry," said Thorn, hoping K'leef hadn't witnessed that disaster at the docks. "But he's been asleep for the last two months. Might deserve a little snack."

K'leef pointed to a pen of sheep a few levels down from the palace. "Think that'll be enough?"

Hades was off in a flash.

Thorn watched him go. "I'll be picking wool out of his teeth for the rest of the week."

"Thought you might be a bit hungry, too." K'leef pointed to a bronze table laden with fruit. "Where's Lily?"

It wasn't just any fruit, but mangoes even more golden than the one he'd paid a crown for. Thorn picked up the fattest. "Mmm?"

"Where's Lilith Shadow, the ruler of Gehenna, descendent of the Prince of Darkness, the mistress of nightmares, the troll friend, the witch queen, whose very name is feared by the seven dukes of hell?"

"Just seven?" Thorn gestured at the big black ship still out at sea. "Seasick. She doesn't travel well. She'll come ashore soon enough. When it's darker."

"Darker? Why?"

"She's changed, K'leef."

K'leef frowned. "I heard her hair's all white. . . ."

"That? Half the girls in Gehenna have dyed their hair white. It's called *fashion*," Thorn said between mouthfuls.

They chatted as they ate, and it felt like they hadn't been apart for a day, let alone six months. K'leef filled his ears with the victories against

Lumina, and Thorn told him about the new cakes Cook had invented, some of which he'd packed for K'leef, some of which he'd already eaten. Then the sun dipped below the horizon, the sky turned a deep purple, and the first stars blinked awake.

"I reckon it's dark enough now," said Thorn.

As if on cue, the shadows trapped between two buildings wrinkled, and a cold wind blew through. A sinister white mist swirled in the growing blackness.

"By the Six . . ." whispered K'leef.

Tendrils of shadow snaked out of the gap between the light and the darkness, between this world and another, rippling over the marble floor. The plants around them withered; the grass shriveled and died. The cold grew deeper, bone-chilling.

"I'd step back if I were you," warned Thorn.

The shadows gave way to a figure, white-haired and ebony-robed, bejeweled with rings, necklaces, and bracelets, and wearing a tall tiara made of silver and bone.

K'leef blinked in disbelief. "Lily?"

"Hello, K'leef." Lily Shadow stepped into the garden and looked around. She pointed to a wooden bucket. "Is anyone using that?"

"No, I don't think so."

"Good." She picked it up. "It's just that I think I'm going to be sick."

# THREE

*I* *should have waited till midnight.*

But she'd been stuck on that ship for two months, and once the city had come into view, she couldn't wait any longer.

*Save the greatest magic for night, when the shadows are deepest,* her father often advised her. *It'll take less of a toll on you then.*

Lily closed her eyes, shutting off the chaos around her, and tried to quell the turmoil in her belly.

Inwardly she smiled. Shadow-stepping was always a risky business, but she'd appeared exactly where she'd planned. Having Thorn to focus on helped, and appearing outside of the palace was far easier than within—it had arcane defenses against such sorcery, and who knows where she might have ended up if she'd tried appearing in the Fire Hall.

"Here," said K'leef, handing her a cup of something white and frosty. "It's sherbert."

Lily drank the icy, fruity liquid. The sour lemon taste was delicious, and it seemed to settle her stomach. Lily smacked her lips. "Got any more?"

"You're turning into Thorn, you know that?" But K'leef refilled her cup.

"Where is he?" Lily looked all around. He'd been there just a few minutes ago.

"Where do you think? Gone to check up on Hades and make sure the beast hasn't snacked on a stable boy by accident."

Typical. That boy loved the old bat more than anything else. She'd just arrived, performed some major magic—impossible for all but the most powerful sorcerers—and he was off.

Fine. Let him spend the night with the stinky bat.

"That was a most impressive entrance. Never seen anyone shadow-step before." K'leef led her into his chambers.

His quarters were huge, especially considering he was only the fourth son of the old sultan. Her parents' rooms were smaller than these.

Palace Djinn couldn't be more different from Castle Gloom. Everything here was bright and airy. The ceilings were high and domed, held up by columns as slender as willow wands. Incense burned in tripods, and rosy smoke scented the air with sweetness.

Mosaics of spiraling flames spread across the floor. The floor shimmered, as if the fire would burst forth any moment. The bronze tables were covered in books, reading being K'leef's favorite pastime, and her gaze fell upon one in particular. One with pages of metal . . .

"Like the place?" asked K'leef.

Lily took off her tiara, adjusted the folds of her skirts, and settled on one of K'leef's many plump cushions. She couldn't appear *too* impressed by someone else's palace. "You need a few more gargoyles."

"You travel through the Twilight, don't you? What's it like?"

"Pretty horrible." Lily drained the second cup of sherbert, just as good as the first.

K'leef sat down next to her. "Tell me."

"It's cold. The kind of coldness you feel in your bones. And sad. The Twilight is a place of regret and longing, K'leef. It's an in-between realm, not for the living, not for the dead. You wouldn't like it."

"And you've been into the Dreamtime, too."

"Yes. I see my father there sometimes."

"I've heard stories about you, Lily."

Lily smiled. "Are there many?"

"Yes." He shifted uncomfortably.

She could guess why. Most of those stories weren't too nice about Lady Shadow. Her family were usually the villains in the tales told at inns and taverns. Not too surprising, given the number of vampires, zombie masters, and blackhearted necromancers that bore the Shadow name. Still, it was strange finding herself in such legendary company already.

"How is Lord Iblis?" asked K'leef. "Er, aside from being a ghost?"

How was he? She didn't know. They met in the Dreamtime or Shadow Library so she could continue her studies with him, but her father's ghost was growing fainter with each visit.

She pushed the thought away. "He's fine."

"So, the Twilight and the Dreamtime. Where else?"

"What do you mean?"

K'leef sat up, excited. "Come on, Lily. Your ancestors went much farther. Deep into the darkness. To the Pit, to hell, to all the realms below."

Lily shook her head. "I'm not suicidal. I don't travel well. Spent most of this journey being seasick."

But when she was in the Twilight, she did sometimes catch glimpses of deeper kingdoms, and their inhabitants. More than once she felt—no, she *knew*—she was being watched.

She finished her third cup of sherbert and paused to examine the empty vessel. The bronze was engraved with minute stars, the rim inlaid with tissue-thin silver. She had nothing like this back in Castle Gloom.

She looked at her tiara, now resting on the table. It was the most extravagant piece of jewelry she had, yet it paled in comparison with the other treasures littering the room.

Lily cleared her throat. She wasn't here to appraise K'leef's wealth. "I'm sorry about your father. Mine always spoke highly of him. Said he was a man of honor, and that was rare nowadays."

K'leef twisted one of his many rings. "He taught me all I know."

Lily sat down next to him. "What happened? Your letters didn't mention him being ill."

K'leef became grim. "The war with Lumina, it was too much for him. He was old, Lily; he shouldn't have gone out on campaign. But he was proud. I think he wanted one last glorious day."

"And that he got. He defeated the duke. I heard he burned the Silver City to the ground."

"Exaggeration, Lily. You shouldn't believe all the tales." He looked at her. "I don't."

"What's that mean?"

K'leef's dark eyes narrowed, and Lily shifted, suddenly uncomfortable under the gaze of her friend.

"I was the first one who showed you how to use magic, remember? In the Shadow Library."

"Of course I remember," Lily replied. She, K'leef, and Thorn had snuck down to the library in Castle Gloom. She hadn't believed, not truly, that she had any sorcery in her blood, but on her initial attempt, she'd summoned a ghost: her recently deceased puppy, Custard.

That was her magic: control of the darkness.

"I owe you everything, K'leef."

"Now look at you," he said. "The witch queen. The one everyone is afraid of. But there's no reason to be, is there?"

She didn't like the way he was peering at her so intently. It was as if he *was* afraid. But of what? Everyone had a little darkness in them.

She got up and inspected the book with the metal pages. The letters, ancient Djinnic, were inlaid silver and gold, but her eyes were drawn to the jeweled bird with outspread wings on the cover. "This is the *Agni Kitab*, isn't it?"

K'leef grinned. "Trust you to know that."

"It's powerful magic. You've come a long way yourself since you were in Gehenna."

He blushed and flames flickered around his ears. "I'm working at it. Sa'if's helping. But I'll never be as good as him, or any of my brothers."

"Come on, K'leef. The *Agni Kitab* isn't for beginners. You've got a lot going for you. You're a sorcerer, a prince, and my best friend."

"Best friend? Really?" K'leef smirked. "Shall I tell Thorn, or will you?"

"*One* of them," Lily corrected, "and Thorn is one of *yours*, so we're all equal best friends."

K'leef was so like her. He and she came from the same world. He had magic in his blood, as she did, and so they understood each other. They were well versed in the houses, who the enemies were, and who could be an ally. They knew that the Six Princes had made the world the way it was and that they, as their descendants, were duty-bound to look after it.

Thorn was her other best friend because he was none of those things. His knowledge of his family tree went as far back as his grandpa and no further. He didn't care about the past, nor much about the future beyond what was for dinner, and he laughed and mocked and acted as though he didn't have a care in the world. He didn't have much respect for—or fear of—the great families, magic, or the Six Princes. It was refreshing.

She frowned, annoyed at herself for comparing K'leef to Thorn. There was no need to, and yet she couldn't help herself. Why?

She picked up the sherbert jug, wanting to think about something else, something safer. "This is Luminean, isn't it? Booty from the war?"

"We came back with a hundred wagons of treasure, some of it magical. The duke gave them to us in exchange for not destroying the Prism Palace. A pile of treasure and a few . . . noble guests."

"Hostages, you mean?" That was the usual deal. Nothing was more effective in making nobles behave than holding a few of their kin. "Anyone I know?"

K'leef's eyes brightened. "Oh, yes."

"You have to be joking. *Him?*"

"He's engaged to one of my sisters, Nargis."

Lily laughed. "That's his third engagement in a year."

"Third?" asked K'leef. "So it's true he was betrothed to a troll?"

"Dott, daughter of the troll king, so an actual princess. The wedding was all set and moving along nicely until the king accidently ate one of the heralds. Thought he was one of the appetizers. We should have realized what was about to happen when he poured gravy over the poor man's head." She couldn't help smiling at the memory. "It was quite funny."

K'leef looked more queasy than amused. "You're House Shadow. Your sense of 'funny' is different from most."

"You had to be there." Lily snapped her fingers and reached into her pocket. "Almost forgot. I have a gift for your brother. I probably won't get a chance to see him till after the coronation, so can I give it to you?" She held out a small, gem-encrusted book.

"What is it?"

"A Djinnic spell book, *The Thoughts of Niran*. How it ended up in the Shadow Library, I'll never know. It has a spell that allows you to create waterproof fire. Useful when trying to get a campfire going in the rain, I suppose."

"One of Niran's books? A rare treasure." He took it gingerly. "Should I wear gloves to handle this?"

Lily laughed. "Beware of Shadows bearing gifts?"

"The story of your great-aunt Gorgon Shadow has spread all the way south. Who was it—her fiancé?"

"*Ex*-fiancé. She was in love with Sir Ebon, a famous sorcerer, but he ended up marrying some golden-haired girl from House Solar. Lady Gorgon gave him a spell book as a wedding gift, to show there were no hard feelings. The book was old, the pages stuck together, so Ebon had to lick his fingers to turn each page. Started reading it that night, and was dead by morning."

"Killed by the poisonous ink," added K'leef. He drummed his fingers on the small book. "Your family has a particular reputation, hasn't it?"

"We're no worse than any other noble house. Better in many ways, actually. We have to be. It's tough to get away with murder when the victim can come back from the grave and hunt down his killer."

K'leef tucked the book away in his robe and stood up. "I have something—some*one*—to show you." He walked over to a brazier. Coals hissed within a tall bronze tripod; weak flames flickered across the surface. K'leef tapped it. "Paz, wake up. We have a guest. You know, the one I told you about."

The hissing grew louder. K'leef banged harder. "Paz! She's here!"

The coals shook as Lily watched. They rolled together and . . . stood up.

Smoke thickened around the black bundle, and the hiss became a voice. "I'm up. What isss it?"

"Just say hello and then you can go back to sleep."

The coals collected into a roughly humanoid shape, just a foot high. Its eyes were two glowing holes, and smoke puffed out of its mouth each time it spoke. "Sssleep? No chance of that now, isss there? You have no ressspect for your eldersss. I should ssspeak with Faisssal. He knowsss how to treat me."

"Great-Uncle Faisal's been ash for seventy years, Paz."

Flames jumped from the creature's head. "Dead?" It sighed, smoke billowing from every crack. "You mortalsss. What'sss the point? Here one minute, gone the next. Like a . . . a . . ."

"Candle?" Lily suggested.

The creature's flames grew. "She'sss got a sssmart mouth, thisss one. Friend of yoursss?"

K'leef smiled proudly. "Yes. This is Lilith Shadow, of Gehenna. Lily, this is Pazuzu."

Lily came closer. Not too much, because Pazuzu burned. "I didn't know House Djinn still had any efreet."

Efreet were fire spirits, beings of the Shardlands. In the past, House Djinn had commanded thousands of them—not small imps like this, but towering giants of fire. During the Battle of the Boiling Sea, a battalion had destroyed the entire fleet of Captain Hammerhead. She smiled at Pazuzu. "A pleasure to meet you."

"Isss it? Maybe for you," said the efreet. "Ssso you're Lilith Shadow? The boy won't shut up about you. Each time he getsss one of your letters, he readsss it to me. Keepsss them tied up with a pretty little ribbon—"

K'leef jumped between them. "Enough, Paz. Lily doesn't want to hear about my filing system."

"Oh, I think I do. So, Paz, where does K'leef keep my letters, exactly?"

The doors burst open, and the room was flooded with silk, jewelry, and dozens of yelling girls. Paz winked out and vanished in a thick puff of smoke.

K'leef groaned. "Oh no . . ."

The girls swirled around her, all talking at once. They spoke in Djinnic, in Gehennish, and a dozen other languages. Lily's head spun as she tried to follow just half the chatter. They gasped, giggled, and pushed and pulled at each other, fighting to be the first to speak to K'leef's guest.

Word had gotten out that the witch queen was here.

"Welcome, Lilith Shadow!"

"My name's Sami! You can stay in my quarters! I've had the walls painted black!"

"No! Stay with me! I've got skulls in mine!"

"She's not living over the latrines! She'll live with me! I have a view of the moon! She'll like that!"

"I do not live over the latrines! That stink's your perfume!"

"Lady Shadow, my cat died! Can you bring it back? Please?"

"Ow! Stop pulling my hair!"

One of the princesses pushed through the throng. "She is staying in her own quarters, and you all know it!" The girl heaved one of her sisters aside to get next to Lily, and then she glared back at the others. "Stop it! All of you! Now!"

There were mutters, quiet swears, and a few awkward shuffles, but they obeyed.

The one in charge gave her hair an imperial flick. "That's better. Behave yourselves. You are princesses of House Djinn, not a bunch of water-brained nymphs, and Lady Shadow is our guest." She turned to Lily and curtsied. "I'm Ameera. It is a pleasure to meet you, great queen."

"Ameera? K'leef's twin sister?"

She smiled, surprised, and slipped her hand through Lily's. "K'leef told you about me?"

"Of course," said Lily. "He said you've been bossing him around since the crib."

Ameera laughed. "True! It's my job to keep him honest, Lily. Can I call you Lily?"

Lily nodded and scanned the crowd for the liveliest—K'leef's favorite. "You're Samira—"

The girl jumped with glee. "But you can call me Sami! All my sisters do!"

"You're Nargis." She bowed her head toward the older girl. "K'leef tells me you just got engaged. Congratulations."

Nargis giggled behind her hands.

Ameera slipped her arm through the crook of Lily's. "Your Djinnic is most excellent, by the way. Who taught you?"

Lily's smile grew stiff. "My uncle. He spent a few years here, using it as a base when he was exploring the Shardlands."

"Your uncle, Pandemonium Shadow? You exiled him, yes?"

"Yes. He . . . broke the law."

What Lily wanted to say was *He killed my parents and brother and tried to murder me, too. Everyone else in Castle Gloom had wanted his head on top of a spike on Lamentation Hill, so I'd been merciful with mere exile.* Yet the pain lingered. Pan had been her hero once upon a time. He'd been the brilliant swordsman and brave explorer who returned from exciting adventures laden with wild tales and gifts galore. Nothing like her parents, who rarely stepped foot outside Gehenna, all because of duty.

Ameera squeezed her arm. "I'm sorry. It was thoughtless of me to bring that up."

Lily spoke to each princess in turn, pulling out relevant details and anecdotes as she did so. Naturally she had studied up on every member of K'leef's family on the way here. What else had there been to do? Besides trying to teach Thorn his letters. And being sick over the railings.

But there was one girl she didn't recognize. She lurked at the back, dressed more like a servant than a princess, in dull, bland hues. "I'm sorry, but you are . . . ?"

The girl bowed. "Kali, Lady Shadow."

Kali? But wasn't that the name of—

"The executioner?"

The girl smiled. "I'm flattered you know of me."

Lily didn't miss the mocking tone. "You have quite a reputation for one so young."

"The same could be said about you."

Some people are born enemies. Lily recognized Kali as one of hers.

Kali came from the far south, from one of the kingdoms that paid tribute to the Sultanate. Her skin was as shiny and black as oil at midnight. Skull tattoos encircled her slim neck, and there was coldness in her eyes, despite the smile. The only bright color was on her nails, which were painted a rich blood-red.

"Oh, ignore Kali," declared Ameera. "She has no manners." Ameera reached over and drew her bejeweled fingers through Lily's white hair. "You are very beautiful, Lily. K'leef didn't tell me *that*."

Lily laughed. "He *did* tell me about you."

Ameera was gorgeous. She had large and intense dark eyes, dusky skin, and glossy hair blacker than a raven's, but all the sisters had those features. They were all equally wealthy, too, and similarly bedecked with gold and gems. Ameera wore earrings that dangled down to her shoulders, and a large ruby stud pierced her nostril. She had golden collars and necklaces, and her sleeveless arms were sheathed from wrist to shoulder with gem-encrusted gold and silver bands. The string of rubies in her hair made Lily's black diamonds seem dull in comparison. Lily pulled at her own cuffs. Next to this Djinnic princess, she felt as shabby as a farm girl.

Ameera's beauty was beyond the mere physical, though. She had a strange, indefinable quality, a presence that was impossible to ignore. Even when surrounded by her sisters, it was she who attracted the eye.

K'leef had written to Lily with tales of his sister. Of how great nobles had courted her, and how four brothers had dueled over her, wiping out half a generation in one family. Yet, as far as she knew, Ameera had refused to be betrothed to anyone. Lily had assumed these stories were fanciful exaggerations, but now, facing her, she could easily believe that men would die for the likes of Ameera.

What had Mother once told her? *A woman's smile can destroy kingdoms.*

"I had heard the Djinnic princesses are the most beautiful in all the New Kingdoms," Lily went on, "and I now see how true that is."

Ameera fanned herself. "We shall be the very best of sisters, I'm sure! Now, we have prepared your quarters. Come with me. Did you bring any servants?"

"Just a few zombies," said Lily.

The room fell silent. Lily remembered, too late, that not everyone felt the same way about zombies as she did. "But they're under strict instructions not to eat any brains while here."

"So it's all fine, then," said Ameera. She clapped to jolt her sisters out of their fearful stupor. "Not that they'd find many brains among this bunch."

Lily looked over to her friend, who'd been pushed to the back of the crowd. "All right with you, K'leef?"

"I cannot defy my *slightly* older sister," he said, hands raised in surrender to Ameera's will. "I'll go check on Thorn. Get some rest, Lily. Tomorrow is a very special day."

Of course. Why else was she here?

Tomorrow they crowned the new sultan.

# FOUR

"How many did he eat?" asked Thorn.

Hades did not look happy. He lay on his back, wings curved around his swollen belly. He didn't smell good at the best of times, but right now, the air around him was especially foul, what with noxious clouds coming out of *both* ends.

"Six sheep and a camel. All the way up to the hump." The stable boy leaned on his bloodied mop. "He made a mess of it, too."

Hades burped and spat out a hoof.

The stable boy sighed. "What shall we do?"

"First thing is to open a few windows and let some air in. He's got a lot of digesting to do, and the smell's only going to get—"

Hades groaned and another cloud erupted. The hay around him shriveled.

"—worse."

K'leef appeared at the stable door. "I've been looking— What in the name of the Six is that smell?"

"He's two hundred years old, K'leef. His bowels don't work the way they used to."

It wasn't a good idea to linger. Even Thorn felt a bit queasy.

They left the boy to deal with Hades and hurried away from the stables. They didn't escape the noxious vapors until they were halfway across the courtyard.

"Poor Hades," said Thorn. "He's not used to foreign food like camel."

"Imagine how distressed he would be if he ate an elephant," said K'leef.

"You heard about that?"

"*Everyone* heard about it. Do you know who was riding that elephant? The ones who got thrown in the sea?"

"Not sure I care." He was used to upsetting nobles back in Gehenna. Why should it be any different here?

K'leef just shook his head. "You never change."

Thorn filled his lungs with the cool, fresh night air. "That bat's going to be useless for a week."

"You were planning on going somewhere?"

Thorn shrugged. "No harm in having a look around, is there? The Shardlands begin no more than ten miles from here. Ain't that right?"

"Only you would want to go sightseeing around the Shardlands."

"They can't be that bad."

K'leef arched an elegant eyebrow. "Not at all. A walk in the park. A park covered in volcanoes, that is, and blasted by storms that melt your bones and make the earth scream in agony. No, not bad at all."

"Yeah, but there's loads of treasure to be found, right?"

K'leef arched his other eyebrow, too. Thorn wished he could do that.

"Treasure? Since when did you care about anything except your next pie?"

"A crown that once sat on the head of one of the Six Princes would buy me a whole lot of pies."

It was all just over that western horizon: the long-abandoned kingdoms of the Six Princes. Where they had lived and ruled before they went to war with each other and the world was divided up. One day he'd see the ruins for himself.

The moon was at its zenith, and through the open gates Thorn saw the city of Nahas below, alive with revelry. The hundred days of mourning were finally over, and people were celebrating. Tomorrow they'd have a new sultan.

"What's your brother like?" Thorn asked.

"Which one? I have . . . seventeen. Only six that count, though."

"Because they're sorcerers?" Thorn scowled. That was all that mattered, wasn't it? Those who could weave spells ruled; the rest just bowed.

K'leef must have heard the quiet disapproval in his response. "It is what it is. And while Sa'if is a powerful sorcerer, he's also a good man. The best I know."

"Kinda thought that was me."

K'leef ignored that comment. "You'll meet him tomorrow, before the coronation. You'll see."

Suddenly, shouts fell from the gatehouse—fearful ones. Guards ran past them and formed up in front of the gates. The captain saluted K'leef as he passed, speaking rapidly in a panicked tone.

"What's wrong?" asked Thorn as the two of them caught up with the guards.

"It seems we're under attack." K'leef blew over his fingers, summoning fire. "Look out there."

This was a side of K'leef Thorn hadn't seen before. The K'leef he remembered liked books and plump cushions, but as fire spread across his hands and his eyes smoldered like coals, Thorn realized there was more to the soft prince than he'd assumed.

"You'd better get inside," K'leef warned.

"And miss a fight? No way."

"Thorn . . ."

"Just someone get me a bow and some arrows."

Figures approached the gate in the darkness. They shambled, they moaned, and they didn't look particularly healthy. Some carried crates, others pulled wagons, and there were a couple with piles of luggage balanced on their heads.

"Relax," said Thorn. "They're ours."

"*Ours?*" asked K'leef. The guards loaded their crossbows.

Thorn shrugged. "Lily's."

The foremost came into the lamplight. Patches of dried yellow skin partially covered his face, and one eye socket was empty. He wore a threadbare gray uniform—it might have once been black—and a sparrow had made a nest in his open skull.

A guard yelled and shot a quarrel through the person's chest, knocking him over.

"What'd you do that for?" Thorn hurried over and helped the man back up. "Hold still and let me . . ." He grabbed the quarrel. The sparrow circled above them, tweeting its outrage.

K'leef instructed the guards to cease shooting and joined Thorn and the victim. "Lily brought zombies?"

"Didn't she tell you?"

"She said something, but I thought she was joking."

"Lily never jokes about her zombies." He wrenched the quarrel out. "You all right, Al?"

"*Rrrhuur,*" said Al. He waved at the sparrow, and it took its place back in his skull. "*Uuurgggh.*"

Thorn patted his back. "Good. Now get the boys to put the luggage over there."

The guards watched, stupefied, as the zombies offloaded the luggage up against the wall. Thorn followed around, collecting any . . . parts. He found a hand. "Get me a needle and some thick twine," he told K'leef. "The salt air has made them rot quicker than usual."

"She brought zombies?" K'leef asked again.

"Why not? See that one with the big gold earrings? That's Eddie. He'd always wanted to be a pirate, but he died before getting to the ocean. Lily thought it would be nice for him to come along."

"She thought she'd take the zombies on holiday?" K'leef sounded more bewildered than ever.

"Once upon a time, that would have sounded strange to me, too. Guess I've been in Gehenna too long."

"Where are we going to put them?" asked K'leef.

"Somewhere downwind. They don't smell so fresh." Thorn counted off the crates and trunks. "All there. Well done, lads. Go and have a lie-down . . . how about over by the wall?"

K'leef shook his head. "Best keep them out of the palace. I'll get a few servants to take Lily's dresses to her rooms. Come on, I've got supper waiting."

They were halfway across the square when the rider galloped in. The two boys jumped back just in time to avoid being trampled.

"Hey, watch it!" Thorn yelled.

The rider reined around and down came a spear, its tip only a foot away from Thorn's chest. The man snarled something in Djinnic, but Thorn understood the meaning. He raised his hands and backed off.

The rider dismounted, and Thorn got a good glare at him.

He'd never seen the like. The man wore a dusty billowing robe. Tucked into the wide black sash around his waist were a dagger and scimitar. His head was bound by a dirty turban, and his face was as wrinkled and as dark as old oak. A scorpion tattoo covered each cheek.

The man jammed his spear into the ground and waited for the rest of his party.

More riders entered, and behind them came a horse-drawn wagon. Its driver was clearly related to the horsemen, but the man seated beside him was no kin.

The passenger was gaunt with hard cheekbones, and he wore patched robes of faded scarlet with gold embroidery at the edges. He wore no turban; his loose, tangled hair was decorated with rings and trinkets, as was his stringy beard. He was half vagabond, half nobleman.

"Who is that?" Thorn asked.

K'leef swore. "Jambiya."

He was also without a weapon, and that meant only one thing. Even these days, when magic was weak and few knew more than a couple of spells, no self-respecting sorcerer wielded so much as a knife. A weapon was a sign of weakness, that you didn't trust your magic to protect you.

He did carry a staff. The driver gave it to him as he dismounted from the wagon bench. For a moment, Thorn wondered if it might be one of the fabled wands of magic; then he realized its purpose was more mundane. The red-robed man used it to tap out ahead of him. He was blind.

K'leef ran up to him. "Brother! I did not expect you."

Jambiya turned his puckered eyelids in K'leef's direction. "K'leef? Why would I not come?"

"I will have rooms prepared for you and your men."

"There are more yet to arrive. A few are still back in the city, enjoying themselves. We have traveled far and hard."

K'leef muttered something like an apology, so Thorn left the two brothers alone to catch up. What interested him were the wagon and the cage upon it.

Four people huddled within it, each one in chains.

Thorn rubbed his wrists. It had been six months since he'd worn shackles, but his skin itched when he saw them.

These folk had to be bad, the worst of the worst, to come here like this.

One of the prisoners shuffled to the bars and held out a hand. "Water?"

Thorn hesitated, looking around to see who might be watching him. The riders might not take kindly to him talking with their prisoners. But they were all distracted, tending to their horses or heading off to find food and soft beds. So he filled a jug from a water butt and brought it over.

The prisoner didn't drink it herself but passed it to another. A child, huddled in the corner.

These were Jambiya's prisoners? A crone, a woman, and two small girls. The woman was pregnant, as in ready-to-drop.

"What did you do?" he asked her.

"Get caught." She stroked her swollen belly. "Jambiya attacked our camp out in the Shardlands."

"You live in the Shardlands?" Thorn approached the bars, curious to meet some nomad folk. "I've heard there's wild magic out there—in the air, the water, and the ground itself. The magic seeps into the bones, in strange ways."

The woman raised an eyebrow. "That's what you've been told?"

"You look normal, though."

She leaned closer so their faces were less than a foot apart. "You think so?"

She rubbed her forehead. The wrinkles began to part. . . .

A pale, rheumy orb appeared under the unpeeling skin.

Thorn stumbled back. "What is it? An eye?"

Her skin closed over it. "Yes, my third eye. But it's practically useless. If it had allowed me to see into the future, we wouldn't have gotten caught." The woman passed the now empty jug back to him. "More."

Thorn glanced back. Jambiya and K'leef were talking intensely, with a hint of anger in their voices. The soldiers were busy stretching their legs. He refilled the jug and brought over an abandoned loaf, which was snatched from him and quickly devoured by the girls.

The woman wiped her long, disheveled hair from her face, revealing dried blood caked on her nose. Clearly she hadn't been captured without a fight. "How about some meat?"

"What did you do? Kill someone?"

She appraised him. "You Gehennish?"

"I suppose." The black outfit was a giveaway.

"They say women are free to make spells there, thanks to the witch queen."

Thorn shook his head. "That ain't entirely true."

"Here, boy, they follow the old laws." She raised her eyes to the tallest tower and pointed. "That's where we're bound."

"There? What is it?"

"It was once called the Phoenix Tower, back when the sultans kept such creatures. But it's the Candle now," she said. "Where they burn witches. High above the city so all can see."

"You're a witch?"

"Yes, and so are my daughters." She gestured at the two girls. "Jambiya is thorough in his cleansing."

Thorn shivered despite the heat. "He's going to burn you all? For what?"

"For being born female." The woman grabbed the bars, and her tone turned urgent. "Your mistress! Go speak with her! See if—"

Someone grabbed Thorn's collar and threw him backward into the dust. He tried to get up, but a stick was pressed hard against his chest.

Jambiya stood over him, snarling. "Do not talk to the prisoners."

Thorn tried to knock the stick aside, but he was held fast. "Let me up. Now."

"You cannot demand anything of me, slave."

"I am no one's slave."

K'leef took Jambiya's arm. "Let him go, Brother. He doesn't know how things are done here."

Jambiya lifted his stick and waved it at his soldiers. "Take the prisoners to the Candle."

K'leef helped Thorn up, muttering, "You shouldn't have done that."

Thorn watched as Jambiya drove the wagon toward the tower. The woman's gaze stayed on Thorn till the doors to the Candle closed behind her.

The Candle was very tall. Higher than the Needle. Bats circled its summit.

K'leef nudged him. "Stop it."

"I'm not doing nothing."

"You've always been a bad liar, Thorn." K'leef frowned. "Look, let me talk with Jambiya. Perhaps he'll be lenient this time. They might get away with just a branding."

*"A branding?"* He shook his head at the thought of hot pokers on bare skin. "It's the same everywhere, isn't it? There's only one law: the law of the forest. The strong rule over the weak. No matter how much we may try to pretend it's otherwise, there's no escaping it."

"I'm sorry, Thorn. But please don't meddle. Not here, not now."

Thorn met his friend's gaze. "Seems to me it was my meddling that got you freed when you were a prisoner. Or have you forgotten?"

"I'm not your enemy, Thorn. I'll speak to Sa'if about the family. But if they broke the law . . ."

"And if Sa'if can't stop him? Then when will Jambiya burn them?"

"After the coronation."

"Yup, that makes sense. You wouldn't want the smell spoiling the party, eh?" Thorn turned away in disgust.

# FIVE

"Who knows, you may even end up with a tan," Thorn said to Lily as he watched Mary fuss over her.

"We Gehennish don't tan."

Thorn was bored out of his mind. "Those new?" he asked, lifting his chin toward her necklace.

"It's not like you to take an interest in my jewelry."

"Those gemstones are kinda hard to miss."

Lily fingered the string of diamonds. "Ameera gave this to me. It's one of the treasures House Djinn received from the Solars. And if you think these are impressive, you should see what she kept for herself."

"Anything besides sparkly things? Like magic swords?" He wouldn't mind one of those. . . .

"Lots of mirrors. Ameera has had the palace filled with them. She's a canny young woman, managing to get herself put in charge of the distribution of the treasures."

"Can't believe she and K'leef are twins. Grandpa said a woman who—"

"Yes," interrupted Lily. "I'm sure he did."

She never let him finish his grandpa stories. "How much longer is this going to take?" he asked. "It's just that everyone's heading down to the coronation now. We'll end up in the back and won't be able to see nothing."

Mary, working on Lily's hair, held an armory's worth of pins in her mouth, but she still managed a sneer. "Feel free to leave at any time, Thorn."

"Can't. Lily wants to keep an eye on me. She's worried about my health."

Lily sighed loudly. "That's one way of putting it."

He grinned. "Mom will be happy to know you're taking such good care of me."

Lily rolled her eyes. "That's me, Lily Shadow, babysitter extraordinaire."

"Can't you just put it in a ponytail?" Thorn suggested, quite reasonably, he thought. "Lily looks real nice in a ponytail."

"I can't go to a coronation with—"

"Hold your head still, girl." Mary stepped back to check her work. "The Medusa style's a bit tricky."

Hadn't there been a story about Medusa Shadow? Thorn couldn't remember it exactly, but it had something to do with snakes. . . .

He peered at the long, complex tresses that Mary had been crafting since dawn. Yes, they did look like snakes, sort of, if the lighting was poor and you squinted a lot.

"How about a bob?" he suggested, determined to speed things up.

Mary choked. "A noble with short hair? What would people think?"

She opened a tub of greasy gloop and, taking a handful, began fixing the tresses in place.

Thorn came a bit closer, though not too near. Mary could be deadly with a pin, and he had the puncture wounds to prove it. "Smells funny. What is it?"

Mary rolled Lily's locks between her hands and warned her, "Don't go near any candles unless you want to spend the next year bald."

"Mary!" Lily jerked away from her.

"And don't nod too much, or it'll all come undone, and I won't have you shaming Gehenna by looking like a farm girl."

Thorn leaned his forehead against a column. "Are you ready?"

There was a knock on the door, and K'leef came in before anyone answered. "Are you ready?" he echoed.

"By the Six . . ." muttered Thorn when he saw K'leef's outfit. "What have they done to you?"

"It's the latest thing." K'leef gave a slow turn.

"For what? Fighting a flock of peacocks?"

"There *are* a lot of feathers . . ." K'leef admitted. Then he added with an aloof sniff, "But it's fashion, something you wouldn't understand."

"Reckon fashion's some sort of punishment nobles give themselves so we peasants have something to laugh about."

Mary waved at them. "Take him, K'leef. Right now."

K'leef adjusted the high collar that gave the impression feathers were sprouting out of his ears. "You have an hour. I saved you a space up at the front."

"Thanks."

"I'm talking to *Lily*. Thorn, you're at the back. You should have gotten there hours ago if you wanted a view."

"That's just great!" Thorn glowered at the two, but Lily couldn't turn to see it, because Mary was still sculpting her. "Come a thousand miles to stare at the back of someone's head. Just. Great."

"Come with me, Thorn," said K'leef.

"Anything's got to be better than this," said Thorn. "Which is real boring. In case I haven't made my point clearly enough."

"Get out, Thorn!" chorused Lily and Mary.

The boys exited, Thorn slamming the door behind them to make more of a point. He looked up and down the corridor. Plenty of hustle and bustle. "Where are we headed?"

K'leef pulled at one of the tall feathers rising from his turban. "You really think this is too much? Wahid's feathers are almost five feet long and covered in gold."

*Why do I hang out with these people? Nobles just aren't normal.* "Where are we going, K'leef?"

Palace Djinn couldn't be more different from Castle Gloom. For one thing, it was sunlit. Rows of latticed windows ran along the long, lofty corridors and cast weird nets of shadow and brightness over the marble and bronze.

Servants dashed and nobles rushed. There was controlled bedlam as last, last, *last*-minute preparations were put in place.

But as they turned one corner, they were showered with sparks.

"Hey!" exclaimed Thorn.

"Ssso thisss isss Thorn? Not impresssed. Not impresssed at all."

K'leef shook his turban. "You almost set fire to my feathers, Paz."

A pile of coals stood in the corridor. It really stood, on a pair of stubby legs, reaching no higher than Thorn's waist. The surface sizzled, ash blew off of it in the faint breeze, a pair of fiery eyes narrowed, and flames flickered over its head instead of hair.

"Thorn, meet Pazuzu. He's my efreet."

The efreet glowered, and smoke hissed from the crack of a mouth. "You're late. Asss usual."

An efreet. Lily had told him about those. And just when he thought zombies were as weird as his life could get.

"What are you ssstaring at?"

"What's got you so hot and bothered?" asked Thorn, not used to being bullied by a burning pile of rocks. "You almost set me on fire."

"*Hot and bothered?* Isss that some kind of joke?"

Thorn raised his hands. "All I'm saying is you need to cool down."

The flames flared. "*Cool down?* You're telling me to cool down? Why don't you just tosss me in the fountain and be done with it?"

"All right. K'leef, you grab its legs."

K'leef stepped between them. "That's enough. Today's not the day for picking fights."

"He'sss waiting, ssso hurry up." Pazuzu turned away, muttering. "If I wasss a hundred yearsss younger, I'd teach you a lessson."

K'leef watched it go, and there was a sorrowful look in his gaze. "Poor Paz. He's lost his spark. He's barely hot enough to cook breakfast now."

"I'm never gonna get used to this place."

They approached a chamber protected by two warriors just as another man was leaving. He stopped when he saw K'leef. "My lord. A grand day, eh?"

"Indeed, Captain," replied K'leef warily. "How go the wedding plans?"

"We are honored that our two houses will be joined. My daughter, Sea Pearl, looks forward to living here. She is already making friends with your sisters." Then he turned to Thorn. "What is it?"

"Er . . . you've got gills. I've never seen a person with gills before."

The man spread out his hands. They were webbed.

House Coral, of course. The water wizards. There were always a few at any port, but none as . . . wet? The captain's skin was, if you looked closely, scaled, and there was an emerald tinge to his hair. His eyes were large and bulbous, but there was nothing comical about his cutlass and scintillating scaled armor.

"I have business to attend to," stated the captain. He marched off.

K'leef nudged him. "It's rude to stare. And be careful—Captain Cuttlefish has spent most of his career as a pirate. That sword's not for show."

"So your brother's getting married?" asked Thorn.

"There'll be a lot of marriages over the next few months. They're the oldest forms of treaty, Thorn. You know that. Sa'if is allowed to have four official wives, and Sea Pearl's lucky—she's the first and will have the highest ranking. But then—"

"Wait up. Four wives?"

"They each get a palace. Then he can have as many concubines as he can manage."

Thorn laughed. "So, they got anyone lined up for you?"

K'leef blushed. "There has been some talk."

"Anyone I know?"

He blushed deeper, and small flames sprouted from his ears. He mumbled something.

"What was that?" Thorn asked, suspicious it *was* someone he knew.

"It'll never happen. She's a ruler, and I'm just son number four. The difference in rank is too great."

"You can't mean Lily?" asked Thorn in disbelief.

Before K'leef could answer, the doors opened and they were ushered inside.

A young man spun around as they entered. "K'leef! And this must be Thorn!"

K'leef grinned. "Thorn, this is Sa'if."

Thorn bowed. "Your Highness."

Sa'if lifted him off the ground with a lung-crushing hug. "Thank you, Thorn, for all you've done for us." He put him down and smiled. "You'll leave here with your pockets full of rubies, I promise."

Now it was Thorn's turn to blush. Sa'if's attention overwhelmed him. There was something magical about the prince, and it was more than mere sorcery. "I was just helping my friend." Then he remembered rule one about royal gifts: never turn them down. "But rubies are good."

Sa'if pulled a gem-studded ring from his little finger and handed it to him. "Yes, they are, aren't they?"

*This would buy me a plot of farmland somewhere sunny. How come Lily never gives me stuff like this?* Thorn nodded his thanks and tucked it away in his sock.

He stepped aside as two servants carried over a cloak of rich red silk.

Sa'if sighed as they put it on him. "It's all rather ridiculous, isn't it?"

"Yeah," Thorn said. "Now you mention it."

"Thorn!" snapped K'leef.

He bit his lip. This was one of those weird tests of diplomacy, and he'd just failed. Lily was trying to teach him, but he still couldn't figure out what was diplomatic and what was a bald-faced lie. "What I meant was, you look really amazing."

Sa'if's wide smile was reassuring. He wiggled his shoe in the air. It had the curliest toes Thorn had ever seen. "These are the Blessed Boots of the Burning Walk. They're to guide me to the right path."

Thorn frowned. "You're making that up."

"Surprisingly, no. The cloak is the Ruby Robe of Righteous Rule. And no, I'm not making that up, either. It was worn by one of my ancestors when he first built the palace here in Nahas. These are his, too." Sa'if tugged at his trousers. "The Pantaloons of Ash, the Desert Hermit. Very special."

"My grandpa has special pants, too," said Thorn. "He's getting on in years, and his gut—"

"That's quite enough, Thorn," interrupted K'leef. "Maybe we can hear about your esteemed grandfather later?"

"Of course." Thorn had plenty of stories about his grandpa. "So what happens next?"

Sa'if straightened his cuffs. "Simple, really. I take the throne and put on the lava crown. If my magic is weak, I burn."

"Burn?"

K'leef slapped his forehead. "Why do you think it's called the lava crown?"

"You nobles are mad. No offense. What if you're having an off day?"

Fire dripped from Sa'if's hands. It poured between his fingertips, spreading over the metal floor, dancing and weaving in serpentine patterns. The heat was intense, stronger than if they were standing before a blacksmith's forge. "Rulers cannot have off days, Thorn." He clapped and the flames vanished.

"I told you he was good," said K'leef proudly.

Sa'if donned a couple more necklaces, then another cloak on top of the red one he was already wearing. "I think that's it." He approached a veiled piece of furniture. "Let's have a look, shall we?"

He pulled off the cloth and stood in front of a full-height mirror. The frame was white wood and lined with platinum. Booty gathered from the Solars, Thorn supposed.

"Hmm, you'd think a Luminean mirror wouldn't be so foggy." Sa'if rubbed the glass with his sleeve. "There, that's better."

Thorn cleared his throat. "Sire, I don't know if K'leef has mentioned some prisoners to you."

"The witches, you mean?" Sa'if frowned at his reflection. "This mirror is too cloudy. The Solars palmed us off with junk."

"They're just four women, sire. Two grown ones and two little girls. They ain't done no one no harm."

"Why do you care so much about them? They're nothing to you." Sa'if turned slowly before the mirror. "K'leef, could you straighten the back of my cloak?"

Thorn bit his tongue. Sa'if seemed more interested in his outfit than the lives of four innocent people. "Sire, please . . ."

"I've been told one of them has a deformity. A third eye?"

"So what of it?" Thorn asked. "She was born that way."

Sa'if glanced at his brother, and there was some unspoken communication between the pair of them. Then he turned to Thorn. "Shardland nomads are strange people, Thorn. They can be dangerous. They don't follow the laws of civilized folk."

"Laws like burning innocent women and children?" snapped Thorn. "Seems to me, such laws we could do without."

*Did I overstep the mark? Didn't do no good insulting a ruler on his coronation day.* But Thorn couldn't help himself.

K'leef just shook his head.

Sa'if's face was a clear, thoughtful mask. "K'leef told me much about you, Thorn."

"Er . . . did he mention I saved his life? More than once?"

"You've got fire in your belly, Thorn. That'll stand you in good stead in this kingdom." Sa'if smiled at him. "Rest easy. The four of them will be freed tomorrow morning and sent on their way."

"Unharmed? No brandings or nothing?"

"Unharmed. On my honor, Thorn. Is that good enough?"

Thorn knew how much the Djinn valued their honor. He nodded. "I'd better get going."

K'leef nodded and took him to the door. "Thanks for coming all this way, Thorn."

Thorn patted the ring tucked in his sock. "The trip's paid for itself."

"Still won't make you pretty."

"Yeah, but I'll be able to buy a better class of friend."

Just like he'd predicted, he ended up in the back. Way, waay, waaay in the back. Thorn jostled with the commoners in the vast courtyard in the heart of Palace Djinn. The sun was high and hot, and there was no shade—the awnings were only for nobles. But he managed to edge his way around to a palm tree and climb up the trunk to get a few feet above everyone's heads.

Over a hundred yards away, on a raised platform, the throne awaited its new occupant. Thorn had expected something made of gold and studded with precious gems, but instead the seat had been carved into a chunk of black rock—cooled lava, he supposed. The thing looked ancient and uncomfortable.

Lined up on either side of the throne were the great and good from many houses. Under one canopy stood a crowd of women, the old sultan's wives and concubines. Some were local, dusky-skinned with jet-black hair, but others were clearly foreign-born from all other kingdoms. One looked prouder than the rest, so he guessed she was the mother of the soon-to-be sultan Sa'if and, incidentally, K'leef and Jambiya.

No wonder she was proud. All her sons were sorcerers.

Lily was easy to spot, all dressed in black. Her tresses did look like serpents from here. Some of the Sultanate's princesses stood with her, Ameera closest and constantly whispering in her ear, and on the opposite side stood Gabriel.

So it was true. Gabriel was being held hostage by the Djinn, to make sure Duke Solar behaved himself. The boy looked . . . well, the way he always looked: like a preening idiot. His silver-blond hair was bound with a platinum band, his white suit shone with bright diamond buttons, and the early sun lit the silver on his belt. A jeweled sword hung from it, which surprised Thorn, until he remembered how useless Gabriel was with a weapon.

*Travel halfway around the world and I still can't escape the Solar boy. What will it take to be rid of him once and for all?* Thorn looked away. The palace was big enough that it would be easy to avoid him until they shipped home. *At least Gabriel isn't engaged to Lily anymore. But what did K'leef mean when he—*

A cacophony of drumming and trumpet blasts burst from all around, and the crowd parted. Sa'if led the procession, followed by his brothers. One tapped his way forward with a stick: Jambiya. He wore simple long, flowing robes, no jewelry, and his eyes were two wrinkled patches of skin. The beard was unkempt, his ragged hair bound by a simple leather band.

The music stopped dead, leaving behind a deep, resonating silence.

The brothers halted at the foot of the platform, and Sa'if proceeded up alone. He took his place on the throne.

Two attendants brought in a bronze stand, upon which sat the crown. It was ugly. Charred, twisted, and dull. It was passed from brother to brother, and then K'leef took it. Even from here Thorn could see his friend biting his lip as he carried it carefully up the steps to the throne.

They exchanged a few words, K'leef and Sa'if, and Thorn saw the older one put the younger at ease with a smile. K'leef turned to face the crowd, holding the crown high.

"Let the Six Princes bless Sa'if, the Sultan Djinn!"

Thorn realized he was holding his breath. As was everyone else.

Ever so carefully, K'leef lowered the crown onto Sa'if's brow. He stepped aside, bowing low, as Sa'if stood up.

The crown began to glow. Flames spat from its crooked spikes.

People cheered.

The crown brightened as the flames rose higher. It blazed to a blinding white.

And Sa'if screamed.

# SIX

"Those screams . . . Did you hear them?" asked Thorn.

It was evening and still there'd been no word about Sa'if's condition. Thorn—and everyone else—had watched in horror as K'leef used his bare hands to tear the fiery crown off his brother's head. It had taken the combined magic of three brothers to put the flames out.

"I was practically standing right next to him," said Lily. "But it was the smell, Thorn. How can anyone stand to watch a burning, with a smell like that?"

"Yeah, I know what you mean. It stains you, don't it?" He sniffed his sleeve. Yes, there it was. He'd dump these clothes the first chance he got.

Sa'if's hideous screams still echoed in his head. They reminded Thorn of the first time he'd shot a deer in Herne's Forest, years ago. His arrow had caught it too high, missing the heart. The creature had stumbled off, and its cries of anguish had made Thorn's blood run cold. His dad eventually tracked it down and finished it off, but Thorn had wept for days after, refusing to pick up a bow.

He'd known that eventually he would have to go out hunting again—it was what you did if you didn't want to starve—but first he'd practiced and practiced until his shoulders had ached and his fingers bled. A clean death: that was what the hunter owed his prey.

"His magic failed him," Thorn said. "Thought that wasn't possible."

Lily's quill scratched the parchment. A pile of already completed letters lay waiting for collection. But she wasn't fooling Thorn. He saw her tears dripping onto the yellow sheets.

He felt so useless. He wanted to do something, even help Mary packing next door, but Lily's maid had ordered him out, not wanting his grubby fingerprints spoiling Lily's fine dresses. So here he was, watching Lily compose in half a dozen languages when he could spell little more than his name in just one. "Who are you writing to?" he asked.

"Everyone. Sa'if's not going to be sultan, even if he survives. There will be consequences throughout the realms. I've . . . I've had experience with this before."

Of course she had. When her family was murdered, it had been a tragedy on two levels: personal and political. Thorn sat down beside her. "I'm sorry."

She smiled, though her brow remained furrowed. "Sable's down at the docks getting everything ready. It's madness."

"When are we leaving?"

"Soon. I'm doing the best I can, but there's no treaty between us and the Sultanate. Nothing official."

"Does that matter?"

She rubbed her forehead. "Oh, Thorn. It matters so much. I don't know where to begin. The Solars will move now. Their most powerful enemy is out of the picture. No one's in charge here, don't you see? If the sultan and I were official allies, then we could keep Lumina under control. The Solars wouldn't try anything with Gehenna to its north and the Sultanate to the south."

"Can't you just band together anyway? Why do you need a treaty? K'leef's our friend. We could stay a while longer and help him."

"A treaty makes things law, Thorn. It gets my nobles on my side. Friendship alone isn't enough of a reason to risk fighting."

Thorn shook his head. "Seems to me that's the *only* reason for fighting."

Lily finished off the letter with a few drops of wax and her seal, the entwined moon crescents. She called to Mary from the next chamber. "Mary, get these to Sable. He'll know what to do."

"You'll be all right for a while?" asked Mary, gathering the papers.

"I have Thorn," Lily said.

Thorn sat up. "You think there'll be trouble?"

"There's always trouble when crowns are involved," Mary said. She waved toward the other room. "Those trunks are ready to go. I'll need some of the zombies to carry them down to the *Shadow's Blade*."

Lily handed over the Skeleton Key. "Put the jewelry boxes in the secure hold and double-lock everything."

Mary looked around the room, her lips pursed. "What a mess."

"Looks pretty tidy to me," said Thorn. "Compared to the squires' dorms, that's for sure."

Lily started on another letter. "I think Mary meant *politically*, Thorn. Not literally."

"Oh." Thorn left such matters to those who cared. "There's a saying back home that . . . *someone* once told me." He saw Lily's fingers tighten on her quill, but he pushed on. "You can only shoot to the horizon, not over it."

"And that means don't worry about tomorrow?"

"Yeah."

"Some days I wish I could, Thorn. I really do." But Lily continued her writing.

Mary put the key in her pocket. "It'll be good to be back home."

Once Mary had left, Lily poured a cup of rose water and handed it to him before filling her own. "Poor K'leef. He worshipped his older brother."

"What happens now?"

"Rules of succession are different here. It doesn't automatically go to the next oldest, but the most powerful in magic. The old sultan had quite a few sons, six of them sorcerers. There're five more to pick from."

"Four. No way does K'leef want that job." He knew his friend well enough to realize the boy would prefer a quiet life. A library full of books and a table piled high with cakes were the extent of K'leef's ambition, and as far as ambitions went, Thorn didn't see much wrong with it.

A soft knock interrupted them. It didn't sound like Mary, and she couldn't have returned so soon.

"Come in," said Lily.

K'leef entered. He looked very different from the proud and happy young man he'd been just that morning. His clothes were the same but now singed and disheveled. The feathers drooped, black and crinkled. His eyes were puffy, but Thorn reckoned he had no tears left. "I tried to save him."

Lily put her arms around him.

They stood there silently for a while. There was nothing else that needed doing. K'leef did not cry, sob, or shake. He just hugged Lily.

"Drink this." Thorn gave him his cup. "And tell us what's going on."

K'leef sat down, unwrapped his turban, and let the burned cloth trail on the floor. "No one knows if he's going to make it through the night," he said, wringing his hands. "We need to decide who will replace him."

Lily sat with him, took his hands in hers. "Who do you think it will be?"

"Jambiya, unless he's contested."

That was very bad news, but it didn't come as a surprise. The rumors had flown faster than falcons through the corridors, and most carried his name. Thorn was gathering a distinct, horrible image of the man. He burned people for the smallest of crimes. Branded them with flames and filled the sky with smoke. Entire villages went to the fire, and now his name was on everyone's lips as the next sultan.

Lily looked worried, almost frightened. Maybe she knew even more than he did about the man they called the Lawgiver.

"Isn't anyone going to try and stop this?" she asked.

"My other brothers are terrified of him, and rightly so. None of them are powerful enough to defeat him."

"How about what's-his-face, the one who was wearing the really big feathers?" Thorn asked.

"Wahid? He's lucky if he can light a candle with his magic."

"Mary was right. What a mess," Thorn declared. "So how will it be decided? Spells at dawn?"

K'leef shook his head. "A trial by fire. It prevents the rivals from actually killing each other for the throne. A challenge is set, and the first one to complete it, or survive it, becomes sultan."

"Sounds stupid."

"It's as good a system as any other," said Lily defensively. "You got any better ideas? How do they do it back in your old village?"

"In Stour? When the head man dies, everyone gathers in the village square and it's a show of hands."

Lily blinked in disbelief. "Everyone?"

"If you've got a house or a field. You have to have roots in the village. Whoever wants to be headman makes a speech. The loser ends up getting thrown in the village pond. For a laugh."

K'leef's look matched Lily's. "So it's just a popularity contest? Nothing to do with ability? Or knowledge?"

"Nope. Every now and then we get the village idiot winning, but that's the way we like it."

Lily shook her head. "Can't see that catching on."

"Whatever the system, it doesn't matter." K'leef frowned. "It'll be Jambiya."

Thorn stopped dead. "What about the four prisoners? They're still gonna be freed tomorrow, right?"

K'leef's despairing look was answer enough.

"But Sa'if said! He promised!" After what had happened today, how could anyone bear even the idea of burning another person, let alone four?

"He promised *us*, Thorn, and what good's our word if Sa'if can't back it up? Jambiya will just laugh in our faces."

"Then do something, K'leef."

"I can't, Thorn!" He stood up. "I'm not like you, don't you understand? I can't go around doing whatever I want, not caring about the consequences. I'm just son number four. Fourth sons sit down at the back and mind their own business." He sank his head into his hands. "Anything else is just trouble."

"So that's it?" said Thorn. "They get smoked tomorrow? You gonna cover 'em in some tar first, make 'em burn quicker? Think those girls'll scream like your brother did?"

"Enough, Thorn!" commanded Lily. "K'leef's right. He can't do anything."

Thorn stood face-to-face with K'leef. "You're nothing but a coward. And to think I risked my neck, saving you. Why did I bother?"

"That's enough, Thorn!" Lily shouted.

Thorn glared at her. "I thought you'd understand." He stepped out into the corridor and shut the door behind him.

He'd reckoned he could count on his friends, but he'd reckoned wrong. They couldn't do anything to save the four prisoners. They had to follow the rules; they were nobles.

*Good thing I ain't.*

# SEVEN

"Thorn! Are you out here?" Lily looked up and down the corridor. Where had he gone? "I'm sorry!"

Typical. He'd run off to have one of his sulks. He was probably headed down to the stables to complain to Hades. Maybe she should follow? The two of them shouldn't argue.

But K'leef was in a bad way, and Lily had to protect him. He wasn't as tough as Thorn.

She needed to speak to Baron Sable; his wife was close to the Djinns. She should help Mary organize the return journey. But what about K'leef, and Thorn . . .

It was her job to look after them all, whether they liked it or not.

The palace felt empty and uncharacteristically gloomy. Only a few servants scurried about, doing their business. As she wandered down the hall, she overheard two of them talking as they lit the lamps.

"This dark sky—it's unnatural, I tell you."

They spotted her and lowered their voices. They whispered in Djinnic, assuming she didn't understand it.

"She brought the Curse of the Six Princes."

"Sa'if invited the witch queen; is it any wonder something went wrong?"

"Can't you be busy somewhere else?" Lily asked in Djinnic. They ran off.

All the world's ills seemed to be her fault. When storms came, why didn't people curse the Feathered Council? When a ship floundered, why didn't they blame the Coral king?

Lily knew why. She was a woman who dared to practice magic, and that was forbidden. It didn't matter that she had saved Gehenna with her spells and her people were grateful for it. Outside of her realm, everyone was convinced that disaster would befall those who broke this, the oldest law of the New Kingdoms.

And it wasn't just that—it was the kind of magic she practiced: necromancy. The sorcery of darkness. Her ability to commune with the dead, to command zombies, frightened people. Would they fuss so much if a girl from House Solar used magic to appear more beautiful? Or a woman in Herne's Forest made the crops grow taller? She doubted it.

She passed a brazier where incense was burning and gazed at the purple smoke writhing off the rocks. It made her think of Paz, K'leef's efreet. Why weren't people as afraid of them as they were of zombies? The undead were harmless and did what they were told.

Now it was zombies, but the Shadows had once commanded creatures far more powerful, the greatest being demons.

Demons were resentful of any mortal who presumed to command them. They could work against you, slyly, wickedly. Still, somehow her ancestors had wrangled four dukes of hell to build the Great Hall in a single night.

What must it be like to have power over such beings?

She shrugged. That was for the storybooks. There hadn't been a successful summoning in hundreds of years.

She heard a noise coming from the other side of a door. Was someone crying?

She tapped gently. "Hello?"

K'leef's sister Sami opened the door, wiping her eyes. "Lily! Please come in."

She invited Lily to join her in a nest of pillows on the floor. "I'm sorry we haven't been better hosts," she said. "No one expected . . ." Her chin began to tremble, and her eyes welled up.

Lily stroked her hair. "I know how much this hurts, Sami. I had a brother once whom I loved more than anything."

"Where is he now?"

"He's with my mother on the Far Shore. One day I'll see them again." Then, realizing this was probably not what Sami wanted to hear right now, she added, "Hopefully Sa'if will be all right."

Sami sniffed and shook her head. "It shouldn't have happened. Not to him."

A small ginger cat strolled in from the adjoining chamber and climbed into Sami's lap. It turned its hazel eyes at Lily, lazily, then nestled in, purring. Sami smiled at it through her tears. "Bonfire misses him."

"Bonfire? That's an interesting name."

Sami glanced around as if making sure they were alone. "Watch." She tickled his nose.

Bonfire twitched and tried to swat her fingers away. But Sami wouldn't be dissuaded. "Show Lady Shadow what you can do, Bonny."

One more tickle and the cat sat up and sneezed.

Flames, no bigger than match lights, emerged from his nostrils.

Sami smiled proudly. "A nomad from the Shardlands sold him to me. The wilderness has a special kind of magic. It . . . changes things."

"So I see," said Lily.

Sami let Bonfire get comfortable again.

Lily brushed one of the cushions aside. They were too soft for her. "Aren't you worried he'll set the room alight?"

"No. Why?"

"Fire spreads rapidly, Sami. And look at all this material around you.

What if Bonfire sneezed over by those curtains? Gauze burns very quickly."

Sami laughed. "I'm not worried about that! I'm not afraid of fire. I could easily—"

Just then, Ameera entered from the other chamber. Sami clammed up and looked sheepish as her older sister knelt in front of her. "You must be tired, Sami. I think perhaps Lady Shadow should let you sleep."

Lily knew when she was being kicked out. She smiled at Sami. "We'll talk about our brothers another time."

Ameera showed her to the door. "You shouldn't bother Sami. She's upset."

"Of course. As are you, I'm sure. Sa'if is your brother, too."

Ameera shot Lily with such a fierce glare, it looked like pure hatred. She pointed stiffly down the corridor. "Your rooms are that way, Lady Shadow."

Lily backed up a few steps. People dealt with adversity in different ways. Lily had been horrible to her servants in the first weeks after her family had been killed. She'd been unable to handle the rage that had filled her to the brim, and she'd hated the whole world for its unfairness. Ameera was just trying to protect her sister.

And yet . . .

Lily was sure Sami had wanted to show her something, something even more special than a fire-sneezing cat.

"Wait. Wait, Lady Shadow." Ameera took her hand. "I'm sorry. It's been a horrible day. You must understand?"

Lily nodded. "Think nothing of it. I'm going back to my quarters now. Preparations need to be made. It's a long way home to Gehenna."

"You're leaving? Already?" She seemed genuinely shocked.

Lily frowned. "Of course."

"Without seeing Nahas? Oh, I had such plans, Lily. We were going to be the very best of friends, and it has all gone wrong."

"I'll write, I promise."

"That's not the same! There are things to see! Please, you've journeyed so far—won't you come with me? Let me show you the city. Please."

She did have a point. When would Lily ever travel this way again? Probably never. And perhaps a few hours out of the palace might help lift her spirits, even temporarily. "I suppose we could have a quick tour. Perhaps tomorrow? I'm sure you want to wait for news about—"

"No!" said Ameera. "I can't stand it any longer. Sa'if's in good hands, and I need a distraction. Let's go now."

Sami's door swung open, and she dashed out. "Yes! Yes! We three will explore the city! It'll be a great adventure! Lily, I'll show you where to buy the best Djinnic Delights in the whole of the New Kingdoms! You'll never eat anything else again!"

Ameera glared at her younger sister. "You were eavesdropping?"

Sami put her small fists on her hips. "Of course. Just like you taught me to."

Ameera shook her head. "No. This is not for little girls. And it's late."

Sami pouted. Then she took on a cunning expression. "If I stay, I'll run around the whole palace shouting how you and Lily sneaked out. Then we'll see how much fun you have in Nahas."

Lily shrugged. "She has us beaten, Ameera."

Ameera grinned. "All right, Sami. But you must obey my every word, do you hear?" She turned back to Lily and said conspiratorially, "Sami is right that we can sneak out. There are secret ways to exit the palace. Can you imagine?"

Lily's grin matched Ameera's own. "Oh, I think I can."

# EIGHT

"We are like your undead!" Ameera laughed. "We only come to life after dark!"

The cool night air brought everyone out, for business and for pleasure. Lily had never seen anything like it, and she couldn't help but stare at all the wonderful activity. It was almost a madness: the noise, the colors, the smells, and the bustle of bodies through the narrow, winding alleys of the Old Town.

Sneaking out had been easy—was there any castle in the New Kingdoms that wasn't riddled with secret passages and hidden doors? But when they exited, they'd found Kali, the Djinn executioner, waiting for them. Instead of sending them back inside, she'd merely commented that some fresh air would be good for them all, so she tagged along.

Each time Lily glanced over, Kali was watching her. Intently, with that sort of look that made the spot between her shoulder blades itch.

But what harm could Kali do, really? Lily was a guest of House Djinn, and there were very clear rules against killing visiting nobles.

Still, those rules did tend to get ignored during times of disorder. . . .

Ameera slipped her arm through Lily's. "What's wrong?"

"Just thinking of some people back home." Lily smiled. "Many of them wanted to come along, but there was only so much room on the ships. Tyburn was *especially* keen."

"Tyburn? Your executioner?" Ameera's grip tightened. "But you can't bring executioners; it's an act of war."

"I know." Lily shrugged. "Tyburn tends to do his own thing, though. He has a habit of turning up most unexpectedly."

The smile on Kali's face stiffened, only for a moment.

Tyburn was a thousand miles away, looking after things in Gehenna. But Kali didn't know that, not for *sure*. It might keep her in her place, worrying that the Shadow executioner may be lurking nearby.

Ameera tugged her along. "Behold Nahas. Isn't it beautiful?"

Lily looked, and her worries about the palace up on the hill faded away.

They entered a sea of people. The stallholders yelled for customers, the customers argued over prices, and Lily's mouth watered at the smell of meals being cooked in vast iron pans. The vibrant colors hurt her eyes. She was so used to somber black that the dazzling array of exotic fruits, bright robes, shining jewels, and golden ornaments blinded and bewildered her. She hung on to Ameera to steady herself.

Ports were always busy places, but here, in this capital, and now, during the night of a coronation, it looked like everyone from the New Kingdoms had turned up. Surprisingly, it didn't seem as though the tragic ceremony had dampened anyone's spirits. Lu Fengese in feathered cloaks pushed past scaled sailors of House Coral, and she spotted visitors in tunics made of leaves and carrying staves decorated with living blossoms. One had skin that was half turned to bark, the sign of a druid from Herne's Forest. There was a nod in greeting as their eyes met, hers of tombstone gray against his of woodland green. Then he disappeared back into the hurly-burly of the market.

"How big is the bazaar?" she asked, trying to keep Ameera in sight among the crowd.

Sami grabbed her hand. "I won't let you get lost. But it's big—bigger than the palace. Don't you have anything like this in Gehenna?"

"The City of Silence is twice the size of Castle Gloom," Lily answered. At *least* twice the size—not that anyone had measured it, for its boundaries changed every year.

"Doesn't it have many people?"

"Many, many thousands. They're just not quite as lively."

Sami frowned, then was distracted by a tray of sparkling jewelry. "Look! I want one!"

Ameera sighed. "I'd better get her something, or else she'll never shut up."

The vendor, smelling a few shiny dinars, adjusted his turban and put on his brightest smile, which was enhanced by his gold fillings. "Ladies, please, come look! I have nothing among these meager trinkets that could possibly match such rare beauty, but perhaps you'll feel some charity toward a poor tradesman?"

"Careful, Fahid, we have a guest to impress," said Ameera. She glanced at the tray and snorted.

The man swept a low bow. "M'lady Ameera! I am honored! Thrice honored that you should bring such fine company! A guest from far-off lands!" He picked up a string of pearls and held them up to Lily. "Mere paste compared to you, lady, but perhaps you have a maid or serving girl who would benefit?"

He knew how to flatter. Her own tradesmen could learn a thing or two from him. "Do you have anything . . . black?"

"Black?" The trader looked puzzled, then, slowly, something lit within his head. He stepped back, staring at her hard. "Black? By the Six . . . the witch queen . . ."

Fear washed all the color from his dark face. The tray rattled as he trembled.

Ameera tutted. "Do not stare so hard, Fahid. Or gaze too deep into her eyes, for they reflect the manner of your death."

He sobbed and sank to his knees in front of Lily. "Please, dread lady, I am but a poor man."

"Is that true about your eyes?" asked Sami, now more interested in Lily than the jewelry. She stood on her tiptoes. "Can I look?"

"Just be careful." Lily tried not to laugh and forced on a serious mask.

Sami frowned as she peered into her pupils. "I think I see a storm. And perhaps an elephant?"

Ameera picked up a small obsidian-headed pin and in its place put a silver coin on the vendor's tray. She twisted a lock of Lily's hair with the ease of a girl with many sisters and slid the pin into place. "Something to remember tonight by."

They moved on, deeper into the crowds. "You frightened that poor man," said Lily.

Ameera smirked. "What of it? You gave him something more precious than gold: a story he can recount again and again. Think of how his children will shiver with delight when he tells them whom he met tonight! Think of how passionately he will hug his wife, having survived the encounter!"

Lily caught her reflection in a curved wall of burnished copper. Was she really so terrifying?

Kali joined her and they both stood there, looking at their warped selves. "People see what they expect to see."

"Reputation cuts both ways," said Lily. "I'm not sure I like mine."

"Really?" Kali stretched her neck to better admire her skull tattoos. "I love mine."

Kali was so different from the dour Tyburn. Or was she? Both relied on their reputations. Tyburn kept Lily's often-fractious nobles in line with his, hardly ever needing to actually draw his sword.

Lily shook her head—she'd long ago given up trying to understand executioners—and caught up with the princesses.

Could it be that the news from the palace hadn't yet filtered down to the commoners? The squares were filled with locals and travelers, and performers entertained on every corner: fire jugglers, fortune-tellers, clowns, and singers. Others threw colored powder into the air so passersby were soon dusted in red, orange, and gold. Ameera paused to buy snacks, inspect some cloth, and chat with the merchants. She'd hear complaints and compliments, offer a word here and there, and move on. Lily couldn't help but admire her easy grace and, if she was being honest, envy it, too. She had watched her father operate in much the same way. Baron Sable had always warned him to surround himself with guards, to keep people at a distance, but Iblis would refuse, saying, "A ruler should not fear his people. If he does, he has failed."

People stared at Lily. They whispered as she passed and cast fearful glances.

*I should be used to this.*

But she wasn't. She died a little each time she saw the frightened looks. How parents drew their children close as she walked by, how crowds parted as they sensed her alien presence.

Ameera slipped her arm through hers. "We're here."

The Street of Storytellers.

The bedlam of the bazaar faded away. This street was dark and quiet, even though it was packed. Listeners gathered in hushed little groups while various men sat with a candle and cup of tea, spinning tales in voices just above a whisper. One man, white-bearded and blind, twisted a stick in his hand as he told of great heroes and doomed lovers. Another man, his hair dyed a shocking red, gestured to indicate the towering height of giants and the undulating flight of fierce dragons.

Others watched from screened windows above. Women and children leaned out, resting their chins on their fists as the stories drifted up to the stars.

Ameera touched Lily's lips with her forefinger and nodded toward a door nestled between two stalls. When she lifted her hand away, Lily tasted cinnamon.

In they went: two princesses, an executioner, and a witch queen.

Sweet incense unfurled from small pots spread throughout the crowded room, making the air thick and heady. Lily stood against the wall by the door, and Ameera hung back with her.

The tale had already begun.

The ceiling sparkled, and Lily saw that it was studded with small shiny objects: coins, pieces of glass, even polished stones. They reflected the single candle flickering in the center of the room, beside the storyteller.

She wore a heavy robe, extravagantly embroidered and strung with rings and coins so that every slight move was enhanced by a soft jingling. More jewelry hung within the plaits of her long hair, as white as Lily's.

She came from the Shardlands—that much was clear from her nomad garb. Which tribe? The tattoos on her cheek were so faded, it was impossible to tell.

The audience was made up entirely of females. Rich, poor, old, and young, all mixed together. Grandmothers sat with young girls on their laps; mothers nursed babies within the shadows; teenagers, their dark eyes wide, listened cross-legged on the carpet, enthralled.

The hairs on the back of Lily's neck prickled as she felt the anticipation. This was something special. And something forbidden.

The woman was using a form of Djinnic that was archaic—something not quite lost, not quite forgotten—and it took Lily a few minutes to get used to it. Eventually the tale became clear, and it was one she knew all too well.

The Six Princes.

The storyteller told them of the high king and his wife from the other world. Here in Nahas, they believed the wife had been a desert spirit. In Gehenna, it was said she was a demoness, a princess of hell. What

mattered was that she was magical, and so were her six sons. She taught each one a different kind of magic, and thus the six great houses of magic were founded, all those unimaginable centuries ago.

"Though she loved her sons equally," continued the old woman, "there was one she loved above them: her precious daughter."

Lily froze. *Daughter?*

There was no daughter. Everyone knew there were Six Princes and that was all.

Feeling dizzy, Lily closed her eyes. It must be the aftereffects of using magic, she thought. That, and weeks of being at sea. She hadn't gotten her land legs back yet. And the incense—it smothered her senses. She turned to the door. She needed some fresh air. . . .

Ameera touched her arm gently. "Please stay. Listen."

The woman took a sip of her tea, then continued. "The high king was old for a mortal, and his time was coming to an end. Who would rule after him? His wife, an immortal, knew that his people would not accept her, so the choice had to be one of their children. And, as all children do, they fought among themselves. The high king laughed to see the sport of it, but the queen fell silent and watchful. The brothers competed in earnest, yet none could defeat their sister. She, being closest to the mother, was the most powerful. It was decided that after the high king, there would be a high queen."

This was not the story Lily knew. "None of this is true."

Ameera cut her a deadly look. "Says who? The legends you read back in Castle Gloom? Legends written by men?"

The room was utterly silent except for the ragged breath of the storyteller. "The brothers could not accept the decree. They waited until their father died, then made a secret pact. Together they confronted their sister, their new queen, and gave her six mortal wounds."

The bard stabbed her chest once for each blow. Lily could almost feel those knives going in. So could the rest of the audience. Even in the dim candlelight she could see tears of anger and sorrow on their faces.

"As her bloodstained crown—their father's crown—rolled across the great hall, the dying queen cursed her siblings. She pronounced there would be no peace between them, or their descendants, until they made amends for their treachery."

The audience held its breath. The storyteller sighed and finished her tea.

A small girl spoke up. "But, mistress, how does the story end?"

The wrinkles around the old woman's eyes deepened. "End, child? This tale has not ended."

She stood and took up her walking stick to leave. She muttered to herself as she made her way through the crowd. Then she paused beside Lily. "At least, not yet."

# NINE

"Are you feeling unwell?" Ameera asked as they came back out in the street.

"Just a little . . . travel-sick. It's been a long journey. I should have stayed in the palace, gotten some rest. . . ."

They'd left the crowded chamber, Lily almost stumbling through the door. She was leaning against the wall, trying to catch her breath and calm her racing heart. Why had that old woman's tale affected her like this?

"Are you all right?" asked Sami. "Kali, go get Lady Shadow a drink."

Lily waved the small girl back. "I'm fine. It was too crowded in there." She stood up and took in some more air. "But I think we should head back to the palace."

She wanted to be away from here. The palace loomed over the city, so they started on their way.

Ameera drew up next to her. "Well?"

"An interesting fairy tale, Ameera."

"Why do you say that? Didn't you hear the story? Do you think—"

"It's not true," snapped Lily, more harshly than she'd intended. "It's just wishful thinking."

"The wishful thinking of half the world's population, Lily. You of all people must recognize the truth of what she was saying." Ameera was deadly serious as they pushed their way back through the oppressive crowds. "That old woman is from a tribe that lives out among the ruins of the Old Kingdom. Their tales are older—and truer—than the fables we've been fed."

Lily almost laughed. Hope came in many strange forms. Women had been forbidden to practice magic for generations. The law was the oldest one of the New Kingdoms, and there was only one penalty, for highborn or low: death by fire. And here she was in the kingdom of fire.

*That's why they stare so. I flout the old law and no one dares to stop me. I've become too powerful.*

*The bear makes his own rules.*

Hold on. Wasn't that one of Thorn's grandpa's sayings? She *must* be sick if she was quoting that mad old man.

She stopped and looked around.

Where was everyone?

*Stupid Lily! Lost in your own head, and now lost in the streets!*

She could navigate the hundreds of corridors in Castle Gloom blindfolded, but here she didn't have a clue as to which way to turn. The houses leaned over the alleyway, cutting the sky to a crooked slice. She didn't even know how she'd gotten here. Had they taken the left alley, or the right? Where were Ameera and Sami? She was all alone.

No, not quite. There were two others.

*Not good.*

The men waited for her with the eagerness of hounds on a leash. One of them wore a leather apron over a wide, rotund torso. His companion leaned against a slanted wall, rubbing his stubbly chin. "You seem lost, m'dear."

Lily shrugged. "No. Not at all. I'll be heading on my way. I think the fireworks are starting soon. Have a good evening." She headed to the left alley.

The bigger man blocked her. Lily noticed the long knife tucked in his waist sash.

Time to use that reputation she didn't want. "I'm Lilith Shadow."

"Are you?" Stubble-chin looked her over, walking around her slowly as if she were some cow at the market. "You're still lost."

Lily frowned. Perhaps he hadn't heard properly. "Lilith Shadow? The witch queen?"

"Oh?"

"I can . . . er, if you look into my eyes you'll see the manner of your death."

"Will I?" The man with the stubble pointed at her throat. "Let's start with the necklace, shall we?"

Lily put her hand over it. "This necklace has been in my family for ten generations. The gems were mined out of the fourth circle of hell by a demon-prince who—"

"Get a move on. Then those rings of yours. Bracelets, too."

The fat man tapped his bald head. Stubble-chin nodded. "And those hair pins. What are the studs? Jet?"

"Black diamonds," said Lily. "The ruler of Gehenna does not wear jet."

He laughed and bowed mockingly. "A thousand pardons, m'lady."

Lily sighed. "Look, I'm tired, and I've had a long day. I don't want to bore you with the details, but it hasn't left me in the very best of moods and certainly not in the mood to be robbed. So, turn around, go home, and shut the door." Lily flexed her fingers. "You have no idea what's *really* out there in the dark."

"And what's that, little girl? Scary monsters?"

"Only one way to find out." She reached out and clawed a sheet of blackness.

The cloth dropped over them, and they sank away until there was nothing but a patch of darkness on the ground. Then that too faded, leaving bare cobblestones.

*Clap. Clap. Clap.*

Kali applauded from her perch on a windowsill above Lily. "Now that was splendid."

"How long have you been up there?"

"Here? The whole time." She dropped the ten feet to the ground. She walked over to where the two men had just been standing and tapped the stones with her boot. "Where did you send them? To some dark, devil-swamped underworld?"

"Want to see for yourself?" Lily snapped. "Was this some sort of joke? Or just for your amusement? I don't perform penny tricks for the crowd."

Kali's gaze cooled. "Don't tempt me to do something unfortunate, Lady Shadow."

"You wouldn't stand a chance."

"Oh?"

"There you are!" Ameera, with Sami in tow, rushed into the space between them and hugged Lily, trapping her arms to her sides. "I was so worried!"

Kali bowed to her, only slightly. "I came looking for Lady Shadow. Her safety is my only concern."

Ameera kissed her executioner. "Thank you. You're a good friend, Kali."

*They're in this together.*

Lily had been an unwitting player in a game of deceit and power. They had set her up, wanting to see if the stories were true. If she was the witch queen they'd heard of.

Why? What did they want from her?

Did they think she was this fabled seventh daughter, returned?

Lily knew what was expected of girls here, and elsewhere. Sit, sew, have babies. The end.

They wanted her to save them from this fate. They wanted the witch queen to wave her magic wand and instantly make them equal to the men in their lives.

But Lily didn't have a magic wand.

*Can't you just cast a little spell?*

*Don't you have some magic for that?*

She knew the look. At home, people—nobles, merchants, and peasants—came to her with one problem or another. At first, it had been all about justice. They'd wanted her and Sable to weigh all the issues and make a decision. Where should the fence go between two farms? Could the mill fees be lowered? Could someone find room for a zombie uncle?

Nowadays they wanted her to wave her fingers in the air and make it all better. She'd tried. When a farmer lost his ox, she'd brought it back to life. Well, sort of. The thing had come back undead. It had decayed, poisoned the well, and killed off the rest of his livestock. And she was lucky no one had drowned the day she had fixed the Bone Bridge with her sorcery. After just one sunny afternoon, the whole thing had collapsed.

Magic wasn't the answer. It was more important to have wisdom and strength of character. Why couldn't they see that?

A flash of light appeared at the tower above the palace. A second or two later, there followed a deep *boom*.

"That's the Candle . . ." said Kali.

"What's going on?" asked Sami. "Has Uncle Ahmed gotten his spells mixed up again?"

Clouds hid the moon, but there was enough light spilling upward from the city to see a giant, winged creature hanging off the tower's roof. Lily cursed.

What had Thorn gone and done now?

# TEN

**T**horn shook the shackles around his wrists. "They're heavier than I remember."

Lily glowered at him. "You're an idiot."

"What did I do wrong?"

She stood on one side, K'leef the other. It was like old times.

Except now they were in a courtyard where palace prisoners were taken to be executed by fire.

Thorn saw Lily looking at the unlit pyre and he smirked. "Not gonna get much use of that today, are they? Their victims flew the coop."

She hissed, loud enough for K'leef to hear. "So, what was your plan?"

"Rescue those women. Which I did."

"And after that?"

"Er . . ."

He winced. It wasn't just the bright morning sunlight that hurt, but the big black eye he'd received when the guards had caught him. The bruise to his ribs ached, too. Oh, and so did his knuckles. He really shouldn't have tried punching the captain, especially while he was in full armor.

Lily looked over at what remained of the Candle. "How much of that Thunderdust did you use?"

"All of it. Blew a great big hole in the wall. And knocked that ugly statue off the top, too." Thorn was eternally grateful to the Eagle Knight, Ying, for giving him the explosive powder back when they had battled Lily's half brother last winter.

"That 'ugly statue' was a famous historical landmark," said K'leef. "The phoenix has protected the palace for three hundred years. My ancestors used them to hunt—did you know that? Great birds of fire, flying—"

Thorn yawned. "Yeah, I get it. Anyway, that dust was the last of my supply. Lily, could you send a letter to Ying asking for another few tubes? Comes in pretty handy."

Lily put her hands on her hips. "Just tell us what happened, Thorn."

Despite the shackles, Thorn clapped. "So, after you two refused to help me, I thought I'd go save those four *innocent* women myself. As always. Hades took a fair bit of persuading—he was still digesting that camel from earlier—but eventually I got him up and away. He latched onto the beak of the phoenix statue while I climbed down to the cell window. Told the pregnant woman, whose name is Kismet in case you was wondering, to stand well back. I shook up the Thunderdust and . . . *bang!* Off it went."

"The whole city saw that," muttered K'leef. "Most thought it was one of the celebratory fireworks gone wrong."

Thorn continued. "The old woman and Kismet got on Hades's back; then he held a girl in each of his claws and flew off. I told him to drop 'em outside the city and come back for me, but . . . he didn't. The lazy fat rat."

Thorn could guess that Hades, tired from the flight and heavy from his meal, had found himself a nice dark cave to snooze in and just left Thorn to his fate. He'd pull the monster's ears hard the next time he saw him.

"I was just leaving quiet like, myself, and then the guards turned up. Pretty angry, they were." He touched his swollen eye. "I tried to explain myself, but none of 'em spoke Gehennish. All I get is a thwack in the face, and here I am."

Lily pressed her knuckles against her temples. "Why do I get a head-ache whenever you come out with one of your plans? Ruling all of Gehenna is easier than dealing with you."

"Grandpa says—"

"Shut up, Thorn, or I swear by the Six I'll send you straight into the Pit."

He narrowed his gaze. "You can't do that."

Her gaze narrowed in return. "Try me."

K'leef straightened up as the far door opened. "*Shh*, both of you."

Jambiya entered. He had discarded his stick and moved across the small courtyard with familiarity. This was his home; he knew his way around, eyes or no eyes.

And in came a monstrous creature behind him.

Tall and man-shaped, the thing was made from smoldering coal. Ash fell with each step, and the skin was cracked, exposing lava within. Flames licked across its body, and Thorn could feel the heat from across the court-yard. It walked in a hazy curtain of superhot air, causing it to appear to waver like a desert mirage. It had no mouth, just a pair of white-hot eyes.

A demon, it had to be. Thorn stared at it, frozen. How was that possible? He thought only Shadows could summon those, and Lily had told him no one had that sort of power anymore. He shot a glance at Lily, who stood watching it, eyes wide with disbelief.

K'leef gulped. "You've awoken Farn?"

Jambiya turned toward the creature. "Do you not have an efreet of your own?"

An efreet? Like Pazuzu? But this Farn was nothing like that small glowing bundle. This monstrosity was almost seven feet tall and so hot Thorn was sweating from a dozen feet away. So it wasn't a demon from the Pit, but that didn't make it any less terrifying.

Farn stood at Jambiya's side, dripping lava over the floor. How could the blind man bear to be so close? If he could handle the efreet, then the lava crown would be no problem. Was that what he was trying to prove?

Thorn pulled at his shirt to let the air in and the sweat drop out.

Jambiya settled himself on the chair. "Bring the prisoner forward."

K'leef cleared his throat. "Brother, I've come to—"

"I have nothing more to say to you, K'leef," snapped Jambiya. "This Gehennish slave broke into the Candle and freed my prisoners: a family of witches."

"They were innocent women," snarled Thorn. "And you were going to burn them."

Jambiya smiled. "So you admit you freed them?"

"Yup." Thorn shook his chain. "And I'd do it again, if needs be."

Lily groaned.

Thorn stuck out his chin. "I *would*. It was wrong for him to take 'em, and it's as simple as that."

Jambiya clapped his hands to summon the nearby guards. "You have admitted guilt, so there is nothing more to discuss. Put him on the pyre. Be quick—my breakfast is getting cold."

"What?" Thorn cried. "You ain't shoving me on that!"

Lily cleared her throat. "Sheik Jambiya? May I speak?"

His distaste was thick. "Ah, the witch queen. I was wondering when you'd try to intervene. I don't know how Gehenna fell so far that they would allow someone like you to rule—a foolish girl—but you have no authority here, m'lady." He practically spat the last word.

"I'm not here to challenge you, Sheik. I'm merely requesting justice."

"You shall see that soon enough."

"The four women whom you imprisoned," Lily went on. "You found them where?"

"In my lands, of course. In one of the villages. It was well known that

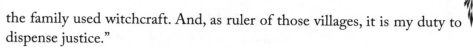

the family used witchcraft. And, as ruler of those villages, it is my duty to dispense justice."

"There's no denying that," Lily replied. "But Thorn's crime was carried out . . . here? In the palace?"

"What of it? And it was more than one crime. He also caused damage to the Candle. Who knows when it can be used again?"

"And that's a bad thing?" muttered Thorn. "Would have been best if the whole thing toppled."

Lily stomped on Thorn's toes. "So, Thorn's crime, if it *is* a crime—"

"Of *course* it's a crime!" Jambiya jumped up. "Take the boy and put him on the pyre!"

"Hey! Let me go!" Thorn struggled as two guards hooked their arms under his armpits and lifted him off his feet. "Hey!"

Thorn kicked out, but the two guards knew their business. They dragged him across the courtyard to the stake surrounded by a pile of wood.

He fought harder. He even snapped his teeth as one wrapped the chains around him. Thorn caught the other hard in the gut with a kick and earned himself a cuff to the side of the head.

Jambiya snapped his fingers. "Farn?"

The massive efreet started toward Thorn. A wave of heat rolled out in front of the creature, and the sticks nearest to it began to smoke.

Thorn pulled at his shackles until his wrists ached, then harder still, until his bones creaked.

Closer came the efreet. Its hands brightened. The black coating broke away from its fingers, revealing something akin to molten rock, white-hot and coated with fire. The air began to crackle.

Thorn looked desperately across the courtyard. "Do something, Lily. . . ."

She walked up to the foot of Jambiya's chair. "Forgive me, as I'm only a foolish girl, but I understood from K'leef that the only person who can pass judgment on a crime committed within the palace itself is the sultan." She stepped nearer still. "Which you are not, Sheik. Sa'if is."

He turned his ruined eyes to hers and said coldly, "Sa'if died at dawn."

"No . . ." whispered K'leef, all color draining from his face. "Why did no one tell me?"

Jambiya sneered. "You were here, with your 'friends,' instead of carrying out your familial duties, Brother."

Thorn glanced at K'leef and saw that he was on the verge of tears. They should have known it was touch and go for Sa'if, but that didn't make his death any easier to accept. He'd been a good man. Unlike this sorry excuse for a sheik.

Jambiya smiled. "I will be declared sultan at noon."

"Stop." K'leef stepped up to his brother.

What was K'leef doing?

Whatever it was, he needed to do it fast. The efreet was almost upon him, and the heat from the monster was unbearable. Breathing became panting as sweat glossed over his bare skin.

"You are not sultan yet," said K'leef. "Not if the title is contested."

Jambiya laughed disdainfully. "*You?* You would challenge me for the lava crown? Perhaps you were away too long and the cold of the north numbed your mind."

"You are not sultan," repeated K'leef.

Thorn couldn't believe it. K'leef was challenging Jambiya for the Sultanate, all to save him. He blushed, ashamed for calling K'leef a coward last night.

"So be it," said Jambiya. He waved toward the pyre. "Farn, desist."

Thorn sank to his knees as the efreet stepped away. The fire within the monster did not die, but it lessened enough for the air around him to become something less than searing. Thorn swallowed great big lungfuls and watched, through eyes covered in dripping sweat, as the thing retreated back to its master.

A guard removed his shackles, and Jambiya stood up, hand outstretched. "Come here, boy. Let us make peace."

Thorn wiped his face with his sleeve, keeping a wary eye on the efreet. But it was a few yards behind Jambiya and no longer radiating at the same intensity it had been a few moments earlier.

Cautiously, Thorn stepped forward and took Jambiya's offered grasp.

Jambiya's smile turned fierce. "You have loyal allies, young Thorn."

"K'leef owes me a favor or two," said Thorn. Then he looked down at his hand, clutched tightly in Jambiya's. "Er . . ."

What was Jambiya doing? Thorn's hand began to tickle. Then itch. The itch grew more intense.

Thorn tried to pull it free. "It hurts. . . ."

K'leef jumped forward. "Let him go, Jambiya!"

Thorn yelled as smoke slipped out from between the clasped hands. The yell rose to a scream. He was burning!

Jambiya let go, and Thorn fell backward.

Lily rushed to him and stared in horror.

The back of his hand was covered with red blisters, from fingertip to wrist. He felt sick looking at it and couldn't stop himself from screaming.

K'leef rushed up and forced it into a jug of ice water. Thorn rocked back and forth, stifling his sobs. By the Six, it hurt so much. . . .

"How dare you!" Lily swore at Jambiya. "You had no right."

Jambiya lifted his nose to sniff the air. "Is there any smell so sweet? Is that not justice?"

"No. That is cruelty." Lily put her arm around Thorn. "Which is base and unbecoming of any prince."

Jambiya sneered, summoned his guards, and left, the efreet plodding behind.

K'leef helped Thorn up. He couldn't trust himself to stand; all he wanted to do was curl up and sob.

"I'll take you to the physician," said K'leef. "He's an expert at dealing with burns. You'll be fine, trust me."

"I'll come with you, Thorn," said Lily, her face filled with concern.

Thorn clutched his hand, tears running down his face. He was in so much pain, it was difficult to focus on anything else. But, through gritted teeth, through his tears, he faced his friend. "Sultan, eh?"

If he wasn't dying of pain, he would have laughed.

Lily looked at the still-smoking pyre. "What happens now?"

# ELEVEN

"**H**ow dare he?" Lily squeezed her fists and all around her the shadows, pale and feeble in the sunlight, shook and trembled.

"Lily . . ." K'leef said.

She should go straight back and face Jambiya. See how good his magic really was. She would tear him to pieces and then rebuild him as a jumbled-up zombie, arms and legs all askew.

She could have dealt with that efreet, too. She was fluent enough in Djinnic to know "Farn" meant "furnace," but it didn't matter how bright and hot it burned. Darkness consumed all things.

Poor Thorn!

"How dare he . . ." Lily muttered again. The things she could do to Jambiya. Perhaps she should march into his dreams and fill them with endless nightmares. Or she could bring in ghosts. . . . Surely there were plenty of victims of his who were all too eager for revenge? Have them haunt his every step. She could do that easily.

He might be blind, but Lily would show him what *true* darkness was.

"Lily. Please."

She turned to K'leef. He stood a few feet away, looking scared. "You need to stop."

Dead birds littered the shriveled grass. Wilted flowers lined the garden path, and the trees nearby had rotted.

Had she done all that?

Lily sighed and let her anger bleed away. "I'm so sorry, K'leef."

"I understand. You couldn't help it."

She picked up a sparrow. "I *must* help it."

Her father had warned her about her temper. *When the powerful lose control, innocents suffer.*

The tiny bird was still warm. Life had left it, but she could still give it an . . . existence. Something this small would take hardly any effort at all.

Then what? Her zombies could hardly walk straight and needed constant rebuilding. There wasn't a night back home when she didn't stumble upon—and often *over*—a dropped-off limb or tread on a popped-out eyeball.

An undead bird would barely be able to fly, and what sort of song would it give? Better not to find out. She placed the bird gently back on the grass. "I'm sorry, K'leef. It won't happen again."

But K'leef wasn't listening. He was now sitting on a stone bench, staring at nothing. "He's dead, Lily. Just like that."

How could she have been so selfish? She'd been so angry at Jambiya, she'd forgotten that her friend had just lost his brother. She sat down next to K'leef and took his hand.

There was nothing to say. No words would make the pain any less, no glib saying could prevent a single tear. Tears had to fall. Sadness had to flow.

And the dead still needed love.

So she sat there quietly, holding K'leef's hand as he was racked with deep sobs.

They were so similar, both in upbringing and in pain. The wound of her family members' deaths was still fresh, and watching K'leef tore it open again.

That day the carts had rolled in with three bodies covered in tarpaulin . . . Baron Sable had told her not to look, but she did anyway. How could she not?

She hadn't been there to witness their suffering, not like K'leef. So for her, the memories of her parents and brother still shone brightly with life. Of her mother laughing, of Dante teasing, and of her father smiling slyly at some mischief of hers.

And from time to time, she was even able to meet with her father still. . . .

"K'leef, do you want to see Sa'if?"

He looked at her, sniffling. "What?"

Was this right? It could make things worse. She'd called on the dead before. It didn't always go well.

K'leef's confusion cleared quickly. "You . . . you could summon him?"

"I could try and find his ghost. It's not the same person, exactly. . . ." She frowned, recalling one of the first times she'd tried. Her servant Rose had been murdered, and Lily had tried to contact her spirit. But she'd been overwhelmed by Rose's fear, pain, and regret, the flood of emotions tied up with Rose's last few, horrific seconds of life.

Lily had gotten a glimpse of the murderer, though—a fleeting look through Rose's own eyes.

"Contacting the dead's not always successful, K'leef."

But his fingers tightened on hers. "Please, Lily. I'd like to speak to Sa'if." There was no mistaking the desperation in his voice. "Even for just one minute."

She looked around the garden. They were alone, and that suited her fine. K'leef understood her powers, but others didn't.

K'leef stood up, shifting from one foot to the other, filled with excitement and apprehension. "Do you want to go inside? Somewhere darker? The palace has underground rooms."

"I like it here. And this is where Sa'if would come, wouldn't he?"

K'leef pointed to a cluster of trees. "That's where he'd pick figs. He loved them. He'd eat them while soaking his feet in the fountain."

"You'd sit with him, too?"

K'leef chuckled softly. "He'd climb up to reach the ones at the top. The leaves stung, but Sa'if didn't mind. He said if he could withstand the fire, then what was a little itch? The ones at the top are the ripest."

"Then let's go over there. It might make things easier."

She kicked off her shoes and folded her immense skirt under to sit cross-legged in the shade of a tree.

The soft wind blew through the garden and dappled sunlight patterned the grass. A hummingbird took a brief interest in them before flitting off to the array of flowers growing semiwild along the paths and the edges of the fountains.

K'leef knelt down opposite her. "Do you want me to do anything? Is this how you contact Iblis?"

"My father's ghost haunts the Shadow Library, where we study together. I can also see him—in a more solid form—in the Dreamtime. The lands of the dead and the Dreamtime overlap, K'leef. I'm sure you'll see Sa'if in your dreams, sooner or later."

"They're just wishful thinking, aren't they?"

"Don't underestimate the power of a wish, K'leef." She pulled the pins out of her hair and let the thick white locks untangle themselves around her shoulders.

She closed her eyes. The cool grass tickled her feet, and the breeze ruffled her hair. She smelled the sticky sweetness of the figs and the faint scents of smoke and incense. Incense burned in every corridor and hallway here. Some of the sticks smoldered in tripods, but most were held by statues that littered the palace in far greater numbers than her own gargoyles at Castle Gloom. Lily idly wondered if K'leef had named the statues as she'd done with the gargoyles back home.

The branches above her creaked. Was it merely the wind?

"Sa'if? Is that you?" she asked.

The air grew colder, and she heard a gasp.

The first thing she saw was K'leef, agog.

Between her and him, a faint shape was taking form. Wisps of ethereal mist wove together in the weak shadows under the tree. The smoke grew thicker until it looked like a man, undefined around the edges.

K'leef stood up slowly and reached out. "Sa'if?"

Vague facial features formed in the cloak of mist. The ghost turned his gaze to K'leef. "Brother."

A ghost was made up of memories and emotions. Content, peaceful, and fulfilled spirits disappeared to the Far Shore without lingering or looking back to the living world. They could still be met, in the Dreamtime, but only when they wished it. Not even the greatest necromancer had successfully summoned a spirit back from the Far Shore.

Lily could tell they didn't have long to talk to Sa'if. His death may have been tragic and horrible, but she sensed the goodness in him, the urge to laugh and love. Sadness, regret, and anger kept the dead from the rest they deserved. Sa'if had none of those shackles. She'd been lucky to find him.

"I'm sorry, Sa'if. I tried to save you, but I wasn't good enough," said K'leef, his heart breaking as well as his voice.

The ghost of Sa'if shook his head. "No one could have saved me, K'leef. My magic failed me."

"Why?" blurted Lily. She hadn't intended to speak, but she couldn't help herself. "It should have been as natural as breathing."

The ghost sighed. "That is a puzzle for the living. It matters not to me."

K'leef's fingers passed through the ghost. "Where are you, Sa'if? What do you see?"

The ghost smiled. "Don't worry for me, Brother. I stand at a quiet beach. Waves are lapping against my ankles, and there is a boat not far away. I shall swim to it, and then? I'll let the current decide."

K'leef sobbed.

"There is a warm sun, but the breeze is cool. I could linger, but in the wind I hear our father's voice calling for me. He whispers your name, too, K'leef. We are all proud of you."

The ghost stepped closer, and his pale, immaterial fingers cupped K'leef's wet cheeks as the ghost looked deep into his eyes. "You would make a good sultan. Kindness is underrated, yet it is the thing we need most. Be just, be brave, and be loyal to those who love you, Brother. But most of all, follow the counsel of your own heart."

"No, Sa'if. Stay a while longer. Just a moment."

The ghost turned to Lily. "There are no lies on this side of the pyre, so I tell you a truth that cannot be questioned, or doubted. My brother has the potential to save our kingdom, with your help."

"Of course I'll help him. Any way I can."

The ghost kissed her forehead. "Bless you, Lady Shadow. For all you have done, for all you will do."

The coldness of his lips burned her skin. She felt a surge of . . . joy, freedom, and love so pure, so bright, she thought she might burst.

But now just the wind moved the branches.

Sa'if was gone.

# TWELVE

"I thought Jambiya had summoned a demon," said Thorn, scratching his hand, trying to reach that itch under the bandage. "Never seen anything like it."

"K'leef said to leave your hand alone," said Lily, sitting at her dressing table. "Does it still hurt?"

Hurt? The pain had been worse than anything he could have imagined. But K'leef's physician had worked wonders. Thorn flexed his fingers. "It's getting better."

"Then leave it alone."

He couldn't. He drew his bow with this hand, and the fingers and thumb were all stiff. He was constantly testing, hoping to feel the old flexibility that meant each arrow would fly true. What if it didn't come back? What if it healed, but healed wrong?

What if he couldn't shoot?

A soft knock interrupted them.

"Come in," said Lily.

It was K'leef. "The funeral's tomorrow," he announced somberly.

Lily got up and took K'leef's hands. "I'm so sorry."

"Thank you, for letting me say good-bye to him." K'leef sniffed.

Lily had told Thorn about summoning Sa'if's ghost. It made perfect sense that she would. She was Lilith Shadow, and ghosts were as common to her day as horse manure was to his.

And K'leef looked . . . better. Less lost and afraid. Lily hadn't told Thorn what they'd spoken about, and it wasn't any of his business, but whatever the ghost had said had changed his fiery friend.

Thorn cleared his throat. "K'leef, I'm sorry, too. For Sa'if, and what I called you. You ain't no coward."

K'leef nodded, obviously moved.

"You're still a fool, though," Thorn went on. "Taking on Jambiya."

"It's not like I want to." K'leef sat down and pulled at the ends of his turban. "What choice did I have? It was either that or watch you go up in smoke."

Thorn went to the window. The docks were just a few miles down the slope. "I've got a brilliant plan for how we can avoid all this."

"Is it as brilliant as your plan to save those four from the tower?" asked Lily.

"I saved 'em, didn't I? So the plan worked. Anyways, about this . . . problem. Face it, Jambiya's after *me*, ain't he? So I'll just run."

Lily rubbed her temples. "This I have to hear."

"I can sneak off easily. Look, we're leaving, right? First things first, we've gotta get your crates back on board the *Shadow's Blade*, and that means we need the zombies."

"Oh, dear . . ." said Lily.

Thorn grinned. "All I need is a bag of raw, fresh offal from the local butcher. As smelly as you can get. I'll shove a handful down my shirt, wrap some runny guts around my neck, then just join Eddie and the rest, moaning and shuffling down the hill. We get on board, and we set sail. Problem *solved*."

Lily stared at him. Probably struck speechless by his cleverness. He pointed at the ship. "We could be gone within the hour."

Lily handed him a jug of sherbert. "Drink this. Your brain's overheating."

He should have known she wouldn't get it. "K'leef?"

"No," said K'leef. "I've challenged Jambiya for the crown. I can't back out now, whether you're here or not. It's—"

Thorn jumped forward, hands out. "Don't say it!"

"—a matter of honor."

Thorn groaned. "Your honor's gonna get you killed. Likely in the next day or two."

"So it will be a trial by fire?" asked Lily.

"I'm afraid so." K'leef sighed.

"Do you know what the challenge is?" asked Thorn. "Something suicidal, I bet."

"They're about to decide, but that's why I'm here. The challenger is allowed two companions."

Thorn stood by his friend. "Seems as I'm the one who got you into this mess, I'd better help get you out of it. You'll need someone with a bit of sense in this trial by stupid."

"Trial by *fire*," said K'leef.

"Whatever."

K'leef arched his eyebrow. "You sure you don't want to take a minute to think about it?"

"Why? If I do that, I might change my mind." He looked back out the window at the empty blue sky. "Be easier if Hades was here, though."

"Still not back?" asked Lily.

He shook his head. Hades didn't know the area. He must have flown over the horizon and gotten himself lost. Though how you could lose sight of a smoking volcano, Thorn had no idea.

Lily volunteered, too. "Of course I'll help. Whatever you need, K'leef."

"No women, I'm sorry," said K'leef.

Lily frowned. "That's ridiculous. I—"

Before she could go on, K'leef said, "No argument there. But I've already got the second companion."

"Who?" asked Lily.

The door opened.

Thorn's heart dropped to his toes. "I've changed my mind."

Gabriel walked in. He looked from K'leef to Thorn to Lily, then back to K'leef. "You told them yet?"

# THIRTEEN

Thorn picked up the bow and examined it. Instead of a single six-foot length of yew, like the ones back home, this was savagely curved, short, and made of various woods glued together. *Composite*—that's what K'leef had called it.

The Djinnic warriors used them on horseback, hence the size. No way could you sit in a saddle and shoot a longbow.

He pulled the string and let it *twang*.

He collected three arrows.

His draw hand felt stiff, thanks to the blisters and the bandages. It still itched like beetles were crawling under his skin.

*Start easy. A hundred paces.*

The target, a straw figure hanging from a hook, had a red circle painted on its chest and a smaller one on its face.

He checked to make sure he was alone in the courtyard.

And loosed.

The arrow passed a foot to the right of the body and thumped into the doorpost.

Thorn stared.

*I missed! I missed by miles.*

He hadn't missed a target in . . . since ever.

His heart was racing, and he felt sweat spread over his palms. No, that was no good. Strange bow, hand injured. What did he expect? That was why he was out here, wasn't it? To check the damage. And practice and practice and practice.

That's all it took. Plenty of people at Castle Gloom thought his skill with the bow was magic, a faint green magic inherited from antler-headed Herne, lord of the forest.

Why was it that if you could do something a little special, everyone thought it had to be magic? That all gifts came from the Six Princes? It irritated him. He didn't owe those ancient sorcerers anything. You aren't born an archer. You become one by shooting thousands of arrows.

Lily was lucky. Sorcery was her birthright; it couldn't be taken away.

He looked at his hand. The skin was still raw, wrinkled and red, but he could move all his fingers and, most importantly, his thumb, just like always. He shook himself out, from his head down to his toes.

*Take your time.*

He licked the fletching and, with a slow, strong inhale, drew the bowstring back a second time.

The arrow flew a foot wide to the left and cracked against the bare stone.

Had Jambiya destroyed him? K'leef had said his hand would soon be back to normal, but it wasn't! He clenched it into a fist, as tight as he could make it. He needed it to work like before. He spat on his palms and rubbed them together. He fidgeted with the bow, feeling for the perfect hold, and took the third arrow.

*Okay, pretend you're back in Herne's Forest, out on your favorite trail. The one that goes by Dryad's Pond. There's the big oak you climbed every day of your tenth summer. Remember the big grain sack you tied to the bough, and the hundreds of arrows you shot that day? Not one of 'em missed.*

*That's where you are. This ain't no different.*

He took ten paces closer. Perhaps the new bow didn't have the range of the longbows back home.

He cursed himself. *That's right, blame the bow. You know there's nothing wrong with the bow. It's your aim that's off.*

He loosed.

The arrow sailed over the wall.

"No!" Thorn smashed the bow against the ground. He hit it again and again until there was nothing left but splinters. He stared at his bleeding hands, pierced by the broken wood. He didn't care now. What good were they if he couldn't shoot?

"I heard the folk of Herne's Forest were famed for their archery. Seems I was wrong."

He whipped around. Someone had seen! "You?"

It was the mango girl from the ship. She sat on the low wall, picking her nails. "Me."

"What are you doing here?"

She jumped down and casually kicked the broken pieces of bow aside. She looked at the target. "It's pretty big. How come you missed?"

"What do you know about it? Look, get lost before some guard sees you and gives you a whipping."

The girl snorted. "I can come and go as I please."

"You still owe me a crown."

"You ate the mango. Money's spent."

There was something else that wasn't right. Her two gold caps were missing, revealing perfectly white teeth, and her clothes, while plain, were good quality.

"Who are you?" Thorn asked.

The far door swung open, and Lily appeared. "Thorn! I've been looking everywhere for you! They're gathering in the Fire Hall. They're about to decide the trial." She stopped as she saw the mango girl. "What's going on?"

"This wharf rat robbed me of a crown," said Thorn. "All I got for it was a mango."

Lily shook her head. "You must be mistaken. This is Kali, the Djinn executioner."

"What?" he exclaimed.

The girl, this Kali, smiled at him in a way he didn't like; there was contempt in her dark eyes. "They said you were someone to be feared, Thorn."

"You were spying on me, weren't you? That whole mango thing—that was just so you could get on board and have a sniff around."

Kali shrugged. "I'd heard you were fond of mangoes." She bowed to Lily. "M'lady."

They watched her leave, and then Lily turned to him. "Don't let her get to you, Thorn. She is a tricky one, I'll admit, but—"

"I can't help with K'leef's trial, Lily!" Thorn cried. "I'm useless. Less than useless." He kicked the remains of the bow. "I can't shoot."

"Of course you can shoot. You're amazing!"

"I ain't!"

"Your hand is hurt. It might take a while to heal."

He shook his head. "And what if it don't? Then what use am I?"

"You think it's your archery that matters?" She frowned. "Thorn, that's never been true. Ever."

"But it's all I'm good at."

She cupped his face in her hands. "I'm counting on you, Thorn."

"Counting on me? For what?" He still felt hopeless, but he did like her hands on his cheeks.

She stepped back, biting her lip. "I don't know where to begin. But Sa'if's death seems . . . odd."

"That's not the word I would have used."

"Did you get a good look at K'leef's hands?" she asked.

"Nope. You were holding them."

Lily smiled to herself. "They're so soft and gentle, Thorn. And he has the long fingers of an artist. . . ."

"I get it. He has soft hands." Did girls really care about that sort of thing? His were as rough as bark.

"But they weren't burned after he handled the lava crown. He's a sorcerer, and his magic automatically kicked in to protect him."

"So?"

"Sa'if was a sorcerer, too. Then why didn't his magic save him?"

"I don't know. . . ."

"Me, neither. It's a mystery."

"Uh-oh. You have that look, Lily."

"I don't have any 'look.'"

"Yes, you do." He raised his nose, pretending to be aloof. "A mystery. Strange magic at work. Secrets. You're a princess of darkness, but you can't stand things *staying* in the dark. You've got to shine that big brain of yours onto it. No matter what it exposes."

"As if you're any different."

"Me?" Thorn prodded his chest. "I mind my own business!"

"Ha! It's a miracle your nose hasn't been snapped off, the way you stick it into other people's affairs! Remember how your hand got burned?"

"All I'm saying is, don't turn the world on its head while I'm away," said Thorn. "Just leave things as you found them. K'leef won't thank you for it if he comes back from the trial all glorious and stuff and finds the city a smoking ruin."

"Is this your clumsy way of saying good-bye? By having us argue?"

"I wasn't arguing."

"I think you— All right. No one here is arguing about anything. Agreed?"

"Agreed." Thorn looked back toward the palace. "So, you'll be staying put, then?"

"Yes. Waiting patiently for you to return, the triumphant hero. Perhaps I'll take up embroidery again. And do some . . . reading."

"Lily . . ."

She grinned. "K'leef has some books about magic. You should see them, Thorn. All engraved on bronze pages, so thin, but very beautiful."

"Bronze?"

"We're in the kingdom of fire, Thorn. Paper spell books don't last long here. The library has burned down four times. Anyway, there's some research I want to do, old legends I want to look into."

"And you read Djinnic, don't you?" He shook his head. "You're so sharp, be careful you don't cut yourself."

Lily took his hand. "Let's go. It's time for the challenge to be announced."

# FOURTEEN

Lily wished she were home. Now more than ever. She wasn't made for traveling. With the passage of time her homesickness got worse, not better.

Thorn, on the other hand, was at home wherever he planted his boots. He made friends just by turning up. How did he do that?

This felt very different from the coronation. The air lay heavy in the corridors, and many of the windows were veiled, adding to the somber mood. Lily slowed down as they neared the throne room, where everyone else was gathered.

"I want you to reconsider our arrangement," said Lily.

Thorn grimaced. "We ain't got an arrangement."

"That's why I want you to reconsider it. Now, Thorn."

"Forget it. No way are you turning me into a zombie."

Lily stood over him, which was easy, since she now had four inches on him. She had sprouted up since her fourteenth birthday. "I never said zombie, and you know it! Why end up dead when there are . . . other options?"

"Name one."

"A ghost? Then you'd have Custard to play with."

"Nope."

"A vampire, then? You'd love being a vampire! You could turn into a bat and go out flying with Hades!"

"And spend my evenings chasing insects? Forget it."

"But vampires are fashionable!"

"A bunch of stuck-up snobs if you ask me."

Why did he always make life so difficult? "Fine. What about a liche?"

"What's a liche?"

"A zombie with brains."

"Do they still rot?"

"Everything rots, Thorn." Then Lily brightened. "But you've got Dr. Byle. He'd keep you all patched up and limber. He's made this ointment that he rubs on the zombies to stop rigor mortis from setting in. It's brilliant for stiff joints. And squeaky doors."

Thorn scratched his hand. "Listen, Lily, I know you mean well, in your weird Gehennish way, but I don't need a 'graveyard get-out clause,' 'cause I ain't planning on dying. Not today, not tomorrow, not here, not in the trials, neither. Got it?"

"Okay. Fine. Just make sure you don't."

"Okay. I won't."

Lily continued. "I'm sending a bat home with some messages. Anything you want to tell your family?"

"Like what?" He met her gaze. "Ain't you gonna take care of 'em?"

"Of course I am. You know that. But don't you want to say something to them? Just in case . . ." Lily twisted her ring.

"Yeah, all right. Tell 'em not to touch my stuff."

"Is that it? Nothing more?"

"There's more. Of course there's more." Thorn pondered. "Tell 'em not to touch my stuff . . . ever."

"Fine. Got it. I'm sure they'll be very moved." Lily stopped in front of the door to the Fire Hall. "There's just one other thing. . . ."

He looked sideways at her, suspicious. "What?"

"I don't want you to take this the wrong way, Thorn. You know I . . . I like you a lot. You are my friend, aren't you?"

"But . . . ?" He narrowed his eyes, as if he was aiming one of his arrows.

"But K'leef is likely to be the next sultan, and if it comes down to saving him or yourself . . . You know what I'm trying to say?"

His eyes went as thin as a blade's edge. "No. I'm just a witless commoner. You need to spell things out for me."

Lily's gaze fell to the floor. "The next sultan, and you noticed that he is very, *very* handsome? He'd make a fine match, and it would make Gehenna so much more powerful. Baron Sable's all for it. His wife is a cousin to the Djinns, and she thinks we could sort out the details pretty quickly."

"What details?"

"The engagement, of course."

"Whaaat?" Thorn pulled his hand free of hers. "So it's true? You're going to marry K'leef?"

"Of course not," she said.

"Phew."

"Not until I'm sixteen," she finished. "Then there'll be a huge wedding." "Aargh!"

Lily burst out laughing. "Honestly, Thorn. You are so easy to tease." Then she became serious. "Look after him, that's all I'm saying."

Thorn scowled at her. "You are a strange, strange girl, Lily Shadow."

"Would you want me any different?"

They entered the Fire Hall. The empty throne dominated the quiet space, a dark tumor at the heart of the kingdom.

Thrones claimed lives, she knew better than most. Yet everyone seemed eager to sit upon one.

How many princes were vying for it today? She looked around the golden room.

It was as large as the Great Hall of Gehenna. But here the columns were thin and elegant and the space brightly lit and colorful. Instead of gargoyles and statues of monsters, these alcoves held mosaics revealing scenes from the life of Prince Djinn, the founder of the Sultanate. She had read about some of them. Him wrestling an efreet in the Shardlands. His capture of the last dragon. The destruction of the first city. Huge flames, lava, and smoke spewed out of the volcano that had once been here. Its eruption had sunk the original Nahas beneath the waves, and the crescent bay was all that remained.

She counted roughly a hundred people in the room, a fraction of the thousands that had cheered for Sa'if outside only a few days ago.

They were clustered in groups around their candidates. Lily and Thorn joined the small band with K'leef.

Gabriel was there, clad in silver armor, his hand clutching the sword on his hip. He greeted her with a scowl. "You took your time."

Lily ignored him and kissed a nervous K'leef. "How are you feeling?"

"Honestly? Violently ill."

Gabriel huffed. "There's nothing to it. The challenge will be set, and you and I"—he glanced at Thorn—"with the assistance of the lower classes, will triumph."

Lily put her hand on Thorn before he could do something unpleasant to the heir of the Lumina. "It's a trial by fire, Gabriel," she said. "It's going to be dangerous. Now, these two are proven heroes, while you're . . . what? A knee-trembling coward?"

Gabriel snorted. "Who saved you at Halloween? Or defeated that treacherous brother of yours in the Battle of Gloom?"

She pointed at Thorn. "Him."

"As I said, with the assistance of the lower classes."

Thorn butted in. "Are you really that deluded?"

"Stop it," snapped K'leef. "We've got to work together. There'll be enough—"

Silence fell over the crowd as the old vizier, Marouf, shuffled up to the throne. He leaned on his staff and paused every few steps.

Gabriel nudged Lily. "One of yours, I suppose?"

"What?"

"A zombie. He looks decrepit enough."

Marouf turned around and spoke, his voice stronger than what anyone would expect to come from his feeble body. "The trial has been decided. The destruction of the old tower was an omen. There has been no phoenix above the palace in almost two hundred years, since the time of Agni, Lord of Flame. We must restore pride and honor to this sullied throne. We must show the New Kingdoms what it means to be the Sultan Djinn. Thus, any of you who wish to wear the lava crown must first claim a phoenix."

People gasped and muttered. A few of the brothers shook their heads, giving up already.

"Can't be done."

"Impossible."

"Might as well ask us to bottle the sun."

K'leef, already pale and sickly, turned a jaundiced yellow. "A phoenix? Is he joking?"

Lily gripped his hand. "You can't give up, K'leef."

"You don't understand. The fire of a phoenix is a thousand times fiercer than the lava crown. Our magic doesn't protect us from it. You get within ten yards of a grown phoenix and you'll be ash in a minute. And it's not like they nest nearby, either."

"So where are they?" asked Thorn, glowering at Gabriel.

"The Shardlands."

"Oh," said Lily. "I see."

The vizier hadn't declared a trial; he had issued a death sentence. The old man raised his hands. "Step forward, claimants for the crown."

Jambiya tapped his way up. His supporters cheered. There were a lot of them, including some from other kingdoms. Lily knew Jambiya had traveled widely, and based on the looks of this bunch, he'd made many strange allies.

There was commotion in another group, and a second young man marched ahead, breaking free of an older woman's grip. She held her hands against her face, trying not to cry.

"Fafnir," said K'leef. "He's good."

*Fafnir?* Lily searched her memory. The red-haired man seemed so different from K'leef, but . . . "His mother is Princess Sif, your father's . . . third wife?"

She looked again at the weeping mother. She was a long way from her original home, with her pale hair and creamy skin, but there was no question that she belonged to House Djinn now. What peace deal had brought her here? K'leef watched his half brother. "If anyone could beat Jambiya, it's Fafnir. But he's a wanderer, like his mother."

"A wanderer?"

"She came here from way up north. There's not a drop of noble blood in her, but I think my father, a warrior, liked the fact that she had seen some of the world. Her people find it hard to settle down, and Fafnir's the same way."

"She was a trader from the Ice Isles, wasn't she? She came selling furs," said Lily. "Gave your father the skin of a dire wolf."

K'leef looked at her, amazed. "How do you know that?"

How did she? She must have read it somewhere. . . .

Thorn laughed. "By the Six, it's a miracle your father got any ruling done, what with all the time he must have spent in the bedchamber."

"Is there anyone else?" asked Marouf.

"It's now or never," muttered K'leef, more to himself than them.

Lily turned her gaze to the two other brothers. Jambiya was twice K'leef's age, well traveled, and an accomplished sorcerer. But he was a ruthless man, perhaps even evil. His plain dress was just a pretense of being humble. He wanted the crown, and Lily was afraid of what he'd do if he got it.

Fafnir was an unknown quantity. He glanced at his group—his mother especially— with doubt and mixed feelings. Why had he put himself forward? To prove something? His name had never come up before. Lily guessed he didn't want the crown, not really. Just like K'leef.

Gabriel lifted K'leef's arm and shouted, "Here! K'leef's doing it, too!"

And that was that.

Stunned, walking as if in a dream, K'leef approached his two brothers. Then the three of them turned to face the crowd. The vizier put his hand on Fafnir's shoulder. "Declare your companions."

Fafnir took a deep breath and called out two names. One was clearly a warrior; the other was a man with the tall, dark features of a nomad.

"He'll be useful in the Shardlands," Lily commented. "Fafnir's clever."

Then came K'leef. "Gabriel, of House Solar, and Thorn, of House Shadow."

Thorn winked at her. "Wish me luck."

Lily's heart skipped a beat to watch him stand beside K'leef. She had gotten used to having him nearby. Gabriel joined them, raising his arms triumphantly as if the cheers were for him rather than K'leef.

The vizier approached Jambiya. "And your companions, Prince?"

His crowd of supporters shuffled around to allow his chosen men through.

Jambiya smiled. "First, I summon Nasr, of the Scorpion tribe."

Another nomad. Jambiya must have guessed that the trial would entail travel to the Shardlands.

Nasr walked forward, his long desert robes sweeping the floor, and bowed before his champion. Jambiya then raised his hand. "And for my second companion . . ."

A man moved to the front, awaiting the call. A man in black.

Lily's blood froze. It wasn't possible.

"I call upon Pandemonium, of House Shadow."

# FIFTEEN

"**I** can't believe it," said Lily the moment she and Thorn left the gathering. She was finding it difficult to catch her breath.

Thorn nodded. "I hardly recognized him, he's changed so much. How long has—"

"Six months."

Six months since she'd discovered that her uncle Pan had murdered her parents and brother in an attempted coup. Six months since he'd tried to kill her, too. Six months since she'd banished him.

"We wouldn't be in this mess if you'd just done what everyone wanted you to do."

"I couldn't kill my own kin, Thorn."

"*He* did."

"And that's how we're different."

Thorn sighed. "You'll regret that mercy, one day. I just hope *I* don't."

He was right. Pan had changed. His hair was short and his beard trim, though grayer than she remembered, and his eyes were sharp again. His wine belly had been replaced by muscle. His slouch was gone, too, the way he used to stand to balance his swollen gut. Now her uncle stood straighter than one of Thorn's arrows.

"How good a fighter is he, Lily?" asked Thorn.

"He was very good." There was no point in pretending otherwise. Who knew how things would play out? "Father was the sorcerer, Pan the warrior. He led our armies, at least until Tyburn arrived on the scene."

"I never thought I'd say it, but I wish Tyburn was here now."

"I couldn't bring him, so I brought you."

"Some replacement."

She'd only gotten a glimpse of Pan, and he'd purposefully not looked in her direction, but her uncle seemed different in another way, too. There was a hardness to him that hadn't been there before.

"We'll just have to avoid crossing his path." Thorn gathered up his bow and quiver. "Time to get going, I think."

Lily glanced at her friend as they walked. Unlike her, he looked completely at ease.

Thorn was wild at heart. He breathed deepest under the open sky. How had they even become friends? They were as different as could be. Lily's world was tombs and darkness and necromancy, the sorcery of death. Thorn's world was hunting in the forest, listening to birdsong, sleeping under the stars, and—

He burped. "Sorry. That last cake might have been one too many."

And stuffing his face. "Cake? For breakfast?"

"That's not a local custom?" he asked.

"You do realize you are heading into the Shardlands, don't you?"

"It's the wilderness, Lily. They're all pretty much the same." Thorn checked his pockets, no doubt for leftover crumbs. "Grandpa says there's simple rules to surviving the wild."

"Go on, then. What does your dear grandpa say?"

"'Stay away from the things wanting to eat you.'"

Lily nodded. "Wise, yet completely useless."

Thorn held up a quarter of a muffin. "And the other one is to eat whenever you can." And so he did.

He was still picking at crumbs when they emerged from the palace and joined K'leef and his horses. Thorn tapped a chest hanging on the back of a mule. "Traveling light, I see. What's in this?"

"Books."

Thorn pursed his lips and gestured at a string of satchels. "And in those? More books?"

"No," snapped K'leef. "Those would be my scrolls."

Thorn rolled his eyes. "And . . ."

K'leef adjusted his turban. "Four maps, the most accurate we have of the Shardlands. Then I've got my blank parchment—and quills and inks, of course. I've brought my measuring gear, too. If we go into uncharted territory, we'll be wanting to record the route."

Thorn grabbed a wooden frame strung with beads. "And we'll be playing music at night?"

"That's an abacus, Thorn. It's for mathematics."

"We're going to die horribly." Thorn looked pleadingly at her. "Tell him to dump this junk, Lily. Please."

She inspected the luggage. "And weaponry, K'leef?"

"Weapons? Why would I have any weapons? I can't fight."

"You are going to the Shardlands. To capture a phoenix." She picked up a cage. "What's this?"

He smiled broadly. "My phoenix cage. I spent all night building it."

"It does look very homemade."

"Thanks."

"It wasn't a compliment. How is this going to trap a phoenix? Aren't they made out of fire?"

"Which is why I've used cold iron." He adjusted the hinges. "I studied the design out of the spell book of Alnniran, my grandfather's grandfather. He was the last to trap a phoenix."

"But he reinforced his cage with a dampening spell," said Lily. "The Enchantment of Sulfur."

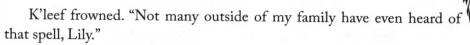

K'leef frowned. "Not many outside of my family have even heard of that spell, Lily."

"Do you know it?" Lily asked.

He shook his head. "Sa'if was trying to teach it to me, but I still had a long way to go."

Lily picked at the thin bars. "Then you may not have used enough cold iron."

"It's all I've got." He fiddled with his turban, retying the end. "There are reports from the nomads that they nest up in the Lava Mountains now. That's where we'll go. That's why I need the maps."

"Oh, I give up!" shouted Thorn, and he stomped off to check his own horse.

Lily helped adjust the saddle. She wanted to do something for him. "Look after yourself, K'leef. If it gets to be too much, come home. The crown's not worth it."

"Someone has to stop Jambiya," K'leef replied. "I've asked Paz to keep an eye on you. If you need anything, just ask him."

The stable doors opened, and out came Gabriel riding a gleaming white horse, followed by six heavily laden mules, and finally two camels, equally burdened.

"Why are you wearing a bonnet, Gabriel?" asked Lily.

"This is not a bonnet. It's a topi, and it's to keep the sun off. Otherwise you end up tanned like a peasant."

"And who are they?"

"My servants."

"You're taking twelve people? On this quest?"

"Of course not." He shifted over and recounted the men lurking in the shade. "There should be fifteen."

Thorn stormed back over. "Lily! Do something!"

She looked up at Gabriel, shielding her eyes from the sunlight blazing off his silver-studded saddle. "Do you really need *all* this?"

"What do you mean? These are the barest essentials!"

She pointed at something bronze tied to a camel. "What's that?"

"My bathtub." He folded his arms. "I am not leaving that here. Someone else might use it while I'm gone."

Thorn grabbed her wrist and dragged her away. When they were alone, he whispered to her, "I'm going to take him out there and lose him. Understood?"

"You can't do that, Thorn." Lily paused. "Not *really*."

"I hear you saying one thing but thinking something else, Lily." He glanced over at Gabriel, who was now issuing instructions to his servants. They were putting out a table and chair. One unfolded a tablecloth.

"It's a miracle he's lasted this long." Lily sighed. "Just make it look like an accident."

"They'll never find the body," said Thorn.

The outer gates began to part. Hot wind rushed in through the widening gap, carrying with it the lifeless scent of desert.

Lily hugged Thorn. She held him tightly, squeezing him as hard as she could, suddenly afraid. She didn't want to let him go. "You take care."

He slipped free. "Of course."

She laughed at his blushing face. "Don't do anything stupid. If you get yourself killed, I'll never forgive you. I'll hunt you into the Twilight, you know that?"

He muttered something, then rose up onto his horse. "Good-bye, Lady Shadow."

"Good-bye, Thorn."

That wasn't what she'd meant to say, but the words had stuck in her throat.

She hoped he already knew what they were.

# THE

# SHARDLANDS

# SIXTEEN

Thorn didn't ride with Gabriel or K'leef. He slipped off his horse—no point tiring it out when they were going so slowly anyway—and joined the straggling line of servants.

Thorn fell in step with one, a gangly boy a few years older, and a foot taller, than himself. There was something familiar about him. . . .

"Do I know you?" he asked.

The boy frowned. "I don't think so, m'lord."

"Not been to the Sword Coast or anything? Herne's Forest?"

"Not been beyond the city until an hour ago." The boy smiled. Then he added, "Sorry, m'lord."

"I ain't a lord. I'm Thorn."

"Merriq," the boy replied as they shook hands.

"That a Djinnic name?"

"No. It's my father's name. He was a famous minstrel."

It couldn't be the same person, could it? Thorn had run across a charlatan named Merrick more than once since leaving Herne's Forest.

"He performed for all the great houses," the boy went on. "Danced with the twelve Solar princesses. They all fell in love with him and the

duke wanted his head, so he ran away, all the way south to the Sultanate."
He smiled ruefully. "At least, that's what he told my mother."

It *was* the same Merrick!

"Then, a month after I was born, he went out, saying he needed a new
string for his lute."

"And never came back?" Thorn guessed.

"And never came back." The boy shrugged. "My grandpa took us in. He
said minstrels were like the wind."

"Meaning they come and go as they please?"

"No." The boy pointed at his backside. "They stink. Said if he ever
showed his scrawny face here again, he'd remove his head."

Thorn nodded. "Sounds to me we're gonna get on just fine, Merrick."

"You can call me Riq."

"Rick?"

He tapped the side of his throat. "No. Riq. With a *q*. Use the back of
your tongue."

"All right, Riq."

"Better." Riq gestured up the line. "What's the story, Thorn?"

"The usual. The nobles have made stupid plans, and it's up to the likes
of us to carry 'em out. We succeed, and we'll be eating mangoes for the rest
of our lives. We fail, and we suffer a forgotten death somewhere in those
sands." Thorn searched the skies. Still empty. "Though I have a bad feeling
I'm going to come back as a zombie."

"Some quaint Gehennish custom? The zombie thing?" Riq looked up,
too. "It isn't going to rain, if that's what you're wondering."

"Nah, just waiting for a friend."

Where was Hades? He should have been back by now. Maybe he'd
gotten lost.

"Hey! Peasant! Come here!"

Gabriel was up front, shouting and waving. He and K'leef had
dismounted.

Riq frowned. "Is he calling for me or you?"

Thorn didn't answer. He just handed Riq the reins and jogged over to his companions. "Can't you manage even five minutes by yourselves?"

K'leef sat with a book open on his lap. "Look at those." He pointed down to some animal tracks in the white sand.

Thorn spread his hand over one of the impressions to measure it. His fingers didn't stretch far enough to span the footpad. And the distance between the forepaws and the hind-paws was over twelve feet. "It's big. Has claws. Never a good combination." He walked over to a flat rock and sniffed. "Yup."

"Yup what?" K'leef continued flicking through the book.

"That sharp smell? It marked its territory."

K'leef paused on an image and showed it to Thorn. "What do you think?"

The paw print on the page matched the one on the ground.

The artist had put a lot of detail into the picture. The teeth, the spiky tail, and the long claws. The creature looked like some big cat, but it bore a humanish face. Just with immense jaws, which were overstuffed with fangs.

"What . . . what is it?" said Gabriel, his voice, and legs, trembling ever so slightly.

K'leef closed his book. "A manticore."

# SEVENTEEN

"**W**hat's that?" asked Thorn, pointing ahead. They'd traveled miles and hadn't yet seen a manticore. But there had been other strange sights, like this one.

The western sky blazed. The horizon flared with bright colors, swirling greens and reds, and spikes of copper and gold. Thunder echoed from far, far away, but within its din Thorn heard, or thought he heard, voices. It gave him the chills.

"Wild magic," replied K'leef. "We're heading deep into the Shardlands, Thorn."

It was dusk and time to camp. They found a patch of stony, flat ground within a low crater, just enough to keep them out of the wind. Gabriel's servants spent the last hour of daylight erecting his white tent. The whole thing was over twenty feet square. He'd brought a carpet, a foldout bed, and a table with four chairs. Plus a dinner set and candelabra. Not that he invited K'leef and Thorn, much less any of the servants, to join him in eating.

Thorn shook open his blanket. It got cold at night here. He kept his eye on the gathering storm clouds. "That something we need to worry about?"

"Oh, yes," said K'leef. "A big storm can change a lot of things: the landscape, the creatures caught in it. Sometimes the effects are only temporary; other times . . ." He drew a pattern on a rock. "Watch this."

The pattern began to glow, as if the lines had cracked the rock, allowing heat to escape. Smoke emerged, and flames sprouted out of the stone, creating an instant campfire.

Thorn tried not to seem impressed. "I've got some powder for making hot chocolate."

But impressed he was. He never got bored of watching sorcery. And K'leef's brand of magic was a welcome change from Lily's necromancy. You could only take so much of zombies and walking skeletons.

Thorn looked at his fingers. Stubby, and calloused from pulling bowstrings and heaving shovels. There was ink under his nails. He could write now—not well, but the letters were starting to make sense. He looked over at K'leef and felt a pang of . . . envy.

K'leef was so talented at impossible things. Thorn was just a commoner. Now he couldn't even shoot straight, what use was he? And how could pulling a bowstring compare to wielding magic?

That's just the way it was, no point worrying about it right now. Thorn scratched at an itch between his shoulder blades using one of his arrows. "We should have camped somewhere else. This place gives me the creeps. Those statues . . ."

"They can't harm you, Thorn," said K'leef as he rolled out his own blanket.

"That's what they always say, right up to the moment they start moving and tear off your arms." Thorn kicked the nearest statue. "Who are they supposed to be, anyway? Took a lot of effort to put these big things out here, in the middle of nowhere."

"It's the Valley of the Gods," said K'leef. "No one comes here now."

"What's this one called?"

K'leef shrugged. "No one remembers. The gods died a long time ago."

Thorn laughed. "The Six Princes hunted 'em down, right? Lily tells me the Bone Throne is made from the spine of one of these gods. Prince Shadow tore it from its back in a battle on the moon."

K'leef made a face. "Why do you talk about the Six like that? Haven't you got any respect? Anyway, they didn't destroy them just to make some furniture. They did it to free humankind from fate. That's why we've got free will and we can decide our own futures without the gods meddling."

"You believe that, do you?" asked Thorn.

"Don't you?"

He shrugged. "Grandpa says the cow don't care why it's being milked, just as long as the farmer has warm hands."

K'leef frowned. "I have no idea what that means."

A roar rolled across the desert.

Gabriel peered out of his tent. "What was that?"

K'leef looked anxious. "The manticore's on the prowl."

"But we're safe here, aren't we?" Gabriel whined. "You've planned for this, haven't you?"

Thorn interrupted. "Why did you come, Gabriel?"

Gabriel tightened the belt of his dressing robe and joined them at the campfire. He winked at K'leef. "Ah, yes, the quest."

"Got sand in your eye?" Thorn asked.

Gabriel winked again. "The quest. Terribly quaint, isn't it?"

K'leef seemed as bemused as Thorn. "What do you mean, Gabriel? Yes, we're on a quest to find a phoenix. You know that."

"Yes, yes. And when we find it and you are crowned, you are obligated to give your companions any reward they ask for. Isn't that right?"

Thorn turned to his friend. This rule hadn't been mentioned to him. "Oh, is it, K'leef?"

K'leef narrowed his gaze. "What do you have in mind, Gabriel?"

Gabriel waved over his shoulder. "To leave this fly-infested cauldron of a country. To go back home, and without your monstrous sister."

K'leef grinned. "Why, don't you like Nargis?"

"No, not in the least." Gabriel craned his neck around. "Come on, there's no need to keep it secret any longer. Where is it?"

"Where's what?"

"The phoenix. You must have it hidden somewhere?"

Thorn took the boy's arm. "Have you gone heat mad? You're not making any sense. Or you're making less sense than normal."

Gabriel laughed. "Quests. So old-fashioned. Father has done hundreds of them. Always comes home victorious. But of course he would."

Gabriel's father, Duke Raphael Solar, was one of the greatest sorcerers of the New Kingdoms. Thorn had heard plenty of stories about him. There was the one about the Golden Hind. . . .

"The most famous is his hunt for the Golden Hind," said Gabriel. "They say he chased it beyond the setting sun and caught it with a rope woven from a sky maiden's golden locks."

Thorn frowned. "Didn't he?"

Gabriel snorted. "Of course not. His huntsmen had caught it two weeks earlier and had it in a pen in the woods. Father put a spear through it while it was tied to a stake."

"And the quest for the Lance of Light?"

"Bashed out by a tin smith from Argent. Father added a touch of glamour magic and that was that."

K'leef sat down. "But he must have defeated the giant of Noland? Twenty feet tall and fought with an oak trunk bedecked with the bones of his enemies?"

Gabriel shook his head. "Five foot tall with stilts and a long cloak. All smoke and mirrors."

Thorn laughed. "I get it. So you think this quest is like that? A setup?"

Gabriel stared at him. "Of course. No one does quests nowadays. Only children believe fairy tales like that. So where is this phoenix? It's just that I want to head back tomorrow morning. This sand gets everywhere." He scratched his crotch. "And I mean *everywhere*."

Thorn glanced at K'leef. "Shall I tell him, or do you want to?"

K'leef, still stunned, shook his head. "You do it."

Thorn smiled. This was going to be fun. In a pathetic way. "Gabriel, listen to me. We don't have no phoenix. Not here, not hidden behind a rock, not stuffed in one of K'leef's chests. The phoenix is out *there*, far into the Shardlands. Past the manticore, past monsters and wild magic and desert nomads who'll cook you for breakfast. Get it? We are on our own." He corrected himself. "On our own with fifteen servants."

"But I can't go into the Shardlands!" said Gabriel. "You don't come back from the Shardlands. Everyone knows that."

"Then we'll be the first to do it, eh?" Thorn slapped his shoulder. "Don't you want your dad to be proud?"

"But I'll get eaten! I'm too important to get eaten!" He looked around wildly and grabbed a servant. "You! Start packing my things! We're going back to Palace Djinn!"

Thorn grimaced. "You sure about that? Manticores hunt at night."

K'leef nodded. "So do rakshasas."

Gabriel gulped. *"Rakshasas?"*

"Shape-changing demons. Most live farther east, but some breeds like the desert. And to them, nothing is tastier than white meat."

Gabriel sobbed.

Thorn sighed. "But worst of all are the . . ." He pondered. "The mobie-dobies."

"Ah, yes," said K'leef. "Twelve feet tall, fangs up to their elbows, and thirty-two eyes. Can't escape them. The, er, mobie-dobies are terrible, hideous things."

"Mouths right on their stomachs," added Thorn. "So big they can swallow a man whole."

"And only one foot," added K'leef. "They can hop a hundred yards."

Thorn frowned at his friend. Even an idiot wouldn't believe something that stupid.

"Mobie-dobies?" whimpered Gabriel. "A hundred yards?"

But there were idiots and then there was Gabriel Solar.

K'leef nodded. "Land on you, and you're paste. *Ker-splat.*"

Gabriel ran off screaming.

K'leef stirred some cocoa powder into the saucepan of milk heating over the fire. "Mobie-dobies? That was the best you could think of?"

They turned toward the wailing coming out of the white tent.

Thorn shrugged. "Pass the cookies."

The sun shone through Thorn's eyelids, but he kept them shut. He was comfortable under his blanket and wanted to chase the end of sleep just a little while longer. He didn't appreciate the brightness, and he didn't appreciate K'leef kicking him, either. "Get lost. I'm asleep."

"Wake up, Thorn."

"Urrgh." He blinked. It was too sunny. "What's up?"

"Looks like the work of mobie-dobies," said K'leef.

"What?"

"Just get up."

Thorn stood up and looked around. "Ah. Not good."

The camp had been cleared out. The servants had taken off with the gear and the animals. A few things were scattered around, including a sleeping Gabriel. He lay snoring in a ditch. They'd stolen his bed right from under him.

Thorn put on his boots—thankfully they hadn't taken those—and inspected the few remaining objects. This was bad. "You just get up?" he asked K'leef.

"A minute ago."

The sun had been up about an hour, but the servants would have run off well before then. Thorn shielded his eyes as he scanned the horizon. Nothing. They were long gone.

K'leef spat, furious. "They took my books, Thorn."

Thorn caught a glimpse of something shiny, half a mile off. "At least they left us the bathtub."

# EIGHTEEN

They found not just the bathtub, but a camel with supplies still tied to it. The servants must have lost the animal in the dark. Thorn unloaded it and checked to see what provisions they still had, while K'leef dealt with a hysterical Gabriel.

Thorn didn't catch all of what Gabriel said, but it did include hunting the treacherous thieves to the gates of hell. Hanging them, drowning them, and putting them on the pyre. And having his executioner, Golgoth, decapitate them, just to be doubly sure.

Food and water were the priority, and Thorn was relieved to find enough to last them a couple of days, as long as they were careful. There was a box of Djinnic Delights, soft fruity candy that just melted in the mouth. He helped himself to a few while the other two shouted at each other. The sweets made him feel a lot better, and his happiness increased when he found his bow and a trio of arrows scattered on the arid ground. Despite his current shooting problems, he didn't feel right without the weapon. With his bow slung across his back and his arrows tucked into his belt, he led the camel over to the campsite. "What's the plan?"

Gabriel waved frantically. "Back to the palace, of course!"

K'leef pointed in the opposite direction. "We're going that way."

"And that direction is ... ?"

"Where we'll find our phoenix."

Thorn looked at each of them. "I dunno if it's the heat that's making me say this, but I agree with Gabbs."

Gabriel glared at him. "How dare you give me a nickname! Or use any name at all! How many times—"

"Shut up," snapped Thorn. "Let the grown-ups speak."

Flabbergasted, Gabriel did indeed shut up.

K'leef smirked. "Never thought I'd witness the day you agreed with ... Gabbs."

"Me neither. But we ain't got enough food for a garden picnic, let alone a journey into the-Six-knows-where."

"I know where we're going." K'leef tapped his forehead. "They may have taken the maps, but I've studied them since I could open a book, Thorn. I've memorized the routes to the Lava Mountains. I'd planned to take the path along Red Ravine, but since we're low on supplies, there's a quicker way."

"Go on. Though I know I'm not going to like it." Thorn emptied some sand from his boot. "Grandpa has a saying: 'Quickest way down hurts the most.'"

"I thought we'd agreed your grandpa's an idiot," K'leef scoffed. "There's a shortcut to the Lava Mountains. Through the Hell Gates."

"And they're called the Hell Gates because ... ?"

"It's across hard desert. It's really hot and on fire—parts of it, anyway. Lots of naphtha wells."

"Nap-what?"

"Thick, sticky oil. Catches fire easily and burns forever. Whole lakes of it out there."

"So why not just call 'em the Hot Gates?"

"They did." K'leef acted all casual and muttered something that, to Thorn, sounded like, "Then the demons moved in."

*"Demons?"* Thorn asked.

*"Demons?"* Gabriel cried.

"They're renegades from the time of the Six. Can't be many of them left by now." K'leef tried to laugh it off. "Come on, Thorn. You're from Gehenna. A couple of demons wouldn't bother the likes of you. Lily must have a dozen working in the kitchens."

"Lily has one, an imp. Good-for-nothing, he is. Two feet tall, eats like a horse—sometimes eats an actual horse—and sleeps six days out of seven."

"Nothing to worry about, then," said K'leef.

Thorn eyed his friend. "You so keen to get yourself killed?"

"I've got to stop Jambiya, Thorn. And I need your help."

Thorn scratched the back of his hand. "All right, K'leef. We go on."

It seemed saving kingdoms was now his full-time occupation.

They packed up everything, including the bathtub. Thorn swore under his breath as they loaded the hideous contraption onto the camel—without any help from Gabriel, of course. The Solar boy was still sulking. Thorn also realized why this particular beast had been abandoned. It would sit down, refuse to get back up, and stare at the boys with aloof contempt. It bit, kicked, and spat huge, phlegmy balls of green slime.

Thorn named it Gobber.

"I thought you were good with animals," said K'leef as they pulled on Gobber's reins in an effort to make him stand. "You ride a giant vampire bat; a miserable camel should be no problem."

"Give me Hades any day of the week," muttered Thorn. Finally, with a mighty heave, they got Gobber up. "Don't know where he's gone."

"He'll come back. He always does."

Thorn inspected the sky for the hundredth time that morning. Nothing.

They walked, Thorn with the camel, Gabriel straggling behind. K'leef led, pointing out landscape features he recognized from his maps and old scrolls. The heat rose with the sun as they passed ruins of old structures, small and not so small.

"These walls are from the time of the Six Princes," K'leef explained. "They're nothing. In the very heart of the Shardlands, they say, are the capitals of the Princes, and beyond that is the high king's palace, the place where magic was born."

"Anyone ever been there?" Thorn asked.

"People claim they have. Can you imagine what it must be like?"

"Dusty?"

K'leef wasn't listening. "To walk the halls the Six walked. To visit the Elemental Library. To see the Garden of Chaos and the Hall of Wishes. My mother used to tell me stories about the golden age of magic."

"My mom used to tell me to clean up after the goats."

K'leef scowled. "You don't have an ounce of imagination, Thorn. Maybe that's why you can't cast spells."

"It's all talk, K'leef. My mom also told me the Six all fought each other for the crown. They wrecked much of the world and the Shardlands—all this decay is their work. They destroyed all that was great about themselves. I ain't got time for folk who'll burn down a forest to cook a rabbit."

"But they were great sorcerers. Where would we be if it wasn't for their magic?"

"Me? I'd still be doing this: looking after the beasts. You, though—you wouldn't be living in a palace."

"Maybe not. But someone would. Magic's coming to an end. This is the age of iron now. Time for swords, not spells." K'leef cast a sideways glance at him. "And it won't be any fairer."

"Nobles will always be nobles," agreed Gabriel. "And peasants will always be peasants. There is an order to the world; that does not change."

Thorn kicked a rock out of his path. Why bother with this talk? It didn't change anything, and yet here he was, arguing with two sorcerous nobles. Not that Gabriel was much of one. Thorn had witnessed him cast a spell once. It had been sad.

Thorn's thoughts about the injustices of the world were interrupted by a roar. "That manticore sounds closer."

Another roar confirmed it. Five, six, miles away. Sniffing around the remains of their abandoned camp, most likely.

Gabriel spoke. "Why can't it go after the servants instead of us?"

"Guess they prefer royal blood," said Thorn. He tugged at the camel's reins. "Come on, you pile of stink. And I thought Hades smelled bad."

"It's not him. Not this time." K'leef took a few steps forward and picked up a pitted lump of rock. He dug his fingers into it, and it crumbled like charcoal. "We need to go around."

"Why?" All he could see was an expanse of ash-covered ground and more of the black, burnt rocks, large and small. Nothing that looked dangerous.

K'leef pulled a tuft of lint from his cloak and rolled it into a small ball. He held it for a second, and it caught fire, burning crisply. He tossed it in front of him. When it landed, it fizzed and sparked. The nearby rocks and stones began to steam and jump, and the gravelly pebbles popped.

Then there was an explosion.

Gobber snorted and Gabriel yelped as the rocks burst, flinging out a halo of white flame that rolled over the ground, igniting more stones until a circle over ten feet wide flamed.

K'leef clapped and the flames began to die down to hissing sprites that jumped across the rocks. They, too, eventually faded away, leaving behind a cloud of smoke and ash.

Thorn brushed his face clean of soot. "Is there nothing out here that doesn't catch fire the moment you look at it?"

K'leef tossed him a pebble. "It's porous. Explosive gas seeps up from vast underground chambers and gets trapped in the rocks. It's called the Devil's Breath."

Thorn sniffed the pitted stone. His eyes began to water as the acidic stench burned through his nostrils. "Should be called the Devil's Farts. That is an evil whiff."

"The bigger the fire, the bigger the explosion." K'leef pointed to a ridge of tan-hued sandstone. "If we can get over there, we should be safe. But it'll add a few hours."

Thorn threw the stone away. "Then we'd better get started."

The wind was picking up, blowing dust in their faces. Behind them broiled strangely colored clouds.

K'leef pointed to a low rocky crest. "We could shelter in those caves."

They moved quickly; even Gobber sensed the danger. They reached the crags just as the storm hit. The wind howled, and swirling sand scoured their skins. Thunder boomed, and the eerie voices that accompanied it turned into wails, tearing at Thorn's mind, making him see things out of the corner of his eye.

Thorn paused at the cave mouth. "Light it up, K'leef. I wanna make sure it ain't some manticore den."

The flame revealed only bare rock and dancing shadows. Gobber folded himself down in the best spot in the back, forcing the boys to squat at the cave opening.

Thorn had never seen anything like this storm. Clouds roiled and expanded; shapes lurked out, then swiftly vanished. Colors flashed, and glowing lights tumbled in the wind, which also carried the sound of screams and cries and laughter. Worst was the sobbing, just within earshot, and so heavy with misery that Thorn found himself weeping. He glanced over to see Gabriel curled up tight, facing the wall.

K'leef sat nearby, his own face traced with tears. "Lost spirits. Nothing more than that."

"Nothing more? It's horrible. Such sorrow . . ."

"Try not to listen to them. They'll drive you beyond despair."

It was true. Thorn's heart was a lead weight in his chest. It was the music of misery. No words—there was no way to understand it and perhaps make the bearing of it easier—but all emotion, all feeling.

Then came the promises.

*Thorn, we're here. . . .*

Ghostly figures emerged from the blazing, hellish lights.

"Lily?" Thorn stumbled to his feet.

*Thorn, we know you miss us, so we came for you.*

Lily smiled at him, just beyond the boundary of the cave.

*Look who I brought.*

She smiled as she summoned his family to him.

His dad, his mom, his siblings.

Lily brushed the hair from his brother Dale's face. A pale smile greeted him, pale and cold and from beyond the grave.

"No!" sobbed Thorn. "What have you done to them?"

*What did you expect, Thorn?*

"You promised, Lily, you promised me!"

Lily laughed, and it was both happy and cruel. *I promised to take care of them, and I have.*

She'd turned his family into undead. His twin sisters stared at him as they stood hand in hand. Heather and Petal. There were flowers woven into their blond locks, and they each held a bunch of withered black roses.

"Why?" asked Thorn.

*Nothing can hurt them now, Thorn. Aren't they perfect?* She clapped with delight.

He had to save them.

"Thorn! Thorn!" K'leef shook him violently. "Ignore them!"

Thorn couldn't. Not with them just beyond the cave entrance, and Lily taunting him. He stepped to the cave mouth, but K'leef held him tighter. "You can't leave, Thorn."

Gabriel rocked back and forth, in his own world of misery. "No, Father, I don't like mirrors. I don't want to see. . . ."

*Thorn, we're waiting for you.*

They needed him, but K'leef wouldn't let go. "You see? They are just illusions, Thorn."

*Come join us, Brother. . . .*

"Get off of me!" Thorn wrestled K'leef, and both boys tumbled to the ground, tugging and pulling at each other. After a few minutes Thorn tried to break away, but K'leef clung to him, his eyes blazing. Flames raged in his pupils, and smoke hissed from between his gritted teeth, as if he'd just been spewed from hell.

The bizarre sight was enough to shake Thorn out of his madness. "All right, K'leef. No need to get so hot and bothered."

K'leef blinked. A laugh burst from him, and all was as before. They helped each other up, and Thorn, his back to the wind and cries, turned to Gabriel.

He was transformed.

His lustrous hair, flawless skin, and brilliant blue eyes had decayed to limp, dull strings, a pockmarked face with crooked teeth, and faded, watery eyes.

This was the true Gabriel. Lily had told Thorn that he used all his magic to look unnaturally handsome. The strain of maintaining the illusion, even when he slept, was enormous. The storm's fury had blasted it away, and there sat a spindly, frail boy with uneven limbs and a thin chest, hardly the stuff of heroes.

"No . . ." Gabriel covered his face in shame. "Don't look at me."

Thorn pushed Gobber's hindquarters aside, just enough to give the three of them room to huddle farther back in the cave.

Thorn stared out into the storm.

And Lily continued to laugh while his family begged for mercy.

# NINETEEN

No one, living, dead, or otherwise, knew the full extent of the Shadow Library in Castle Gloom. Passages led out to all points of the compass, stairs sent explorers upward to gallery after gallery, and stairs took them down to one scroll-filled catacomb after another. Entire chambers had been lost to time, decay, and to abominations that had seeped out from one magical page or another, malevolent, bloodthirsty, and territorial.

Lily knew of the lost Hall of Harrowing Whispers, for example, where Moloch Shadow had tried—and only partially succeeded in—summoning a demon. Moloch's ghost still haunted the dark and bloody chamber, eternally repeating the spell he hadn't quite gotten right, as if one day he might remember the missing phrase that had led to his destruction.

Maps could not be relied upon, because the Shadow Library was not a constant construct. Rooms moved and sometimes disappeared entirely to return centuries later, with an unlucky reader now a skeleton slumped over the faded pages of a spell book.

But one creature was doing his best to explore every corner of the endless library, and he came scurrying out of a passageway at the sound of Lily's heels clicking on the marble flagstones.

Lily crouched and patted her lap. "Custard! Here, boy!"

The black Labrador puppy yapped excitedly and leaped onto her lap. He rolled over, and Lily tickled his belly mercilessly. "Miss me, Custie?"

He wagged his short tail.

"I'll take that as a yes, then?" She put the dog down. "Where is he?"

Custard dashed between two forever-high pillars of books. Beyond them a figure sat at a table, a small moon orb glowing above him.

Lily didn't have to be wary of anything here, for this was not the library itself, but a dream of the library. And she would never be afraid of this man, who rose from his chair and smiled warmly. "Lily."

Her father haunted the Shadow Library back home, and Lily could see him there whenever she wanted to. But in the Dreamtime, he was real—flesh and bone and breath—not the faded ether of a ghost. They only met this way when he chose to.

"Something is worrying you," said Iblis Shadow as he freed her from a hug. "How are things in the Sultanate?"

"Sa'if is dead. And Thorn blew up the Candle."

"Ah." He pushed out a chair for her. A strange gesture, since they both knew this was a dream. "Sit down. Tell me everything."

Custard settled on her lap, and Lily idly brushed his fur as she went over the main events of the last few days, primarily the coronation.

"I summoned his ghost, for K'leef's sake. He wanted to say good-bye to his brother."

Iblis patted her hand. "You did well. Such summoning isn't easy, even for an accomplished necromancer. Did the ghost give you any hint about why he hadn't been able to protect himself?"

"No. He was looking to the Far Shore. I couldn't keep him lingering long." Then Lily added, "But something strange has happened since. I know things, things I don't remember learning. When K'leef showed me a cage he built for a phoenix, I knew more about the spells to complete it than he did."

"You might have come across something in your studies?"

Lily shook her head. "And things about his family, too. Private things. They're in my memory, but they're not my own."

Iblis's eyes widened. "It's a gift from Sa'if. I've heard about this before, but not in a long time. Blessings of the Dead."

"It's magic?" asked Lily. She hadn't come across such a phrase.

"It is far older than what we might call sorcery. We Shadows are more open to receiving such gifts, because we don't build barriers against the dead the way other cultures do. It was probably a sign that Sa'if was grateful to you, for being such a good friend to K'leef."

Lily shivered. "So I have some of Sa'if's memories?"

"Some of his knowledge. Don't be afraid, Lily. What he gave you was because of the love he felt for his brother. A love he recognized in you, too."

"Love?" Lily felt her face redden. "I don't feel that way about K'leef." It felt odd to even mention love and K'leef in the same sentence.

"There are many types of love, Lily." Iblis sighed. "And there is a great magic in it."

The longing in his tone was unmistakable. After death he hadn't gone to the Far Shore like her mother and brother, Dante. He had remained in the Shadow Library so she could visit him whenever she needed some guidance. But for how much longer could she expect him to be at her beck and call? The stronger she became, both as a witch and as a ruler, the less often she needed to consult him. And as much as she couldn't bear the thought of him leaving her, she knew that keeping him from his wife and son was unfair and cruel. Her father deserved peace.

Time to get to the heart of the matter. "What do you think about Sa'if's death?"

"The more important question is, what do *you* think?"

"I've thought and thought and thought about it, but none of it makes any sense. Sa'if's magic should have saved him."

"Do you know why the Sultanate uses the lava crown?"

Lily shrugged. It was the first thing she'd read up on. "To test one's magic. Only a sorcerer of fire can wear it and survive."

"And we know Sa'if was a very skillful sorcerer of fire, until that moment."

Lily met her dad's gray gaze. "Until his magic failed . . . or he was no longer a sorcerer?"

Iblis nodded slowly. "If you eliminate all other options, what else are you left with?"

"That he lost his magic? Is that even possible?"

"It must be, because that is what happened."

Lily looked at the shelves around her. They reached far up into the darkness and went on forever. But the books and scrolls they contained were figments of her imagination, and as such, they couldn't provide any answers. She needed the real library. "Sa'if lost his magic the very moment he needed it most. That is too much of a coincidence to be an accident."

"I agree."

She bit her lip, hesitating over the thought that would create chaos. But there was no escaping it. "He was murdered."

Iblis nodded. "So it would seem."

"It has to be Jambiya," said Lily. "He found some way to block Sa'if's magic."

"Sa'if has other siblings, too, Lily. It could have been any one of them."

"Only five of Sa'if's brothers are sorcerers, and putting aside K'leef, that leaves four. It's one of them. It has to be."

"Whoever it is, they'll make a move against K'leef now that he's taking part in the trial."

Lily's blood ran cold. If someone were after K'leef, he'd have to go through Thorn to get to him.

"I need to find the killer." She put the sleeping Custard on the table. "I have to wake up now, Father."

"Is that everything?"

She frowned. "What do you mean?"

Iblis walked over to one of the many busts of the ancient family members that littered the library. "There's no hiding in dreams, Lily. You know that."

"I'm not hiding anything."

"Oh, no? Have a good look at this face." He pointed to the sculpture.

"Why? I know it's Dagon Shadow. He's in . . ." Lily's voice faltered as Iblis stepped aside and full light fell onto the bust.

It was Pan, her uncle.

Iblis gestured at the statue in the alcove. "And that should be Earl Tannin Shadow, yet he has the face of my brother. What aren't you telling me? Pan's very much on your mind."

"He's here. He's working for Jambiya."

The room shook and books fell from the shelves. Custard woke and fled. The polished surface of the table splintered, flicking needle-sharp slivers across the room.

Lily touched her father's hand.

Iblis unclenched his fists, and all became quiet again. "I'm sorry, Lily."

"No need to be, Father. But that's why I didn't want to tell you."

He was fading. His pain was stealing him from her.

"What shall I do, Father?" *What shall I do to the man who killed you and our family?*

He put his palm softly against her cheek, and Lily watched a tear fall down her father's own.

And then she woke up.

# TWENTY

*Who killed Sa'if?*

The question plagued Lily. She had some of Sa'if's memories, but none that were helping.

With so many people in mourning or preoccupied by the trial by fire, Lily was reduced to consulting with Pazuzu about Sa'if and his brothers. She knew it was dangerous to talk too plainly in the open corridor, where anyone could hear, so she had to patiently endure some irrelevant stories from the efreet.

"He was hisss father'sss mossst brilliant ssstudent," Paz told her. "Weaving fire from the moment he could walk." The small smoldering creature chuckled, pumping clouds of smoke and ash from his glowing mouth while recounting the chaos Sa'if had once created during the Festival of the Candles, igniting thousands of wicks simultaneously and covering many of the guests with dripping wax.

The efreet had many more tales, and he was desperate to share them with someone, but Lily couldn't spare the time. "Could you tell me more about Jambiya? I'm worried about K'leef having to compete against him," she said. "K'leef hadn't finished learning from Sa'if, and now he's—"

"K'leef could be asss great as Sssa'if wasss, if he had ambition." Paz sighed, and the air around him shimmered with the heat. "But he isss content with hisss booksss."

"K'leef has other, better qualities than ambition. Qualities that would see him through any ordinary trial by fire, I'm sure of it. But this time, someone might try to—"

The old efreet's head grew brighter with flames. "He looksss up to you. Do you know that?"

That brought her up short. "Really? Why?"

The efreet hissed, "He hasss alwaysss been led by bosssy women."

*"Bossy?"* She hated that word.

"I mean . . . confident women. Ameera commanded him with her firsssst wordsss. They grew up so clossse, until hisss training began. Then he had lesss time and she, lessss patience."

"Ameera's quite a character," agreed Lily. "I think it would be hard for anyone to stand up to her."

The efreet didn't reply. He just hopped off his brazier and made his way to the door. "There are choresss I musssst attend to."

"The palace would fall down if it weren't for you, I'm sure."

Paz turned. His eyes glowed brighter, and his laugh was the sound of rocks banging together. "Quite right. I am beginning to like you, Lilith of Houssse Shadow."

Lily walked in the opposite direction, as baffled as ever. She still had no clue about the murderer's identity. And if Sa'if was such a powerful sorcerer, how could he have been thwarted?

Magic was instinctual. Sure, you needed to concentrate to create some effects, but the first thing magic did was protect the sorcerer. Its defensive power acted like a natural reflex. She knew this from firsthand experience. When her uncle Pan had tried to kill her in an attempt to take over the country, she'd unintentionally shadow-stepped. She'd sunk into the darkness and out of the mortal world into the Twilight, the shadow realm between life and death. She hadn't studied that spell—she'd never even seen anyone do it—but she'd needed to escape and her magic let her.

Lily knew well that magic was both a blessing and a curse. Thorn seemed to get along fine without it. . . . In fact, he was more content with his lot in life than she was with hers. Most of the time.

They were linked, she and Thorn. Some weird strand connected them; any miles separating them didn't seem to matter. One time her father had claimed that he could find his way back to her mother from anywhere. *I just let my heart do the searching, and with a step I'd be with her.*

Lily blushed. She didn't feel *that* way about Thorn. Not really. She was just . . . very fond of him. Everyone was. He was that sort of boy. Even Tyburn had said something nice about Thorn, once.

So, while it was doubtful that she could leap immediately to Thorn's side wherever he might be, she guessed that, if she wanted to, she could at least head in the right direction.

But she wasn't here to weigh Thorn's merits, odd and uncouth though they were. She was here to solve Sa'if's *murder*.

Magic ruled the world. And it was the sorcerers who sat on the thrones and wore the crowns. It didn't matter if they were wise, or good, or even vaguely competent—and plenty had been none of these things. What mattered was their ability with spells. It was the *only* thing that mattered.

Sa'if's magic should have saved him. Using magic was like breathing. You couldn't stop breathing.

*Unless someone suffocated you.*

Someone had stopped Sa'if's magic. But how?

With cold iron? That was the usual way to cancel out a sorcerer's powers. The prison cells beneath Castle Gloom had cold iron bars for that very reason.

But if cold iron had been present, then the other sorcerers would have been affected, too, and K'leef and his brothers had used their magic to remove the lava crown. So cold iron wasn't the answer.

Then what was?

She had no idea. Yet.

Which was why she found herself standing outside the doors to Sa'if's chambers.

The candles that usually lit the corridor had been extinguished and covered with cloth. The wind moved through here, rustling the gauze window curtains and whispering sorrows at the passing of a good man.

His quarters were locked. Of course they were.

And the Skeleton Key was with Mary.

She could go get it. Made of the forefinger of the Scarlet Trickster, the legendary thief, the key could open any lock, both mundane and magical. She used it to enter the Shadow Library, as all her ancestors had done before her.

Mary was down at the docks; that would be a long round-trip, and Lily wanted to solve the mystery of Sa'if's murder *now*. She was convinced that the answer was on the other side of these doors.

People broke into forbidden rooms all the time, and without the use of a magic key. There had to be another way.

What would Thorn do?

Something half-foolish, half-heroic. Which would be . . .

There was an open window at the end of the corridor. She leaned out of it and saw a ledge running along the exterior of the palace. Her eyes followed it to one of the balconies off of Sa'if's chambers, where a curtain billowed outward in the light breeze. Which meant there was another open window. . . . It was practically an invitation.

*Come on, Lily. You've climbed over every roof of Castle Gloom. This is nothing.*

But as she edged out onto the ledge, it didn't feel like nothing. It felt very high, and the ledge felt very narrow.

She rested her back against the warm stone. Anyone looking up would have seen a strange black moth clinging to the radiant red marble.

*One step at a time. And don't look down.*

Lily slowly shuffled along the smooth wall. There wasn't a groove or crack to dig her fingers into, unlike in the weathered walls of Gloom.

After what seemed like hours but was only minutes, the balcony was a few feet away. She reached out carefully, trying hard not to lose her balance, and sighed with relief as her hand found the bronze balustrade. She gripped it firmly and swung herself over, sighing even more deeply when both of her feet were planted on the polished stone.

That hadn't been so hard.

Still, she'd leave through the door.

The ceiling rose forty or fifty feet and was held in place with delicate-looking columns laced with gold leaf. The furniture, carved from rosewood or deep chestnut, was exquisite. "Are you here, Sa'if?" she whispered.

She doubted he lingered within these walls, but she extended her fingers anyway. If she felt his spirit in the passing breeze, she could grasp it.

But she didn't. He was at peace; he had crossed to the Far Shore.

Some glass crunched under her heel. Frowning, she looked down and saw shards of a broken mirror. There it was on the wall in front of her—a large one framed in white.

The glass remaining in the frame was foggy. Strange. Judging from the design, it was clearly from Lumina and made of the very best quality silver. Lumineans were famed for their mirrors.

She glanced at the ornate frame. The workmanship was beautiful, the maker clearly a master. Then why put in such faulty glass?

There were diamonds on the dressing table, and the chairs were made of ivory. Now, looking anew, she saw that these were some of the treasures bartered by Duke Solar for a humiliating peace. Cloaks of white fur hung over a door.

Lily had broken things when her parents and Dante had died. She'd torn down the curtains, too, and ripped up her mourning dress. It was natural that someone would want to take out their anger on something, especially something from the enemy.

A piece of jewelry caught her attention. Crouching down beside a chair, Lily picked up a small ruby earring. The princes wore earrings, but this was dainty and very finely wrought, perfect for the delicate earlobes of some princess. She pocketed it.

She stood, turned, and came face-to-face with Kali.

Kali glanced over her shoulder to the door. "Those doors were locked."

Lily knew the best defense was a good offense. "Spying on me, Lady Kali?"

Kali gasped. "Spying? My dear Lady Shadow, why ever would I need to spy on someone as noble as yourself? I'm sure every breath you take is born from a breast of the purest virtue, and every action—"

"What is it that you want?" Lily snapped. Kali's mockery was starting to get to her. If she'd wanted constant sarcasm, she would have kept Thorn behind.

Kali bowed. "Princess Ameera would like the pleasure of your company."

# TWENTY-ONE

"**T**hank the Six you're here!" Sami grabbed Lily's hand and dragged her in. "My other sisters are sooo boring!"

"I can't stay long. I've got to prepare for the journey home once the trial is over. Getting the ship ready is turning out to be quite difficult."

Ameera sat up from her cushion. "Don't worry about that. I'll have a word with the vizier. Go speak to him, Kali. Tell him to find some extra hands for our guests."

And with that the executioner left.

*Ameera wants to help me. Then why don't I trust her?*

The princess led Lily to a row of trunks lined up in the garden. "I've collected some gifts for you. A few things to help you remember your visit."

Lily stared. "So much? I really couldn't, Ameera, but thank you. I have nothing so valuable to give in return. It would be an unfair gift."

Ameera's brow furrowed. "They are gifts given freely. We are nobles, not merchants. We are not in the business of trading."

Lily looked over the trunks. One was piled with silk finer than any she'd ever felt before. Another had boxes of jewelry stacked within it, some holding rings, others with bracelets, and so on. Perfume bottles filled the third, neatly arranged in padded racks. Then there was a chest full of vellum and inks and quills.

"You will write to me?" asked Ameera anxiously.

Lily picked out a quill. The feather had a silvery sheen. "Is this from a Pegasus?"

"Do you like it?"

"I'm overwhelmed, Ameera. How can I repay you?"

Ameera held her hand between her own. "By being my friend, Lily."

"Of . . . of course." Yet Lily pulled gently away. Ameera wanted something from her, and it was more than friendship. All the charm, attention, and gifts, they were not for free. Ameera expected payment. But what could a princess of Djinn want from a kingdom as poor as Gehenna? "I'll have Mary take these to the docks."

Sami pulled out a length of silk. "Don't you want to try these on? Look, they're all black!"

The three of them played at dressing up in Ameera's suite. Sami danced around in this dress and that one and put on a skull mask to make Lily feel more at home. She decked Lily out in rubies and amber and fire opals, despite Lily's protests.

Lily sank into a cushion, gasping after being twirled around and around. "I've never worn anything so soft."

Sami had laughed when she'd seen Lily's corset, and Ameera had shaken her head in disbelief that anyone would wear something so restrictive. They'd dressed Lily as one of them, in flowing black silk and gauze, freeing her stomach entirely, perhaps *too* entirely.

Ameera patted her own bare midriff and the ring piercing her belly button. "You should decorate yours. I could get a needle, and we could do it right now."

"Er, maybe not right now," said Lily, covering her belly protectively.

She admired her bracelets. "But thank you for all these. I don't have glittery things like this back home."

Not for the first time, Lily felt out of place. She'd never criticize her own craftsmen, but they were used to working with tin and iron and pewter. Few had the skill of the jewelers of the Sultanate, who had fashioned a bracelet for her that looked like tiny entwined silver bones.

Sami just stared. "Your skin is so white. Do you have no sun at all in Gehenna?"

"No, not much."

Ameera leaned over, resting her chin on her delicate fists. "You're here now. You should wear whatever you want. Try this." She held out her own red shawl.

"I only wear black, Ameera."

"But you have a choice, no?"

Lily removed the tiara she'd been given. "Rulers have less choice than you imagine."

"But if you wore, say, red, who would stop you? No one. *You* make the rules, Lily. And you break them when it suits you."

Lily didn't like the way this was going. There was something too pointed in Ameera's questions. What was she after?

"You wouldn't have burned those witches, would you?" Ameera's eyes brightened. "Because you are one. You're the witch queen."

"Thorn took care of that before I could," said Lily. "Burning women, or anyone, for using magic is wrong. It's that simple."

Ameera nodded. "Which is why we need you, Lily."

"Need me for what?" She retrieved her familiar black dress from the table. Dress-up time was over. It was time to stop pretending and go back to being who she really was: Lilith of House Shadow, corset and all. When she collected the dress, she found a small book underneath. She picked it up, recognizing the metal sheets. "This is the *Agni Kitab*. Wasn't K'leef studying it?"

Ameera smiled. "Yes. I took it."

"Why, Ameera?"

Ameera gestured at Sami. "You show her, Sami."

Sami licked her finger and frowned. A flame sprang from her fingertip, and she wrote her name in the air. As the last of the fiery letters blazed and died, she turned to Lily, grinning. "Easy-peasy."

"We can all do it—that and more, Lily." Ameera jumped up, filling her hands with glowing light. "We've been studying in secret. We're witches, just like you."

"Where is this going, Ameera?"

"Why shouldn't we rule, Lily? Us, instead of them? Why should it be them?"

"Your brothers?"

"*Men.*" Ameera spat the word.

Lily's mind whirled with questions and mixed emotions. Did K'leef know about his sisters' abilities and ambitions? If Jambiya found out . . . "That fairy tale about the seventh princess has taken you down a dangerous path, Ameera. Let's pretend this conversation never happened."

She wasn't listening. "With your support, I could become the new sultan! Think about it, Lily! You in the north; me in the south. We would be the best of friends. The best of allies. Then who knows where that would lead?"

Lily knew all too well. "War, that's where. You can't force people to accept—"

Ameera backed away. "Oh, I see. You *like* being the witch queen, don't you? Lilith Shadow, the dreaded ruler of Gehenna. You don't want us to become like you. Then you wouldn't be special anymore."

"You're a thousand miles off the mark, Ameera." Lily removed the red shawl. "I'm leaving before this goes any further."

Ameera sighed. "No need to run off. I thought you would understand, but I was wrong. That is all." She picked up a necklace. "I had this made for you, before you came. The rubies have been carved into tiny skulls. I thought you'd like it. Try it on, please. Then you can go."

Lily took the necklace. Anything to get this over and done with. She held up a hand mirror. "It looks lovely. Now can I—"

"No, you can't see it properly in that small thing. Use the bigger one." She led Lily to the corner of the room.

A white drape covered the full-length mirror. Lily pulled the cloth free. "From Lumina, too?"

Sami joined her. "You look beautiful. You should go now."

"Let her look *properly*," said Ameera.

Sami's eyes filled with tears. "No, Ameera, please don't."

The glass was foggy.

Something stirred within her mind. She saw an image of a noble prince rubbing his sleeve against such a mirror and smiling at the reflections within. He was flanked by his brother K'leef, and the peasant boy he admired, Thorn.

This wasn't her memory—it was Sa'if's. Why was it emerging now?

Was it a warning?

"Sa'if had a mirror just like this," said Lily softly.

The gasp from Sami gave her all the information she needed.

Lily winced as she momentarily felt what it was like to put on the lava crown. This Blessings of the Dead thing *hurt*.

She rubbed her scalp instinctively and turned to consider Ameera. The princess was covered in jewelry, from golden rings on her toes to a diamond tiara on her head, and yet, there was something missing. Four ruby earrings hung from her left ear, but from the right there were only three. Lily drew the earring from her dress pocket and tossed it at her. "I found this in Sa'if's room."

"I didn't mean for it to happen," said Ameera, unable to meet her gaze.

"You took his magic, just when he needed it most. How?"

Ameera glanced over to the mirror. Then she frowned, knowing she'd given it away.

*This is a trap.*

Lily stepped away from the mirror and toward the door. One quick dash and she'd be out. She made a move and—

A wall of fire, twenty feet high, burst up from the marble floor. The stone cracked under the heat, and the nearby curtains combusted. The flames formed rough humanoid shapes and came running toward Lily.

"Stop her!" Ameera ordered them.

Sami crouched behind the couch, crying, "Let her go, Ameera! She's my friend!"

Lily stumbled back from the heat. How could Ameera be so powerful? K'leef couldn't cast such a spell, and he was good! Ameera was going all out to kill her.

Lily extended her hands, seeking the magical forces that kept the flames alive. Ameera's own life force animated them, much like Lily did with the zombies. Lily felt the invisible puppet strings between Ameera and the fire creatures. Strings made out of life.

Lily cut them with a snip of her fingers. The flames vanished.

Ameera groaned and collapsed on her knees, clutching her heart. Sami screamed in terror.

Ameera gasped. "What . . . ?"

"Enough, Ameera," Lily warned. "I don't want to hurt you."

Once Ameera had caught her breath, she said, "Oh, Lily. If only we could be allies. Can't you see how we could rebuild the world?"

"I don't have that ambition," said Lily. "To rebuild, you have to destroy what stood there before. I won't do that."

Legs wobbling, Ameera stood up. She'd recovered more quickly than Lily had expected. This wasn't over. Lily kept her guard up even as Ameera poured herself and Sami a sherbert.

Ameera took a sip and smacked her lips. "Can you blame a prisoner

for wanting to destroy her prison? Or a slave for trying to break the chains she wears?"

"You wear only gold, Ameera."

She scowled. "A gold chain is still a chain." She blew flames across her fingers, and burning darts dashed off. Lily swatted them aside, but her sleeves smoldered.

"Leave Lily alone!" protested Sami.

How could Ameera be this skillful? How long had she been studying, in secret, to learn such magic?

*You of all people should know.*

But Lily could sense that Ameera's magic was waning. She'd pushed herself as far as she could go, and there wasn't anything left in reserve. It was time to finish this.

Lily drew on her necromantic energies. The flowers around her shriveled as a terrible, graveyard cold spread out across the chamber, extinguishing Ameera's remaining flames. Then the shadows came alive, summoned into service. They spread across the walls and over the furniture—chill, long fingers grasping at Ameera's hair and clothing and binding themselves around her limbs.

Lily watched as Ameera was pinned up against the wall. "Good. Now you just—"

She cried out as something bit into her back. Lily swung around just as Kali raised her knife to stab again, her eyes blazing and a cruel, frenzied grin locked on her face. The second slash tore into her sleeve and pierced the flesh beneath.

Rage flooded Lily. Rage and fear.

She let go of her necromancy.

The knife rusted, then crumbled to powder. The handle rotted away in Kali's hand and turned to dust.

But that wasn't enough.

Kali's black skin, so taunt, so young and fresh, began to wrinkle as the flesh softened and the muscles withered. Her dark hair faded to gray. . . .

Sami ran between them. "Lily, no!"

Lily blinked. Kali lay curled on the ground, her body twisted by old age. Even her clothes had suffered, turning to drab, pale rags hanging over a skeletal frame.

Kali looked up, glaring with volcanic fury. "What have you done to me?" she croaked.

Her nails were as long and curved as claws, her gums pulled back so her teeth, big and yellow, appeared more like fangs now. The only brightness in her puckered mouth was her swollen red tongue.

Kali managed to get to her feet. With a murderous scream, she raked her nails across Lily's arm and went to grab her throat. Sami shouted and tried to pull them apart, but Kali had gone berserk. Despite her now crippled body, she was fuelled by pure hatred and attacked with wild, savage fury.

"Kill her!" yelled Ameera.

Kali clawed at her again. Lily ducked but was rewarded with a kick in the stomach. As Lily gasped for breath, Kali grabbed a new knife from the dining table.

*I have to flee.*

Ameera had escaped the tendrils of darkness and was standing by the mirror. Why? Was she trying to hide behind it? She was rocking it, trying to push it over. What was she thinking? That she'd crush Lily? She was too far out of range.

Kali advanced, bent over like some hideous spindly insect, her thin fingers locked around a gold-hilted knife.

*Time to leave.*

Lily whipped her hands to opposite corners and pulled the shadows around her like a cloak. A cold wind tore through the room. Kali charged again, but Lily entered the black folds. She looked back in time to see the mirror totter as Ameera gave it a final push.

Then Lily sank into the protective darkness.

# TWENTY-TWO

**L**ily's head spun as the howling winds of the Twilight assaulted her. The first few seconds of moving between realms—shadow-stepping—were always disorienting, no matter how many times she did it. She gritted her teeth to focus on the world around her.

She was surrounded by decay, loneliness, and cold. This was the land between the mortal world and that of the dead, and no living person had the right to be here, not even Lady Shadow.

An icy storm whirled around her, hurling clouds of misery across a gray sky marbled with black light from a black sun. The wind carried ancient curses, forgotten vows, and endless despair. The Twilight was formed of raw, dark emotions. The path was paved with broken promises, and it wound through the crumbling ruins of regret. She didn't want to linger, for this place was not uninhabited.

The specters sensed her; she saw them come crawling out of the dark places. They knew her now, knew what she was capable of, so they were cautious. But they were still eager. They could not resist the warm breath of the living.

Other malformed spirits lurked in the woe-drenched landscape. Some had forms that were spindly or grossly obese, depending on the lives they'd led. Some no longer looked human at all, being so vile and evil that their minds had corrupted their bodies like a pestilence.

They were gathering, having learned their lessons from her earlier visits. Perhaps they hoped to overwhelm her by sheer number. How many would it take to bring her down?

Cracks opened up in the sky with a groan. There were beings beyond this plane, and Lily felt their inquisitive eyes upon her. Her father had once told her proudly that the dukes of hell had taken an interest in her.

She needed to find Thorn and K'leef, tell them what she knew: that Ameera had killed her own brother. Ameera wanted the lava crown for herself, and she was powerful. . . .

The sound of shattering glass echoed over the Twilight, and the fog around her thickened. Lily lost her footing and fell.

And fell and fell and fell . . .

She didn't have time for this. She had to find them!

And fell and . . .

Hit the hard, gritty ground.

Lily lay there, aching and trying to catch her breath. The travel nausea was rising out of her stomach. Her head pounded. She was weak after her battle against Ameera and Kali.

The cut on her back burned, but a quick brush with her palm told her it was just a small slice through the skin, almost dry already. The nail scratches along her arm were equally superficial.

She sat up. Where was she now?

Broken rock, dusty hills, and bare, spindly trees in all directions. The sky rumbled and weird colors flashed on the horizon. Spirits added their malevolent curses to the wind.

*The Shardlands.*

But where in the Shardlands?

She stood up and brushed herself off. It was cold out here at night, and she'd escaped wearing only a flowing silk skirt and a short top, the dress of a court princess rather than garb suitable for exploring the ruins of the Old Kingdom. And so much uncomfortable jewelry. She took off necklaces, bangles, and bracelets she'd been given and dropped them in the gravel, keeping only a few rings she'd brought with her from Gehenna.

Had Ameera broken that second mirror, too? Why?

Lily trembled. Shadow-stepping always left her exhausted, and she'd fallen out of the Twilight more suddenly than expected.

Up ahead was a camp with a glowing fire and some horses standing nearby. She could make out at least two people, one in robes. K'leef?

She couldn't believe her luck. She raised her hand and called out. "Hey there! It's me!"

One figure turned around. With his back to the fire, all she saw was a blocky silhouette. "Thorn?" Maybe that's why she had landed here. He and she were connected. . . .

The figure approached, drawing a sword. He walked cautiously, then stopped a few feet away. She could see him clearly now in the light of the moon.

*No, no, no . . .*

He smiled and pointed the sword at her heart. "Nice of you to join us, Niece," said Pandemonium Shadow.

# TWENTY-THREE

Thorn awoke with a long, deep moan. Sleep had come, somehow, despite the storm. Yet as he woke, he shivered. Those phantasms had been so real, so believable, that he'd almost gone out into the chaos to confront them.

"Peasant," said Gabriel, kicking him.

"Get off," muttered Thorn. *Oww.* He was so stiff, every bone locked at an odd angle. He turned his head carefully, loosening his neck and spine one vertebra at a time.

K'leef stood at the cave mouth. "Good morning."

Thorn joined him. "It don't look it."

Ash filled the air and coated the ground, turning it black and gray. The patches of sky visible through the ash clouds radiated a bloody crimson. The earth had cracked open, and it was spewing fire and lava, and the stench of brimstone.

"How can this be the same place as last night?" asked Thorn. "It's impossible."

"That's wild magic for you. Thank the Six we had shelter."

The ground shook, and a column of lava erupted from a newly formed tear, gushing higher than forty feet and showering the surrounding area with steaming black pumice. K'leef partially unwrapped his turban and covered his mouth with a strip of cloth. "Don't let the ash get in your lungs."

Thorn started loading up Gobber. "What happened last night?" he asked K'leef.

"We're in the Shardlands, Thorn. Reality's been left far behind."

*Reality* . . . Had Lily turned his family into zombies or not? Of course she hadn't. Lily was his best friend; she'd never do anything to hurt him.

But Lily could do it if she wanted to. She could summon the undead, disappear into shadows, and travel through the Twilight and Dreamtime. She was getting more powerful every day. Sure, she was still that nervous, wanting-to-please girl he'd met in the courtyard, all that time ago, but for how much longer?

He helped K'leef lift the bathtub. "By the way, that was a pretty neat trick you did, when we were wrestling. I thought you was going to burn up—and take me with you."

K'leef touched one of his singed eyebrows and smiled sheepishly. "I've never done that before. The magic is surging. It's weird, but I can sense it buzzing in my blood." He exhaled a roll of flame. "It feels pretty great, Thorn. Pretty great. But it's wild—makes you powerful one moment, powerless the next."

"Yeah. Lily told me there's always a downside."

K'leef nodded. "If I'm not careful, I could blow up. Completely combust and not be able to put it out. More than one of my ancestors has gone that way. It makes life a little dicey."

"What about him?" Thorn gestured toward Gabriel. "Could using too much magic leave him ugly forever?"

The Solar boy was brushing his hair, which magic had restored to its usual shiny platinum blond. Each strand was in exactly the right place. He swept a glistening silver cape over his shoulders, tied his bonnet in place, then looked over at them. "I'm finished. You can put the chest up now."

Thorn tugged his forelock. "Yes, m'lord."

Once the bags were loaded, the three of them left the safety of the cave and headed toward the distant mountains. Thorn carefully picked his way through the broken streams of lava and hot ash, and it wasn't long before he was soaked in sweat. He wished they'd brought a sorcerer from House Coral. At least then they'd always have something to drink. Their water was getting dangerously low.

K'leef chucked a stone into a lava pool. It spluttered with fire before sinking. "Is it my imagination, or are these streams getting bigger?"

Thorn cursed. "They're joining up. Like tributaries of a river."

"Which means?"

Thorn shielded his eyes from the ash. What was that ahead? The air shimmered, yet he could see . . . "We're dead."

A few hundred yards later, they slid down a slope to the edge of a river. A river of lava.

Gobber folded his legs and settled himself down on the bank.

Rocks, dislodged upstream, bobbed in the flow. Flames ran like ribbons across its surface, and there were continuous spurts and small eruptions.

Thorn groaned. "We need to go back the way we came."

"But the opposite bank's only over there!" declared K'leef. "It can't be more than a hundred yards away!"

"Feel free to swim across anytime you want, K'leef."

"Er, peasant . . ."

Thorn sighed. "What now, Gabbs? Want a piggyback ride?"

The beast watched them from the top of the ridge, grinning.

It was twice as big as a lion; brown patches speckled its fur and ash powdered its thick mane. A fang-filled mouth almost split the face in half. It swished its spiked tail, dragging the long ivory needles back and forth

through the blackened earth. It shook its massive shoulders and roared, as if already proclaiming its victory.

There was a thud as Gabriel fainted.

Thorn managed to nock an arrow, despite his shaking hands.

The manticore had them trapped.

# TWENTY-FOUR

The arrow trembled on the string. Thorn couldn't stop the sweat from blurring his sight.

*It's huge! You can't miss!*

"Shoot it!" yelled K'leef.

He tried to slow his breath, control his racing heart. He could do it. It was only a few yards away, there was no cross wind, and the arrow was stalk-straight.

Why wouldn't his fingers work? They seemed locked.

"Shoot it!"

Gobber charged the manticore. He galloped up the slope and lashed out with his front legs. The manticore rose on its own hind legs to slash with its wicked front claws.

Gobber bit its ear as the monster clawed his back, tearing off the baggage and scoring red wounds in the camel's hump.

Thorn jumped aside and dropped his arrow as the chest full of Gabriel's clothing bounced past, smashing open and sending silk underwear into the lava. They burst into flame and floated above the river like fiery butterflies.

The manticore swatted the camel's face, and Gobber stumbled aside.

After one final kick, the dromedary dashed off. The monster roared angrily, then turned its attention back to the three boys.

Thorn scurried on his hands and knees to the fallen arrow.

"Thorn!" shouted K'leef.

He spun, and it just . . . happened.

His eye, hand, the arrow, and the distance between him and his target merged into a seamless, instinctual reaction. Even as he released the bowstring Thorn knew where the arrow would go.

It flew true into the monster's left eye. The manticore snarled and snapped the arrow off with a flick of its paw. Oily yellow mucus dribbled out of the wound, but otherwise the creature didn't seem bothered by it.

Thorn drew another arrow, and this one slipped easily onto the bowstring. All his previous fears and doubts about his ability had vanished. The arrow would strike exactly where he wanted. Like always.

What good would it do, though? Eye shots usually ended things, but that one hadn't fazed the beast.

K'leef wove his hands through the air and fiery darts shot out, some striking the creature's flank, others disappearing into the ash. The fur smoked, but the manticore kept coming.

Thorn stepped sideways, seeking the other eye. If he could blind it . . .

The creature wasn't stupid. It circled, too, keeping its face turned, denying Thorn a shot. It flicked its tail.

"Look out!" yelled K'leef.

Thorn dove as the spikes hissed through the air. K'leef hurled another volley of flames.

The manticore pounced, and Thorn jammed his bow into the manticore's mouth as it went for his neck. The fangs glistened with spit, inches from his face, and the long red tongue lashed eagerly. The bow began to crack. . . .

It snapped, and Thorn jabbed the broken halves down the manticore's throat. The beast sprang back, blood dripping from its torn gullet. Thorn scrambled back to his feet and joined K'leef, who was standing over the still-unconscious Gabriel.

"Maybe we can throw *him* at it," suggested Thorn. "Gabriel won't feel a thing."

"Then what?"

Back across the ash plains? Through the Valley of the Gods? With the manticore snapping at their heels? If only they could get across that river! Thorn laughed bitterly. Yeah, in a fireproof boat. As if . . .

He looked at the bronze bathtub.

"Get Gabriel." He rolled the tub to the edge of the river.

"You can't be serious!" cried K'leef. But he picked up the Solar boy.

Thorn glanced back. The manticore had spat the broken bow out of its mouth. Blood dripped from its black lips, and it was growling angrily. It swung its tail, looking for another shot.

The tub bobbed, and the metal hissed as it settled into the lava. It didn't feel too steady. If it tipped over . . .

Thorn jumped in as the tail lashed. Spikes clattered against the metal, and one brushed his shoulder, tearing his tunic but missing the flesh. "Come on, K'leef!"

"I don't believe I'm doing this." K'leef and Gabriel fell in together as Thorn fumbled for Gabriel's sword.

The manticore roared and leaped at them.

Thorn pushed off the bank.

The manticore tried to twist in midair. It screamed as it splashed into the lava, its legs and belly catching fire. It beat at the flames, succeeding only in spreading them further. Then it clambered out of the river, shaking and smoking blackly. The smell of burning fur stank in Thorn's nostrils, yet he grinned.

The manticore paced up and down the bank, roaring with fury. It was hurt but not mortally wounded—it was beyond tough. It sat down and started licking its singed paws.

Thorn pushed at a rock with the sword, using it to punt across. "We've made it. I don't believe it, but we made it."

"Thorn . . ." K'leef cradled Gabriel. The Solar boy's white tunic was red. There was a spike sticking out of his chest.

# TWENTY-FIVE

"**T**horn was right." Lily shook her shackles. "These things are heavy."

"Be thankful they're just around your wrists and not your neck." Jambiya chewed on a strip of desert rat.

"I am *so* grateful."

Jambiya scowled. "Wit in a woman is perverse and unnatural. What kind of creature did your brother raise, Earl Shadow?"

Pan said nothing, but Lily saw a flash of anger in his eyes.

They traveled light, a horse each and a spare for supplies that Lily was now riding. Their nomad guide, Nasr, clearly knew his business. He was constantly supplying food and finding waterholes. They were taking their time, going slowly and carefully.

And a hundred paces behind strode Farn, each of his steps sizzling the earth beneath. The efreet flared, casting off wings of fire from its shoulders, and it dripped lava from the cracks that scarred its rock-encrusted black skin.

She employed zombies, she hosted ghosts, and she walked through other people's nightmares in the Dreamtime, but she could not get over her fear of Farn. Even from this distance her flesh prickled with the heat, and she felt his pitiless glowing white eyes on her and her alone.

The background magic of the Shardlands only made the creature stronger, and hotter. How could you defeat something like that? Farn could melt an iceberg.

She nudged her mount a few paces closer to the blind prince.

"K'leef probably has his phoenix by now," she said. "Sultan K'leef. I like the sound of that."

Jambiya picked some flesh from between his teeth. "Boy's given up by now, I'm sure. Like Fafnir did."

"Fafnir gave up?" Lily gasped. "Why?"

Jambiya shrugged. "He was weak and ill-suited to the Shardlands."

"Unlike you?" she said. "But that doesn't matter. I think you should free me now."

"And why should I do that?"

"You have no right. I've done nothing wrong."

"Nothing wrong?" Jambiya snarled. "You are the greatest criminal in all the New Kingdoms! A witch who uses her magic openly, defying all that is just and decent. An abomination."

There was no point in arguing with a fanatic. Lily looked to her uncle. Jambiya raised his stick, somehow sensing her intention. "Oh, don't think you have an ally there. You exiled him, did you not? Cast him out of Gehenna dressed in nothing but rags."

"I was merciful," said Lily. "Others wanted him executed. Remember, Uncle? We stood right there, up on Execution Hill, with Tyburn and his ax. You were on your knees, begging."

"I was a different man then," Pan answered, scowling. "Weak."

There was no denying that.

*Now look at him.* The drunk was gone, and in his place was a warrior.

The years had fallen off him. He was tall and proud and no longer puffy. Pan flexed his fingers around his sword. He was dressed not like a noble, but a mercenary, in plain armor with unadorned, functional weapons and nothing extra. All business. A brutal business.

What was in this alliance for him?

Fame? Fortune? A title?

All those things, once Jambiya became sultan.

But Pan would always be an exile from his homeland.

And what were they going to do with her?

Jambiya wanted her dead, so why wasn't she already? It's not as if anyone would ever find out, not here in the wilderness. Had Pan prevented it? No, she wasn't alive out of some lingering loyalty from Pan. Something else kept her breathing.

*He needs me. For what?*

The answer was obvious. Despite Jambiya's casual dismissal of K'leef, she knew her friend had a chance of winning. With her as hostage, Jambiya could blackmail K'leef, perhaps even trade her for a phoenix if K'leef succeeded and he didn't.

But would K'leef make that choice?

He'd hand over the phoenix to save her, she had no doubt about that. But instead of that making her feel better, it made her feel worse. She was a bargaining chip, her only value being what she could be traded for, like a farmer's prize cow. The same was true for many a royal princess.

Lily twisted the links of her chains angrily. The dull *clack* told her they were forged from cold iron. She wouldn't be casting any spells with these on.

Where were her friends?

Having nothing better to do, Lily settled herself as best she could and let her thoughts wander back home.

She'd left Gehenna on a foggy morning, so she hadn't even gotten to see Castle Gloom on that last day. Just a few dim torches had lit the road—those and the ethereal glow of the few ghosts lurking on the borders of the City of Silence, the vast graveyard beside her home. Aside from them, the only beings to notice her had been the crows that nested on Lamentation Hill, the execution ground.

Lily missed her home dearly. It was a physical ache for the cobwebs, the macabre statues, and the bats that inhabited every nook and cranny. Would she ever walk the dark corridors again, hear the soft wailing of the zombies? Spend winter evenings sewing their parts back on?

*I went too far. Too far from home, too far with my ambitions.*

She should have predicted that people outside her realm would not accept her. After all, half of her own subjects whispered behind her back, seeing her as a freak of nature, an uppity female, or just simply too young to hold the reins of power. She could think of a dozen nobles who'd rather park their backsides in the throne. They'd send Jambiya a crateful of black diamonds if she just *happened* to disappear.

*Face it, Lily, how many friends do you really have? Not counting the dead ones?*

It wasn't a long list, and the top two were somewhere out there, deep in the Shardlands.

Jambiya spoke. "Your uncle tells me you have many other great treasures in Castle Gloom."

"And that's where they'll stay."

She hadn't brought any of them with her. Not the Mantle of Sorrows, nor her magic books or potions. She'd only brought the Skeleton Key because it would make unpacking her trunks easier, and that was now with Mary.

The key was useful in discovering secrets, and Lily liked discovering secrets. Like the one she'd been struggling with for days.

Ameera had killed Sa'if. She was a sorceress of no mean ability. And Jambiya had no idea.

How would it play out? Would Jambiya return triumphant only to face an army of his sisters? Would the Sultanate be torn apart by civil war?

Was there no peace to be found anywhere?

Lily couldn't deny the truth that she had, unwittingly, played her own part in it all. Ameera was merely following in her footsteps. Lily, of all people, knew how the princesses felt.

The nomad, Nasr, held her reins, leading her as if she were a five-year-old on her first pony.

Like most nomads, he bore the side effects of the wild magic that contaminated the Shardlands. Chitinous folds covered his forehead and overhung his eyes. His hands were also layered with hard skin, and below his wrists were a pair of small pincers, the vestigial remains of his original scorpion ancestor.

"Scorpion tribe, yes?" she asked him as they plodded along. "They say the Scorpions are some of the best hunters out in the Shardlands. Almost as great as the Vipers."

He spat a wad of phlegm between them. "Vipers? Who says Viper is greater than the Scorpion?"

"It's just what I've heard. . . ."

"Then you have heard lies." Nasr picked at an old scar on his left cheek. "A child of the Scorpion tribe could easily kill even the greatest Viper warrior. Everyone knows this."

"But they are the best explorers. The Vipers know all the routes through the Shardlands. I've heard, from honest people, that the Vipers even know where the high king's city is."

Nasr glared so angrily at her, she might as well have slapped him. "Prince Jambiya trusts me, Nasr of the Scorpion, known as the Red Scorpion, not some slithering green thing. What prospers better in the Shardlands than a Scorpion? Does any of Viper know where the phoenixes nest?"

"Of course. In the Lava Mountains. Even I know that."

"Then you, like a typical woman, know nothing. They abandoned their nests there twenty years past." Nasr gestured southward. "The last of the fire birds now live beyond the Weeping Stones."

"Never heard of them."

He grunted. "As I said, you know nothing."

This was bad. K'leef had bet everything on the Lava Mountains. He was going the wrong way and didn't know it.

"These stones—a long ride from here, are they?"

Nasr growled. "No more questions."

Lily held up her chains. "I'm not going anywhere. What difference does it make if you tell me or not?"

Nasr glanced over at Jambiya and Pan; they were a hundred paces away. "Another day, perhaps two. We have to pass the Haunts first."

"The Haunts? Sounds like my kind of place."

"The place is cursed."

"They usually are. Have you seen the creatures that live there? Actually with your own eyes?" If they were undead, she'd have an advantage. Old spirits remembered House Shadow, and the loyalty they owed it. It was useful being able to call in favors from thousands of years ago.

"Creatures foul and unnatural," snapped Nasr. "They feast on blood and marrow. They are ruled by an immortal demoness who lives in a cavern of bones."

"Sounds like Great-Aunt Morrigan," said Lily. "Kept her husband's skull beside her bed for years. Told me they'd have little chats after midnight."

Nasr shivered, then spurred his horse away.

"Suit yourself," said Lily. She'd never understand why people found death so frightening. Surely she wasn't the only child who had skull-shaped cakes for her birthday?

She hadn't even celebrated her last birthday, just a few weeks ago. Fourteen now. Wasn't life supposed to be figured out by the time you turned fourteen? She'd been ruling Gehenna for a year, and with each day, it seemed to get harder, not easier. Mary said it gave her gray hairs just trying to balance the books, blaming Cook for paying the millers too much and selling their bread for too little. Lily had to do much more than that as queen . . . but she didn't have to worry about gray hairs, not with her all-white locks.

The others had stopped at a ridge. Lily came up beside her uncle.

Below them was a small camp of nomads, their tents protected by the outcropping. Several warriors waved up at them.

"Reinforcements, eh?" asked Lily. "Isn't that against the rules, Uncle?"

Winged creatures circled above them. Not birds, and not bats, either. Their wings were leathery and the color of pale flesh, lined with red veins. Their beaks were wicked hooks, and their bodies were scaled. Farther on, just on the edge of the horizon, Lily made out a dark, crooked line of cliffs. Their sheer walls were pitted with caves, which she knew wouldn't be empty. No, here in the Shardlands, you had to expect the worst. Lily couldn't suppress a shiver. The landscape reeked of foreboding.

Pan tipped his spear toward the high rock face. "The Haunts."

# TWENTY-SIX

*P*ut one foot in front of the other. That's all that matters. Just keep going.

But each step was harder than the last. Thorn's legs felt as heavy as anchors, and his feet dragged through the ash, because he didn't have the strength to lift them. His shoulders and arms screamed in protest of all the pulling.

They took turns, but he was sure he had dragged Gabriel twice as long as K'leef had. It seemed to him that the Djinnic prince would take just a few steps before declaring his shift over.

They'd found enough pieces of wood to build a makeshift sled, using turban cloth and belts to hold it together. They'd even managed to patch Gabriel up. For the time being, at least.

*Can't believe he's still alive.*

*Won't be for long, though. For all of us.*

Hardly any water, no food, and no idea where they were headed.

Thorn coughed and tried to produce enough saliva to clear the ash from his mouth. A few drips of black spittle made it out.

A small part of him, that traitorous part, urged him to sit down and let it just happen. The end.

*Keep going.*

*Give up.*

*You can do it.*

*Who do you think you are?*

*I'm the bat rider.*

*You're the stable cleaner.*

*I've saved kingdoms and rescued princesses. I'm a hero.*

*You're a peasant. Always have been, always will be.*

Thorn shook his head. Out, out, out with the bad thoughts.

"K'leef, come back here. I've gotta rest awhile." Thorn lowered the sled and felt a foot taller. Wow, he could dance now, freed of the weight. Dance his way back home. All he had to do was abandon Gabriel.

K'leef, who'd been scouting ahead, shuffled back and dropped to the ground. He shook the waterskin. "Half-empty."

"Or half-full," said Thorn. "Pass it here." He took a mouthful and handed it back to his friend.

K'leef shook his head. "I'm not thirsty. Why don't you save it till later?"

"Drink it, K'leef."

The prince stared at the waterskin. "What's the point of sharing it, Thorn? That might keep you going for another day."

"Keep *me* going? This ain't about me." Thorn pushed the skin into K'leef's chest. "Drink, and I don't want no more of this talk."

K'leef wanted to give up. Thorn saw it in his eyes and the way he slumped. But pride, or honor, kept him going. He wanted Thorn's blessing to quit, but Thorn wasn't about to grant it.

Thorn laughed. "So, we ain't discussed my reward for helping you."

K'leef smirked. "Oh, right. What is it you desire? The hand of a princess?"

Thorn grimaced. "Why would I want only her hand?"

"It's a figure of speech, Thorn. You get all of her."

"Oh? It's just that I work with zombies, and sometimes a hand is all you get."

"A princess's hand in marriage is the traditional reward. But then, so are a few chests of gold. A noble title or two. That's pretty common."

"Sir Thorn Batrider. I like the sound of that." Thorn slapped his neck. "These insects are worse than that manticore. I swear by the Six, they're draining me dry."

"Just try and ignore them."

Thorn waved the insects away from Gabriel's wound. "If I had a handful of elfwort, we could fix him up, no problem."

K'leef blinked. "Elfwort? We have that back at the palace. Each jar costs fifty dinar."

Thorn whistled. "Fifty? Ain't worth nothing back home. It grows all over Herne's Forest. We use it to make poultices. Even chew on it to cure toothaches."

Elfwort and a sprig of stalker fern. Rub that over your skin and you could stop worrying about any insects. The smell of it scared them off better than . . .

Better than what?

Thorn frowned. He used to know all the herbs and plants. . . . How could he forget one? He sighed, his heart suddenly heavy with homesickness. He was slowly losing touch with where he'd come from. He hadn't thought that possible.

"Have a sleep," said K'leef. "I'll wake you up in an hour; then we'll swap and I'll pull the sled."

"Only an hour, all right? We want to get to those hills before dark," said Thorn. "They could shelter us for the night."

K'leef went to check on Gabriel, and Thorn closed his eyes.

"Peasant. Peasant . . ."

Thorn blinked. "What?"

"I'm dying, aren't I?" Gabriel's eyes fluttered open. "Tell me the truth. I can take it."

"Yup. Reckon in the next few hours." Thorn wiped his face semi-clean. "By nightfall for sure."

Gabriel wailed. "Why did you tell me that?"

"You asked! And if it makes you feel any better, we won't be far behind you."

Gabriel wiped his eyes, though the tears were too precious to waste. "I . . . I have things to do."

"Like what?"

"You're not interested, not really."

Thorn shrugged. "I ain't in any rush. Tell me."

"The way I was with you, it was wrong. I know that now. I should have treated you differently."

What? Was Gabriel apologizing?

"I was too soft," Gabriel continued. "You need thrashing on a regular basis. You're a terrible servant. And really very ugly. No offense."

"Er . . ."

"Is that why they all like you? Is that why you have so many friends and I . . . don't have any?"

"Because I'm ugly?"

Gabriel sighed. "Yes. They feel sorry for you. The shape of your nose would make most children scream. And then there's your hair. A worldwide tragedy. But they envy my handsomeness, my elegance and sense of style. I intimidate them with my perfection."

"Maybe. Might also be because you have the personality of a skunk. You always act so superior. Like everyone else is beneath you and only there to make your life easier."

Gabriel lifted himself up onto his elbows. "That's the way of the world, peasant! There are those who rule: me. And there are those who serve: you."

"In case you've forgotten, this ain't your kingdom, it's K'leef's. You're his hostage, remember?"

Gabriel lay back down, saying nothing.

Where was K'leef, anyway?

"Gabriel, have you seen K'leef?"

The Solar boy didn't respond. He was moping.

Thorn stood up, suddenly afraid. "K'leef!"

Then he saw the waterskin. He picked it up. Still half-full.

*No, he didn't. . . .*

"K'leef! K'leef!"

Thorn looked in every direction. "K'leef! Come back here right now!"

He saw the footprints in the dust and followed them. But he only got thirty paces before they disappeared. The wind had done its work.

"K'leef!" Thorn shouted, even as it dawned on him it would be in vain.

He'd never find him. K'leef's ancestors had come out of the desert, and he'd gone to them.

Thorn wanted to cry, but he didn't have enough water left in his body. "Good-bye, K'leef. May you find shade under Herne's Tree."

"Where's K'leef?" asked Gabriel when Thorn returned.

"Gone."

"Then go find him! I order you to go find him!"

Thorn handed Gabriel the water. "Don't finish it. It's all we've got."

Thorn scanned the horizon, but the ash whirling in the wind obscured everything beyond a hundred feet.

Gabriel sobbed, dropping the skin. "It's empty."

He'd finished it. Thorn knew he would. "Leave it. Less to carry."

They struggled on, Thorn supporting the Solar boy, until Gabriel's wound reopened and he started bleeding. Thorn put him down against an ancient stone pillar, as much out of the wind as he could manage, which wasn't much.

It was strange how Gabriel's clothes remained perfectly clean, aside from the patch of red spreading slowly over his chest. Thorn was a dusty gray from head to toe.

They sat huddled together, trying to keep the stinging grit out of their eyes.

"I want my mother," said Gabriel. It was barely a whisper but nevertheless powerful. "She always made things better."

"That's what moms do."

Gabriel gripped Thorn's hand with a strength Thorn didn't think he had. His blue eyes were losing their light. "You'll stay with me?"

Thorn nodded. It wouldn't be long now. For either of them.

"She used to sing this song, when I was little," continued Gabriel. "I . . . I haven't heard it in years. Father thought I needed toughening up, so he sent her far away."

"That's sad," said Thorn simply.

"I wanted to make my father proud." Gabriel stuck out his chin. "To see that I could be brave. I didn't cry when she left."

"How old were you?"

"Five. It was my birthday. Mr. Funny cried, but I didn't. I was a brave boy."

His grip was weakening, and his head lolled. His skin, always pale, was turning bluish.

Thorn spoke. "You remember the song?"

"No." Gabriel turned slowly to face Thorn. "You know any?"

"None suitable for a noble. Just 'The Old Duke's Longsword.'"

Gabriel laughed. It was a sad, chest-shaking wheeze. "Sing it."

"I ain't got much of a singing voice. Grandpa always said it was worse than his pig choir. People paid a penny each to hear them whistle a tune at the midsummer fair. But I could give it a try." Thorn tried to clear his throat, but it was too dry. *"The old duke's got a mighty longsword, so the maids do declare. . . ."*

Thorn sang the four verses he knew, not sure if they were in the right order, and added a few lines his grandpa had made up.

He was about to repeat it, when Gabriel fell against his shoulder. His last breath was a giggle.

The glamour that Gabriel wore faded. His hair turned lank, his skin became loose and jaundiced, and his white clothes lost their lustrous sheen, becoming stained, dusty, and torn.

Thorn tried to get up, but he couldn't. He'd reached his limits, too. And where could he go, anyway? This was as good a place as any to die.

The stone he was leaning against was some sort of marker. It must have been taller once—the crack ten feet up proved it. How many thousands of years had it stood here? The letters on it were worn, but he bet Lily could have made sense of them. Then she'd spend the next hour boring him stupid about their historical significance.

He should've been thinking about his family, but it wasn't they who dominated what was likely to be the last hour of his life.

It was that strange girl dressed all in black. And covered with jewelry. So much jewelry. She'd explain that this ring was in honor of that ancestor, and that necklace was worn on Tuesdays because of some reason from five hundred years ago, and the bracelets, well, she had long arms and short sleeves. She was always growing out of her outfits, keeping Mary busy making new ones.

Funny that now, when he had no future, the future was all Thorn could think about. He'd never get to take her to Herne's Forest, the place where he'd been born. Perhaps that was for the best. Herne's Forest was the domain of the druids, and they weren't too friendly with other sorcerers. He could only imagine the chaos Lily would create dealing with them. Still, he would have liked to show her the immense trees he'd climbed, the peaceful groves where he'd picnicked, and the streams he and his brothers and sisters had splashed in during the summer.

*I'll see Lily in the Twilight.*

When he did, he'd say he was sorry for not keeping his promise. He'd tried not to die. He wished he'd told her things when he'd had the chance. His feelings, his dreams. Stupid things, really.

He lay down. *Might as well get comfortable.*

The wind picked up—steady, repetitive gusts that blew waves of ash across the lifeless landscape. He could hear the spirits crying. Was it the ghosts, waiting for him?

By the Six, the land of the dead *stank*. It was like rotting. . . .

The gusts grew stronger, and he blinked.

Giant wings flapped above him and beady red eyes shone, wild and fierce and bright with life, through the blurry haze.

Talons, each saber-long, clicked on the stony ground and those tremendous wings folded. Hades looked him over, then bent down and nudged his cheek.

"About time," said Thorn. Then he passed out.

# TWENTY-SEVEN

Cold water settled on his brow, and he felt moisture on his parched mouth, stinging his dry, cracked lips. Eyes still closed, head lost in delirium, Thorn slurped greedily.

"Careful," spoke a nearby voice. "Just a few drops at a time."

Thorn tried to peel his eyelids open, but they wouldn't cooperate. Fine. He preferred the dark. "More."

He sucked on a damp cloth, not minding the sand that seemed to coat the inside of his throat as he swallowed. He sat up and tried his eyelids again. This time they parted.

Above him stood a huge, black, hairy winged monster.

Thorn's aching cheeks broke out into a bigger-than-manticore grin. "Hey, boy."

Hades looked down at him, not that impressed, and sniffed. Then he almost licked Thorn's face off.

Thorn drew his fingers through the thick, spiky fur, and pressed himself deep into it. That familiar smell, the bat's warmth, and the *thud thud thud* of his heart, a hammer that pounded against him . . . there was nothing better.

"How did you find me?" he asked the bat.

"*We* found you."

Thorn focused on the others in here—wherever *here* was—and saw a woman squatting opposite him. "Didn't I save your life a few days ago?" he asked.

"Consider the favor returned," said Kismet. She pressed her hands on her knees to stand up. It had been less than a week since Thorn had freed her from the Candle, but her bump had grown since. The baby was in a hurry to come out.

She was out of her torn rags now and dressed in a long skirt, high boots, and a caftan embroidered with all kinds of weird shapes and swirling patterns. A coin-studded bandana covered her forehead, hiding the third eye he'd seen back in the courtyard. She wore as much jewelry as any of K'leef's sisters, but while they wore gems that could buy whole cities, Kismet's rocks were merely that—stones that had been painted and polished and threaded to make necklaces and bracelets. What precious metal she had was minimal, but she wore rings on all her fingers and her earlobes were stretched from the weight of her many earrings.

Only rulers put this much effort into their appearance.

He took the jug and drank until it was empty. Gritty water had never tasted so good. "Got anything to eat? I could murder a roast chicken right about now."

"Only meat around here is desert rat. I've got some turning on the spit," said Kismet. "Tastes like chicken."

"Bring it over, then." He was alive. He had Hades, and he was hungry. It was turning out to be a good day after all. Thorn grabbed the first skewer from Kismet and tore at the meat. She was right—it did taste like chicken. Didn't take long before all that was left was bone, which he used to pick the stringy fat stuck between his teeth. He sucked on a thighbone as he looked around.

Fifteen family-sized tents covered a slope that led down to a flat landscape broken up by old ruins. Behind him was a line of cliffs, and above that, a cloudy night sky. He didn't like the look of those clouds. They could boil up into another storm. The air brewed with trouble. "Where am I?"

Kismet handed him another skewer of rat. "With my tribe."

"This tribe got a name?"

"The Accursed," she replied wryly. "It's not a name we like, but that's what the other tribes call us."

"There a reason for that name?" Then he put his hand up, stopping her. "Yeah, I bet there is, and finding out's gonna spoil my day. Right now, I want to make the most of being alive. And speaking of being alive, you rescue anyone else besides me?"

"Yes. We found a blond boy. He's asleep."

So Gabriel hadn't died after all. The Solar boy's constitution was stronger than Thorn had thought. He was surprised not to feel too disappointed.

"But your other friend's eager to speak with you," Kismet went on.

"K'leef? He's here?" The day had just gotten a thousand times better.

Just then the Djinnic boy came walking up the slope toward him. He looked like he'd been dragged from certain death on the Shardlands. When he got close, he touched the red patches of wind-burned skin on his cheeks. "Don't laugh until you've seen yourself in the mirror."

Thorn shrugged. "Yeah, but I ain't never *been* pretty. As you've pointed out more than once."

Kismet handed him a bundle of clothes. "Finish your food, then get changed. I have some business to attend to." She brushed Hades's cheek and said to him, "You can leave them, too."

Thorn sat up. "You can't command my—"

Hades shot up into the clouds.

Kismet raised an eyebrow. "You were going to say something?"

What had just happened? Hades hardly listened to *him* most of the time, and yet he'd just done what this woman had asked, without any fussing, snarling, or attempting to bite her head off. She must've put a spell on him.

Thorn changed into his new clothes: baggy trousers, loose shirt, and sashes to hold it all together, and then a coat with cut sleeves, even more baggy. If the wind blew up, he'd probably sail away. Then . . . "A turban?"

"It'll protect you from the sun." K'leef helped him wrap it on. "Anyone ever tell you you've a funny-shaped head?"

"Not so tight," Thorn complained. "You know where we are?"

K'leef's eyes lit up. "Let me show you."

They were in a wide valley, with cliffs on either side. But within the valley was a whole city—a vast, ruined, empty city. The silence was eerie; the wind blew softly, as if loath to disturb the solitude. Even the cliff faces looked as if they had once been inhabited. They were carved with extravagant doorways and columns and huge friezes. Statues that shamed the ones he'd seen in Castle Gloom lined the roads, some as wide as rivers.

"I've never . . . Who built all this?" he asked, gazing at the towers sculpted from glass.

"Who else? The Six Princes." K'leef brushed the ash off the marble road, revealing a mosaic of swirling colors and mysterious writing under their feet. "We're deep in the Old Kingdom now, Thorn."

Thorn gulped. "It's too much."

"Too much splendor, you mean? Imagine what it looked like ten thousand years ago, when it was new and the streets were filled with people."

Thorn jerked his thumb over his shoulder. "And what do you know about them? The Accursed?"

"A tribe ruled by women," said K'leef. "Women said to have the gift of prophecy."

The camp covered a good few acres, but it was still dwarfed by the scale of the city they'd pitched beside. But why not stay in the city itself? There was plenty of shelter to be found there. Horses and camels were penned in one of the nearby squares, and two women collected water from a well.

Goats roamed, as they tended to do, and children played hide-and-seek among the rocks, but they did not venture beyond shouting distance of the tents.

A sudden cry behind them made Thorn and K'leef jump aside.

Some tribe members rode past. They were all equipped with hide armor, spears, and wickedly curved bows. But they weren't on horses— they rode giant lizards, green and brown and some red. Each beast was decorated— No, they changed color as they moved, patterns rippling across their shimmering scales. They rushed up a slope, easily climbing over the rocks and the sheer cliff face, to settle on a wide ledge.

"Giant salamanders," said Thorn, awestruck. "Lily told me they lived way out in the Shardlands. Never knew you could ride 'em. That's unbelievable."

K'leef laughed. "Says the boy who flies on a giant vampire bat."

"Yeah, but still . . ." He became distracted by a commotion on the ledge. "Something's up."

"Leave it to them, Thorn." K'leef stopped by a memorial stone and began inspecting it. "Look at this. It's in honor of a sorcerer. Says it's—"

"Bored already." Thorn saw Kismet talking to another group of warriors. She glanced in the boys' direction. It was a look Thorn had seen on Lily's face a hundred times before. That was all Thorn needed. "I'm going to find out what's happening."

He started walking toward Kismet.

"Thorn!" shouted K'leef. "You can't meddle in—"

Thorn paused and looked back over his shoulder. "Thought you knew me better by now."

K'leef hitched up his pants and followed. "Just wait a minute, then."

First they needed to get past one of the big salamanders. Thorn was sure the monster's jaws could take his head off pretty easily, even though it had no teeth, just a crusted beak of sorts. A high crest speckled with gold and silver spots rose from between its eyes to run halfway down its spine, and the saddle was nestled just below the shoulders. A young woman sat cross-legged upon it, chewing a fistful of cabbage leaves. Thorn glanced up at her. "May I?"

She nodded.

The salamander closed its eyes as Thorn ran his hand across its scales. They changed from red to orange to yellow and back again. The crest shivered, and the woman laughed. She said something in Djinnic.

"She says you're lucky he hasn't bitten your hand off," translated K'leef. "Salamanders are surly beasts."

"If I can handle Hades, I think I can handle an overgrown gecko." Thorn was from Herne's Forest. His people had a knack for dealing with animals, and he was better at it than most of them. He felt even more confident now, after hanging around monsters so long.

Kismet approached them with a party of warriors in tow. "Why are you here in the Shardlands?"

Thorn let K'leef answer. It was a ruler-to-ruler thing.

"I'm on a trial by fire," said the prince.

She narrowed her gaze. "I thought Sa'if was going to be the new sultan?"

"He died," said K'leef. "It's down to me and my brothers Fafnir and Jambiya."

"I didn't expect this." Kismet looked up at the ridge with a worried expression. "Someone's approaching."

"So?" asked Thorn.

Kismet was about to say something but stopped herself. She shook her head and backed away. "We don't want any trouble."

K'leef didn't let her go. "Who is it? Do you know?"

She shrugged. "It's none of our concern."

*She's hiding something. What?* Thorn scanned the cliff tops. He made out a few salamanders up on one ridge, well hidden, as they'd changed their color to rocky gray. "Can we see for ourselves, then?"

Kismet grunted. "Aliyah will take you up."

The woman finished her cabbage and picked up the reins of her sala-mander. She twitched it around to face the watchers on the ridge. Then she motioned for the boys to climb on behind her.

K'leef paled. "Do we really have to . . . ?"

Thorn grabbed his arm. "Come on, it'll be fun."

And up they went. Straight up. The salamander, like most lizards, could cling to sheer surfaces and the vertical cliff wall was no challenge.

The lurching ride was a bit like being on the deck of a ship in storm-tossed waves. Thorn was a little queasy by the time they hit the top, and K'leef was slightly green, too. But it was preferable to walking up the steep hundred-foot trail, especially when both of them were still weak from trekking through the desert. A week of lying around doing nothing but eating steak and cake was what they needed, not more wandering in the Shardlands dining on rat.

The boys dismounted, their legs shaking, and hauled themselves onto a rock.

It was a perfect lookout spot. They could now see that this valley was just one among many; the whole landscape was broken ridges and cliffs. A chasm in the earth offered the easiest passage between valleys, and that's what they were peering down into. At the mouth of the next valley was another camp—smaller than theirs—and Thorn's eyes were sharp enough to see the campfires glinting off armor and sword blades.

"Any idea who they are?" he asked.

"Scorpion tribe." K'leef pointed at two wings of riders. "That's a pincer formation. Tents on either flank, guarding the main one, which is where you'll find the chief."

Chief? There was someone down there, dressed in red robes. "Could that be . . . Jambiya?"

It had to be. There was Farn, smoldering in the dying light of the evening. The monstrous efreet sat away from the main camp, wreathed in flames.

K'leef squinted. "I don't know what he'd be doing here. The Lava Mountains are in the other direction. We're here because we got off course...."

"Maybe he knows something we don't. Which wouldn't be difficult, since we know nothing."

"The books said—"

"Yeah, yeah, yeah." Thorn shuffled forward, to the very edge of the cliff, for a better look. One member of the Scorpion tribe was pushing along another figure.... "Oh no."

"What?"

"It's Lily." Thorn caught the flash of the metal around Lily's wrists. He knew they weren't bracelets. "She's their prisoner."

# TWENTY-EIGHT

"**S**he is not my problem," Kismet said after Thorn and K'leef had told her about Lily.

"But I saved you and your family," Thorn replied.

"And I saved you and your two friends." Kismet rubbed her belly. "Whatever debt I had toward you has been paid."

Thorn pointed at Gabriel. "He doesn't count! You could have left him!"

"Hey!" Gabriel lay on a mattress nearby, still weak from his injury but hungry. He was already on his fourth skewer. "This is good, what is it?"

"Chicken," everybody said at once.

Others sat around the camp, including Kismet's wrinkled old mother. She kept her beady eyes on Thorn, and he didn't like it. The warriors, too, just listened to Thorn's pleading, offering nothing. Eventually, Thorn stood up, kicked sand into the fire, and stormed off to a rock far from everyone. Though he did stop to grab another stick of rat on the way.

K'leef followed a few moments later. "So how are we going to rescue her?"

Thorn peered across the camp. "It would be a lot easier if we had ten or twenty of them helping."

K'leef shook his head. "They'd only cramp your style." He snapped his fingers and a spiky bush burst into flame. "Can I suggest something?"

"Go on."

"We rescue Lily and get out of there. No heroics."

"Of course."

K'leef stared at him so hard it made Thorn blush. "Thorn, I know what you're thinking. You've got too honest a face."

"I ain't thinking nothing."

"Rubbish. You're thinking that Jambiya needs to be taught a lesson. I don't disagree, but now's not the time."

Thorn scratched his knuckles. "Easy for you to say. He didn't try and melt your hand."

"If you want my help, then you've got to agree to this."

"Who says I need anyone's help?" said Thorn. "Give me a bow, an arrow, and a giant bat, and I can solve most problems."

"Thorn . . ."

"All right. It *might* be easier if there was a distraction. You may come in useful. For a change."

Aliyah walked over. She said a few words in Djinnic and held out a bow and quiver full of long shafted arrows.

K'leef laughed, then translated. "She says Kismet told her to give you these."

"Am I really that predictable?" But Thorn took them with a nod of thanks. The bow was typical Djinnic, compact and highly curved, and the arrow shafts were straight, with neat fletching. He touched the tip of an arrow to test its sharpness. "Can't get decent iron out here? Bone arrowheads aren't bad, but they can shatter."

Aliyah must have picked up the dismissive tone. She spoke again, and K'leef translated. He pointed at one of the arrows. "Not these. And they may serve you better against the things of the Shardlands."

"What's that supposed to mean?"

"It means Aliyah knows her business better than you do, Thorn."

Still, he felt a lot better—whole—with the quiver slung over his back and bow resting in his fist. He gave the bowstring a thrum. "Beautiful sound, ain't it?"

"Only to you, forest boy."

Hades responded right away to Thorn's whistle. He sensed that Thorn wanted to make trouble, and he was eager to join in.

"What's the plan?" asked K'leef.

"You distract them with your magic. While they're looking left, I'll come in from the right and free Lily. Open up them shackles, and then we're out of there."

"And Hades?"

"He'll grab you and take off. Lily and I will shadow-step." Thorn slipped onto Hades's back. "We'll be back before someone tells Gabriel what he's really been chewing on." He held out his arm and helped K'leef climb up behind him. "Best you hold on tight and try not to look down."

"It can't be— WHOA!"

Up and up they rose, Hades carrying the bulk of both boys without too much effort but with plenty of grumbling. The monster had lost some weight while being out here, which wasn't necessarily a bad thing. Predators needed to maintain a fine balance of being lean enough to want to hunt but not so lean as to become weak. Right now Hades *soared*.

Over the cliffs they went, K'leef howling with joy and a dash of fear as he squeezed his arms around Thorn's waist. Thorn nudged the bat with his knees—there was no saddle on Hades—and they crossed the valley and headed toward the camp where Jambiya had settled down for the night. It was the perfect setting for trouble—cloudy and cold, making men want to nestle down in their blankets and stare at the fire. Beyond the cast of those flames, the rest was utter darkness. Hades, despite his immense size, drifted in the wind as silently as a feather.

They circled over the camp.

What was shadow-stepping like? Thorn wondered. He'd never actually gone on one of those journeys with Lily. He hadn't wanted to—the thought of traveling through the Twilight made him break out in goose bumps. But this plan was a good one. Nice and simple.

He'd been in chains before, and to avoid that happening again, he'd made a point of learning how to escape them. The blacksmith at Castle Gloom had shown him how to pop the locks off a shackle. He'd then practiced until he could open it in less than a minute with a slim knife, like the one now tucked in his sash.

The cuffs would be made out of cold iron—otherwise they wouldn't be able to hold Lily—but the mechanism would be the same as any other.

He wouldn't complicate things by trying to take on Jambiya. But if that scum did come into his sights and an arrow found its way heading in his direction . . .

"You ready?" Thorn asked K'leef.

"To save Lily?" His friend grinned. "You're never going to let her forget this, are you?"

"Nope." Thorn patted Hades's cheek. "Put me down there."

He slipped off Hades and dropped the last ten feet. The bat, his load cut in half, jerked up, then powered higher with another wingbeat and was gone.

Thorn crouched behind a boulder.

*Get Lily and get out.*

Most of the tribesmen were asleep now, all wrapped in their blankets next to their little fires.

Which one was Lily? Everyone looked the same from here.

He unwrapped the end of his turban, covered as much of his face as possible, then wandered into the camp. It was time to rescue a princess.

And yeah, he was never going to let Lily forget it.

# TWENTY-NINE

*I* *need to get out of here.*

Lily glanced around the camp. There wouldn't be a better opportunity than right now. Jambiya was busy making plans, leaving her under the guard of one of the new nomads.

Her magic would be at its most powerful on a night so dark. She could probably shadow-step hundreds of miles. But first she needed these cuffs off.

Guard duty was boring. It was a job passed to the lowest-ranking person, usually the least able. The man watching her had hand-me-down armor, and his spear wasn't even straight. A patchy beard did little to hide a face cratered with sores. He wore two different style boots, one exposing his toes. The only clean item he had was the bandage around his right arm.

She sucked her teeth and gestured to it. "Looks nasty."

"It is nothing."

"How did you get it? A fight?"

A flicker of a smile crossed his lips. "I slew a ghul."

"Wow. A ghul? That is no mean feat." Lily frowned with concern. "You've had it treated, right? For infection?"

He hesitated. "Of course. I washed the wound before I wrapped it up."

"Good. That's all I wanted to know. Glad you keep sprigs of, er, rot-root handy."

Now he looked worried. "Rot-root?"

Lily shrugged, acting as if this was no big deal. "Of course. It grows everywhere in Gehenna, practically a weed. Everyone knows you clean out ghul bites with rot-root. Stops you from becoming one yourself."

Tales grew in the telling. Gehenna was a kingdom of ghosts and ghouls and all breeds of graveyard monsters. But one myth persisted: If you got bitten by an undead creature, you'd become one yourself. The story usually involved vampires and zombies—maybe because they had teeth. It was utterly ridiculous; anyone giving it a moment's thought would realize that it made no sense. If it were true, then there'd be no living people left in Gehenna by now. Yet some stories stuck.

The nomad scratched the wound.

Lily wrinkled her nose. "Itchy? That's how it begins."

He forced himself to stop. "It is nothing!"

"I'm sure you're right. But tell me this: Is your throat feeling a bit dry?"

He clutched his neck. He was truly afraid now.

*Of course it is, you fool. Think how much smoke you've been breathing in the last few hours.*

He looked at her desperately. "What will happen to me?"

Lily glanced over at Jambiya. "He won't want a ghul in his band, will he? I suspect your lord will . . . well, you know."

The nomad gulped as his future suddenly became very bright. With flames.

Lily sighed. "It's a simple spell to fix the decay."

"Do you know this spell?" he asked, pleading.

"I am the witch queen," Lily snapped. "Of course I know it."

"Please, my lady. I have family. . . ."

Lily shook her head. "No. I can't cast a spell. Jambiya will sense me using magic and then what? He'll kill me. Both of us."

The nomad pointed to a large boulder some distance away. "There? Will he detect you using it from there?"

Lily frowned. "Perhaps, perhaps not. How about there?" She pointed to another cluster of rocks, coincidently nearer the cliff face.

He got up and looked over at another one of the nomads. "The girl wishes to relieve herself."

His companion nodded, not that he seemed particularly interested in what Lily wanted while he picked the flesh off his grilled rat.

The nomad prodded Lily with the butt of his spear. "Move."

They walked to the rocks, and as soon as they were out of sight, the man frantically unwrapped his bandage. Lily inspected the wound, only a small gash, and gasped. "By the Six . . ."

"What? Tell me!"

"It's worse than I thought. You'll need a new bandage—this one's contaminated. We'll use your turban."

He pulled it off and shook it until it was a long ribbon.

Lily directed him to sit down. "Relax. The more you worry, the faster the poison will spread. Take a deep, slow breath. Close your eyes."

He did.

Lily quietly picked up a rock and raised it above his bare head. "*Relax.* It'll be fine in just one moment. . . ."

*Thud!*

The man slumped to the ground a moment after Lily struck.

Crouching, hidden from view of the camp, she estimated the distance to the cliffs. They were about a hundred yards away, and there were plenty of caves to hide in. Then she could take her time getting the shackles off.

Another nomad approached, and she ducked back down behind her boulder. She picked up another rock, just in case. Why couldn't they all just go to sleep and make life easier for her?

She tightened her grip on the rock and waited.

"You gonna come out anytime soon, or are you still taking care of business?"

Lily jumped up. "Thorn?"

The nomad pulled the cloth from his face. "Who else?"

"Thorn!"

"Shh!" he snapped. They both hid back down. He winked. "I'm here to rescue you."

"You're lucky I didn't knock your brains out," she said, tossing the rock aside. "And I do not need rescuing. I was making my escape perfectly well by myself until you interrupted it."

"Escape? Dressed like that?" He looked her up and down. "And why *are* you dressed like that, with your belly showing an' all?"

"I suppose, since you're here, you might as well get these off," she said, holding up the shackles. He didn't respond. She shook them again. "My outfit distracting you, Thorn?"

"Er . . . what?" He shook his head. "The shackles. Right."

He twisted his knife into the lock, and with a few swift turns they came undone.

What a relief. Her fingers tingled as the blood started flowing back into them again. "So did you actually have a plan, or were you making it up as you went along, as usual?"

"Of course I had a plan," he snapped.

"Well?"

A series of explosions went off to their left. One after the other, each and every campfire blew up into an inferno, shooting burning debris a dozen feet into the night sky so the camp was suddenly lit with small shooting stars.

"That plan," said Thorn proudly.

Men ran and shouted, and a horse bolted through the campsite, knocking one of the smaller nomads head over heels.

"That K'leef is getting better every day," said Thorn. "This next part's up to you, Lily." He nocked an arrow and loosed it in one fluid move. The arrow cut through another horse's tether, and it, too, galloped free, adding to the chaos.

Jambiya yelled orders at his men. Then he turned toward the fires and held out his hands, palms facing outward.

The flames waved and pulled. They jumped through the air and spiraled over and over, gathering themselves like so many burning threads until they formed a long ribbon, heading toward Jambiya's open hands.

A hellish shriek overhead made the men dive into the dirt. Hades swooped low and fast over the camp, claws outstretched. He grabbed a figure out of the dark, threw his wings down mightily, and took off before the spears and arrows flew after him.

The mighty efreet, Farn, was up and lumbering through the camp. But its presence was making things worse as it sought to protect its master. His merest touch ignited tents and the guide ropes. More horses panicked as the creature surrounded itself with flames.

"Thorn!" screamed Lily.

Her uncle charged at them, sword drawn.

Thorn's next arrow lodged itself in Pan's calf, and he stumbled. He glared at Thorn and broke the shaft, while yelling at the others to stop them. He wasn't giving up.

"The shadows are deepest there," said Lily, pointing at a crevasse in the cliff wall.

Thorn laughed with glee. Horses bolted and nomads chased after them; other men were busy using blankets to extinguish small fires, and Farn had gotten itself wrapped up in the blazing folds of a tent. Thorn was loving the chaos.

"Hold tight, Thorn. I don't want to lose you in the Twilight."

He did as she said.

Lily sliced her hand through the air, ripping the Veil between the lands of the living and those of the dead, opening a doorway into the Twilight. There'd be a blast of freezing air and then . . .

Nothing.

Lily did it again. Still nothing.

She stared at the shadows. "It's not possible. . . ."

Pan limped toward them with five others beside him. All looked ready to kill. One smoldered.

Thorn looked back anxiously. "Get a move on, Lily. . . ."

"I can't." Her voice cracked as she clawed uselessly at the darkness. "My magic's not working!"

# THIRTY

What was happening?

Magic could fluctuate out in the Shardlands. The wild storms altered reality, and what else was magic but an agent for change?

Could that be it? Yet K'leef's and Jambiya's fire sorcery was working. . . . Then why not hers?

They ran into a fissure in the cliff. The roaring flames behind them lit up the cave entrance, but then, as they made their way deeper inside, the light dimmed to a faint glow and finally, complete darkness.

That didn't bother her. Lily had grown up in Castle Gloom. Even without light, she could sense where the winding walls were by the subtlest air movements, and as in the castle ruins, her feet stayed steady on the pitted and rocky ground.

"Come out, Lily! You're too old for hide-and-seek!"

Uncle Pan had grown up in Castle Gloom, too. Darkness was no handicap to him, either.

"Do you know where you're going?" Thorn whispered.

"Shhh!"

"It's darker here. Try your little spell again."

"It doesn't work," Lily snapped. "None of it."

She felt as if she'd been pulled inside out.

The last spell she'd used was the shadow-step to flee from the palace. So why couldn't she do it now? With all this darkness, it should be easy!

A light shone from around the corner, and boots scuffed on the gravel.

They crouched down behind a rock as a nomad waved a torch in their direction.

Lily held her breath, wishing for deeper shadows. Surely the nomad could see them? They were only five feet apart.

But he just grunted and turned back the way he'd come.

Both of them sighed with relief when he left. They waited for Pan to venture in, but he never appeared. *He must be searching another cave.*

Thorn peered farther along the crooked path. "Keep going? We might make it out the other side."

"What other side?"

He told her about Kismet and her camp in the ancient city.

"From the time of the Six Princes? Are you sure?" It sounded incredible. To walk the actual streets they'd trodden!

"That's what K'leef told me, and I guess he'd know." He tore his turban into strips and wrapped them into a bundle around two arrows. A minute later, using his flint and tufts of cotton, he lit the cloth on fire, which gave them a few yards' worth of light. "Waste of two perfectly good arrows," he grumbled.

She looked around. The cave walls were strange. Despite their crookedness and all the cracks, they were too evenly proportioned to be natural. "Someone chiseled this tunnel."

"Hmm?" Thorn was riffling through his quiver. "Eight left. Let's try and avoid any big battles, eh?"

And this gravel. Most of it was ash and dust blown in from the desert, but under that layer lay small, faded squares of stone and tile, all delicately inlaid by master craftsmen a long time ago. Castle Gloom had similar designs in its older halls. There were gaps in the walls that, if you looked at them skew-eyed, might appear to have once been window openings.

Were these cliffs natural, or were they buildings so old and decayed that they had melded into shapeless rock? No one knew exactly when the Six Princes had reigned—it was back when the sun was young and the world not yet fully formed—so could these be the homes and palaces of the ancients? Wax sagged over time; did stone do the same?

"The war . . ." she whispered.

"Hmm?"

"When the high king died, the six sons fought for the crown. All the marvels of the golden age of magic were destroyed by their rivalry. Seas boiled, populations were turned to stone, the sun grew black, and the crows all died. Mountains shifted, and they say the world turned on its axis. Storms scoured the earth, flattening kingdoms. It was a cataclysm, and we're descended from those who survived. Haven't you ever wondered why so much of our world is empty?"

"Not really." Thorn puffed on the flames of his makeshift torch to give it more life. "Let's go. I reckon we've got an hour before this winks out, and I ain't got the arrows to spare for admiring the decorations."

Lily sighed. "You don't have any interest in the past, do you?"

"I'm focused on us having a future, Lily. Even if it's just another hour."

"Lead the way, faithful servant."

He bowed. "As you wish, m'lady."

How did he do it? He knew his north from his south even here, deep inside a mountain. Thorn inspected the dust and found mouse paw prints where Lily just saw faint scratches. He could smell the difference between stale, trapped air and fresh desert wind from outside.

"It's like magic, what you do."

Thorn was sniffing the ground. "It's just paying attention. Something's been this way, not too long ago. Something rotten."

"Rotten?"

He nodded. "I've been around zombies long enough to know the smell, Lily. You're too used to it, so you don't notice. I've said it plenty of times, ain't I? You need to get out more, spend some time out in Spindlewood and Bone-Tree Forest. Give your nose some exercise."

"I'll start exercising it the moment we get back home." She couldn't quite conceal the tremble in her voice. This wasn't the best news, not now. "Zombies?"

"Nothing you can't handle."

Could she handle them without her magic?

They entered a chamber where the ceiling had partially caved in, making it feel tomb-like. Even for someone raised in Castle Gloom, the silence was eerie. Lily felt that she—they—didn't belong, that the living were trespassers here.

Was that the sound of wind blowing through cracks, or the ancient souls whispering? Something awful had happened, and the pain of it still lingered, even after all this time.

"They didn't want to die," she said.

"Reckon that's what all the dead say. Nobody does. Grandpa . . ." He looked around at the dusty ruins. "Never mind. Another time."

They came to a large underground square. Lily approached a broken column with letters and symbols carved into it. Bones were scattered all around.

Lily traced her fingers over the deep grooves, her brow furrowed as she deciphered the language of the Old Kingdom. It wasn't easy, but one name came up again and again. "This is Al Na'im, one of the jeweled cities."

"That a good thing or a bad thing?"

"It means 'a place of delights,' roughly. Its citizens didn't want to take part in the war; they refused to ally themselves with one prince or the other. So all six descended upon it." She couldn't stop the tears. "The stories are awful, Thorn."

"The more I learn about the Six Princes, the more I hate 'em."

She turned to him sharply. "Don't say that. They were great, great men. They made our world what it is."

"Great fools, more like." Thorn inspected a bone. "And it seems to me the world survived in spite of 'em, not because of 'em."

"Will you put that down?"

"Nope." He wrapped the remains of his turban around the top of it. "This is a thighbone, but I wouldn't like to meet the person it belonged to. Must've been seven feet tall, easy."

Lily shrugged. "They say the people of that age were taller, more handsome, and nobler than those of today. They lived for hundreds of years, and even the lowliest beggar was richer than Duke Solar."

"And yet they fouled it all up. Hooray for them."

How could he be so dismissive? So ignorant? Lily reminded herself that Thorn hadn't had a proper education. When they got back to Gehenna, she'd show him the books and tell him some of the tales. Then he'd understand, and he'd come to feel the same way about the Six Princes as she did.

And yet, as she looked at the ruins, she couldn't help wondering if Thorn had a point.

Her best artists could never match the splendor of the art here, not even if they worked for a hundred years. How were they able to sculpt marble so delicately, or make glass so thin and yet so strong? So much had been lost forever because of the ambitions and rivalry of six brothers. Men who should have stood by each other no matter what. Instead, they had made a war that lasted hundreds of years and almost destroyed the world.

They were great and they were terrible. Perhaps one could not exist without the other?

"Let's keep going through," she suggested.

So they did, reentering the winding tunnels.

And they found their first dead body.

Thorn poked it with the tip of his bow. "One of them nomads."

The dead man's face was frozen in terror, ashen, his lips drawn back in a scream that never made it out. Lily wondered if he was howling in the lands of the dead even now. Dark purple bruises encircled his throat. He'd been strangled, with long fingers. . . .

Lily jumped at the scream. More cries and yells joined it. Then came the sounds of fighting from the branch heading left. Thorn pointed right. "Thataway."

There was a time to be curious, and a time to escape. This was one of those run-far-away times. "Go! Don't wait for me."

The screams grew louder, wilder, and more desperate. Someone sobbed, another begged and then gave a cry that ended with a hideous gurgle. Torchlight flickered behind them, then wavered, and was snuffed out.

The path sloped steeply upward. Soon they were scurrying hand over hand, Lily's skirt tearing and her knees bleeding on the sharp rock.

"Shall I get behind and push?" Thorn muttered.

"You'll get nowhere near my behind." Lily cursed as a jagged edge sliced her fingertips.

"Then move it."

Lily spun around as a yell echoed down the dark passageway. A figure stumbled around the corner, flailing with his sword.

Something dark and bony leaped at him, and he slashed its face, a blow that would have killed a man but barely scratched whatever this was. Yet it backed off, waiting for its companions. Their snarls warned Lily that they were not far behind.

The warrior sagged, and Lily could see it was taking all his strength just to hold his weapon aloft.

"We've got to help him." Lily skidded down the slope.

"No, we don't!" Thorn shouted in despair. "Lily!"

Lily dashed a few yards to catch up with the man. He turned just as Lily grabbed him. "Come with—"

Their eyes met, and she gasped at his most familiar face.

# THIRTY-ONE

L ily blinked again. Uncle Pan!

"Put the sword down!" Thorn stood there, bow drawn.

"What are you doing, Thorn?" Lily cried.

"Outta the way!" he yelled back. Then, to Pan, "Sword down, or by the Six, I will shoot!"

The arrow zipped over her right shoulder.

Horrified, she turned, expecting to see her uncle dead. Instead, one of the creatures lay behind them, an arrow buried in its eye socket. It stumbled a few paces before collapsing.

Thorn pointed his second arrow at Pan. "The next one goes in *your* eyeball. Drop the sword."

Pan complied, and the heavy blade clanged on the stone floor.

Lily ventured over to the dead creature.

It was human, or had been once. But its spine was so bent it scurried on all fours, on limbs long and bony, and with fingers filled with a macabre strength. Dirt and dried blood had turned the ragged nails black and broken, and crooked teeth lined the puckered gums.

"A ghul," she said.

Ghuls were cowardly creatures that ambushed lone travelers in remote places and dined on their flesh. She had studied them and knew that whole tribes of them dwelled out here. With little else to eat in the Shardlands, it wasn't surprising that they had turned to eating the flesh of the dead— even their own. Over time and generations, they had evolved into something not quite alive and not quite dead.

The magic of the Shardlands altered all of its inhabitants sooner or later, and in unpredictable ways.

Lily turned to her uncle. "Can you walk unaided?"

"I'll manage," he replied.

Thorn muttered under his breath, and even she didn't understand why she was helping her uncle, but the three scrambled up the slope and down the other side. They hobbled on for . . . how long? Lily had no idea, but eventually the creatures' shouts and screams died away, and the three of them slowed down.

Pan limped to the side of the path, pale and panting, and sat down on a pile of rubble. Blood soaked the crude bandage around his leg.

Thorn yanked her around to face him. "You've done some all-out crazy things since I've known you, but this is the craziest. What were you thinking? You should have left him!"

"I couldn't! He's my uncle!"

Thorn threw up his hands in frustration. "You are impossible!"

Pan laughed. "I can hear you, you know."

Thorn scowled. "That leg giving you trouble?"

Pan nodded.

Thorn smiled. "Good. With any luck you'll bleed to death, and that will be that."

But Lily helped unwind the turban cloth her uncle had used as a bandage. The wound looked clean—disabling but not fatal. Thorn could put an arrow through one of Mary's hoop earrings at a hundred paces during a hurricane, so Lily knew he'd done this on purpose. No matter how much he threatened, Thorn wasn't a killer. Pan's running had loosened the cloth, that was all. She retied it, adding her own scarf to increase the pressure and reduce the leakage.

"Thank you, Niece." Pan stood up, testing it. "I think I can walk now."

Thorn pointed back the way they'd come. "Off you go, then."

Lily scowled at her friend. "Ignore him, Uncle."

Thorn plucked his bowstring. "I'm never gonna complain about Gabriel ever again."

Thorn wasn't wrong to mistrust her uncle. Pan had murdered her parents and brother and tried to kill her. Nothing was ever going to change that, or make the loss any less painful. But without them, he was all the family she had left. She couldn't leave him to die, despite his crimes and treachery.

She and Pan took the lead while Thorn held back, constantly checking behind him, as tense as his bowstring.

"Al Na'im," said Pan eventually. "Isn't it?"

"Yes."

"Do you know how many years I spent looking for the City of Delights? The fortunes I wasted on fake maps and phony guides . . . This one time, I—"

"Stop talking. I'm not interested."

He shrugged. "You're in charge, Lily."

Thorn snorted, and Lily knew there was a huge "I told you so" on its way from him.

Yet no one knew the Shardlands better than Pan. Obsession was too small a word for how her uncle felt about the ruins of the Old Kingdom. Lily had sat listening to his tales so often, she'd almost believed she'd been there with him, exploring ancient tombs and digging for buried cities. When her father had become Lord Shadow, Pan had gathered his armor and a handful of men and left, promising to return laden with treasure and with a pet dragon for her. He had come back with neither, but that hadn't mattered to her. It had to him. The failure had made him feel useless, a feeling that grew in intensity the more powerful his brother—his *younger* brother—became.

His drinking had been amusing, at first. Pan the clown, acting out duels and wild stories while he stumbled around the Great Hall. Eventually the laughter faded and was replaced with uncomfortable silences and mockery. Lily remembered dying inside when she'd overheard the servants laughing not with him but *at* him as they dragged the unconscious Pan to his bed.

When had his sense of worthlessness become poisonous? When had his envy of his brother turned into thoughts of murder?

Could she have done something? Said something, anything, that might have made a difference? Should she have told Pan how much he meant to her? Reminded him that when she'd been small and frightened, it was he she'd gone to? That he was her hero?

But what had that adoration accomplished? It had not stopped him from ripping her heart out.

She was House Shadow. She thought she was familiar with darkness, but there were dark places within people that she could never hope to understand.

The rest of her family were in their tombs, and here he was, alive.

Not merely alive, but vital. Lean, fierce, dangerous, and clear-eyed. The exile had made him new again.

"You look well, Lily," he said. "I've heard about what you've accomplished in Gehenna."

She didn't respond.

"Your father would be proud."

"Don't speak about him," Lily warned. "Don't you *dare*."

"Lily . . ."

Cold rage gripped her. "I saved you from execution, because I didn't know who you really were. If I had, things might have turned out differently."

"I know you, Lily."

"You think you do. I've changed."

"Not in the ways that matter," he replied.

"You think I was weak to let you go. That's what everyone says. Baron Sable would take your head off if he were here."

"Mercy is not the same as weakness."

Thorn spoke. "Lily, can I have a word?"

Pan rubbed his calf. "It would be good to rest a minute. Go on."

"She doesn't need your permission," Thorn snapped.

They walked a few yards ahead. Thorn kept his eyes on Pan as he spoke. "Don't listen to him. He's just a fox trying to get you out of the coop."

"That's one of your grandpa's quotes, isn't it?"

He glowered. "My grandpa's over seventy, and do you know how many people in Stour are that old? Just him. So he's been doing something right, don't you think?"

"I know what you're saying. Pan is trying to flatter me, make me drop my guard," said Lily.

"Good. So don't you fall for it. Whatever he tells you, they're all just lies. No matter how much you want 'em to be true."

"I'm not stupid, Thorn."

"You should have killed him when you could."

She'd had enough. "Go on, then. Shoot him. You can't miss from this distance."

Thorn's gaze hardened. "I ain't your executioner, Lady Shadow."

*Not yet, Thorn.*

Tyburn was her executioner. But no executioner lasted forever. She knew Tyburn had his eye on Thorn as a successor, though he hadn't yet shared his plan with Lily—Tyburn didn't share much with anyone. But it made sense.

Thorn was a born hunter. It was a small step to move from hunting deer to hunting men.

How would it happen? How did executioners train their replacements?

It would begin with a first kill. Thorn would have to cross that threshold, take the life of another human being. Then, knowing he could do it, would other assassinations be . . . easier?

What would become of Thorn, this boy she knew?

She smiled suddenly.

He frowned. "What?"

"Never change, Thorn."

He laughed. "'Cause I'm so perfect already?"

"That remains to be seen," she replied. "So, where are we?"

He put his hand against the wall. "Feel this. It's warm."

"So?"

"Sunlight's been on it. Came in from up there, somewhere." He pointed.

All she could see were broken rocks and deep shadows. "You sure?"

"We need to climb. There'll be a way out of here yet."

This wasn't ideal. "What about Pan? He can't climb with that leg."

"He'd better. I ain't giving him a piggyback."

They talked it through with Pan. Thorn would be in the lead, and he'd try to pick the easiest way up. "Hold on tight," he advised Pan, "and don't look down." Then he brushed his hands. "Ready?"

"If we're so close to the outside, why don't you just use your magic, Lily?" asked Pan. "I've seen you shadow-step, remember?"

"I do. You were trying to kill me," said Lily.

"Then it'll be easy. Take young Thorn, then take me. I'll wait right here."

"My magic is not for your convenience, Uncle. We climb."

Thorn scrambled up the wall and onto the broken roof like a squirrel. He was forty feet up before he turned around and called down to her. "You next, Lily."

"What about my uncle?"

"He goes last. That way, if he falls, he doesn't take anyone down with him."

Pan laughed. "You're full of heart, Thorn."

Lily climbed. Thorn called out instructions, telling her to feel for a handhold on her left, to wedge her foot into this crack or balance on that ledge. It wasn't long before she was sweating. She shook out her hands one at a time to get rid of the ache.

"Now you know how I feel after holding a quill all morning," said Thorn. "It's just the same."

"Hardly. If you make a spelling mistake, you don't plummet a hundred feet to your death."

"It levels out in another few yards. We're almost there. Can you feel the breeze?"

Yes, she could. It was fresh and cool.

The slope flattened, and they crawled. Thorn whooped from ahead.

A few moments later, he helped Lily to her feet. He spread out his arms. "Now how good am I?"

They were out. Stars and moonlight shone upon a vast ruined city and the sprawling nomad camp beside it. They smelled cooking fires and heard the sounds of drums and singing.

"Pretty good," said Lily, refreshing herself with deep breaths of night air. "Now be even better and go help my uncle."

# THIRTY-TWO

Thorn led them down the cliff, taking a steep, zigzagging path just wide enough for a mountain goat. Lily looked pale—paler than usual—as she gazed down, but she firmed up her lips and descended without complaint—though she did sigh loudly when she reached the bottom.

Sadly, Pan made it, too.

"The camp's right there," said Thorn. "They call themselves the Accursed."

"I've heard tales about them," said Lily. "Didn't know they were real."

Screams could be heard coming from Kismet's tent. There was only one reason for her to be making noises like that. "Looks like her baby's gonna make an early appearance."

Armed nomads approached, and the old crone, Kismet's mom. She waved the warriors back and gave Lily a once-over. "You must be the witch queen."

"Kismet will want to speak with her," Thorn said. "But seeing as she's busy right now, how about something to eat?"

The old woman replied with a curt laugh. "Kismet's done this before.

Give her an hour or two, and then we'll talk." She gestured to a nearby campfire. "That's yours."

"And him?" Thorn motioned to Pan.

The old woman glanced at him. "Chain him up."

Lily was about to argue, but Thorn stopped her. "This ain't the time nor place, Lily."

Glowering but saying nothing, Lily backed off.

They led Pan away, and Thorn headed straight to the campfire. K'leef was there, tending the flames. He got up and hugged Lily—a bit too tightly for Thorn's liking. Gabriel was asleep on the ground nearby, under thick blankets.

Thorn picked up a stick of the usual desert meal and handed it to Lily. She accepted it unenthusiastically. "It looks like a rat."

"Nothing wrong with your eyes." He took one for himself, and they all sat down. "How's Gabbs?"

"Alive. Spends most of his waking hours moaning about his mattress not being soft enough." K'leef opened a bag of dates and shared them. "Just gone to sleep now."

"And Hades?"

"See for yourself."

Hades was perched up on a ridge, his chest turned toward the moon. Clouds of bats swirled around him, but he ignored them. His eyes shone, two gleaming red beads. Thorn sighed. "He's homesick."

K'leef scooted closer to the two of them. "So what took you so long?"

Lily put down her half-eaten rodent. "My magic's not working."

"That's not possible," said K'leef. Then he looked uncertain. "Is it?"

"That's what I thought. That's what everyone thinks, but we're all wrong, K'leef. What happened to me also happened to Sa'if. His magic was stolen, and he didn't even realize it." She took his hand. "He didn't die by accident. He was murdered."

K'leef stared at her in shock and disbelief. "Who . . . ? How?"

Lily bit her lip. "I'm not sure how to tell you this. . . . I think it was Ameera."

Thorn watched his friend go pale. This battle for the lava crown was turning into a bloodbath for his family.

K'leef shook his head. "It can't be. You're wrong. Why would she—"

"She's a sorceress," Lily blurted. "So is Sami and, I suspect, many of your other sisters. Ameera's leading a coup. She wants the lava crown for herself."

"That's ridiculous!" said K'leef, his eyes blazing. "How could Ameera and the rest learn magic without anyone finding out?"

Lily looked at him. "I did."

Thorn threw aside his meat-stripped rat bones, keeping a rib to pick at his teeth. "She's your twin; her blood's the same as yours. Why shouldn't she be just as good at magic as you? What's the difference? Aside from being a girl?"

K'leef stood up and started pacing. "If it's true, then what am I supposed to do when I get back? Fight my own sister? I grew up with her!"

Thorn looked over to where Pan sat, chained to a thick post hammered deep into the ground. "Siblings fight more than most."

K'leef sank back down next to Lily. "When did you last use magic?"

"Shadow-stepping away from Ameera." She frowned. "It was a trap, K'leef. She invited me over. There was a foggy mirror. She wanted me to look into it."

K'leef frowned. "The mirror in Sa'if's room was foggy, too."

"Sounds like Capture Glass," said Gabriel, rolling onto his side to face them.

Lily threw her rat at him. "You've been listening this whole time?"

Gabriel smirked. "I was trying to sleep, but you have a particularly grating voice. No wonder the dead can't rest when you're around."

"Hold up, Lily. Don't hit him just yet." Thorn met Gabriel's cool gaze. "Capture Glass?"

Gabriel propped up his head with his hand. "It's old sorcery—no one knows how to make it now—but it used to be a punishment for sorcerers who broke the law. They faced the mirror, and the reflection took their magic. Made them . . . powerless."

Lily stifled a gasp. "Did they ever get their magic back?"

"They could get in front of the mirror again," said Gabriel. "Unless, of course, the mirror was broken. That was the worst punishment you could inflict on a sorcerer."

Lily's next question was barely above a whisper. "Then what happened?"

"They lost their magic." Gabriel yawned. "Forever."

# THIRTY-THREE

*N*o, no, no, no . . .

"You have to be wrong," said Lily. She grabbed Gabriel and shook him. "You have to be wrong!"

"Lily!" K'leef pulled her away. "Gabriel's wounds—they'll reopen."

Lily held her hands out in front of her. She stared at the shadows that swayed all around her. She stretched out her fingers. . . .

*Just one. If I can just hold one, then I won't care about anything else.*

Holding her breath, she slowly closed her hand.

*Just one. Please. Just one . . .*

The shadows danced, free of her.

Gabriel sat up on his elbows. "How does it feel, Lily? To be so . . . ordinary?"

"Shut up," snarled Thorn.

Lily felt like she was suffocating. Her heart pounded against her ribs; the blood rushing to her head made her dizzy. It was as if the ground were falling apart beneath her feet. "It can't be true."

Someone grabbed hold of her. Bewildered, it took her a moment to realize it was Thorn. "There's a way of solving this," he said.

She pulled away. "Oh, I didn't realize you were an expert in sorcery all of a sudden. Did you find the crown of the high king while you were wandering? That must be it!"

He grimaced under her sarcasm. "There *has* to be a way."

"Does there? You know that for certain?" She couldn't control the despair rising in her. "Tell me how you *know*, Thorn."

K'leef stood with them. "You can't give up hope, Lily. That's what Thorn means."

She closed her eyes. She wanted the world to stop swaying. "Yes, you're right. Hope. There has to be hope."

But what if there wasn't? What hope had there been for Sa'if?

*Stop thinking like that.*

She steadied herself before opening her eyes.

They were her best friends in the world. The boy from the Sultanate, so fine and handsome and clever, and Thorn. Rough, smelly, crude, and honest Thorn.

She smiled at them. "I'm sorry."

Thorn smiled back. "Yeah, I know."

K'leef dropped his voice. "Until we sort this out, it has to be our secret. No one must know what's befallen Lily. It could make our position . . . awkward. People fear and respect the witch queen, and we need that."

Thorn glanced down at Gabriel. "You hear that, Gabbs? Our secret."

The Solar boy made a sour face, but Lily knew he'd stay silent. His life depended on them.

Kismet's screams and moans gave way to an abrupt silence, and then the sudden wail of a newborn. The sound raised cheers and singing from the nomads. The old woman came out a few minutes later. She was tired but happy. "It's a boy."

Thorn winked. "I told you."

The old woman gave him a queer look. "Got some sorcery in your blood, eh?"

"What's his name?" Lily asked.

The old woman looked back at the tent. "Name? Let's see him survive a week or two first; then we'll think about a name. Kismet wants to see you."

"Shouldn't she be resting?"

The old woman laughed. "Girl, one day you'll learn there's no rest for mothers. Not with the first baby, not with the tenth. Go see her now while the baby's quiet. He's had a busy day."

Thorn hesitated. "I'll wait here."

"Kismet wants to see all of you, and that goes for your uncle, too."

They followed the old woman back to the tent.

They were changing the sheets on the bed. Kismet sat on one side, sweaty and flushed, but relieved, a small bluish baby feeding at her breast.

Lily gave one of her rings to Kismet. "May the Six bless your son with long life and good fortune."

The tent flap opened and in came Pan, shackled. A nomad pushed him forward. Pan smiled, wriggled off a ring of his own, and stepped forward. "May the Six—"

The nomad snarled and touched him with his spear.

Pan held out the small trinket. "A gift, for the newborn."

It was as if he was still a noble, delivering largesse to his people. It wasn't his right. But then, was it Lily's? She wasn't a sorcerer anymore. She was . . . just like Pan.

Sheets refreshed, Kismet settled back down in her bed, and one of her daughters rearranged the pillows while cooing over her new brother. Beneath Kismet's disheveled hair, Lily spotted the third eye twitching, looking this way and that.

What did it see? The Accursed were prophets, able to foretell the future. How far did Kismet's vision extend? Did she glimpse the mere shapes and hues of destiny, or something clearer? Could she envision a time when Lily would recover her magic?

Kismet spoke. "The camp is moving at dawn. Our location has been compromised."

"Where will you go?" asked Lily.

If Kismet knew—and Lily assumed she did—she wasn't saying.

"You could come with us," said K'leef. "I'm on a trial by fire, a quest to find a phoenix. If you help me, I'll make sure you're well rewarded."

Kismet smiled. "A phoenix? I'd like to see one of those. But you're talking about the deep Shardlands. The nomads don't venture there."

"Is it any worse than here?" Thorn asked. "I mean, we've met manticores already."

"Much worse."

"Do you know where the phoenixes nest?" asked K'leef.

Kismet shook her head. "It has been a long time since they appeared in any of our—"

"I know where they are," said Pan.

*No, no, no.*

But he had their attention now. That was why Pan came in here, acting so in charge: he was.

Pan stood in front of K'leef. "If I help you find them, what's my reward?"

"Don't trust him, K'leef!" Thorn pushed his way between them. "He's sworn to your brother. He'll run away the moment our backs are turned. If he doesn't murder us in our sleep first."

Pan sneered. "I wouldn't need to wait till you were asleep, boy."

"I'd like to see you—"

Pan pushed his nomad guard with one hand and stole a knife from him with the other. The point was at Thorn's throat before he could move.

Pan's sneer twisted to a wolfish smile. "See?"

"Let Thorn go, Uncle."

There was a tense moment when Lily thought Pan would open Thorn's neck, but then Pan flipped the knife over and handed it back to the embarrassed nomad. "As you command, Lady Shadow."

K'leef sighed with relief. "That little demonstration doesn't make me want to trust you, Earl Shadow."

"Trust? Why should I expect you to trust me? But you need me, and I need you. As much as I enjoy all this camping under the stars, I'm a man of stone and mortar, preferably castle-sized. You give me lands and a title, and I'll get you your phoenix."

Thorn rubbed his neck. "This the same deal you struck with Jambiya?"

"So what if it is?" Pan stuck his thumb out. "As far as I know, Jambiya's dead, a meal for those ghuls. I have no loyalty to dead men." He stepped into the center of the tent. "None of you know how to fight. I do. Without your maps, K'leef, you'll spend years wandering aimlessly. You need me."

Thorn still looked like he'd eaten something rotten. "And you need to get rich, be a noble once more. You'll have everything you lost."

"He'll never have a home," said Lily. "You can put him in a palace, but it'll never be home. He's lost that forever."

Was this all Kismet's doing? Lily knew the tales, of how the womenfolk of the Accursed would weave the destiny of others. They weren't about gazing into crystal balls and flipping over tarot cards; they were subtler than that.

Who was in charge? K'leef, Pan, or this woman with a newborn suckling at her breast? The fate of kingdoms was being manipulated, and not in a way Lily liked. They should refuse her uncle, but where would that leave them?

*Without a phoenix, that's where.*

K'leef looked into Lily's eyes. If she shook her head, he wouldn't make the bargain.

Feeling sick to her stomach, she nodded.

Pan smiled at her. "Together again, eh?"

Kismet laughed. "It seems you have a pact. Now get some sleep. Best you leave at dawn and try to get some miles done before noon."

The old woman cackled. "Ah, the Six bless this endeavor."

"Yeah. Great," said Thorn miserably.

Did Pan feel any pain or remorse? Did he suffer for what he did to her and her family? Had she made a mistake by merely exiling him? Out here there was danger in every direction, and yet they were relying on the very man who'd murdered her family, and tried to kill her.

"What's the route?" asked K'leef.

Pan gestured behind him. "We go south. There's a valley I know from a few years back. Once we're through that, we'll find your phoenixes, m'lord."

K'leef's eyes brightened. "What's beyond this valley?"

"Ruins. One of the capitals of the Old Kingdom."

Lily's heart skipped a beat. "Which capital?"

"You'll be pleased, Lily. We're going home. It's the city built by Prince Shadow himself." He smiled, but there was no amusement in it. "Necropolis."

# NECROPOLIS

# THIRTY-FOUR

"**K**ill the witch!"

The cries echoed from all around her, as if the castle itself demanded her death.

"Kill the witch!"

"I see her! Hurry, brothers!"

Lily ran through the empty corridors of Castle Gloom. "Someone help me!"

Where were they? There should have been servants and soldiers and maids all around, but the castle was empty.

"Help me!"

Howls rose up behind her. Howls and mocking, vicious laughter.

*They're coming!*

Lily turned the corner to the Great Hall, and there stood Mary. Thank the Six! She ran into her arms. "Mary . . ."

Her old nanny stroked her long hair. "Hush, child. Hush. I will take care of everything."

She was safe now. Mary always looked after her.

"Ow!" Lily cried. Mary had grabbed her hair and wound it into a rope. "Let go!"

"But, sweetness, you need to die," Mary said, smiling. "I did warn you it would come to this."

Lily fought against her. "Let go! Please, you have to!"

They were getting closer. She could hear their running feet.

Lily wove the shadows out of the dark corners. They fell around Mary, and the old woman cried out as they tore her away. "Lily! I love you, Lily!"

Lily sobbed as Mary disappeared. She hadn't wanted to do that, not to her. . . .

But she didn't have time to grieve; she needed to get away. She fumbled for the Skeleton Key and tapped it against the massive doors of the Great Hall. The demons and devils carved into the doors seemed to glare down at her, as if she didn't belong. But this was her home. She'd been born here. She had as much right to Castle Gloom as anyone. Why didn't they understand that?

The door resisted her, a final barrier to what was rightly hers.

"Open!" Lily screamed, beating her fists against the leering demons.

Every muscle straining, she managed to push the doors apart enough to slip through, but she didn't have the strength to close them behind her.

An empty throne awaited.

Next to it lay a crown, discarded on the floor.

Her crown.

It was a simple thing, made from bones, twigs, water, lightning, fire, and sunlight. She stumbled across the hall and gathered it in her hands, clutching it against her as she sank into the throne. She was too tired to go any farther.

And they entered.

Six of them. People she knew; people she loved.

Dante came first, sword in hand. "You shouldn't have run, Sister. Did you think you could escape all of us?" He stared at the crown, and greed flared in his gray eyes. He tightened his grasp on the sword. "Give that to me."

Lily held the crown closer. "It was given to me, Dante. Father picked me."

Then came Gabriel, in a shining white tunic studded with pearls. "He is an old fool, giving the crown to a *girl*."

"Girls have no right to rule. They are weak creatures of emotion," spoke the next, the red-robed K'leef. Flames licked across his skin.

"Help me, K'leef, I thought you were my friend," said Lily.

How could she fight them? She cared for them all. Yet they were acting like strangers. Dante, her brother, was threatening her with a sword.

"Hold her," said Ying, the Eagle Knight, dressed in a cloak of blue feathers.

"No!" Lily leaped up, but someone grabbed her wrists from behind. She twisted around and saw—

"Tyburn!" she cried. "Why?"

The grim executioner wrestled her back onto the throne. "It is my duty to protect the kingdom, m'lady."

"But I'm trying to make things better."

It was no use. Tyburn held her on one side, and a young man in shimmering scale armor held her on the other, trapping her arms, forcing her into the seat. She snarled at Tyburn. "So, are you going to kill me?"

"No. There is a new executioner."

Dante turned to the sixth boy. "Do your duty."

Thorn stepped through the doorway, wearing an outfit of green, his bow ever ready. He drew out an arrow.

"No, Thorn, you can't!" Lily begged, her heart breaking.

Thorn licked the feathers, taking all the time in the world, then nocked the arrow and pulled the bowstring back using his unique thumb draw. Their eyes met, and he smiled. "It's for the best, Lily."

He shot.

Lily gasped. She woke, heart pounding and hand clenched against her chest, the place where Thorn's arrow had struck.

Struck and killed her.

*They betrayed me. All of them.*

The very people she loved most in the world had conspired to kill her. And why? Because she was a girl. For no better reason than that. She had done no evil, harmed no one, yet she'd been sentenced to death for her gender.

*Because you are a witch.*

Lily got up, angry. It had been two days since they'd left the nomads, and her dreams were getting more vivid and more disturbing. The first night she'd dreamt of being chased, the faces of her pursuers obscure, the halls formless and insubstantial. Tonight, though . . .

Was it the Shardlands? Was the water she drank making her imagine things? No one could measure the amount of magic soaked in the soil, or radiating from the rocks.

Trails of multicolored lights wove across the sky to the south. She'd never seen anything like it. Wild magic so thick that it polluted the very air. How was it possible that a war from thousands of years ago could still leave its trace on the fabric of the world?

Surely, with all this magic around her, she could make something happen? But even as she began to stretch out her hand, Lily stopped herself. The disappointment of failing again would be too painful.

She pulled her woolen caftan closer around her shoulders. Kismet had given her a change of clothes, transforming Lily from a princess to a nomad. She liked the look. The boots were as well made as any from back home, and the tassels of her skirts swished as she walked. They'd strung a necklace of rat skulls for her, and wearing it made Lily feel *much* better. No outfit was complete without a few bones.

It was, of course, all black.

Thorn slept a few feet from her, arms spread out and face up to the stars as if trying to embrace them. K'leef lay a little farther off, snoring under his own blankets, his turban unwrapped and covering his eyes. Smoke rolled out between his lips. His magic was growing more powerful each day.

She thought back to her hideous nightmare. The tale of the high queen had infected her mind. The dream was her version of the tale, casting herself as the victim and those closest to her as her enemies.

These two were her best friends, and both had risked their lives for her. How could she think, even for a second, they'd betray her?

"Bad dream?" Pan sat against a rock, feeding the fire with twigs. His boots were off, but he still wore his armor. His sword lay beside him, blade bare. "Just like when you were little."

Lily's heart skipped a beat. The dream had left her feeling raw. If anyone would betray her, it would be Pan. But he was right—it *was* just like when she was little.

Mother and Father were always too busy to show much concern about her nightmares. And Mary, preoccupied with running the castle, made light of them. Lily was a Shadow—she couldn't suffer nightmares; she *made* nightmares. Pan, though, was sympathetic. So when she was scared, Lily went to her brave uncle, who would, dressed in full armor and sword resting beside him, sleep at her door. Only later did Lily realize how uncomfortable sleeping in armor could be, but she never had nightmares when he was protecting her.

That was a long time ago.

Lily sat opposite him and peered in the saucepan over the fire rock. There was enough hot chocolate left for a cup. She poured it.

Pan chuckled to himself. "What was that cuddly toy you were frightened of? Mrs. Fluffy?"

"Fluffykins," said Lily. "I thought she was trying to eat me. She had big teeth and would never stay in her box."

"You know that was Dante? He'd come in when you were asleep and put her at the foot of your bed. The boy was mischief. Whatever happened to that toy?"

"I took her for a swimming lesson in the moat," said Lily. "With a brick."

He laughed. "Isn't that what Duchess Hel did to her first husband?"

"First, third, and fourth. You'd think they would've learned their lesson sooner," said Lily. "Or at least drained the moat."

He gazed into the small fire. "I can't ask for your forgiveness, Lily."

"Good. I'll never give it."

Some things were unforgiveable.

"Have you spoken to Iblis? About . . . you know?"

"About how you murdered him, his wife, and his son?" snapped Lily. "Never. But I've seen the hideous, malformed specters that lurk in the Twilight for all eternity. Always hungry for something they'll never have. Crazed with hatred they can't get rid of. You know exactly what I mean. You summoned them, after all."

"I remember."

"You'll be one of them, sooner or later," she said. "And I won't forgive you then, either."

Lily thought she saw him shiver. As well he might. The Twilight was a bitter limbo with no comfort and no warmth.

"You were a hero once, Uncle. What happened?"

He looked at her and pain radiated from his eyes. "I honestly don't know." He cleared his throat gruffly, wanting to move on, like her. "Tomorrow we'll reach the outskirts of Necropolis. There's a street of tombs, but it'll be safe enough if we reach them early. Most have been emptied by tomb robbers over the centuries, and their occupants have been . . . dealt with. But the city itself, that's unexplored. We'll be relying on you from then on."

"Me?"

"You're the necromancer, Lily, not I." He flexed his fingers. "These were made for holding swords, not weaving spells. It's the city of death, so it'll need a Shadow to deal with it, a *real* Shadow."

"Uncle, I . . . I don't know. . . ."

"Is there any cocoa left?" Thorn came over, blanket over his shoulders, and squatted down next to her. He looked in the pot. "Go get us some, Pan. It's in the pannier, the one with the red tassels."

Pan got up. "The red tassels?"

"I think." Thorn's eyes narrowed. "Maybe one of the others. It may take a while to find."

Pan, still barefoot, walked off to the horses and the supplies. As soon as he was out of earshot, Thorn turned on her. "What were you thinking?"

"What?"

"Don't play all innocent with me, Lily. You were going to tell him you'd lost your magic."

She faltered, caught between denying it and realizing she'd been about to confess the truth to her uncle. "He'll find out the moment we face our first undead threat. Then what are we going to do? He's counting on my magic to see us through this."

Thorn scowled. "So far I've managed well enough without using a single spell. And we'll manage this, too."

"I can't do anything without magic, Thorn!" she snapped. "Nothing!"

"Poor you. Stuck with being normal like the rest of us. Boo-hoo. How will you ever survive?"

"Sarcasm doesn't suit you, Thorn."

"Maybe I need more practice? Anyway, we are here and we've got a job to do and we're going to do it. But don't think for a second that man over there is interested in anything but his own greed. You of all people know that!"

"But . . . but he's family, Thorn. You don't understand what he once was to me."

"I don't care about then. He's a mercenary now. The only reason he hasn't abandoned us is because he thinks he has a chance at fame and fortune in getting those flaming birds." Thorn glanced over. Pan was still busy searching the bags. "He's got no loyalty. The moment things turn tough, he'll be off, if he doesn't murder us first. He's here because he thinks you've still got your magic. If you want us to succeed, you've got to let him keep on believing that. Understood?"

"You're getting cunning in your old age, Thorn." Lily handed him her half-empty mug. "Lying didn't come so easily to you, once."

"I've learned it by hanging around nobles. My *betters*." He finished the hot chocolate. "That was sarcasm, too."

The four of them crossed the hard red earth with Hades soaring high above. Thorn rode between her and Pan, making sure the communication between her and her uncle was kept to a minimum. K'leef more often than not rode ahead, either to scout out the landscape or merely stay far away from the family feud. Lily sympathized—he'd have to deal with something worse once he returned to Nahas.

The sand had given way to sunbaked stone, and the wind sent scouring clouds of grit against them. Lily kept her eyes on the sky and the crackling storms on the horizon. The clouds rumbled and pulsed with vibrant colors, warning that it was no mere lightning at work, but the wildest of magics.

Time was fluid out here; it could be stretched and compressed. The limits of reality, fragile in the Shardlands already, could be more easily broken the deeper they went.

Mary had told her tales of adventurers who had ventured far into this unnatural wilderness, seemingly only for a week, and returned home to discover that a hundred years had passed and everyone they'd known was gone.

"Hold up." Thorn reined in his horse. "People ahead."

Lily shielded her eyes. "They're not moving."

"They're waiting for us?"

Lily spurred her horse forward. It ran lightly over the cracked surface, sure-footed and smooth, as was the way with all the horses of the Sultanate.

Hades flew overhead, circling the strangely quiet crowd that awaited them. It looked like there were hundreds of them. Most were on foot, but some sat on steeds that were just as motionless.

"Hello!" Lily cried from twenty yards away, pulling her horse to a walk. "My name is . . ."

Now she knew why they waited so patiently. They'd been waiting patiently for a long time and would continue to wait far into the future.

Thorn trotted up beside her. "Statues?"

A whole army of figures, of all types: male, female, adult, child, and elder. Some stood straight and impassive; others were twisted, their faces masks of pain and fear. Each fold, crease, wrinkle, and fingernail was perfect.

"Who made all these?" said Thorn. "And why leave 'em out here?"

Lily dismounted. "No one made them. These must be the Weeping Stones."

She stopped by a girl who was posed running, looking over her shoulder. She was holding a dog in her arms.

The figures were tall, elegant, and handsome. Their clothes weren't of today; they wore long flowing robes. Most men had tight beards, and the women were richly jeweled with rings, necklaces, and bracelets.

"They're people," said Lily. "Real people."

"Can't be. Look at 'em. People don't look like that. The men are almost seven feet tall!"

"They're from another age, Thorn."

Lily examined the girl's face. Her eyes were huge; the terror was obvious. What had she seen in that last moment before she'd been transformed into stone? How long had she been trapped like this?

Thorn gazed, too, horrified. "I once saw a druid turn a leaf to stone, but that was as much as he could manage, and he needed a jug of cider afterward. But this? Why do this to 'em? What was their crime?"

"Being on the wrong side."

Lily surveyed the rest. Thousands, all fleeing in one direction. They'd fled with just the clothes on their backs; there'd been no time to bring anything else. One man, strong-limbed and running, carried an old woman piggyback-style. She had her head buried in his long, wavy hair, and her thin fingers were digging into his shoulders. The man's face was a mask of grim determination.

"I'm glad that magic doesn't exist anymore," said Thorn. "I never realized how evil it was."

"It was war. People died. It happens now, too."

"Not like this. One spell—that's all it took." Thorn paused. "Are they dead? Or are they still in there somewhere?"

"The Six Princes were great men," said Lily. "They had the power to change the world."

"And look what they did to it."

"They were running away . . ." said Lily, more to herself than anyone. She peered into the distance, in the direction from which the statues were fleeing.

The direction they were headed.

K'leef joined them. "Do you want to turn back? I wouldn't blame you if you did."

They'd come too far by now, but there might be worse things ahead. Could she face them? What horrors of the past loomed in Necropolis?

Both boys waited for her answer.

"We need to stop Jambiya," she said finally.

Thorn gestured behind them. "He could be dead, killed at the Haunts. Who knows?"

"But then there's Ameera," Lily added. "She's killed Sa'if already. If you return home without a phoenix, she might use that against you, as proof that you don't have what it takes to be sultan."

Thorn stepped warily around one of the statues, as if he feared it might come back to life. "But if we keep going, we could end up like this bunch."

K'leef faced his friend. "You knew the risks, Thorn."

"There's a big difference between seeing a wolf's paw print and its teeth."

"So do you want to go back?" Lily asked.

"Me?" Thorn sighed and turned to face the way they'd come. "Y'know, hardly anyone leaves my village. You go more than ten miles from Stour and you're some great explorer. Now that I've left, I've got a hunger for seeing what's over the next horizon. I ain't stopping."

Lily took off her most precious ring, one studded with black diamonds, and placed it carefully on the girl's little finger. "I'm sorry. I hope you've reached a restful place."

"Why bother, Lily?" K'leef asked. "The sands will bury them soon enough."

Lily said nothing in reply, just remounted her horse.

They wove their way through the petrified crowd. K'leef was right; the desert was already claiming them. Some were already knee-deep in sand and would be submerged soon. Eventually it would be as though these people had never existed.

Lily was determined not to allow that. She looked at the face of each one she passed, fixing it in her memory. The Gehennish honored the dead by remembering them. She would do the same for this strange, abandoned throng. There was not enough jewelry on her to gift them all, but she gave them her shining tears.

# THIRTY-FIVE

Thorn trotted his horse up to K'leef, keeping a wary eye on the two Shadows. "Lily's upset."

"Understandable, given the situation."

"Shouldn't we do something?"

K'leef frowned. "Like what?"

Thorn tried to sound oh-so-casual. "We could . . . misplace Pan?"

"Thorn . . ."

He sighed. "Would this be a matter of honor? If it is, I don't want to hear it. All I'm saying is Lily's been crying, and it's because of her uncle."

"I'm not entirely sure it's just because of him. We're headed to Necropolis, the heart of Prince Shadow's kingdom."

"I always thought he was born and raised in Gehenna."

K'leef slowed down so he could search for signs of phoenixes around the crags and boulders. He pointed ahead. "See those ruins?"

"Yeah. So?"

"This is the Old Kingdom. The Six Princes were born here, in palaces that have been lost to age and destruction so all that remains are those broken buildings. Places like Castle Gloom and Nahas are merely poor replicas of what the Old Kingdom was. It's here that mankind learned magic. Prince Shadow only went to Gehenna afterward."

"After he and his brothers destroyed all this, right?"

K'leef frowned the same way Lily did when anyone criticized their ancestors. "This is where the six brothers were taught magic by their otherworldly mother."

"The elf queen," said Thorn. That's the story he knew. "And Herne was her favorite."

"She was a desert spirit," stated K'leef. "As anyone within a thousand miles of here will tell you, it was Djinn who was her best student. And we're not going to discuss this anymore."

Right. Everyone had their own opinion, depending on where they were from. The people of House Coral believed she'd been a mermaid, captured in the high king's nets when he was nothing but a penniless fisherman. Lily was convinced she'd been a demoness of some sort. In the end, what difference did it really make? But everyone wanted to believe they were more special than everyone else. Grandpa had a saying for that, but Thorn didn't reckon it was suitable for K'leef's delicate ears. "So, what was this Necropolis like?"

K'leef settled himself more comfortably in his saddle, which Thorn envied. His own backside was aching something awful, and his inner thighs felt like they'd been scrubbed with sandpaper. "After the high king died, as all mortals do, his kingdom was divided among his six sons. Necropolis was Prince Shadow's capital. Like all the magic capitals, it was splendid. People passed easily back and forth across the Veil. Death itself had been conquered. They say it was imprisoned in a hole under Prince Shadow's throne of bones."

"Sounds uncomfortable," Thorn replied, trying to find an unbruised part of his buttocks to rest upon. "But you're being poetic, ain't you?"

"Poetic?"

Thorn brightened. "It's like the song, 'The Old Duke's Longsword.' What it's really about is—"

"It's better in the original Djinnic. Here it's 'The Old Sultan's Scimitar.' You see, it's bent in a funny way, and no one can make it straight." It was hard to tell, but it looked like K'leef was blushing.

"Interesting variation. Anyway, K'leef, as you were saying, Death's in this pit. . . ."

"Yes. In the pit. So, the Six-Sided War broke out between the brothers. They all wanted the high king's crown. Prince Coral drowned cities under his tidal waves. Prince Herne split the world open with massive earthquakes, and my ancestor burned the very clouds. But as more people died, Prince Shadow's armies grew greater and greater. Everyone the other princes killed became another soldier in his battalions. He had ranks upon ranks of not only undead, but also other creatures of darkness. He had summoned great demons, terrifying devils, and—"

"Devils and demons? Ain't they the same?"

"No, very different," said K'leef.

"How?"

"No one's ever found out and survived. Still, very different. Hasn't Lily explained all this to you? Castle Gloom was built by demons, under the command of the prince. But the last to have a demonic servant was Telane Shadow. I think he took her as his bride. Didn't work out. Marriage is a tricky enough business for mortals."

All this talk made Thorn's skin grow cold. He was just about used to the undead that lurked in every dark corner of Castle Gloom, but he wasn't sure he could stand the idea of demons and their like. "The Shadows are strange, ain't they?"

"But that's what's so appealing, isn't it?" K'leef glanced back at Lily. "They fascinate us."

Thorn kicked K'leef's boot to get his attention off her. "Back to the war, K'leef? Tell me about Prince Shadow."

"It looked as though he was going to win. So the other five formed a temporary truce and went after him."

"One against the rest? That hardly seems fair."

K'leef glanced at him. "You hunt bears with one dog, or a pack?"

"Neither. Poor use of dogs. We hunt bears with these." Thorn patted his quiver. "But I see your point. One arrow ain't usually enough for a bear."

K'leef continued. "They were about to corner him here, in his capital. Think about it. This was Prince Shadow's home. His wife and children all lived here. He knew what his brothers would do to them if they were taken alive."

A shiver traveled up Thorn's spine. "Let me guess: Death before dishonor?"

K'leef nodded. "When his brothers rode in, their victory was a hollow one indeed. There was not one person still alive, except for Prince Shadow, lonely and heartbroken on his throne. The pit underneath was empty. He'd freed Death and unleashed it on his own people. He wanted to die himself, to be with his family on the Far Shore, but Death has a cruel sense of humor, it seems, and did not take him. Death wanted Prince Shadow to forever feel the pain of losing everyone he loved. That's when the prince went into exile, far away to the very ends of the earth."

"Gehenna." That made sense; it was the most forsaken place in the New Kingdoms.

K'leef cleared his throat. "That's the story I know. And that's why you don't want to be in Necropolis when the sun goes down."

"I ain't sure I want to be there at all."

K'leef stopped and pointed ahead. "Look."

Thorn squinted. "What?"

"There! Did you see it?"

What was he . . .

A line of fire slashed the clouds, just above the horizon, then winked out. A moment later, he saw it again—it trailed in a long, winding spiral, rising up and dipping before vanishing again.

"Is that what I think it is?"

Hades swooped overhead, crying out a challenge. He beat his wings, angry that there was an intruder in the sky, *his* sky.

The flames burst out again, fiercer than before, and changed colors beyond the red and yellow to pure white and eye-aching blue.

"We've found them," whispered K'leef, awestruck. "We've found the phoenixes."

# THIRTY-SIX

"**S**o that's Necropolis?" said Thorn, squinting into the distance. "It don't look like much from here."

He glanced around. No one was listening but Hades. And he wasn't sure about Hades, either. The big bat's attention was on the fiery trails left by the phoenixes. One lip rose in a sullen snarl.

The others were back down the slope, drawing in the sand.

"Hey! I was just sayin' that the city—"

"Whatever," snapped Lily. She sat on her haunches, focusing on the crude map before her. "I don't think the Avenue of Horror runs beside the Heartache Canal. I remember it being more west." She used a long bone to redraw the route. "This way."

K'leef scowled. "My maps were more up-to-date than your storybooks, Lily. The Ruby Warlock said the canal went south, not west. Past the Temple of the Dead Gods."

Pan shook his head. "The Ruby Warlock was a fool and a liar. The nomads said he never went more than a day's ride from Nahas. Would sit out, enjoy their hospitality for a month or two, then come back with some new wild tale."

Flames crossed K'leef's forehead. "The Ruby Warlock is a famous ancestor of mine. He's one of the greats."

"One of the great charlatans," said Pan. He took the bone and drew a deep line across the others. "The canal cuts this way—past the towers. That's how you'll get your phoenixes, young man."

Thorn peered over Lily's shoulder. Lines crisscrossed everywhere. "Why don't I just—"

"Just a moment, Thorn." Lily laid out three rocks. "But we can all agree that the Skull Towers are here, yes?"

"No," said K'leef, glaring at Pan. "The Ruby Warlock, famed throughout the New Kingdoms as one of the *greatest explorers ever*, swore the Skull Towers had been demolished. That pile to the east is the Catacomb of Exiles, not the Skull Towers."

"Look," interrupted Thorn. "I could—"

Pan pointed at a stone. "Wait, is that the Gate to the Path of Misfortune, or the Hallowed Hall of Countless Horrors and Three Delights?"

"Neither. It's just a pebble." Lily picked it up and threw it aside. "Sorry."

He'd had enough. Thorn stepped over Lily onto the middle of the map. "Me and Hades will take a look."

Lily stood up and brushed the sand off her skirt. "Why didn't you say so earlier? Honestly, Thorn . . ."

K'leef clapped him on his shoulder. "I knew I brought you here for a reason."

"Yeah? I thought I came just for fun."

"This is where you belong, Thorn. When certain death looms and the kingdom's all in peril and disaster's on the horizon."

"It don't sound so much fun when you put it that way." Thorn gazed over to the faint line of wall and the trails of light above it. They were still many miles away, but there was no missing the dancing comets of fire.

How many birds were there? At least two, maybe more.

"Hades and I might be able to find them," he said, "but how are we gonna hold 'em?"

The cage had disappeared along with the thieving servants, and Thorn couldn't think of any other way to trap a phoenix.

"There's no turning back now." K'leef turned his hands over, and flames wrapped through his fingers. "First find them; then we'll come up with a plan for keeping them."

Hades hissed through his nostrils. Those small red eyes of his kept watch on the flames cutting the sky.

Thorn stroked the big beast's furry chest. "They bother you, huh?"

Hades stared down at him.

"Not used to someone else ruling the skies?" teased Thorn.

Hades gave him a closer look at his immense fangs. He didn't find Thorn's comment funny.

Lily and Pan approached. She looked over at the far walls. "Just take a quick look around, then come right back. Find out which tower the phoenixes nest in."

What were the two of them up to? Was she taking Pan's advice? "You asking me or ordering me, Lady Shadow?"

She frowned. "You're an idiot," she said, and walked off.

Thorn bristled. What had he said? Nobles—nothing they did made any sense.

"She's right. You are an idiot," said Pan.

"If I want your opinion, I'll ask. And guess what? I'll never ask."

Pan didn't leave. Instead he stared at Thorn, as if trying to read what was going on behind his eyes. "That chip on your shoulder will grow heavier until it breaks you, or you drop it. This comes from a man who knows."

"Like I said, I'm not interested in your opinion, Pan. I can call you Pan, can't I? You're not a lord or nothing anymore, are you?"

Pan scowled. "No one has stepped in Necropolis for thousands of years.

We don't know what might be lurking in there. So be careful. If there's a hint of trouble, get out."

"I know how to look after myself." He patted the bat's cheek. "Ready, Hades?"

He leaped up into position. Ah, now this was better. "I'll be back in an hour."

⁓

Hades picked up the heat rising off the sunbaked stone and rose in wide, languid circles to gain some height.

The Shardlands. Who would have thought, even a year ago, he'd end up here? Last spring, he'd been back in Herne's Forest, heading out with Dad before dawn with bows, axes, and a handful of traps. Sometimes one of his siblings would come along, too. Usually it was Pagan, who was the next oldest, and sometimes it was Heather—she had a gift for finding trails and the choicest forest mushrooms and berries. But more often than not, it was just the pair of them.

Did he miss those days? Would he want to go back to how it used to be?

Thorn grinned. What? And lose the chance to fly on the greatest animal there ever was? And to see all this? He rubbed Hades in his favorite spot, right between his big ears. Hades growled contentedly.

All right, Necropolis was bigger than he'd thought.

A whole lot bigger.

The city sprawled. The hills he'd thought were at the far edge were actually a line of palaces; Necropolis stretched on and on after that. There were squares and roads and palaces spreading far beyond the main walls. You didn't see that very often nowadays. People preferred to live within walls for safety. Even his hometown, Stour, had a ditch and simple hazel hurdle fence surrounding it.

That told him there had been peace here, for a long time.

The streets were wide, the houses magnificent, the statues and columns gigantic and, even after all this time, breathtaking in their grandeur. Hades skimmed over a row of crouching stone scorpions, each one sitting on a plinth over thirty feet high, their stingers arching over the road, poised as if to strike an unwary traveler. The black stone was pitted by age and the elements, yet it still sparkled.

He understood Lily a bit better now, seeing the home of her ancestor. No wonder she always spoke of Prince Shadow with such awe, and why she struggled to find any fault in him. How could you not be proud?

The nobles of the New Kingdoms lived in the shadow of giants: the Six Princes. No matter how much they achieved, their accomplishments were small compared to the sorcerers of the past. How must that feel, knowing the best was all behind you?

That wasn't the way he lived. When he wasn't hunting with his dad, he was busy in the garden with his mom and the rest of his brothers and sisters. There was good coin working in the local farms, too. Planting in the spring, reaping in the fall.

Things *grew* where he came from. Today it might be nothing but a handful of seeds, but tomorrow promised golden stalks and mighty oak trees. He'd been raised looking for the riches in his future, not looking back at ancient glories.

They flew over the walls into the heart of Necropolis.

Giants had to have lived here. The towers were double the height of the Needle, narrower and more elegant, too, with hundreds of gargoyles roosted on each. Bridges as thin as knives arched between them, hundreds of feet above the ground, and Lily's Great Hall could have fit inside any one of the palaces twice over. The ground was not covered by mere cobblestones or flagstones, but wild, endless mosaics that formed weird, mesmerizing patterns of dark and light.

Lily had a word for this kind of architecture: sinister. Like Castle Gloom, which was meant to frighten visitors. It made your skin turn cold, and the hairs on the back of your neck rise up. Despite its lack of windows, the place was drafty, and a chill breeze would raise goose bumps, made all the worse by the suspicion that it was the breath of a passing ghost.

You got used to it, mostly.

There was so much to see here, it made Thorn's head spin. He needed to explore at ground level, where he could concentrate on the details. The view from up high was too overwhelming.

"Let's settle down there," he said, nudging Hades in the side with his left knee. Hades resisted.

*He wants to go after the phoenixes.*

"No, not yet. We're to keep out of trouble, understand?"

The bat swooped, and a few moments later, his claws clinked on the black shoulders of a toppled statue.

Thorn counted out his arrows and double-checked his bow. The bone-tipped arrows were standing up to the travels better than he'd feared. None had chipped—a common problem with bone; each remained needle-sharp.

Thorn addressed Hades. "Let me look around a bit. You just stay here, and *don't touch anything.* Got it?"

Hades blinked. He got it.

Thorn set off.

Wind moaned through the arches, dragging along dust and a chill ambience. Thorn shivered. It felt as if he were being watched, but there was no one lurking in the empty doorways or peering through the narrow, tall windows. He thought he caught a glimpse of someone just beyond the dark wall opening, but it turned out to be a shadow created by the shifting clouds.

Over time, magic had deteriorated. Today's sorcerers were like infants compared to those who had built all this.

He thought back to the frozen statues out in the desert. Maybe being smaller and weaker was better. Today's sorcerers couldn't cause such widespread damage.

His arrow nocked, Thorn crept along the silent, ancient streets. That spot between his shoulder blades itched—as if there were eyes upon it—but the only company was the wind, which whispered eerie, fractured threats and malevolent promises.

The wind also carried with it the sharp sting of the Devil's Breath, the deadly gas he'd encountered back in the desert. It seeped up through the cracks and crevasses that scarred the city, and Thorn wondered if, given Necropolis's history, there was a simpler reason it was called the Devil's Breath.

Thorn spun at a groaning noise, the bowstring drawn to his cheek, but it was just a door swinging on its rusty hinges. He paused at the doorway and peered in.

They looked like mounds of silk at first. After his eyes adjusted to the semidarkness, he realized what they really were: skeletons covered in dusty cobwebs.

They knelt in a circle, still holding hands. Two bigger people—the parents—facing each other, and two children between them. Their once-fine clothes were now moldy rags, but each of them wore enough jewelry to buy Thorn ten acres of rich farmland and the livestock to fill it. The woman's bracelet alone would get him a dozen sheep with change.

*She don't need it.*

Yet nothing could tempt Thorn to cross that threshold, no matter how big his eyes grew at the treasure scattered a few feet inside. The plates of silver and gold, the gem-encrusted books, all so near, but untouchable.

He'd been in Gehenna long enough to know the dangers of robbing the dead.

On he went.

Yet there was some activity, of sorts, within Necropolis. The fountains gurgled. The aqueducts that crisscrossed the city still brought water down from some reservoir up in the mountains. It wouldn't take much to make this place habitable. There was water; there was shelter. Yet nothing grew here. Life shunned it.

Except the phoenixes.

They flew directly overhead, filling the shadowy streets with their fiery light. It seemed very wrong that they, creatures filled with brilliance, would nest here, in so lonely a place.

He watched as a pair of them spiraled around each other, one blazing with orange and gold, the other blue and white, their flames entwining as they headed toward a lone tower. They blew flames over its roof until it glowed; then they settled down.

*So that's their nest.*

Thorn scanned ahead. It seemed clear, so off he went. Down this street, across that square, along the edge of a park, the fiery tower always in sight.

How far was it? It looked so close! Was this more wild magic? Maybe the city wasn't measured by normal means. He glanced back, hoping he'd be able to find his way back to Hades. It was getting darker, and the others were waiting for him.

He reached the phoenix tower and looked up and up and up and up.

The summit of the tower glowed like a volcano. Thorn felt the heat even down here. Then he caught sight of something shiny among the debris on the ground.

It was a curved piece of gold.

*Now that'll come in handy.*

Thorn reached for it, then yelled as he touched the metal.

It was burning hot!

He sucked his fingers until they stopped pulsing.

Gold was gold, and this piece obviously didn't belong to anybody. He wasn't going to leave it.

Smaller pieces lay around, all each equally hot to the touch. Thorn undid his turban and wrapped up a few. The cloth smoked. He stole one final glance at the tower, then ran, cradling the treasure against his chest.

They'd lost the phoenix cage, but Thorn had something better.

A plan.

# THIRTY-SEVEN

"**W**hat do you think?" Thorn unraveled his find dramatically. The gold pieces clattered on the ground, hissing when they touched the cooler stone.

Lily, Pan, and K'leef gathered around.

Hands on hips, Thorn smiled. "Well?"

K'leef whispered over his open palms, then picked up a small piece. His fingers smoked, but whatever magic he was using prevented them from getting burnt. "Strange. Gold doesn't usually retain heat this long, not without melting. And the curves . . . Is it a vase?"

Thorn grinned. "Guess again."

Lily leaned over K'leef's shoulder. "Some bowl? A container of sorts?"

"Yeah." Thorn clapped. "It's an eggshell."

K'leef still didn't get it. "So?"

"So I saw the phoenixes blowing flames over their nest. Keeping it warm. Our chickens do the same thing by sitting on their eggs—keeping 'em warm till they hatch. So this piece of shell tells me there's at least one chick up there, and I reckon there's another at least. Why catch a live phoenix when we can grab an egg instead?"

K'leef's eyes lit up. "Take that home, wait for it to hatch, and we've done it."

"Exactly. We pop it in a furnace or something until it cracks. Then you'll have your phoenix and the lava crown. As easy as that."

Pan interrupted. "Phoenixes only lay every hundred years. You can bet this pair won't let us just grab one of their precious eggs and ride off."

"You're right," said Thorn, enjoying this. "So we'll need you to make a distraction while I swoop in with K'leef. Hades can carry the both of us, as long as it ain't too far."

"What's that supposed to mean?" snapped K'leef.

Thorn glanced at the boy's rotund frame. "It means you can either fly or have double-helpings at meals, but not both."

K'leef patted his belly. "It's just reserves."

Pan was standing, looking over at the city. "You want me to play tag with a pair of phoenixes?"

"Yup."

Lily had her not-amused face on. "They'll kill him."

"Probably," agreed Thorn. "So?"

Lily's not-amused face became an angry face. "We need a better plan."

"There ain't one, and time's running out. Look at the sun, Lily. Only another few hours till sunset, and we need to be long gone from here by then."

The shadows were lengthening, quicker than they liked.

"What about me?" Lily asked.

Thorn grimaced. "You stay here."

"Where it's safe?" said Lily.

"If you put it like that, then, yeah. Where it's safe."

Her eyes narrowed. "And why should I do that?"

"Because you shouldn't be here in the first place, Lily!" he snapped. "K'leef's after a crown, your uncle's after fame and glory, and I'm here . . . that doesn't matter. You were supposed to stay back in Nahas."

"Until Ameera tried to assassinate me. Or don't you remember?"

K'leef looked ashamed. "I'll take care of her when we get back."

Thorn wasn't finished. "You're the ruler of a kingdom; assassins are an occupational hazard. You've dealt with them before. Hasn't she, Pan?"

Pan didn't rise to the bait. "Thorn's right. You best wait here, Lily."

Thorn wasn't proud of himself, but he knew Lily was trapped. What he didn't want to do was blame it on her magic, or lack of it. Even if she were up to full strength, what good would it do her here? This was Necropolis, thick with magic beyond the abilities of any sorcerer alive. If anything went wrong, her spells wouldn't make a difference.

Thorn turned to the others. "Come on. We're running out of time."

K'leef nodded. "I'll use my magic to dampen down the heat from the nest. As long as the phoenixes aren't around, we should be able to grab an egg."

Pan handed Thorn his quiver. "You've got this all planned out, haven't you?"

"It ain't the first time I've stolen eggs out of a nest."

Pan picked up Thorn's bow. "Is there any end to your talents, young Thorn?"

"Give me that."

Pan held it aloft. "Such a simple weapon—so crude, yet so powerful. A piece of wood, some string . . ."

The bowstring twanged apart.

"Oops," said Pan.

"You broke it on purpose!"

Thorn yelled and swung the bow at Pan, but he sidestepped and shoved Thorn off his feet.

Pan put his boot on Thorn's chest and sword tip to his throat.

"Either of you try something and the boy dies," Pan stated.

Flames licked K'leef's angry brow. "What's the point of all this?" he asked.

He didn't need to wait more than a few seconds before the point revealed itself.

Thorn cursed, and K'leef stumbled back as the men came out of hiding. They seemed to emerge out of the sand itself, or crawl from between the rocks and broken buildings. Seven nomads of the Scorpion tribe, armed and itching for them to try something stupid. The nomads looked like they had suffered. Some were injured; all had taken a battering.

Jambiya entered the camp, tapping his way over the rubble. "Well done, my friend."

Thorn glared at Lily. The mightiest "I told you so" waited on the very tip of his tongue.

Lily looked up at her uncle, her own gaze as cold as midwinter ice. "Traitor." She slapped him.

How could they have let this happen? Thorn should have done something when he had the chance! Now all he could do was lie helpless in the dirt.

Then Hades joined in.

# THIRTY-EIGHT

Add a giant bat to any fight and what you get is chaos. The wings covered over fifty feet, and the small camp was engulfed.

While all eyes were on Hades, Lily acted.

She barged into one of the nomads, grabbing for his sword, a move so unexpected he practically dropped it into her hand.

There was a high-pitched scream and a very unpleasant crunch that sounded a lot like the noise a head might make if it got itself between the jaws of a giant bat. A moment later, Lily ducked as the decapitated corpse of one of the Scorpion tribesmen went flying past.

Messy, but predictable.

Other people might be squeamish around a headless body, but Lily was Gehennish, born and bred. She had learned to sew by practicing on old One-Eyed Ron, the family zombie.

No one paid attention to her, not with Hades trying to snack on Jambiya.

An arch of flame burst up around them. Lily spun away from it and swung the sword wildly side to side, almost toppling over with the weight of it.

*What am I doing?*

"Hades!" she yelled. "Grab Thorn!"

Thorn tried to run past the two nomads blocking him. "I'm not going without you!"

"Hades! Take Thorn!"

The bat wanted to fight, but he was clumsy on the ground. Now that the shock was over, the nomads had him surrounded. Sooner or later, one of them would get a spear or sword into him, with or without the help of Jambiya's magical flames. Hades shrieked, snapped, and swiped with his wings, but he wasn't going to win this.

"Hades!" Lily commanded once more. "Take Thorn!"

The bat buffeted one of the Scorpion tribesmen aside, snatched Thorn's collar in his teeth, and beat down once, a huge thrust that smothered them with stinging sand.

"No!" Thorn yelled. "Put me down!"

A few seconds later, they were far out of range of the spears, arrows, and fiery blasts.

"Run, Lily!" K'leef shouted. "I'll hold them back!"

He'd summoned a wall of fire, over ten feet tall and bonfire-intense. The magic soaking the Shardlands was feeding K'leef's power.

But it was feeding Jambiya's, too.

Lily hesitated, trapped between loyalty to her friend and the wisdom of his words.

Who was stronger out of the two brothers? She didn't know.

And who was the more ruthless?

That she did.

As if to prove her point, K'leef started backing off. He didn't want to hurt his brother, while Jambiya was going for the kill. Any second now, K'leef would hesitate, drop his guard . . .

She grabbed him. "We are leaving!"

"Lily!" yelled K'leef. As he stumbled backward, he threw out one final blaze. The entire camp combusted. The nomads dove for cover, and even Jambiya, immune to flames through his own magic, gasped as his robes caught fire.

"That'll keep him busy for a while," K'leef said, trying to suppress a grin.

They ran, Lily leading the way. The ruins grew denser as they headed toward the city itself. Lily glanced back, fearing pursuit, but she saw no one. They didn't stop until they'd been running for ten minutes.

Both of them collapsed, panting hard. Lily caught her breath first. "That was amazing. A full fire wall! Remember when you could hardly light a candle?"

"I think I'm going to be sick."

Lily sprang up onto a boulder as flames poured out of K'leef's mouth. He vomited fire for a good minute, then finally burped out a cloud of smoke. "Sorry."

She didn't get down. "You finished?"

"I've burned my boots." He wiggled his now bare toes.

Lily peeked over the side of a wall. It didn't look like anyone had spotted K'leef's little bonfire of sick, but it was probably a good idea to keep moving. "Let's go."

"But the stones are sharp, Lily!"

"Stop it. You're sounding like Gabriel." She pulled off his turban and tore it in half. "Wrap up your dainty little toes."

"I can't believe we escaped," said K'leef as he set to binding.

"Jambiya captured me once already. No way was I going to allow it a second time." Lily clambered to the top of a statue to have a look. She couldn't see Hades or Thorn anywhere. "I'm not one of those helpless princesses."

K'leef laughed. "No, you certainly aren't."

By the Six, she hated those stories! The ones with a simpering princess, an evil witch—usually one of her relatives—and a heroic prince or a handsome peasant who thought, just by killing the monster, he basically got to own the idiot princess. There were never enough zombies in those tales, and if they did appear, they were always villains!

Real life wasn't like that at all. Take K'leef, who was a prince but didn't look like he was capable of saving anyone right now. Peasantwise there was Thorn, but he was no one's idea of handsome.

She made a much more interesting heroine. The witch queen who lived with the undead, conversed with her father's ghost, and kept her brother in an eternal sleep in a tall tower covered with cobwebs. All true, as it happened.

K'leef's face clouded as he looked behind them. "You didn't see Farn, did you?"

With all that had happened, it was only now that she realized the efreet hadn't been part of the ambush. "It would be too much to hope it had been destroyed, somehow?"

"Only way I know of putting out an efreet is by chaining it to an anchor and sinking it a thousand fathoms deep."

So was Farn lurking out there somewhere?

Why was nothing easy? Just for once?

"My fires aren't going to keep Jambiya and Pan at bay for long," K'leef said. "Nothing's going to stop them from completing this quest—and trying to kill us."

"You got a plan for catching a live phoenix?" asked Lily.

He shook his head. "I bet Thorn's grandpa would have something to say about this predicament."

"This would have never happened if I'd been allowed to bring Tyburn."

K'leef scowled. "And you know as well as anyone that bringing your own executioner to a foreign kingdom is illegal."

"But still." Lily sighed. "Could you imagine it? Seeing him come strolling over that hill right now?"

They both looked over at the hill. No one came. Strolling or otherwise.

"Oh, well." Why was she was still holding the nomad's sword? She dropped it in a crevasse. "I'd settle for Baron Sable. He taught my uncle how to sword-fight."

"Who was better?"

"If you had asked me six months ago, I would have said the baron, no question. But now?"

"Mary would sort this mess out," said K'leef. "Send Jambiya to bed without supper."

They were without any of their allies. The only one within in a thousand miles was a stubborn peasant boy. . . .

Lily gazed over at Necropolis. "What do you think Thorn's going to do?"

K'leef's black hair fell to his shoulders in soft ringlets, and Lily almost laughed. He was actually quite beautiful. A funny thing to think of, right here, right now. But maybe you needed to look for the smallest good things even in the worst situations. "I don't mean this as an insult," K'leef said, "but Thorn's not that clever, is he?"

"True. But he has a ridiculous amount of courage. You might even say too much."

K'leef nodded. "So he's going to do something brave but foolish. Agreed?"

They both looked off at the distant, fire-lit tower.

"He's going after the phoenix egg," said K'leef.

"We need to stop him."

"How?"

She frowned. "I'm merely listing our problems. Solutions will present themselves. At some point."

"Better be some point soon. According to the Ruby Warlock, one should never linger in Necropolis after dark."

"Did he say why?"

"No, because he didn't linger to find out."

"Now that's as useless as one of Thorn's grandpa's sayings." The tower looked to be miles away. "How much do you want those eggs, K'leef?"

He spat sooty phlegm on the ground. "I wish I'd never gone on this stupid quest."

"Then let's forget about it and go home. We'll find some other way of keeping Jambiya off the throne. But first we have to get Thorn."

# THIRTY-NINE

"**P**ut me down, you smelly lump of fur!"

Hades did not obey. He carried Thorn higher, and farther, from his friends.

"We can't leave them, Hades!"

Thorn wriggled in the bat's grip, not caring that he was hundreds of feet above ground. He couldn't just abandon them! "Let go, Hades!"

Hades squeezed his claws another inch deeper into Thorn's shoulders.

"Ow! That hurts!"

But he stopped wriggling, and Hades took the pressure off.

And they flew.

"Let me up," he said. "I'm tired of hanging here like one of your sheep."

Hades opened one claw, and Thorn swung over to the bat's side. Balancing on the bat's curled leg, he hoisted himself swiftly up onto Hades's back, right between his shoulder blades.

"I should have sold you to the circus when I had the chance."

Hades snorted in reply. He knew Thorn too well to take his threats seriously. Thorn knew him, too. He couldn't imagine life without the smelly old bat.

Thorn shuffled forward and rested his elbows just above Hades's neck. "I guess we can't head back. Jambiya will have his archers on the lookout for us."

So what *could* he do? There was no way he would abandon Lily and K'leef, and no way he could beat Jambiya. But at least he still had Hades, his bow, and, oh, a handful of arrows. He pulled the spare bowstring from his boot and restrung his weapon.

Hades began to circle.

"You tired?" Thorn should have realized sooner. Hades hadn't eaten a proper meal in days, and Thorn had been pushing him too hard. They settled down in the ruins.

A mournful wind swept across the ancient flagstones, and the black iron statues groaned on their high plinths. They were pitted with rust yet proud. He'd seen statues like this back in Castle Gloom, in the Shadow Library. Huge, otherworldly, and inhuman. He must appear like a mouse in comparison, and that grated on him. People shouldn't be made to feel so . . . small.

Sure, there were bigger oaks in Herne's Forest. Grandpa said there was one, deep in the heart of Herne's Forest, so tall it held up the sky.

But an oak had earned it, starting off as a minute sapling, then spending centuries rising, surviving bitter winters and blistering summers, the floods and the droughts to become what it was. An oak had a right to be proud.

*You've been away from home too long.*

Home. Where was that? Herne's Forest, or Castle Gloom? Both were thousands of miles away.

Nothing grew here, nor had anything in hundreds of centuries. The soil was bitter and lifeless. It wasn't merely dead but seeping with a hatred of the living. That intuition made his skin crawl. Thorn had spent countless days lying on cool grass, gazing at clouds drifting by and listening to bees buzzing from flower to flower. His dad had once said that if Thorn listened carefully he would hear the roots growing deep into the earth, and when that happened, he'd have learned all there was to know about the forest. Thorn had lain there, ear pressed down, trying to understand the secrets of all green things.

What secrets were there here? What wisdom?

Thorn grunted. None he could see or hear. If they had been wise, they wouldn't have destroyed themselves.

And over what? A crown. A mere circlet of metal that any blacksmith could have knocked out in an afternoon. He never understood why people wanted to mind other people's business when there weren't enough hours in the day to mind their own.

Look at Lily. More and more she was getting others to do the things she should be doing because she was too busy getting involved in the affairs of others. Others who might not appreciate her involvement. This whole trip was a perfect example. She should have stayed in Castle Gloom and he with her.

"Leave the crowing to the cockerel."

Hades rustled his wings.

"Just one of Grandpa's sayings," said Thorn, brushing grit out of one of the leathery folds.

Hades sneered. It seemed he didn't think much of his grandpa, either.

All this pondering was getting him nowhere. He needed to save K'leef and Lily. They weren't capable of saving themselves. Lily was too dangerous to Jambiya, with or without her magic, and K'leef's stupid honor probably had him tangled in knots.

But he knew what Jambiya wanted.

Thorn spotted the bright flames above the tallest tower as the pair of phoenixes did their aerial dance over their nest.

There was only one solution: swap the egg for his two friends. He didn't really care what type of ruler Jambiya would be as long as he was on the other side of the world when he put on that lava crown. K'leef could come to Gehenna with them.

But to make all this happen, he needed an egg box.

The place reminded him of Castle Gloom, and that was big enough. But this city . . . it seemed endless. The streets went on forever. He was also awestruck at the true height of the buildings all around him.

But its emptiness made him cold and uneasy; he was constantly glancing over his shoulder. Hades glided alongside him, swooping from one perch to another. When the bat clung to the outstretched arm of one statue, even Hades looked small.

Men couldn't have built all this. Each doorway was a work of art, intricately carved and inlaid with mother-of-pearl, beaten silver, and delicate gemstones. The walls, though worn by exposure, still displayed extravagant friezes of past battles and tales now long forgotten.

So, whose work was it? Demons and devils that Prince Shadow would have summoned and bound to his service? What was the place like, back when such creatures walked alongside everyday folk? And the undead. Castle Gloom had more than its fair share of zombies and ghosts, but Necropolis must have heaved with the multitude of such creatures. Plenty of the buildings here were windowless, like Castle Gloom. The ideal dwellings for vampires and their kin.

Why had he thought that? Now he was scaring himself. Sunset wasn't far away.

Thorn slipped into a house through an open door. The front hall was an atrium, open to the sky, and there was a dry pool in the center, the dust within it partially hiding a mosaic of chatting skulls and dancing skeletons. There were couches, the cushions long since rotted away, and a skeleton reclined on one, its skull slumped on a forearm as if it had drifted to sleep after a heavy meal and never woken. A glass vial was still clutched within its bony fingers.

Had the inhabitants known they were doomed? Had some decided to choose their own manner of death, dining on lavish dishes and enjoying rich wines instead of facing the armies that waited beyond the walls?

Thorn shook his head. He would never give up like that. There was always a way out if you were brave enough—or desperate enough, like a fox with a leg caught in a snare.

This place gave him the creeps. He didn't want to stay any longer, but he needed a box.

It was in a bedroom that he found one. He didn't recognize the wood, but it was thick and solid. He opened the lid and tipped out jewelry and coins.

There. Enough space for a melon. He just hoped the phoenix egg would fit . . . and the spirits wouldn't mind him taking it.

It had rings at either end, and he knotted a leather strap through them and hung the box from his shoulders. Then he hurried back onto the street.

Narrow blades of darkness cut the city from west to east. The top of the phoenix tower glowed brighter, contrasting with the darkening sky and . . .

Thorn spotted a golden glow of firelight ahead of him. It formed a humanish outline on the wall.

"K'leef?" Had his friend escaped?

The figure rounded the corner and, upon seeing Thorn, flared as lava-filled veins pulsed with unimaginable heat.

Why did it have to be him? Thorn sighed. "Been looking for me, Farn?"

# FORTY

Thorn's first instinct was to hop onto Hades's back and fly far away. Instead, he waved Hades off as he circled overhead. The bat hissed angrily but stayed aloft and watchful.

Arrows would do no good against the efreet. They'd turn to ash ten paces from the creature. But if Thorn didn't do something now, Farn would dog their steps all the way back to Nahas and, one night or another, catch them.

Farn waited, its white eyes pulsing with anticipation. Lava dripped from its fingertips and flames rippled across its blackened shell.

Thorn took a step back.

Farn edged forward.

Thorn could lose the fire monster in the endless streets and countless houses and palaces if he wanted to. How could it find him? It lacked the tools of tracking: it couldn't hear, feel, taste, or smell. When you were without any one of the five senses, you needed to compensate in other ways, like Hades did, using his big ears to overcome his weak eyes. But Farn's eyes were limited, too. They were tiny and set deep into its head, so it could probably only see what was right in front of it. Step a few paces left or right and you'd vanish.

Thorn's dad had taught him how important the other senses, beyond sight, were to predator and prey. At night, vision was useless; it was your ears and your nose that kept you out of the bear's belly.

Thorn knew the tang left by wolves. The scent of their spray on trees lingered for days, even to a nose as weak as his. And he knew how to mask his own scent with fern and mud so he could get close enough to a deer to touch it.

Yeah, everyone except hunters underestimated how important smell could be to a successful hunt.

Thorn sniffed the air. There was just the smallest acidic sting, as if someone had been slicing lemons—foul and decaying lemons. The odor was drifting in from the west.

He looked back at Farn. "What are you waiting for?" Then he turned and ran.

And so did Farn.

By the Six, the efreet was fast! Thorn dashed over a wall, and Farn smashed straight through it, hurling molten brick everywhere.

This wasn't fair! Thorn had thought it could only plod along. Running wasn't allowed!

The ground shook under the efreet's thundering footsteps, and the air on Thorn's back burned.

Hades shrieked but couldn't get to him. The alleyway was too narrow.

Farn made it wider by charging down it without pause. The buildings cracked, and a gargoyle tumbled onto the efreet's head, disintegrating into a million pieces on impact. Farn did not falter a single step.

This wasn't going how he'd planned.

"Argh!" Thorn's caftan burst into flames. He stumbled and almost dropped his box as Farn hooked its fingers on the garment's hem. Thorn wriggled out of it just before Farn turned him into a roast. The efreet searched the burning cloak as if expecting someone to still be inside it. Thorn didn't linger long enough for the fire creature to realize its mistake.

Which way? This place was more confusing than Castle Gloom. Was it past the iron statue of the vampire on horseback? Or along the path lined with skulls? The trouble was, all the paths in Necropolis seemed to be lined with skulls.

He tried to control his heaving chest with a few deep breaths.

Farn wasn't far behind. The vampire statue began steaming in the heated air.

*Stop running like a panicked deer. Calm down.*

Thorn closed his eyes and concentrated on the smells around him.

He could identify the not-so-fresh stink of his sweat; the hot city dust, which made him want to sneeze; the melting iron statue nearby; and the sulfurous odor of Farn. But there was also something else—sharp, stinging, and . . .

Thorn opened his eyes, looked to his left, and saw a large sunken square. Of course.

He ran, jumping down one broad step after another until he reached the cracked expanse, which measured more than a hundred feet across. Extravagant twisted columns lined the perimeter and were crowned with—what else?—grinning skulls.

Here the smell was thick and made his eyes run. Great, jagged fissures had turned the once-pristine floor into a treacherous mix of pits and slopes. Huge slabs of stone slanted downward into the darkness, and Thorn struggled to keep his footing. He didn't want to know how deep those crevasses went.

The ground shook as Farn landed behind him.

Hades circled over the open square. The bat twitched his claws, but Thorn ordered him to stay back.

This was it.

He slowed down and turned to face the monstrous efreet. "Okay, I give up," he said, panting. "I can't go any farther. You win. Come and get me."

Farn marched forward. The air around the creature began to shimmer and pop.

Thorn leaned against a large slab of marble. "I'm so, sooo tired. Can't take another step. Honestly."

Hades circled lower.

Farn began to tremble. It started in the arms and legs. The efreet raised its hands and stared at them as the lava spluttered and expanded from within, widening the cracks in its crusty exterior.

Now its chest pulsed. Fresh cracks appeared across its torso, spitting out burning rock.

Thorn smiled. "It's the Devil's Breath. You'd know that if you had a nose."

He whistled, and Hades swooped. Thorn hooked his arm over a claw, and the pair of them rose twenty feet instantly.

Farn's arm burst apart, and lava spewed from its open shoulder socket.

"Better take us higher," said Thorn. "When it blows, it's going to—"

Too late. There was a blinding, deafening explosion, which threw Hades into a tailspin. Thorn lost his balance and began to fall free of the bat.

The whole square was filled with Devil's Breath, and one after another the deep crevasses, where the gas lay thickest, burst into flame.

Hades managed to clamp Thorn's leg between his jaws just before they were toasted. The bat lifted clear of the fiery pits now covering the square.

Of Farn, nothing remained.

Thorn clambered back into his usual spot on Hades's back. Huge clouds of smoke smothered them both, and Hades climbed higher and higher to get free. As soon as they reached clean air, boy and bat gulped it greedily. Then Thorn checked for damage. Thankfully, the bat hadn't suffered any burns. Aside from losing his own eyebrows, he seemed okay, too. His bow was whole, the arrows were still in their quiver, and the box was sooty but intact.

In the distance, the phoenixes spun in their fiery dance in the dusk.

Thorn nudged the bat with his knee. "Come on, Hades. This marshmallow roast is over."

# FORTY-ONE

"**W**hat was that?" Lily stared at the huge column of fire in the distance. "Jambiya?"

"It can't be. He couldn't make a fire that big." K'leef frowned. "And the noise . . . That wasn't a spell. I'm sure of it."

Lily narrowed her eyes. She thought she'd seen something within the clouds of smoke. Now she couldn't be sure.

"We need to get a move on," said K'leef.

"This way," said Lily. They didn't have time to investigate the fire. "We go along the Avenue of Endless Tears, past the Halls of Ancestors, and under the Arch of the Moon."

"You sure?" asked K'leef.

"I'm very sure." *Tales of Necropolis* had been her favorite book when she was small. Mary must have read it to her a thousand times. Sometimes Lily had forced her to read it several times in one night. The book had been lavishly illustrated, the margins crowded with images of ghosts and bats. She'd copied her favorite images onto scraps of parchment and, once, on an ancient scroll bearing the Spell of the Seven Witches, ruining its magic forever.

But most of all she'd admired the foldout map at the front.

Now, was the Street of the Ghast-Born down on the left, or straight ahead? She closed her eyes and tried to recall those quiet, candlelit nights with her on Mary's lap and the book open before them. She pictured the map. . . .

"Left. I'm certain it's left."

They continued on, staying alert to sounds and changes in the light. There were so many stories about this city, too many to absorb in a hundred lifetimes. To actually be here, that was something beyond her wildest dreams. How many people had searched in vain for Necropolis? Every Shadow had longed to visit the city once ruled by the founder of the family, the greatest necromancer who had ever lived. Everything Lily was had come from him.

Except . . . now her magic was gone.

She wouldn't think about that. She was still a Shadow, no matter what. The blood of the prince flowed through her, and one day, she would regain her spells. No matter how long it took.

She saw the arching tails of the scorpions rising over the roofs of a row of storehouses.

K'leef whistled softly. "Avenue of the Scorpions. Which way to the towers?"

"Not sure," she admitted. "I thought we'd be near the Garden of Misery, but that's way over there. And I can't find the Well of Mothers' Grief."

"Isn't it beside Pale Heart Palace?" suggested K'leef, pointing at the towering building ahead of them.

"Maybe. Shall we try?"

It was as good a plan as any, taking a shortcut through the palace itself. The tower was easy enough to spot, with the phoenix fires lighting it, but they didn't have Hades to fly them over the buildings that blocked their way.

They entered through a vast courtyard. The steps leading to the open gates were carved out of the bones of giants, and the columns were crowned with huge skulls.

"It gets a bit repetitive, don't you think?" K'leef tapped the doorposts, each designed as a skeleton with raised arms.

"Why mess with perfection?" Lily replied. As far as she was concerned, it was impossible to criticize anything about House Shadow, especially here.

They reached the top of the stairs. The great demon doors were wide open. Still, Lily hesitated before stepping inside. Those demons were locked in iron and stone, but would they awaken if she tried to enter?

She gulped but put her foot over the threshold.

The demons remained where they were, and she sighed with relief. "Come on, K'leef."

What would they find within Pale Heart Palace? Treasures? Magical artifacts from the Age of the Six? Perhaps she would discover Prince Shadow's own library. The one in Castle Gloom held only a few shelves of knowledge compared to the one in Necropolis. And such spells! Prince Shadow had been able to alter the path of the moon itself.

She wanted to explore every corridor, search every room and hall. Then . . .

She spun around. "Did you see that?"

"Hmm?"

Lily took a few steps down a side hallway. She was sure she'd seen something. . . . "There!"

A figure, a person, ran from a dark corner and vanished after taking a left turn.

"There!"

"What?" K'leef screwed up his eyes. "I didn't see anything."

"Come on." Lily picked up the pace. "Now, K'leef!"

They dashed around the corner, and Lily began to run. Who could it be? Was it Thorn? No, he wouldn't run from them. There was someone new here; she had to find out who it was.

"Slow down, Lily!" panted K'leef.

"Wait!" Lily turned another corner just in time to see the figure disappear through a door. "Stop! We need to talk!"

"Lily! Where are you?" K'leef's cries echoed from this way and that. She turned but didn't see him. He couldn't be far behind.

"Lily . . . Lily . . ." The shouts faded.

She tried to retrace her steps, but it did no good. That wall hadn't been there before, had it?

The palace was changing. It was trapping her . . . or guiding her.

*The only way is forward.*

Every few yards there was a new marvel, like lanterns that floated in the air, their flames long extinguished and their metal rusty orange and green.

She entered another hall.

Mirrors the size of ships' sails ran along both walls. Lily's reflection fell into the glass, multiplied infinite times.

She rubbed her fingers over the dusty surface and peered in. Her reflection stared back, but it looked slightly different. It gazed at her with its own intelligence, showing features that were better proportioned and more elegant, and clothes that were cleaner, better cut, and made from finer materials. It was a superior version of herself.

Her reflections varied even more the deeper they went into the mirror world. They were older, or younger; they wore strange hair and clothing styles. Some versions weren't even female. Far, far in the back she met the gaze of herself as an old man. He tipped his hat at her.

On any other day, that might have felt odd. Lily just waved back. It seemed the polite thing to do.

Which way should she go? The palace went on forever.

A whisper drifted into the hall. The words were too faint for her to understand, but the sound was distinct enough to lead Lily to a doorway.

The black marble door was partially ajar.

Lily pushed it open wider. Despite the age and dust and sand, the door swung easily and silently.

Into a throne room.

A cracked, crystalline dome covered the circular hall. Light shone down into the center and onto the throne, a giant, high-backed piece of obsidian.

A man still sat upon it.

He looked young, about the same age as she, but his eyes were dark and old, very old. He wore the rich black clothes of a Shadow noble: a velvet cape and trousers, tall leather boots, and a silk tunic embroidered with patterns.

He smiled. "I've been waiting a long time for you, Lady Shadow."

# FORTY-TWO

*C*ould this be the ghost of Prince Shadow? Her heart leaped with hope—and abject fear—at the idea.

"Do you . . . do you know me?" Lily stammered.

The boy stood. "I know *of* you. The underworld praises your name, and your deeds have come to the ears of the great and terrible."

"That's nice," she replied cautiously. "And you are . . . ?"

He bowed. "I am Bitter Promise."

"That's not a real name."

"Names have power; surely a Shadow understands that more than most?" His dark eyes glistened. "My kind only reveal their names to their very closest friends, and masters."

Lily caught her breath. "A demon?"

"Let's agree I come from somewhere very far away."

"Far away" was one way of putting it. Lily had gone into the Twilight, the area between the world of the living and the dead. She'd also explored the Dreamtime, that patchwork kingdom made of everyone's dreams. But Bitter Promise had come from a place much, much farther than either of those.

She squinted at him to get a better look. There hadn't been a demon around in centuries. Commanding the undead and raising zombies from the grave was child's play compared to summoning such creatures from their own realm. She wouldn't even know how to start.

But she *did* know that you couldn't trust them. They were lords of deceit.

And granters of wishes.

"What do you want?" she asked, still keeping a wary distance between them both. "And what have you done with K'leef?"

"Your companion? Nothing. I merely wanted a few minutes to talk with you privately."

As he approached her, he changed. His body and clothes transformed so Bitter Promise became a young, dark-haired woman, not unlike Lily herself—or how she used to be before her magic had turned her hair white. They could be sisters.

"Don't do that."

"Why not?" answered Bitter Promise. "I want us to be friends. Allies. I can help you, Lady Shadow. Help you regain what you have lost—regain that, and so much more."

"My magic?" Lily's pulse raced.

"I was bound in the service of your ancestor, Prince Shadow. That is why I am here. I serve House Shadow. I could serve you."

Lily tried to gather herself. "How?"

Bitter Promise's eyes darkened, and their endless depth frightened Lily. "Think, Lady Shadow. What is the oldest law of the New Kingdoms?"

"Women cannot practice magic. The penalty is death by fire."

"Think hard. What difference would it make if they could? Why are men so afraid? They are afraid because women would be *more powerful*. Are you not proof of that?"

"I have no magic at all."

The girl's smile was cold and sly. "I can fix that. I can teach you everything the high queen knew."

"So it is true; there was a high queen." Strange that she couldn't believe it when others had told her yet somehow she believed it from the lips of this demon. "What happened to her?"

Bitter Promise smoothed her long black hair. "I was there when they killed her. All six of them came for her. They hunted her through the corridors of the palace until they drove her here. Then, one by one, they plunged their swords into her. She could have destroyed them easily. But she chose not to."

"Why not?"

"Love."

Lily's lungs felt squeezed within her chest. This was her terrible dream. All of them coming for her, and her unable, unwilling, to defend herself. "Then what happened?"

"The Six passed a law forbidding women to practice magic. They were afraid that others would one day learn what their sister knew."

"And what was that?"

"She knew of a magic that surpassed all that of her brothers. Beyond the command of fire, water, earth, air, light, and darkness. The seventh sorcery."

"There is no . . ."

The girl grabbed Lily's arm. "Stop it! Stop thinking within the walls that men have built around you! The prison they've made of your mind! We can be free, Lady Shadow!"

Lily wrenched herself away. "Freedom? Is that what you want?"

The demon pouted. "I have been a slave for countless millennia. Freedom is a small thing to you, but in return I will make you so, so great."

"What would you do with your freedom?" Lily asked. "Go home?"

"Eventually. But I would seek some pleasures first."

Lily could imagine. An unbound demon was a terrible thing. For Bitter Promise, pleasures would take the form of blood, slaughter, and carnage.

But these things existed already. What difference would one demon make? And she would have her magic back . . . her magic and more.

Bitter Promise stepped aside from the throne. "This has been empty too long. It could be yours. All you need do is take a little step."

"Prince Shadow's throne . . ."

She'd seen many paintings of it, but they'd all been from the artist's imagination. This was the real thing. Simpler than she'd expected, yet, strangely, more powerful because of that.

"A kiss—one simple kiss—is all it will require. I will be free, and you will be restored with all the magic you have lost, and more." Bitter Promise stepped closer, and Lily noticed how sharp the creature's teeth were. "I promise."

Lily backed away. "And that would be a bitter one, right?"

"What?"

Lily backed away from the throne and Bitter Promise. "The deal. There are many tales about the bad deals we mortals have made with your kind, as well as other creatures: fairies, spirits, and mermaids. They always end poorly for us. We get what we want, but the cost is too high."

"Such tales are for weaklings, not the bold like yourself." Bitter Promise scowled. "You could have everything you ever dreamed of. More power than any other sorcerer alive."

"I don't want it."

"You're happy to live the rest of your life as a mere mortal? Without any spellcraft?"

"I didn't say that," Lily replied. "By the way, your name, Bitter Promise—you didn't pick it yourself, did you? Prince Shadow gave it to you."

"What of it?"

"It's not a name. It's a warning to anyone who might cross your path."

"You will regret this decision," snarled the demon. "And sooner than you—"

"Lily!"

K'leef stumbled into the hall, and Bitter Promise disappeared. K'leef rested his hands on his knees as he gathered his breath. "Found you."

Lily hugged her friend. "Thank you."

"Er, that's all right. Is everything okay?"

Lily faltered. "I was lost. And worried."

K'leef didn't look convinced. "Did you find it? The thing you were chasing?"

She shook her head. "It was nothing. My imagination. Trick of the light, perhaps."

"Hmm. Perhaps." K'leef took her hand. "Come on. We need to find Thorn."

She let him lead her out, but Lily stopped at the door and looked back. The throne sat empty except for its bitter promise of power.

# FORTY-THREE

**T**horn rested his elbows on Hades's head as he pondered how to get the egg. The phoenixes were fast, agile in the air, and made of fire. Hades was old. But he was still as swift and cunning as a snake. And his wickedly long claws could tear through steel.

The phoenixes hunted as a pair, just like some hawks. One would drive the prey into the clutches of the other. As long as Hades didn't fall for that and he stayed ahead of them, maybe he could outdistance them and double back to the nest.

Thorn bit his lip. It wasn't much of a plan, but it was getting dark.

He didn't need to tell Hades any of this; the bat knew what he was thinking. Hades dropped off the perch—one of Necropolis's spiky towers— and spread out his wings as he picked up speed. Thorn checked his quiver and thrummed his bowstring. The sound calmed him.

Up and up they went, toward the comfort of the moon. In this twilight, Hades was almost invisible. Gliding down, he'd also be utterly silent. The phoenixes wouldn't know what hit 'em.

Thorn readied his first arrow. He wasn't planning to damage the birds, just dissuade them from getting too close. The last thing he wanted was a singed Hades. Burning fur *stank*.

The phoenixes danced below them. They swooped and spun around each other, creating beautiful patterns of fire. The colors included brilliant greens and blues as well as bright yellow, gold, and red. They fanned flames over their nest, warming the eggs like a hen over her own. They lived on top of the highest tower in all Necropolis. They must have thought themselves safe from everything. Thorn grinned. "Time to put the bat among the pigeons."

Hades dove.

# FORTY-FOUR

As Thorn had predicted, the phoenixes didn't know Hades was there until he was right on top of them. Thorn and Hades felt their heat even from a dozen yards away. When they swept close to the birds, it was like they had charged through a forest fire. Hades roared as he used the beat of his mighty wings to buffet the phoenixes aside; then he spun away.

The phoenixes screamed their rage and gave chase.

"That got their attention," Thorn commented.

Dragons, from the stories he knew, breathed fire. Phoenixes trailed it. It fell from their wings, rippling to the side as they beat them, but they could not throw their flames forward, and that gave Hades his advantage. The bat wove through the towers, never using the same route twice. The phoenixes followed, just as swift, but unable to get ahead, unable to attack. That made them only more furious—they were used to ruling the skies over Necropolis. A few times they paused—having chased Hades across the city, they were on the verge of heading back to the nest—and Thorn taunted them with an arrow. Hades zipped between them, close enough to fuel their rage and urge them to continue their chase.

But the phoenixes knew the city better than Hades, and they knew how to hunt.

Thorn glanced back and saw just one behind him.

Where was the other? Thorn turned his head in all directions. How could they have lost it?

"This is bad. . . ."

Hades curled under a bridge spanning two lofty towers.

The heat hit them first. Thorn yelled as if he'd been showered with burning coals, and Hades screamed, spinning sideways just as a comet of white flame blazed past, ripping into his left wing. Thorn grabbed hold desperately, staring in fear as the phoenixes reunited. They sensed victory.

The bat dropped as the thin membrane on his wing tore and the fur on his chest smoked. He beat hard, but that only made things worse as a wave of fire swept over them from a passing phoenix.

It lasted just a fraction of a second, but that fraction was agony. Thorn gasped for air as they broke away. It felt as if every inch of him had been pierced—another second and he would have ignited. If a phoenix scored a direct hit, he'd be ash.

The two birds circled back, close now, and created a wall of fire between them. If Thorn didn't break them up, Hades would soon be engulfed in flame.

Thorn flexed his aching fingers. He had one opportunity to make a shot. It had to be up close so the phoenix couldn't dodge it. If he missed . . .

*I don't miss.*

Hades, hissing angrily, tried to fly faster, but the torn skin on his left wing flapped in the wind, making him less aerodynamic. They weren't going to outdistance the pair of raptors.

The heat beat on Thorn's back as the phoenixes closed in.

One shot was all he needed. Leaning over Hades, Thorn slipped his arrow into place. There weren't many left in his quiver.

The heat became agonizing.

*Not yet. Not yet.*

His clothes started smoldering.

*Not yet. . . .*

The tips of Hades's fur caught fire.

Thorn turned, bowstring pulled to his cheek.

The phoenix glared, just yards from him. The eyes of the creature were two blinding spots of sun, too painful to meet; its crest was a crown of fire that blazed intense blue. Its body was coated with silver and gold feathers that rippled with heat, and its wide, shimmering wings streamed flames. Its beak opened as the phoenix prepared to tear Thorn apart.

Thorn loosed.

The phoenix screamed as the arrow flew straight down its gullet. The bird broke formation, and the second bird hesitated and almost crashed into a wall.

Hades gave a sudden surge, and they were away.

Thorn let out a sigh. That was as close to death as he ever wanted to get. "Hades, you okay?" He stroked the bat's smoking shoulder.

Hades snarled.

"Yeah, this plan ain't working."

Hades was slower now, the air dragging through the tear in his wing, and both phoenixes were gaining—clearly the arrow hadn't done any real harm—determined to regain their dominance over the skies.

"Not good." Thorn hunkered down on Hades, cutting down the air resistance as much as he could. "Watch out!"

A series of arches spanning two buildings was dead ahead. Hades pulled in his wings just enough to get through. Then he doubled back, surprising the birds, but not for long. They were side by side now, looking to finish them off once and for all.

Then Thorn saw the water.

This wasn't a bridge—it was an aqueduct. Water still ran along the gullies. He'd seen the flowing fountains when he was on the ground.

Somewhere in the distance there was a stream or a river, still feeding the city, even after all this time.

How big was the source of the water? He had no idea.

"Turn around!" he yelled. "Now!"

As the wind rushed against him, Hades pushed himself harder to try to create a gap between him and the fiery hunters.

The columns supporting the aqueduct were slender and old. A few of them leaned at odd angles, and water trickled down through cracks in the disjointed stone.

Thorn picked one. "There!"

He jumped.

There was a brief moment of free fall; then he hit the path of water, bouncing, sliding, and splashing along, making sure every bone got a bashing and his head received a few good knocks before he locked his fingers on a jutting piece of stone. At least the water cooled his scorched flesh.

He stumbled to his feet, standing waist-deep in the gully of water. The phoenixes arced around the far edge of a building, so close to one another that their wing tips touched, forming an inescapable line of flames.

Thorn pulled himself over the edge of the channel, shimmied down one of the columns, and sat with his back against it. Then he placed the soles of both feet against another column—the one that was already tilted at a dangerous angle—and pushed with all his might.

"Move," he snarled as he kicked loose a brick. "Move!"

Hades hovered nearby, watching. If Thorn failed, the bat didn't have enough speed now to get away.

The stone groaned as the bricks shifted. Dust fell out of old cracks, and water splashed down from the gully overhead.

Another few inches . . .

The heat wave built in intensity. The phoenixes were so bright that it hurt to look at them.

Thorn slammed his feet against the stone. "Move!"

The column cracked.

"Move!"

The heat was unbearable. The phoenixes would fly through the arches any second now and Thorn would go up in smoke.

Teeth gritted, and using every ounce of strength and determination he had, he heaved one last time. "Move!"

The column crumbled, unable to withstand both the pressure at its side and the weight above.

Water cascaded down as the aqueduct broke apart, not just in that spot, but all along, as the loss of that one column destroyed the integrity of the whole. The noise of shattering stone was deafening.

The narrow arch Thorn was on gave way. There was loose stone and water everywhere.

The phoenixes screamed as the spray hit them. They hissed and filled the air with steam. Trapped by the falling stone and water, they tumbled down, spinning uncontrollably as their flames began to flicker and go out.

Hades snatched Thorn out of his free fall, and a moment later, he'd clambered back into place on the bat, gasping but relieved.

The phoenixes were down, their flames extinguished. Thorn clapped, then flung his arms around Hades's neck. "That wasn't so hard, was it?"

The deep rumble from Hades's throat sounded like he disagreed.

"Ah, you love it really."

Hades cried out and did a victory roll. He did love it.

Would the phoenixes rise again? They were known for that, after all. How long would it take? An hour? Maybe only minutes?

*Assume the worst and make it minutes.*

Thorn swiveled his head until he spotted the phoenixes' nest, still glowing orange with heat. It was easy to spot now that the sun had set.

The shadows of the city below were long and deep.

And, unless his eyes were deceiving him, *things* were stirring within them. . . .

# FORTY-FIVE

"Thorn!" Lily yelled, waving. "Thorn!"

"He's too high up, Lily. He can't see us." K'leef snapped his fingers. "I could create a fire. . . ."

"And have Jambiya spot it? No." She climbed down off the wall she'd been standing on. "We know where Thorn's headed."

She'd watched the whole battle, her heart in her mouth. She'd screamed warnings and curses from down here, urged Thorn to duck and Hades to weave, and cheered when the aqueduct had collapsed.

"That boy . . ." she muttered. Thorn took way too many risks.

K'leef smiled. "I know."

"Would you have thought of the aqueduct?" she asked.

"Maybe. Maybe not. It must be hard to concentrate when two phoenixes are about to burn your backside."

"He's too stupid to be afraid," said Lily. "That's Thorn's problem."

She wasn't. She'd been terrified for him. Not that she'd ever let him know that. He might get the wrong idea.

*Oh, who am I kidding?*

He was always on her mind, one way or another. No one stood up to her like him, no one tormented her like him, and no one gave her as much joy as him. He didn't know it. She couldn't let him know, because . . .

Because she was Lilith of House Shadow, ruler of Gehenna, and he was just Thorn.

*Names have power.* That's what Bitter Promise had said. And they had weight, too. Hers weighed heavily on every aspect of her life. It represented all her past, and all her future. Thorn flew among the clouds—he was free. Lily lived among the tombs of her heritage, with a name too heavy to let her take flight.

Thorn's twin sisters were named Petal and Heather. There would be Lilys in his village of Stour, too—girls from Herne's Forest were often named after flowers.

But her name was Lilith, and that wasn't a flower. It meant "Mother of Monsters." She fooled herself sometimes that she could be simply "Lily," a flower of graveyards and tombs. There was no escape, no way to pretend she could be anything other than what she was.

Thorn circled over the phoenix tower. He slid off Hades and dropped into the nest.

"He's done it," said K'leef. He grabbed Lily and swung her around. "He's done it!"

Lily laughed as they hugged with joy and relief. All the dangers and the hardships now seemed worth it. Thorn had the phoenix; K'leef would be Sultan Djinn.

"Did you ever doubt?" she asked.

"That Thorn . . ." K'leef shook his head in wonder. "There's no one like him."

She swelled with pride. There wasn't. No one caused trouble like him, no one took risks like him, and no one achieved the impossible like him.

He proved that you didn't need to be a sorcerer to do miraculous things.

K'leef let her go, and she spun on her heels and collapsed, laughing, in the dust. K'leef performed a little foot shuffle. "Remember when we first met? How we danced?"

"How you kicked my shins, you mean?"

He did a pirouette. "What do you think?"

"Best stick to the sorcery, K'leef."

The whip hissed from out of the dark and cracked across his face. K'leef fell instantly.

Lily jumped up but was struck across the back of the knees and fell down beside her stunned friend. K'leef groaned from the blinding cut across his forehead.

"Stay down, Lily," ordered Pan. "When will you learn?"

Jambiya arrived with a handful of nomads—only five remained of his original host. One wound his whip into a loop that he slung over his shoulder.

"You've lost, Brother," muttered K'leef, still in the dust and wincing with pain.

"Oh?" Jambiya turned around, arms spread. "Where is your phoenix?"

"Thorn has it," said Lily. "And he's part of K'leef's team, remember?"

"There is a vast difference between getting a prize and holding on to it."

"You'll ransom us for the bird?" exclaimed K'leef. "Where is your honor?"

"K'leef, do you know how naive you sound? *Honor?* It's a joke." Jambiya flexed his fingers, and the tips glowed. "And you are a fool if you think I will leave you alive this time."

But Lily wasn't paying them any attention. Flames were growing in the distance. "No . . ."

Pan followed her gaze, frowning. "What?"

The two phoenixes erupted over the ruins of the aqueduct. They circled once, then flew toward the nest.

"Thorn!" Lily yelled, even though it was useless at this distance. "Thorn! They're coming back!"

Jambiya smiled. "Now that doesn't sound good."

Lily struggled to her feet. "THORN!"

What was he doing? The plan was to grab the egg and get out! Hades rested on another tower, battered and burned, unaware of the danger swooping in from behind.

"Thorn!"

Then she saw him—his head poked up above the edge of the nest. He held something glowing in his arms.

"He has the phoenix egg . . ." said K'leef.

Hades spread out his wings. He tipped off the tower and glided toward his friend.

The phoenixes hit Hades unawares. He shrieked as they burned him, and Lily screamed as the bat fell in the sky, trailing smoke and fire.

Thorn stumbled back and dropped the egg. He then gathered his bow. Arrow after arrow arched through the air, each one a perfect shot—as ever—but the shafts were consumed by fire before they hit. The two phoenixes circled above the nest, shrieking their rage at this intruder.

"Thorn!" Lily screamed.

The phoenixes hurled wave after wave of fire over the nest with each beat of their wings. The nest turned from red to gold to an unbearable white, too painful to look upon. The stone at the top of the tower bubbled.

She screamed his name until her voice cracked.

Lily sank to the ground. It couldn't be.

The phoenixes stopped their attack. They rose up over the nest and did their strange dance of fire over it. The danger was passed; the intruder was no more.

Jambiya dabbed the sweat off his brow. "You could feel it from here, couldn't you? I can only imagine what it must have felt like in the nest. But you can be sure it was painless. The boy was ash before—"

"No!" Lily slammed her fists on the ground.

The flames thickened on Jambiya's palms. "It is over, Lady Shadow. I told you that one day you would be punished for your . . . unnaturalness. That day is here."

The nomads stepped back. One held K'leef by the throat.

Lily lowered her head.

Thorn was dead.

And now it was her turn.

But not on her knees.

She stood up and straightened her dress. She brushed the dust from her sleeves. "The lava crown will not rest long on your head, Jambiya. They'll know. They'll know the throne's not rightly yours. It may take a year, it may take ten, but eventually"—she looked over at her uncle—"all traitors reveal themselves."

"Perhaps," Jambiya snarled as he summoned the flames. "But *you'll* never know."

Lily glared at him, defiant till the end.

*Mother, Father, Dante . . . I'm coming.*

But it was Thorn she pictured as the heat intensified. Thorn with his bright green eyes, cheeky smile, and always-dirty face.

Jambiya hurled the fireball.

# FORTY-SIX

"**N**o!"
Lily was thrown off her feet. Fire fanned all around her. The flames licked her back, burning, enveloping her in pain.

*How am I still alive?*

"Run, Lily!"

She stumbled up, tripping and falling over the rubble.

*I should be dead!*

"Run!"

Pan! He stood there, between her and Jambiya. Flames engulfed him; he'd blocked the attack with his own body.

How could he still be standing? Jambiya poured more flames on him, and the air around them roared and pulsed with unbearable heat. The sand at his feet bubbled and blackened.

The nomad holding K'leef retreated, unable to stand the horrific sight and smell of burning flesh.

"Uncle!"

He looked back, just for a moment. His skin was black and peeling away from his face; his armor glowed a fierce, hissing red. "Run . . ." he croaked.

"Stop!" Lily screamed.

Jambiya, wearing a hideous grimace, did not listen. He spread his hands, and another wave of fire erupted over her uncle, melting his armor. Pan buckled but did not fall, using his sword to hold himself up.

Then, unbelievably, he moved—one step, then another, faltering, shaking, each movement an unimaginable agony, yet he approached Jambiya and raised his blade, even as his skin burned on the metal.

With one last cry, Pan stabbed it into Jambiya's chest, driving it through till the point exited the sorcerer's back.

"Uncle!" She had to save him. He was the only Shadow she had left.

"No, Lily!" K'leef pulled her back.

"Let me go!"

Jambiya roared. Flames spewed from his mouth and the wound in his chest. He grabbed hold of Pan and drove more fire through her uncle's body. The flames swirled around them, creating a barrier of devastating heat.

Pan pushed once more, driving his blade deeper, and finally, both men fell, the fire extinguished. Jambiya trembled, turned black, and crumbled to ash.

"Lily . . . are you . . . all right?"

It was Pan. His body was burned horribly, his armor had melted over him, and yet somehow he lived.

"Uncle!" Lily ran to him.

He sighed as she gently cradled his head. Smoke seeped from his cracked skin, and he was almost too hot to hold, but Lily ignored the pain. Her tears hissed as they fell upon his cheeks. "Why?"

# FORTY-SEVEN

"No, no, no, no." Lily held Pan's hand, squeezing it for all she was worth, as if she could pass her life into his. "Please, Uncle, stay with me. You have to stay."

He shivered despite the heat and smoke rising out of his blackened body. His cracked lips formed a weak smile. "Lily . . ."

"You'll be all right. I promise. I promise."

*He has to be. Life can't be this cruel.*

Pan's smile turned into a grimace as he fought the immeasurable pain. "Salome . . . always said . . ."

"We'll talk about Mother later. Just rest. Don't worry, I'll take care of everything."

His eyes glazed over; whatever he was seeing now wasn't in this world. ". . . said a lady had to have three things . . . grace, wit . . ."

"And brave knights. Brave knights."

His laugh was a hideous, croaking gasp. "Brave knights willing . . . to die for her. That's what she said, Lily. Remember?"

"Don't think like that."

Her heart had been ripped apart once before. She never thought she would feel the same pain ever again. Yet here it was. How? This man had murdered all she'd loved, and yet she couldn't bear the thought of him leaving her.

K'leef knelt down beside her, letting his tears join hers.

"So like her, Lily. You're so like her," Pan went on. "You have those three things."

"I don't want them," Lily replied.

Pan shook. "Oh, Lily, I can't face them. How can I? After what I did . . ."

"They'll forgive you, Uncle. I know they will."

He looked at her, desperately afraid. "Some things can't be . . . Some things are beyond forgiveness."

She ached at the price of it all. She'd never wanted to be ruler; the crown was no reward—it was a curse.

Lily brushed the crinkled hair from Pan's tortured face. His eyes brightened, and he relaxed, as if all pain was passing. He smiled. "Lily, I see . . . look . . ."

Then a sigh escaped him, and the eyes quieted, yet the smile remained. Whatever Pan had seen in that last moment had made him glad.

Lily kissed her uncle's forehead. His exile was over.

"Lily. You need to get up." K'leef stood over her. "They're coming."

"Who? There's no one left. . . ."

He didn't answer.

Lights blinked in some of the windows, as faint as the first stars of the evening. She heard murmuring voices, too—sounding distant but numerous. And the shadows moved. Dark figures crossed the streets and the walls.

Misty shapes emerged from the ruins, the ancient doorways, and the bones. They swirled softly, animated by a force the living couldn't feel. They took the forms of men, women, and children. They wore robes and jewels of the finest quality, now reduced to ethereal memory.

They had tarried too long. In all the chaos, Lily had forgotten the ancient warning.

*Do not linger in Necropolis after dark.*

And so they had come, for it was their city.

The dead.

# FORTY-EIGHT

A nomad—one of Jambiya's small band—tried to attack the encroaching mass. He slashed and stabbed with his scimitar, but the keen blade passed through the spirits, for they were not made of mortal flesh. They gazed, dull and pitilessly, as his blows grew more and more frantic. He yelled and cursed, and then his eyes widened and the fury morphed into terror.

One of the ghosts reached out and sank its fingers into the man's chest.

His clothes began to rot. His black hair was washed through with gray, and his dark, tough skin wrinkled as the muscles beneath withered. Patches of rust bloomed on his bright blade, and then the weapon corroded. Even when he was just a skin-clad skeleton, some weak, feeble life remained. He tried to struggle free, but how could he? He was ancient now. The ghosts surrounded him, drawing out his life essence, and then he sagged and all that remained were some dusty bones within a pile of moldy, faded cloth.

"Stay close!" K'leef grabbed Lily's hand and swept a circle of flame around them both.

The ghosts backed away, but there were other victims to their immortal hunger. The few remaining nomads tried to run for it. They climbed over the walls, even as the spirits floated toward them straight through the cracked marble. They fled down alleys and along the street, even as the ghosts drifted out of the buildings and gathered in dark corners of the city, and there were many dark corners.

"I can't keep . . . this . . . up. . . ." K'leef strained to hold the horde back. His flames spluttered and fizzed. His barrier cracked.

The ghosts drew closer.

A chill wind blew over them, and the flames flickered. K'leef stood, defiant, jaw clenched, as he urged more energy, more magic, out of his body. Smoke hissed from his skin and darts of fire flew from his eyes. She tightened her grip, ignoring the heat.

But he was exhausted from fighting his brother, and the undead were beyond counting. Any second now they would be overwhelmed.

They'd come so far, suffered so much, and this was how it ended.

Lily gritted her teeth. Let it end. What was left for her in this world anyway? Soon she'd be with them all. Her family, and that surly boy with the cocky smile . . . She so desperately wanted to see Thorn again.

The breeze grew stronger, and on it came a familiar smell, the stink of old fur. . . .

"So, who wants to be rescued?"

Hades, his fur still smoking, dipped a few yards out of the sky and hooked Lily and K'leef in his claws.

Thorn nudged the big bat with his knees, and Lily's stomach dropped as they launched moonward.

The ghosts surged forward through the fading wall of fire, but with each massive wingbeat, they rose farther away.

Thorn looked down at her. "Miss me?"

# FORTY-NINE

"**Y**ou should be dead!" said Lily. Then she hugged Thorn with all her might. "Never, ever do that again!"

Hades hadn't carried them far—he couldn't. One wing was torn, and the poor bat had bleeding gashes across his body. They looked bad; the skin around them was red and blistered.

K'leef slapped Thorn on the back. "You had us worried."

Thorn shrugged. "Ah, it was no big deal."

"Really?" she asked, eyebrow arched.

"No. It was actually amazing. I think, given all the *amazing* things I've already done, this must be the most amazing of all of them. I expect a pretty long poem out of this."

"Immortal fame and glory?" asked K'leef.

"Yup. And a castle."

Lily circled him. His clothes were burned. His hair was singed black, he'd lost his eyebrows, and his clothes were filthy with soot. But his skin shimmered. Thorn's skin never shimmered, even after his weekly bath. "Well?"

"Er . . . well what?"

"You're glowing, Thorn."

"You noticed that?" He rubbed his bare arm. "It's fading, a bit. But I think that's why I'm alive instead of . . . not alive."

K'leef frowned. "Just tell us what happened."

"I had the egg," he said. "I had it, and it was a lot hotter than I expected, and . . . er . . . I dropped it."

Lily groaned. "The phoenix egg? The fate of the Sultanate rested on that egg, Thorn! How could you?"

"It was really hot!" he complained. "I tried to catch it, but, you know, catching eggs is hard. I squeezed it too much and it, well, just, er . . . broke. Yolk went everywhere. All over me—I even swallowed some. Tasted disgusting. Really, really foul."

"Then what?" asked K'leef.

"Then Mommy and Daddy turned up and blasted fire all over the nest, with me still in it. I just blacked out. I only just woke up a few minutes ago. Fortunately for me, the parents had flown the coop. I saw the two of you in trouble, as usual, and I reckoned you needed saving. By me." He smiled. "As usual."

"That's it!" K'leef snapped his fingers. "The yolk—it protected you from the phoenix fire. You are stupidly lucky, Thorn."

Lily hugged him again. "It was a fair trade: you for the phoenix. Let's get going."

Thorn frowned. "What do you mean?"

"Oh, no, Thorn. We are going home now. We are not still after a phoenix. Forget it."

He shrugged. "If you say so. Then I'd better say good-bye."

"Good-bye?" Lily asked.

Thorn whistled.

What was he up to now?

A small bundle of fire appeared from a window ledge above them. It shook and sparked and then . . . spread its wings. It tottered, waving those small wings awkwardly, then, tilted off into the air. It flapped hard and drifted a bit left and right before finding its rhythm. Then it circled over the three of them, showering them with minute, multicolored fairy lights before settling on the top of a wall. It gave a small cry of delight.

"There was more than just yolk in that egg," said Thorn. "And before you ask, Lily, the answer is 'nope.' You are *never* gonna hear the end of this."

Lily approached the small bird. "Is this what I think it is?"

It hiccupped a flame.

"A phoenix chick," said Thorn. "Ain't named her yet."

"You can tell it's a her?"

Thorn frowned at her. "Of course. It's obvious."

The bird flapped her small wings, excited by the attention.

"Her flames are still quite weak." K'leef held out his hand, and the phoenix, hesitating only for a moment, jumped on. K'leef winced; clearly the bird was hot. Then he smiled. "I've never seen anything so beautiful. How are you controlling her?"

"I ain't. She's just taken it on herself to tag along. She can leave anytime she wants."

But the chick clearly didn't want to, even with the phoenixes flying overhead.

How did Thorn do it? Lily shrugged to herself. Why even try to understand him? He'd always be a mystery to her.

They stood side by side, her best friends in the whole world. The prince of Djinn and the peasant boy of Herne's Forest. They were as different as could be.

K'leef. Handsome, elegant, studious, and a sorcerer.

And Thorn, none of those things.

It seemed to her that her life hadn't really started until he had come around. The Lily she was now was due to him and all his uncouth, untactful, and insolent ways.

K'leef was more right than he knew: there really wasn't anyone like him.

Suddenly the bird squawked and flew up to hide in a window.

"Hey!" shouted Thorn. "Come back down here!"

K'leef backed away. "We've got company...."

The ghosts had found them.

There were wraiths, formed of misery and regret: thin shadowy creatures so ancient that their true forms had been long forgotten, even by themselves. There were ghuls that nested in crevasses and hunted the few brave and foolish adventurers that sometimes, somehow, made their way to the dark city. There were specters that had come through the Veil, which was thin and easily breached in places like this.

And the forlorn spirits. Those who had trusted and served Lily's legendary ancestor, Prince Shadow. They had died for him in countless numbers and still lingered, trapped by their unjust deaths.

The boys gathered on either side of Lily—K'leef on her left, Thorn on the right. Thorn scanned the approaching ethereal crowd, arrow ready. "I have eight arrows left."

"Eight? What use are eight arrows against this horde?" asked K'leef.

"Feel free to sweep them all away with your spells," snapped Thorn. "Anytime you like."

"Magic's not like that!"

Thorn scoffed. "You're about as much use as pants on a pig."

"Let me guess: your grandpa?" asked Lily.

Thorn loosed an arrow into the nearest ghost. It vanished in a swirl of sparkling mist. He drew another and smiled. "Yeah. That's one of his favorite sayings. You ain't heard it before?"

"We can discuss it later," Lily said.

"Suit yourself. Just not sure how much 'later' we've got."

Lily searched around and spotted an empty alley. "Run."

Thorn flicked an arrow through another ghost as he spun on his heels and ran. K'leef plodded heavily behind. Smoke puffed out of his nostrils and minute fires danced on his fingertips, subconscious reactions to all the magic shaking up his system. She just hoped he didn't burst into flames.

If only she had her—

*No. What's the point? I don't. We'll just have to figure out another way.*

But she'd gotten used to it, hadn't she? Less than a year—that's all the time that had passed since she'd summoned Custard's ghost, her first spell. The magic had come without training, just through sheer will, and regret. Since then she'd worked and studied and practiced—and wrestled with— her sorcery. She'd grown used to it. Not using it constantly, but having it there, like a shield and sword on the wall of an old fortress. Ready in case the need should arise.

*I will get my magic back. No matter how long it takes.*

But she needed to survive the here and now, and the chances of that suddenly diminished when they turned the corner and entered the ruins of a square.

There were three other exits, each spilling out countless ghosts. In the center stood the bottom half of a statue; the top half was rubble on the ground. When it was whole, it must have been hundreds of feet tall— the cracked half head was the size of a barn. Lily wondered if it might be Prince Shadow himself. Thorn scrabbled up the face. He balanced a foot on the nose and reached down for Lily's hand. "Come on."

He hauled her up and K'leef a moment later. Thorn's energy and strength never seemed to flag. The boy just kept on going. He was bursting with life.

Hades swooped overhead, but the ghosts were now crawling over the buildings like ants, leaving him no room to land. They piled over the walls and statue fragments, a sea of spirits.

"Get back!" yelled K'leef. Flames poured from his palms and swept away dozens of the undead, but it didn't last long, and as the fire died out, there were as many ghosts as before. Thorn's bowstring hummed again and again, and each arrow found its mark, but soon he would have none left.

Lily, balanced on a broken piece of marble, looked out over the square and despaired.

The dead covered every inch of it. They crept across the floor and coated the buildings like ivy. Hades landed and tore at them, but they were as unsubstantial as mist and they began to climb over him, sucking his strength with their coldness.

There was no escape.

# FIFTY

The ghosts poured in from all directions. They rose out of the stones and the thick fog. K'leef stumbled, exhausted and all his magic spent, and Thorn held his bow like a staff, ready to swipe at the undead surrounding them. He snarled, wild with a desperate fury, yelling at the hungry spirits.

Even with her magic Lily would never have been able to take them all, and now what chance did she have? She was a Shadow only in name.

A name that had lasted thousands of years, and would end here.

Mary would never know what happened; she'd wonder and wait till her last days. She'd always hope, despite the passage of years, that Lily would come back, and she'd never be willing to accept the possibility that Lily and her two friends were bones in the dust.

Would Lily linger in the Twilight, like her father? Or would she be trapped here, with these poor spirits?

Hades screamed and beat against the ghosts, but they were all over him and his attacks were becoming sluggish. Soon it would be too much even for the valiant bat.

"One . . . one more big spell . . ." K'leef gasped. "Enough . . . to let you make a run . . ." But the boy was on his knees, and Lily doubted he could light a match. She held his hand, and he smiled up at her. "I'm sorry, Lily."

"Come on! Try me!" roared Thorn, swinging his bow wildly at the creeping creatures. One of the ghosts grabbed the stave, and it rotted away in seconds. Thorn threw the remaining splinters at it. Then he backed up to join his friends, grinning. "This is exciting, isn't it?"

She laughed and took his hand, too. Why not? "You never, ever give up, do you?"

"Give up? This is just the start!" He hurled a rock into the mass of encroaching death. It went straight through to bounce down along the road. He shrugged. "Ah, well."

Hades was now under a mass of glowing mist; the ghosts had overwhelmed him. He still struggled and snapped, but it wouldn't be long before they'd rob him of his life force. They swarmed over the old bat, feasting.

Thorn squeezed her hand. "Got a plan, Lady Shadow?"

"Oh, Lady Shadow is it now?"

"What? I always call you 'Lady Shadow'!"

"Ha!" *Now* he used her title and family name. But she wasn't much of a Shadow, not anymore. It was just a name. An ancient, soon-to-be-wiped-out name . . .

*But names have power. . . .*

They had a magic of their own. Lily thought back to the way people reacted when they heard hers: with awe and dread. She'd hardly ever needed to use her necromancy; the name alone was enough.

But would it be enough here?

There was only one way to find out. She released her hold on her two friends and stepped toward the ghosts.

"Lily!" Thorn yelled. "What are you doing?"

"My name is Lilith Hecate Shadow!" Lily cried. "And that is a name you all know well! I am a child of the great Prince Shadow, your lord and master! His blood runs in these veins!"

Did they hesitate? She couldn't be sure. There were so many, she felt like a person standing on a rock in high tide, the sea rising all around her.

"You are creatures of the darkness, creatures spilled from the Twilight, that place between life and death. Look back and ask about me—I am well known. Go to the Pit, and you will hear my name whispered by the dukes of hell!"

She stood up straighter, defying them. "Ask the specters, who fear me. Ask the zombies, who serve me. Ask the shades of Castle Gloom, who are my friends and allies. Ask the dread monsters, who follow at my heels."

That was an odd way to describe Custard, but it was technically correct.

Lily glared at the spirits. "Go ask them what I do to those who defy my will!"

She stepped closer toward the ghosts, head aloft, arms loose by her side. If they wanted her, they just needed to reach out. . . .

They parted before her.

"I don't believe it . . ." whispered Thorn from a few paces behind her.

Of course it was a bluff. She had no power, but her name did. Power that stretched back to the very founding of this capital.

The ghosts didn't remember much—how could they? They were the bitter remnants of a crime committed in the days of legend. They did not recall their old lives, their friends and loved ones. But they still remembered the name Shadow.

They feared it and, even now, served those who bore it.

Hades tore free of the ghosts and soared into the night sky with a raging cry. He swooped down over the dead once, then rose up to settle himself, panting and watchful, on a tower.

Lily could still feel the nearest spirits sucking life and warmth from

her. But she could not let herself shiver; she would not show any weakness. They needed to believe that she was the rightful heir to their prince, and his sorcery still lived in her.

"Stay close to me," she warned her two friends. "We're leaving."

As she'd hoped, the ghosts parted before her as she led Thorn and K'leef out. Lily looked into the spirits' faces, into the empty eyes that were so hopeless, so sad, and so lost. They had been abandoned by their ruler and forgotten by his descendants.

Loyal till death and beyond. It broke her heart to see the useless devotion they had to her. They were hers to command.

An army of undead, the likes of which the world had never seen in thousands of years. Who could stop them? The thought of it made her head spin. She thought of the high queen, the words of Kismet. Was this her destiny, after all? To be the high queen?

She only needed to give the command and the crown of the New Kingdoms could be hers.

But there was only one command she could give. No one should serve forever.

"Go," she told them kindly. "You are free now. You have been loyal long enough."

That was all it took.

Dappled with starlight, the ghosts of Necropolis finally found peace. The ones closest reached out to touch her.

In the distance, soft, sparkling lights carpeted the city.

The starlight gathered around her, each one a departing soul. This was no dark presence, full of anger and misery. She felt joy and gratitude. She glimpsed old memories, of families of Necropolis when it had been filled with sunlight and life.

Her heart swelled as a comforting warmth spread through every fiber. It surrounded her, encased her like the embrace of her mother. The people of Necropolis shone all around; everywhere she looked she saw the light of a brilliant soul.

They whispered to her, words in languages that hadn't been spoken in thousands of years, so old that even she did not understand them, but she knew what they meant. There was thanks, affection, and, most of all, an overwhelming love, unlike any she'd ever experienced.

Each spirit held her for a moment, shining brightly; then, one by one, they disappeared.

Lily didn't need her sorcery to know the difference between mere retreating to the half realms and true departure to the Far Shore. They would not be returning.

Thorn watched, agog. "You've done it, Lily. You saved us."

"And them," added K'leef. "You saved all of us."

"They're gone . . ." said Lily, stunned. All of them. Not one lingered on this side of the Veil.

*How do I know that?*

Shadows stirred around her. Not those made by the moonlight, or the flames of the phoenix, but those she willed to come forth. They rippled across the ground and settled upon her shoulders.

"Your magic . . . but how?" asked K'leef.

Blessings of the Dead. What else could it be? It had happened when she'd summoned Sa'if to say good-bye to his brother, and it had happened now. But this time the effect on her was a thousand times more powerful.

She smiled at her Djinnic friend. "There'll be plenty of time for me to explain later."

Hades shrieked overhead. A swirl of fire spun over him, then dove down to settle on a bone perch. As the small phoenix shook its wings, flaming motes fell off its feathers. It looked at them expectantly, blinking its brilliant glowing golden eyes.

K'leef walked up to it and let out a soft whistle. The bird hopped onto his outstretched forearm. The sleeve creased and blackened and turned to ash, but K'leef's magic protected his flesh. He stroked the phoenix's head, and the bird seemed to chuckle.

"She likes you," said Thorn.

K'leef blushed. "But she's your pet. I can't take her."

"Pet? That phoenix ain't anyone's pet." Thorn looked over at Hades. "Besides, I'm busy enough dealing with this monster."

Lily hooked her arm through K'leef's. "What will you call her?"

K'leef let the phoenix fly. It was newborn and wanted to explore.

"Almudhannab," he said.

Lily nodded. "That's a good name."

"What's it mean?" asked Thorn.

K'leef smiled widely as the bird wove through the night sky. "Comet."

# THE LAVA CROWN

# FIFTY-ONE

"Ameera's waiting," said Thorn as he and Hades landed next to Lily and K'leef. "She's brought her sisters."

K'leef steadied his horse. "What does she want?"

"A fight."

Thorn idly flicked sand from Hades's ears. He couldn't wait to get back to Gehenna. He reckoned he'd be shaking sand out of his skin for the next six months.

But first there was the matter of a treacherous sister to be dealt with. . . .

"What are you waiting for?" asked Gabriel. "Have her chained and executed. It's the only way. That'll set an example for the rest."

Thorn met Lily's gaze. He knew how she was feeling. Of all the people likely to survive the Shardlands, Gabriel should have been at the bottom of the list. Yet here he was, being as pompous and unpleasant as ever, and looking as splendid as always on his white horse. He was dressed for a parade, his tunic pearl white and his buttons polished silver, his hair that unnatural pale blond, and his eyes a brilliant sapphire. It was all magic, of course—the clothes were nothing but rags and hide, the buttons were made of cheap tin, and the steed was a bony donkey. Thorn had seen behind Gabriel's mask. Too bad Gabriel's magic wasn't good for anything more than mere vanity.

It had taken them two weeks to get back from the Shardlands. They'd sent word ahead that K'leef had captured a phoenix and therefore was the new sultan. Now they were just a few miles out of Nahas.

Ameera had chosen a good spot for a confrontation: outside of the city, where there would be no one but her sisters around. The land was barren except for a few boulders and dusty trees, none of them large enough to hide any ambushers.

The sun lingered just above the sea, as if eager to witness the scene before allowing the night to come. But even the smallest stones left long shadows, something Ameera might regret.

"What do you think, Lily?" asked K'leef.

She sat alongside him on her own fire steed, looking every inch the desert princess. "You're the sultan, K'leef. This needs to be your decision, and yours alone."

Thorn admired her for not saying anything more about Ameera. It was only natural that she would want revenge—Ameera had robbed her of her magic. But Lily had suggested nothing of the sort, leaving the heavy think-ing to K'leef. He needed to get used to it if he wanted to be sultan. Which, as everyone knew, he really didn't.

K'leef furrowed his brow. "What about the executioner? Did you see her?"

Thorn shrugged. "Kali wasn't with them."

"Did you have a good look?"

That wasn't even worth answering. K'leef had sent him ahead to do some scouting from the air, and now he didn't trust his word? Thorn drew his bow and twitched a string. "I could go back and put a few arrows among them, if you'd like."

K'leef's gaze darkened. "I am not having you shoot my sisters."

"No harm in scaring 'em a little. The Six know our little party will only make 'em laugh."

It wasn't much of a procession, hardly the glorious march of a victorious new ruler. Behind them were a few ragged-looking riders on salamanders leading three weary mules and a wagon.

Thorn still wasn't happy that Kismet had invited herself along. He was even less happy about the way she and Lily had been talking together the last few nights, switching to Djinnic whenever he tried to sit nearby and listen. Something was brewing between the pair of them.

He grimaced, looking back at the wagon. "Kismet should have stayed back at the camp. Dragging a newborn across the Shardlands is not right."

"Kismet knows what she's doing," said Lily.

"Yeah, I bet she does."

Lily shot him a cold glare but stayed silent. They'd been arguing about Kismet for pretty much the whole journey back.

Ah, well. What did it matter? He could smell the salty sea air. K'leef had promised them his very best ship, and in a few days, they'd be riding the waves and Kismet would be headed back to her tribe.

Comet lit the dawn gray with blazing colors. She swooped and spun overhead, and Hades growled as she drew close. The bird replied with a petulant shriek but flew off a few dozen yards.

The two of them, Comet and Hades, kept a wary distance from each other. Comet—young, excitable, eager to show off and fill the sky with her bright flames—would circle the grouchy bat, wanting to play. She'd singed his fur on a couple of occasions, and the last time, Hades had chased her through the clouds and buffeted her with his giant wings, almost putting her out. Comet had learned her lesson. For a day or two at least.

"She just wants to be friends," said Thorn.

Hades sniffed. Clearly he was too old and proud to indulge in the phoenix's silly games. Still, Thorn noticed how the bat watched the bird from the corner of his small eyes. Even with his poor eyesight, it was impossible for him to miss the blazing Comet.

So here they were: a peasant boy, a princess of darkness, a brand-new sultan, the idiot son of Duke Solar, and a bunch of nomads, about to take on all the princesses of House Djinn. Thorn twirled a shaft between his fingers. He toyed with the idea of "accidentally" loosing an arrow toward them but then realized Lily was watching him.

"No, you don't," she warned.

"You're no fun at all," said Thorn.

"Nothing's going to get resolved with us just watching. Come on." And with that K'leef dismounted and walked toward his sisters.

Lily followed and, after returning his arrow to the quiver, so did Thorn.

The battle for the Sultanate was about to begin.

⁓◌

If Ameera was afraid or impressed, she didn't show it. The other sisters whispered and pointed at the phoenix until Ameera snapped at them. Then they all stood in tense silence.

Ameera met them halfway between the two parties. She looked at Thorn and Lily indifferently. Nobles were good at hiding their feelings. She smiled at her twin brother. "So? Shall we fight now, K'leef?" Flames licked her fingers.

"Where's Kali?" Thorn asked. He could imagine the executioner hiding under the sand, daggers at the ready.

Ameera stared hard at Lily. "Your necromancy transformed her into a crippled old woman. She left—I don't know where."

Thorn relaxed a little. With Jambiya, Pan, and now Kali out of the picture, maybe he could finally stop checking his back.

K'leef gazed past her. "And what of our sisters? Will they join in?"

"They are all sorcerers, too," she replied. "If they wish to fight by my side . . . I will not stop them."

"K'leef has a phoenix," added Thorn. "He won the trial by fire."

Ameera shrugged. "The trials are a foolish old tradition. He caught a phoenix. So what? Does that make K'leef one inch the better ruler?"

"It proves he has courage and knows what it is to defy death. You done anything like that?"

He didn't bother listening to whatever she had to say.

Ameera's sisters watched them. Some looked anxious; some looked ready for a fight. They'd picked her side and didn't expect any pity or mercy.

The lava crown was a bloody piece of headgear. How many were already dead because of it? And how many more might find themselves on the funeral pyre before the day ended?

"I don't want to fight you," said K'leef. "You're my sister."

Ameera sneered. "Then what? You'll give me the crown?"

"No."

This was a different K'leef. This one had some steel in his spine.

So there would be a battle. There was no other way to end this. Ameera's ambition was too great, and she'd committed too many crimes to just give up.

Thorn settled his grip upon his bow. The arrows rested in the quiver, but he could sense the journeys ahead of them. Two or three might make enough mischief among the other sisters to force them to back off, perhaps just enough to tip the balance in K'leef's favor.

"You must pay for what you did to Sa'if," said K'leef. "And Lily."

Ameera lowered her gaze. "I thought only to weaken Sa'if, not rob him of all his magic. It was only meant to be a little crack in the mirror."

Her remorse seemed sincere, not that Thorn cared.

K'leef folded his arms. "And what about Lady Shadow?"

Ameera's eyes hardened. "You should have been my ally, Lily. But when you refused our offer, I knew you were too dangerous, to all of us. I had to destroy you for the good of the Sultanate."

*And yet, you didn't destroy her.* Ameera had no idea that the dead of Necropolis had given Lily their blessings, and she was more—much more—than she had once been.

K'leef spoke. "The people will not forgive you for what you did to Sa'if."

"The people?" Ameera sneered. "They will get on with their own lives. They will forget."

"But will you?" Lily asked. "Or will Sa'if's murder haunt you every day of your life, and beyond?"

Ameera grew pale. "What's done is done."

Lily wasn't finished, and there was a cold smile on her lips that Thorn, if he didn't know her so well, would have found frightening. "We went to Necropolis," said Lily, drawing closer to the Djinnic princess. "The city of the dead. There were ghosts, ghuls, specters, and creatures whose names we dare not say out loud. But they spoke to me, Ameera. Do you know what they said?"

Ameera tried to back away, but Lily grabbed her wrist.

Was it his imagination, or had the air grown colder?

"Let me go. . . ."

Lily didn't. Instead, she pulled Ameera toward her. "You killed your brother. Someone who loved you, sheltered you, honored you every day of his life. He went to the Far Shore. I saw him leave. But do you know where you are destined for?"

"Let me go!" But Ameera couldn't get free.

"I shall tell you." Lily whispered in the princess's jeweled ear.

Thorn couldn't hear Lily's words, but even he shivered as Ameera's eyes widened and a deep moan escaped her lips. She began to tremble.

What was Lily saying to her?

He really didn't want to know.

Ameera broke free with a scream. She fell to her knees, sobbing.

K'leef stared at his crumpled sister. "What did you tell her, Lily?"

"You don't want to know."

The other sisters were terrified, having seen their leader fall. They didn't dare approach.

Like Thorn, the princesses had been raised on horror stories about House Shadow. They'd been warned of the nameless, terrible deeds the Shadows would perform on children who had not been good.

And here stood such a Shadow, and they had been far from good.

The Shadow name held a dreadful power.

"What have I done?" whispered Ameera.

Lily crouched down beside her. "As you said, what's done is done. But you can make amends."

"For killing my own brother?"

Thorn hadn't been there when Pan had sacrificed himself for Lily, but they'd talked about it one night. Lily was convinced that Pan had finally made restitution for his crime. Her eyes had shone with starry tears when she told Thorn, "I know Dante and my mother will welcome him."

Lily helped Ameera up.

All the princess's defiance had fallen away. Ameera cringed as she looked up at her brother and asked in a desperate voice, "What must I do, K'leef?"

He smiled at her. "Do something that would make our brother proud."

"But what is that?"

"That is for you to find out, Sister. But the answer is not in Nahas."

"Exile, then?" she asked, shocked.

"Freedom," K'leef replied.

The old Ameera reasserted herself. She drew herself up straight, raised her head, and wiped away the tears. "Very well."

How could she be so calm all of a sudden?

He'd never understand nobles.

But he didn't want to. Only one noble mattered to him.

Lily caught his glance and smiled.

Did she know how he felt about her? He wished he had pretty words like K'leef's, but Thorn was just a simple peasant boy more used to wrestling sheep than swapping feelings with princesses.

All he knew was that nothing made his day more complete than being with her at the end of it.

Ameera returned from saying good-bye to her sisters. "What will happen to them? They are all sorcerers, K'leef. The old law—"

"Is the reason for all this suffering," said K'leef. "Women will practice magic freely in the Sultanate."

"You really mean that?" asked Ameera. It looked like she didn't know whether to cry or laugh. "Of course you do. It's a matter of honor, isn't it?"

"Ruling a kingdom is a tricky business. I shall need all my sisters to help me."

Comet circled overhead, shrieking and spilling flames from her wingtips. She flew over the heads of the princesses, and all of them ducked. Except one.

Comet flapped down and settled on Sami's outstretched arm. She giggled, clearly entranced—and unharmed—by the fiery bird.

K'leef smiled wryly. "And perhaps I shall need Sami's help most of all."

# FIFTY-TWO

"K'leef won't last a week," said Thorn.

"Hmm?" Mary stood in the center of the room, surrounded by trunks and crates, hands on her hips, doing that rocking thing she did when she was thinking. "Did you say something?"

"K'leef's head is in the clouds. Bet he won't last a week."

Mary laughed. "He's survived this long, Thorn. That young man may surprise us yet."

The ships were loaded with stores, goods, and zombies. Baron Sable was down by the quay making last-minute preparations for their dawn departure. This was Thorn's final night in the Sultanate, so he'd thought he'd make the most of it and stay at the palace. One more night sleeping on silk before two months in a ropy hammock.

He picked a chair that wasn't covered in clothes. "Where's Lily?"

Mary shrugged as she searched through a pile of dresses. "No idea. But you'd better go find her. I need to tick off all the gifts before I pack them."

Thorn set off.

Lily was probably with Sami, thanking her for the presents. By now, he knew the palace well. He could take a shortcut across the courtyard to the women's quarters.

Turned out he didn't need to. Lily was in the courtyard, tending Hades.

This time of night the place was quiet except for a pair of sleepy guards at the gate.

The bat looked down at him and burped. Thorn patted the swollen belly. "Stocking up for the journey, eh?"

Lily pulled some stringy fat from the monster's chin. "He's getting a taste for camel."

Thorn looked at her. "Can't wait to be off."

"I miss Gehenna so much, Thorn."

"It's your home," said Thorn. "It's where you belong."

"Until this trip, I'd never been out of Castle Gloom for more than a week." She sighed and looked north. "The leaves will be gold by the time you return."

"Good, I can't wait for winter. I tell you, I'm going to walk barefoot in the snow. It'll be great to be cold again."

"You squires still have your snowman contests?"

Thorn brightened. "Of course. Mine was taller than nine feet last year. And also I've got, y'know, Mom, Dad, and the rest waiting for me."

"Did you miss them while you were here?"

"No." Thorn met her gaze. "Not when I was with you."

Lily shook her head. "This is going to be hard, Thorn."

"The sea voyage? Maybe you won't get so seasick this time around."

"No, not that." Lily looked down at her feet. "I wish you hadn't found me. I left you a letter. . . . K'leef was going to give it to you tomorrow."

Thorn lifted her chin, his heart pounding. "We are going home, Lily. You, me. All of us."

"No, Thorn. Not all of us."

Thorn felt rage rising in his chest. "This has to do with Kismet, don't it? What rubbish has she been telling you?"

"Not just her, but the dead. That there is—"

"The dead?"

"Yes, and the dead don't lie, Thorn. The ghosts in Necropolis knew of the high queen. Of there being a seventh sorcery." Lily's eyes grew bright with excitement. "We know she was real, Thorn. And there may be a way to learn her magic. To weave spells that haven't been used in thousands of years."

"But you've got your magic back, Lily." He spoke carefully, trying to mask the pain in his words. "Why do you need more?"

"I'm the witch queen, Thorn. And K'leef has brought an end to the old law. Women can now practice sorcery here without fear. This is the beginning of something . . . something great." Lily turned toward the gate. "There are lands I must explore beyond even the Shardlands. Realms the high queen once ruled."

There was no point arguing. "All right, if that's the way it's gonna be."

"Don't be angry, Thorn. I'll be back as soon as—"

"Let me grab some more arrows, and we'll be off."

"Wait. You'd . . . you'd come with me?" Lily stammered.

"I thought you knew me by now."

She jumped forward and trapped him in a tight embrace, one her troll friend Dott would have been proud of. Thorn felt his ribs squeeze in, but he didn't care. Lily trembled for a moment, and he thought he heard a sob, but it couldn't be. Not Lily. He knew she didn't feel that way about him, even if he wished it otherwise.

This was the way it should be, Thorn and Lily, side by side. He felt ready to take on the Six Princes.

"Why do you stick with me?" she whispered.

"Because I . . ." Thorn swallowed. He wanted to tell her why, but the word, that short word, just couldn't be pushed through his lips. If he told her how he felt, actually told her, there'd be no taking it back. He could take on manticores, efreets, and phoenixes, and people thought his courage had no limits, but it did. He couldn't admit how he felt to Lily. "Because I serve you, Lily."

Lily stepped back, and slowly her hands slipped down until she held him by just his fingertips. "I'd like you to come with me, Thorn. I'd like that very much."

"Good. So just let me—"

"But I can't take you," she said. "I need you to go back to Gehenna."

He stared. Thorn's throat constricted, and he was barely able to drag out enough breath to speak. "Why?"

"It wouldn't be fair, Thorn. This is a search for magic, the magic of the high queen, and I couldn't bear to put you in any more danger."

"I'd do it for you, Lily. I would."

"I know. And I can't allow myself to be that selfish. I want you to come, but that's unfair." Despite her smile, her eyes were sad. "Go back to Castle Gloom. Keep an eye on Mary. You know how . . . attached to me she is. And you must continue your training with Tyburn."

"When will you be back? How long will it take?"

"You know I can't answer that, Thorn." She kissed him. "Good-bye, my dearest friend."

The night breeze grew colder, and the darkness around her thickened. Thorn sensed the Veil opening, the barrier between this world and the lands of darkness. How far was she going?

"It don't matter where you go," he said. "I'll be right behind."

"Thorn . . ."

Tears swelled as he spoke. "You can't get rid of me, Lily. I'll follow you."

"I'll be going places even Hades can't reach."

"I'll find a way. I always do."

She looked at the gathering darkness, then back at him, scowling. "You are very irritating."

"Then I take that as a yes?"

"Traveling through the Twilight's not like traveling on Hades, Thorn."

He stared. "We can't leave Hades behind!"

Lily threw up her hands. "I don't believe it! Anyone else you want to bring along?"

Thorn looked back at the old bat. "Nope. I think Hades will be enough."

Hades rubbed his chin on the top of Thorn's head; the sharp bristles scratched his forehead. The bat's rough tongue licked him.

More than two hundred years had gone by since Hades had first fluttered over Castle Gloom. For decades, he had served House Shadow in times of war. The big monster was scored with wounds, ancient and not so ancient. Thorn traced his hand over the long sword slash near Hades's neck, and the three puncture marks caused by a trident during a battle against House Coral. The scars, at least a century old, were now just faint white spots where the fur had never fully grown back. His recent injuries from the phoenixes, including his torn left wing, had been sewn up, and he seemed no worse for wear.

Ever since Thorn had awoken Hades from his years-long hibernation, the bat had been free to do as he pleased. It just so happened that his pleasures usually coincided with what Thorn wanted. Thorn didn't own Hades—how could anyone own such a creature?—but everywhere he went, so did Hades.

And that would never change.

"You get on first," he told Lily. "I'll sit behind so you don't slide off."

She sighed and hitched up her skirts. She didn't have Thorn's nimbleness in climbing on, and there was a bit of scooting before she found a comfortable position between the bat's shoulders. Lily blew a white strand from her face. "Come on, then."

Thorn swung himself up behind her.

Lily spread out her hand and a shimmering patch of darkness grew before them, first the size of a door, then wider until it was bigger than a castle gate.

Hades began to beat his wings, and he rose to the tips of his claws. His fur stood on end as he faced the black portal. He hissed.

"Is Hades scared?" Lily asked.

"*Scared?*" Thorn laughed. "He's warning whatever's out there that he's coming and they'd better run."

Lily turned her head to him. "Hold on tight."

He locked his arms around Lily's waist as Hades took to wing. The bat rose up and took a big circle over Palace Djinn.

Thorn looked down at the fires and the celebrations in Nahas as they honored their new sultan.

"Sultan K'leef," he said. "Who would have believed it?"

Then Hades banked and tucked in his wings.

"Ready?" asked Lily.

"Lead the way, Lady Shadow."

Thorn's heart pounded. He didn't know what lay ahead. More adventure. More mystery. More danger.

But he didn't care. He had Lily, he had Hades, and that was all that mattered.

Hades roared as he dove into the portal. Lily gasped, and then the three of them vanished into the all-consuming darkness.

# ACKNOWLEDGMENTS

Writing is a kind of magic. These semi-random lines of ink can transport us, make us weep, laugh, rage, and ponder, sometimes well after the covers have closed. If I have taken you, however briefly, away from your day-to-day and into the company of Thorn, Lily, and the indomitable Hades, then I have done all I ever aspired to do.

But this magic was not accomplished alone. All sorcerers need help—just ask Lily. My help came from some of the most magical people I know.

First, always, is Sarah Davies of the Greenhouse Literary Agency, my mentor, my first (and often most dread) reader, and my friend. I would not be here without her.

Then, certainly a sorceress of the greatest power and wisdom, is my editor, Stephanie Lurie. This little dark trilogy was her doing, and I still feel a thrill each time I remember I am edited by her at Disney Hyperion. The publishing house has some history with princesses, after all.

My family has been a constant source of inspiration. My wife gave me the courage to follow the path of shadows, pushing me to explore all those dark places of my imagination and bring out what lurked there. My eldest daughter was my sounding board for all the wild adventures and strange inhabitants of Gehenna and the New Kingdoms. My youngest reminded me of what heroes are: stubborn, bold, and devoted. I can never express how much you fill my heart each and every day.

Thanks to Alison and Ruth, who persevered through many pages with their cunning eyes and heads. You made me appear far more accomplished than I really am! Gabriel would be proud.

I must give special thanks to my sisters and parents. This saga is about kinship—of blood, and by adoption. All that is good about family is because of them.

I have been incredibly lucky to have the support of other writers, many my heroes. Rick Riordan needs no introduction and is every bit as great in real life as you'd hope your heroes to be. Jonathan Stroud has inspired me since before I started writing, and each new tale of his brings the household to a complete halt. Then there is my local conclave, Natasha Ngan, Alex Bell, Jane Hardstaff, Ali Standish, Louie Stowell, and James Noble. All are writers of rare talent, and friends of the truest hearts. I hope you know what you mean to me.

In the end, my biggest thanks go to you, the reader! My heroes only truly live within you. No author can possess those whom he or she creates, mainly because we have seen them rise from nothing, from the random ideas and thoughts that were eventually filtered down to leave the darkest of princesses and the most loyal of outlaws. You ultimately own the characters and bring meaning to their existence. So, on behalf of Lilith of House Shadow and Thorn of Herne's Forest, we thank you.

Good night and sweet dreams,
Josh